GARCÍA'S HEART

—

GARCÍA'S

LIAM DURCAN

HEART

a novel

MCCLELLAND AND STEWART

LIBRARY AND ARCHIVES CANADA CATALOGUING IN PUBLICATION

Durcan, Liam
García's heart / Liam Durcan.

ISBN 978-0-7710-2940-0

I. Title.

PS8607.U73G37 2007   c813'.6   C2006-905097-X

We acknowledge the financial support of the Government of Canada through the Book Publishing Industry Development Program and that of the Government of Ontario through the Ontario Media Development Corporation's Ontario Book Initiative. We further acknowledge the support of the Canada Council for the Arts and the Ontario Arts Council for our publishing program.

While the activities of Battalion 316 described herein are based on documented fact, the characters are fictitious and the book is a work of fiction.

TYPESET IN GARAMOND BE BY M&S, TORONTO
PRINTED AND BOUND IN CANADA

This book is printed on acid-free paper that is 100% ancient-forest friendly (100% post-consumer recycled).

McCLELLAND & STEWART LTD.
75 Sherbourne Street
Toronto, Ontario
M5A 2P9
www.mcclelland.com

1   2   3   4   5   11   10   09   08   07

To Florence, Niall, and Julia

—

Every angel is terrible.
And still, alas
Knowing all that
I serenade you.

RILKE

GARCÍA'S HEART

—

ONE

—

"Going to see the Angel?" the cab driver said, and smiled like a man who knew for certain he'd won a bet.

All Patrick Lazerenko had done was to get into the cab and ask to go to the tribunal building at Churchillplein. The real destination was obvious to the cab driver. At this time of year, with the hotels catering almost exclusively to dark-suited people on official business, Patrick had the look of a tourist. Standing among a group of businessmen in the lobby of the Hotel Metropole and watching them disperse into the Den Haag drizzle, he had already begun to feel conspicuous, almost wishing he could pick up a briefcase and join their ranks for a day of bloodless regulatory triumph. Other than business, there wasn't much reason to be in Den Haag in November. What was left of the tulips had been interred for weeks, and the jazz festival was a memory of someone else's summer. Patrick wasn't surprised by what the cab driver said. The only public spectacle was taking place at the War Crimes Tribunal building where a man who had come to be known as the Angel of Lepaterique was on trial. It annoyed him to be so easily gauged, and he almost leaned forward to tell the cabbie to mind his own business, but instead he just nodded and said "Yes" in a squeaky voice, a bubble of last night's sleep still clinging to a vocal cord.

Patrick didn't enjoy travelling and this trip hadn't begun well. He'd slept poorly on the flight from Logan – sometimes extra legroom isn't the issue – and the attentions of the first-class stewardesses, which he thought he'd gotten used to, felt like the clumsy interventions of a special-needs teacher. There had been delays with the trains from Schiphol, saddling him with an extra hour to study the fairly limited palate of greys offered by the skies around Amsterdam. He'd assumed it was raining but hadn't bothered to go up to the window to check. By early evening he had arrived in Den Haag and a half-hour later found himself propped up against the reservations counter of the Hotel Metropole, trying to stay awake through the surprisingly elaborate process of check-in, craving the chance to close his eyes, hallucinatory bursts of REM sleep intruding and almost tripping him up as he concentrated to sign his name. Hours later, he awoke in a dark, compact room, got up to undress and then went back to bed, returning to a dream where everything seemed to slowly spin. He awoke again, coming to the surface of sleep's muddy pond for a breath of air that was really the voice of his wake-up call. It was past ten when he finally got out of bed.

As if obliged to point out that Den Haag had more to offer than genocidal criminals, the taxi driver mentioned a few local landmarks worth seeing as they stopped and started through traffic. "The old city," the driver said for clarification, taking pains to make eye contact with Patrick in the rear-view mirror. Patrick thought he must have seen some of this already – cobbled streets and a foreign style of architecture, the theme-park reassurances of European cities – details glimpsed on the ride from the train station. But maybe that was Amsterdam. Or Brussels, from last year. Here, along Johan de Wittlaan Boulevard, the taxi driver explained that it was mostly hotels. Many looked nicer than the Metropole.

The traffic was made up almost entirely of trucks, other taxis, and what appeared to be a scattered fleet of black S-class Mercedes. Every time he looked through the windows into the back seats of other cars, he saw people talking into their mobile phones. He could remember when the sight of all these people talking on their phones would have seemed sophisticated, but that was another time. Now the world was filled with people for whom the choice of ring tone was the truest declaration of personality. Even his *mother* – every digital clock in her house perpetually blinking 12:00, the Greenwich Mean Time of the technologically impaired – had a phone. Now, seeing someone just sitting in a back seat doing nothing made him wonder what was wrong, if they'd lost their phone or had no one to talk to.

A light rain began to fall and the brake lights of the taxis ahead blurred between swipes of the wiper blades. He wondered whether all roads leading to the courthouse were similarly crammed, full of taxis ferrying people with purpose, pouring toward a place where the truth was wrung out. In Boston, he spent almost all his time at work, where he had become used to being the most focused person in the room, the most highly trained, with the most declared competency, so travelling north on Johan de Wittlaan he felt detached, a guest species accidentally transported into the midst of a bustling, exotic ecosystem. If not for the circumstances, it would have been refreshing.

The cab manoeuvred to an outer lane and without warning pulled into a parking lot. A tall, black iron fence with a gateway stood in front of them.

"This is it?"

The taxi driver tilted his head and pulled his shoulders up into a shrug that acknowledged the anticlimax of arrival.

"You'll need your passport."

Patrick fished some new Euros out of his wallet. He got out of the cab and thanked the driver, who said, "Good luck in there" in a tone bleached of any sarcasm or sympathy. The rain had stopped and Patrick took his first good look around. He faced a fence of wrought-iron bars, a cartoonish accessory to the moment, lacking only the clang of a cellblock door being slammed.

To his left across a plaza, in a spot the gods had obviously chosen to take a great jagged crap, the Congress Centrum loomed like a postmodern mother ship. A huge fountain fronted it, its pool duly reflecting the Congress Centrum's facade and another oblong swatch of grey Dutch sky hanging at an awkward angle. It reminded him of a Zeppelin crashing to earth.

He turned around and looked through the iron fence again. Had he not been dropped off in front of it, he would have passed the tribunal building without a second thought. It was smaller than he imagined it would be; three storeys of neo-classical granite, a design Albert Speer's mother would be proud of, without any marking to indicate what went on inside. He had read that the tribunal building once belonged to an insurance company, which now, looking at it, made complete aesthetic sense. Once past the gate, he was ushered into a guardhouse a short distance from the entrance. There, he presented his Canadian passport to a UN official in a kiosk and received a blue ticket stamped with the date.

He was a physician – at the tribunal that designation alone would make people assume a professional interest in forensics, which he would deny – and as such, he was entitled to a special tribunal pass, a pink ticket, instead of the blue one. But it wasn't as though a pink-ticket holder was granted any special privileges, no all-access pass to go behind the scenes and meet the star of the show. All the pink ticket meant was having to fill out forms and list credentials, so he'd decided to skip it.

It satisfied him to come to the tribunal that morning as a nameless citizen, happy to be mistaken for another tourist cruising through the zoo to see what monsters had been let out for display. He wanted to be a nobody in the gallery, as anonymous as a person can be after showing his passport and declaring an interest in such proceedings. He cleared security – a series of metal detectors and several stern questions as he emptied his pockets and took off his belt; an elaborate exercise, but nothing more strenuous than boarding an overseas flight – and after presenting his passport and the blue ticket again, he was finally free to climb the stairs to the visitors' gallery.

Patrick eyed the small radio receivers used for simultaneous translation of court proceedings that sat in a rack just outside the entrance to the gallery. He picked one up and, for the first time since leaving Boston twenty hours before, felt an uneasiness that until that moment had been suppressed by the details of travel. He paused and then went in.

Patrick braced himself to see his friend sitting there, unspeaking, dressed in that plain blue shirt that the world had seen him wear in the television coverage, but to his relief the booth where the accused would be seated was empty. There were sixty or so spectators in the gallery, and he found a place, dividing the big plush pout of the folded auditorium seat. He put on the earphones and waited to hear that detached form of language known as translator-talk, a cousin dialect to Dutch taximan-speak, but there was only a faint staticky hissing. Below the gallery, a man who looked to be in his fifties was on the witness stand, motionless and silent. Beside the witness, three justices dressed in black robes were reviewing documents. Patrick had memorized their names and was trying to match them with the faces he saw. The prosecution and defence teams were also intently flipping through large black binders. No one was saying anything and it looked to Patrick like a study group of honour students. He recognized one of Hernan's appointed lawyers, Marcello di Costini, staring down through a pair of dauntingly stylish glasses at the pages before him. Patrick had come across the lawyer's photo on the tribunal's Web site, where he'd spent hours reviewing Hernan's case information sheet, but it didn't do the man justice. Even in a moment like this, as the lawyer joined his colleague in a search through another binder, Patrick could see that di Costini was one of those for whom charisma was just another dominant trait, like his height, or his wit, or his wind-blown hair that had likely been styled by a ride through the countryside in an Alfa Romeo convertible. He would have been jealous if not for the fact that he had spoken several times to di Costini and found him interesting and good-humoured in the face of his client's recent turn in behaviour. Hernan García de la Cruz, after entering a plea of not guilty, was refusing to speak to anyone, including Marcello.

Hernan's silence – a stance interpreted in various media outlets as either principled, canny, or arrogant – had become the big, inexplicable development of the proceedings. After the initial incredulity and tactical regrouping, Marcello seemed to have taken his client's vow of silence in stride: "He is the first client I am certain will not perjure himself," he had said to Patrick about a month before, during one of their first telephone conversations.

This was not to say that Hernan had disengaged from the trial. On most days that the tribunal was in session, the television camera showed him seated in the defendant's bullet-proof glass kiosk, scribbling the occasional note that he allowed no one, not his family, not the judges, not di Costini, to see. To Patrick, watching from the safety of an over-designed living room in Boston, Hernan's recent appearances on the evening news revealed a man who had undergone a radical physical change – a deterioration accompanied his silence, causing alarm and adding urgency to Patrick's thoughts of going to Den Haag. The man had aged. When he was shown being moved into and out of the courtroom, Hernan walked like a man crossing an icy road. The features of his face were traced deeper, as if by concession to the demands of public villainy, making every expression more severe.

The lawyers sat at tables arranged into a triangle. They continued to speak quietly among themselves, until one of the justices found the transcript of previous testimony they had all been looking for. Each of the participants kicked into sudden motion, as if the line of text was a power cord restoring current.

A lawyer for the prosecution approached the witness – number C-129 according to the updated docket – and asked him in English how long the electrical shocks had been applied to his feet. There was a pause as the man, weathered skin drawn over broad Indian facial features, listened to the translation. He spoke, another brief silence followed, and then an English translation skipped along after his Spanish reply. "I don't know how long it took, but it was more than fifty times. I lost consciousness a few times."

The witness sat impassively as he was asked to recount his experiences of internment and interrogation just outside the town of Lepaterique during the months of January and February 1982. He described the details of the cruelty he endured in the same way that Patrick had often heard the details of a traffic accident related. A clinical description: what happened, when, and how. Throughout, the witness referred to "the doctor" and when asked for a clarification, García's full name was pronounced. The details. Facts without any reaction. Patrick was used to this, the facts shouldn't have affected him – his job demanded a fairly strict detachment – but the lack of anger in witness C-129's voice, the absence of tears on those cheeks, only amplified the effect of his testimony. Patrick hadn't expected that he could just sit down and start hearing details like this. He'd thought it would be different, more dramatic; maybe it was the diet of television where adults felt free to cry on camera if they'd so much as been denied an upgrade on a flight to the Caribbean. More likely, Patrick thought, he needed some indiscriminate out-pouring of emotion to undermine the witness's testimony, to make it attributable to the embellishments of some *campesino* with a grudge and a faulty memory. There were no windows in the tribunal chamber or in the gallery – a security decision, he thought – and this added to the room feeling sealed and increasingly airless. He became aware of the faintly ridiculous sound of himself panting and made the effort to breathe more deeply, only to revert minutes later to shallow, almost gulping breaths. It was a mistake to come here.

Patrick removed his earphones and looked around the courtroom in dismay. He'd spent five years hoping it wouldn't come to this, as though the accusations against Hernan were some sort of illness with a prognosis vague enough to offer hope. But as time passed, the possibilities narrowed until the trial became real and then inevitable. The day had arrived and the arraignment had been set and this place was the only logical conclusion for Hernan García's story.

And yet there were moments when he still felt inclined to *root* for him, the Angel of Lepaterique, a man with a history that had led to the death of his wife and had come to haunt his children. Patrick had not seen Hernan in more than ten years, and since then only on television surrounded by police or immigration officials or captioned by some news channel feed as a war criminal. *A real war criminal.* In a media cycle gorged with every form of criminality, Patrick could understand how a war crimes trial could seem reassuring, almost nostalgic. Balkan field marshals and Hutu warlords had been publicly tried in the very building in which he sat, the details of their genocidal acts transcribed and deliberated over and a judgment rendered. In the emporium of modern atrocity – airplanes piercing the perfect glass skin of American buildings, the videotaped farewell speech of the most recent suicide bomber – images of war criminals had become a relief, a rare example of evil being called to account for itself and where good was considered to have triumphed.

And now, in the face of incontrovertible evidence, Patrick was reduced to hoping tortured Hondurans would reveal themselves as less-than-credible witnesses. But the facts of the case were clear. Indians from the mountainous northern regions, university professors, activists from Tegucigalpa, all survivors of the civil war, were lined up and waiting to testify. Other figures from deep inside the regime were also due to appear, many with personal histories in the internecine wars of Honduras so shadowy that it was unclear who should be shown the witness stand and who deserved the defendant's chair. But García was the star. In the last five years the world had come to know the story of Hernan García's life, a life Patrick had not been aware of, one so incongruous with the decent and generous man Patrick had known, the man who had made him want to become a doctor.

Going to the tribunal had been based on more than just personal considerations; as the founder and chief scientific officer of Neuronaut, a biotech company that offered "the cognitive approach to marketing," Patrick Lazerenko had faced considerable opposition when he announced that, with little notice, he was going to need three weeks away. In another country. At a war crimes trial. When he told the other four people on the board (the official term for the three MBAS who had started Neuronaut with him and the CEO they had poached from another company), their first reaction was a deep, broadloom silence, the type of silence that his recent entrepreneurial experience had taught him to associate with the imminent decision to contact a lawyer. Then there was shouting. The case for making him stay was presented to Patrick by Marc-André, the only one of his colleagues who could contain himself long enough to speak in complete sentences. Yes, Patrick assured them, he was a team player and yes, he was aware of the tenuous nature of the Globomart deal and the issues involved in the latest campaign. Globomart Inc. was their biggest client, their breakthrough client, and now, according to all involved, their oxygen and water. Globomart, Marc-André said, knowing exactly which card to play, wouldn't want Patrick to go.

Famously founded by the Olafson brothers of Medina, Minnesota, Globomart took pains and spent a great deal of money to cultivate a corporate image of success based on hard work and moral probity. The image make-over – the pains and money, the strategically stealthy philanthropy (somehow always discovered in the act) – was necessary because Globomart had a reputation for being "results oriented" in its business approach, which was the diplomatic way of saying it treated its competitors as Genghis Khan treated his enemies. Globomart, simply put, was the biggest retailer in the world and the company acted like it, bare-knuckling across the American business landscape.

It was logical that Globomart, paying Neuronaut large sums of money to analyze its most recent advertising campaign, would fully expect the Chief Scientific Officer to be on-site, ready to troubleshoot. Marc-André reminded them all that for Patrick to simply be out of the office was troublesome. For the only person who knew the science to be away in another country, *indefinitely*, was a slap in their billionaire Lutheran faces. Marc-André had turned to the other people in the room: "And we haven't even brought up *why* he needs to go. Who wants to be the one to explain to the Olafsons that he's going to a war crimes trial? Public relations-wise, this is a worst-case scenario. Welcome to Chernobyl."

At this point the other two founding board members, Jessica Stallins and Steve Zaks – or "Steve Zaks from Baltimore," as he inexplicably liked to call himself – both began frantically pacing around the main meeting room as if they had been suddenly transported to the listing promenade deck of the ss *Titanic*. Jeremy Bancroft, who had been parachuted in as CEO just five months before, sat motionless and listened. At one point, when the discussions got heated, he took a long, almost thirsty look out the window in the direction of the Charles River.

Marc-André continued pressing Patrick – if he thought the Olafsons didn't appreciate him disappearing at this critical phase, he should try imagining how the shareholders would react. Just mentioning the shareholders – evoking images from their inaugural meeting one year ago where they had stormed the ballroom, commandeered microphones, and forced him to answer endless questions – made Patrick wince. Marc-André reminded him that the shareholders loved nothing more than to punish flighty moves like this, and their desertion could be sudden and would cause the very ground beneath them to crumble. Marc-André finished his summation, sat down beside Patrick, and, knowing his colleague would understand French, whispered in his most irritating Parisian accent: "*Tu restes, cowboy.*"

Then something quite unusual happened. Bancroft said that he, for one, supported Patrick making the trip, and the room rolled into another silence. Even though he was the CEO and had been incredibly quick to absorb the technological details behind Neuronaut, Bancroft was still the outsider and had not yet imposed himself in that CEO-way on "internal" issues like this. It was like watching a stepfather's first foray into an old and foreign family squabble. The stepchildren were all a bit stunned.

"It isn't Patrick, but his ideas, that are indispensable," Bancroft said, and Patrick remembered thinking that he would have preferred a simple, autocratic edict rather than the business school clichés. "We can't afford to be so dependent on the physical presence of one person, can we? It would be valuable to prove that to Globomart. Besides, Patrick has brought somebody on board specifically to handle data situations like this when he's inaccessible."

"Sanjay?" Jessica said, alarm and disbelief fusing in her voice.

Sanjay Gopal was a post-doc from his old lab, hired two months before on Patrick's recommendation. On paper, Sanjay was perfect: brains and drive and a monthly student loan statement heavy with the weight of mounting interest. He was also, despite his designation as protegé, miserable in the office where his recent arrival and prepubescent appearance combined with the insecurity of the business-types to bleed credibility from him. Sanjay had offered his resignation three times in the last month; with a bit of supportive psychotherapy and an implied challenge to his intelligence – motivational tactics Patrick had mastered as a thesis supervisor – he agreed to stay.

Jessica looked around for support but all eyes were on Bancroft as he held up his right hand and leaned forward ever so slightly, a CEO-grade gesture that was authoritative and commiserating at the same time. It was nothing and yet it was perfect, a boardroom martial arts move that disarmed his colleagues and made Patrick understand why they were paying him.

"We need to prove to our clients, to our shareholders, that we're more than a boutique operation. We can't be dependent on one person. Patrick trusts Sanjay. I think we should all trust Sanjay."

Jessica groaned and Marc-André put his head in his hands. Bancroft turned to Patrick, obviously looking for a peacemaking gesture, some quick concession offered from the victorious party. Patrick promised he'd be available, e-mail, phone, whatever, no limitations. This was, after all, the way the world usually did business, he reminded everyone. Jessica, apparently still wordless, snorted. The other two seethed. But Bancroft agreed with him. Bancroft knew it was Patrick's expertise that drove the company, just as he understood it was Patrick who had taken the biggest risks – quitting his university job and going to court to win the right to take his research results into the private sector. He knew who had made all of them wealthy in the last year.

Nobody said a word when Patrick tried to give his assurances. He'd thought Bancroft would be the swing vote, but, looking at the people around the table, he realized he'd been wrong. Bancroft was the only vote, and he had voted for Patrick. Sanjay was his voice in his absence. He'd be leaving on Monday.

Explaining the situation to Heather – the woman he'd been seeing for the last year – was tougher. He would have preferred to say nothing, to let her assume it was nothing more than a business trip that became unexpectedly prolonged, but she had seen an information package about the tribunal lying around the condo and she had begun to comment on the books he read, books about – as she put it – "people who do terrible things." He started off by admitting that he knew

Hernan García personally, which, to his surprise, she was relieved to hear. (Apparently, it made those books and his interest in the details of the trial less creepy.) And if she'd been quietly miffed that he hadn't confided in her, her anger found its fullest voice when he told her he had a ticket for Den Haag and needed to pack his bags. Several hours of interrogation ensued, always narrowing down to the same question: "Why are you going?" The most convenient response, the one he settled on, was actually the truth. Hernan's lawyer had asked him to come. She left without saying goodbye.

During that first telephone conversation, di Costini hadn't volunteered how he had found out what Patrick did for a living or how he got his number, and Patrick never asked, assuming the decision to call had been one of Hernan's last requests before he chose to stop speaking. Only later did di Costini let it slip that it had been Celia, Hernan's daughter, who asked him to approach Patrick. This complicated matters for Patrick, making him think that this was a more personal appeal from the Garcías. But as the calls from di Costini continued, increasing in frequency, it became apparent to Patrick why he was being contacted.

At first the questions were vague ("Could Hernan have a brain problem?") before becoming progressively, frighteningly, sophisticated ("But if brain activity is largely determined, and determined by physical attributes of brain structure, then where is his decision-making capacity? Where is his intent?"). He was impressed by the lawyer's interest in neuroscience and flattered by his suggestion that Patrick come to Den Haag to continue the discussion in person. It hadn't occurred to Patrick that anyone would take a biological approach to Hernan's defence. Marcello was asking questions Patrick had begun to ask himself, questions that intrigued him and made him uneasy at the same time. Of course, the facts of the case remained.

Hoping to find some brain malformation that could potentially explain aberrant moral reasoning, Marcello even had Hernan undergo an MRI ("Ridiculously normal, can you believe it?" Marcello hissed). Patrick had never mentioned any of this to Heather. If she were around when Marcello called, Patrick would cover the phone and mouth the word "Business" before finding a door to close.

Initially he had declined di Costini's invitation to meet in Den Haag, deciding it was better to keep his distance from the Garcías and their problems. But he made the mistake of watching the news. It started with a glimpse of Hernan during an international update, and in no time he was searching through the newspapers, until finally he was running through the posted transcripts of the trial on the tribunal's Web site, all the time telling himself he was only keeping informed, overestimating his detachment even as it waned and then vanished altogether. After the first two weeks of proceedings, watching the evidence mount, he realized this might be the last time he would be able to see Hernan. He decided to take di Costini up on his offer.

Patrick stared up at the ceiling of the auditorium, from which one of those huge UN-certified mobiles hung. Mysterious symbols (geometric shapes, representations of people, a cow with what looked to be a lightning bolt shot through it) floated through space above the oblivious participants. He scanned the ceiling and counted fire sprinklers that were like little toadstools pocking the great smooth face of the ceiling at regular intervals, another marking of grand institutional design. He imagined the spray from the sprinklers soaking the blue industrial carpet until it buckled into a wave pattern, the water peeling paint and warping wood and popping out the mahogany inlays. The mobile would whirr about as the deluge continued, slowing as it dripped before settling into a frozen, rusted grimace. But now, it only sat there. A nebula system slowly precessing in silence.

One of di Costini's colleagues stood and addressed the justices. The first thing Patrick noticed, aside from her unnaturally good posture, was how young she looked. Early thirties, maybe still in her twenties. He watched her trying to argue a procedural point, interrupted by a flurry of words – di Costini stood, as did another lawyer who had been seated at the other table – the argument ending with the chief justice of the tribunal rebuking the young lawyer and di Costini. She sat, and Patrick continued to watch her in her chair until his attention drifted back to di Costini. This was a place of contentiousness, Patrick was reminded, a place where every word had repercussions. To an outsider, the tribunal was daunting. A body of knowledge and a system of rules, all foreign to him at first. But he'd told himself before he came to Den Haag that the trial was like anything, that it could be reduced to facts and principles. Anything could be broken down and understood, its threat defused. He had become a student of the tribunal, learning that, in contrast to all the disputed histories that can arise in the aftermath of a civil war, the birth of the tribunal itself had been surprisingly smooth and uncontested. The International Tribunal for Crimes in Honduras had been established by the United Nations along the lines of the ad hoc tribunals for Rwanda and the former Yugoslavia. Various attempts at reconciling atrocities committed in the civil war in Honduras had failed, and the government, continually stung by the international community's hectoring and increasingly slow-to-arrive economic development cheques, threw up its hands. All it took was the added carrot of upcoming G8 talks on debt forgiveness, and the president of Honduras almost sprained a wrist in the rush to sign the agreement granting authority to the UN. Once it became somebody else's problem, the pace of activity picked up dramatically. There were arrests in Tegucigalpa and Florida and, finally, in Canada. Deportations were fast-tracked and the planes touched down long enough on the tarmac at Tegucigalpa for a ceremonial refuelling and repatriation before taking off for Den Haag. It didn't stop there, of course. The archives of the secret police were opened and there were names named. More arrests followed, and some scores were settled along less explicit jurisdictional lines. The period of relative calm in the 1990s was replaced by the familiar sound of gunshots heard throughout the night from anywhere in Tegucigalpa. Hernan García wasn't implicated in these first wild weeks of reckoning. By the time they thought to look for him, he had already been gone fifteen years.

Marcello di Costini now rose and approached the bench where he conferred with the three tribunal judges. Four heads leaned in toward something being said. There was some sort of agreement that the prosecution team appeared to have no objection to. It was easier to bear without the earphones, without the words deadening all the possibilities.

Patrick was glad that Hernan García was absent. He had wanted to see the chambers without having him there; ideally, he would have liked the gallery empty, to be able to sit and in some way demystify the place and its strange customs before having to face Hernan here in his new role as a criminal. He wanted to separate the place from the man, and in that way limit all the accusations to that little glass booth, that aquarium where a new species of Hernan García could be contained. But listening to the testimony, that plainsong of physical horror and depravity, made him despair that nothing was capable of detoxifying this place. He put the earphones back on.

Patrick scoured the gallery for a face that he could recognize, not holding out too much hope that he'd immediately find any of the Garcías. That's when he saw Elyse Brenman sitting on the far bank of seats. When Patrick had first met Elyse, she was still a reporter for a Montreal newspaper, knocking on his door to interview him for one of a series of articles she was writing about the fresh allegations made against local corner store owner Hernan García. The articles became a book called *The Angel of Lepaterique*, and the book became a best-seller and now Elyse didn't work for the newspaper any more. He hadn't thought she'd be here, and it was only after spotting her that it seemed logical: the story hadn't yet come to a conclusion. She wore jeans and a cloth jacket, and with the knapsack at her feet she could have passed for a student in a lecture hall, taking notes and lifting her gaze occasionally in the direction of the tribunal judges. He lowered his head and began fiddling with the earphone cord, trying to roll it up, bringing his attention back to the proceedings.

Witness C-129 finished his testimony and was escorted from the stand. The door used for trial participants closed behind him. Patrick had read that the defendants were caged in an ultra-secure holding cell under the building but he knew nothing about the witnesses. Would C-129 be dispatched back home now? Just a quick Den Haag cameo, get it all off your chest and then a cab back to the airport? It was a bit cold. He hoped that they at least had a room for witnesses somewhere in the tribunal building – for some reason an anteroom resembling a business-class lounge in an airport came to mind – where they could put their feet up and get a handshake from a local dignitary or maybe have a drink while they sat through the mandatory debriefing from a UN-approved psychiatrist.

The chief justice declared a recess until the next morning. Patrick waited for the clap of a gavel, but that was an American thing. This was definitely not an American thing. The lawyers just got up and placed their large binders into larger briefcases. The crowd rose and some stretched in silence, as though they had just sat through a disappointing movie or a game where the home team lost, not unexpectedly, by a couple of goals. Maybe they had all come to see Hernan. It was an odd crowd: mostly people on their own who studied each other as they put on their coats. Some exchanged a word or two of greeting, and he began to think that there was such a thing as "regulars" here, lonelies who had set up shop on the banks of this foul river. He moved quickly to be the first at the door, not wanting to come across Elyse Brenman as he ducked through the crowd.

Outside, Patrick decided against waiting for a cab and risking ambush by Elyse, opting instead for a brisk walk. It was not yet four o'clock and already getting dark, darker than it would have been in Boston for that time of day in mid-November. Other than that, Den Haag could have been Boston's sister city. The air was a big bowl, sharp with sea smells, and a fog had installed itself, squatting most thickly in empty areas of the public parks. Placemat-sized wads of leaves clotted the sidewalks. All that was missing was a Red Sox fan staggering through the mist, muttering about something epic and trying to find the train to Newton. He pulled his jacket up to his chin and headed back up Johan de Wittlaan, looking for the Hotel Metropole's corporate symbol floating in the fog. No luck.

Eventually, the Metropole appeared out of the darkness across the boulevard, its lobby of marble and glass glowing like a festive Las Vegas crypt. As he passed through the lobby, a tall man waved him down from behind the front desk. Up close, Patrick saw the man wore a name tag that said "Edwin." Edwin was not a happy man. Tragically prominent ears sat on either side of his head like satellite dishes, picking up bad vibes from the entire Metropole constellation. Apparently Patrick was the cause of that day's crisis. Edwin told him that the front desk had received numerous calls for him, incessant calls, some quite provocative and rude. He was requested to turn on his cell phone and check his e-mail. "Immediately, please," Edwin said, lowering his gaze to emphasize the obvious seriousness of his request. And with that, Patrick was dismissed. While he hadn't been hungry before, speaking with Edwin stirred an appetite in him, and instead of rushing off to comply with Edwin's wishes, he turned and let the concierge watch as he walked over to the Metropole's deserted restaurant, where he proceeded to eat an early dinner with deliberate, almost malicious leisure. But he began to feel ashamed of himself before the meal was over. This was the extent of his defiance, he scolded himself, churlishness. Passive-aggressive dining, all to spite his colleagues and put an officious concierge in his place. It was a short journey from the restaurant to the bar. It wasn't stalling, he told himself as he ordered a scotch, the bar was simply a transition phase, a recuperative moment.

But Patrick couldn't help dreading the thought of all those messages lining up in his inbox, each communication dense with the thinly veiled wrath of his partners, still upset that he'd chosen to disappear just when the Globomart project was launching, cursing his technical indispensability, and not believing for a moment that Sanjay was up to the task.

After a second scotch, the feelings of nostalgia for Boston and everyone at Neuronaut began creeping onto the surrounding barstools to keep him company. They were the closest he had to friends. He remembered how Bancroft had called him into his office, weeks before he'd publicly endorsed Patrick's decision to leave. Bancroft had sat him down to tell him that he'd heard about "his troubles" and what was going on in The Hague and said he would help in any way he could if Patrick needed anything. He was friendly and vague, with a tone somewhere between a guidance counsellor and a distracted older brother. Patrick asked Bancroft how he'd found out – for all his scotch-induced reveries of the people at Neuronaut, he'd never actually confided in anyone there – and Bancroft told him he'd read *The Angel of Lepaterique* that summer, that he knew about Hernan and all the Garcías and Patrick himself.

"A damn shame," Bancroft said, and Patrick nodded, unsure of what his boss found most shameful.

The bartender stationed himself at the other end of the bar, diverting his attention from the glasses he wiped only to register the business people as they came and went. The other patrons gathered in clusters that broke up and reformed as the evening passed. Patrick listened to conversations and was able to pick up the rough rhythm of joke telling, a prosody that was unmistakable, even in Dutch or German. It occurred to

him as he eavesdropped on another Hans regale another
Jurgen that he was not yet part of this type of life, this nightly
fellowship gathering in hub cities across the corporate world.
He always thought it was chummy and a little slurred and
pleasantly benign and that he'd enjoy it. He was far more
familiar with academics in situations like this, loosed in a bar
in a foreign town between plenary sessions of some world
congress, without their spouses or departmental colleagues or
post-docs to rein them in; after about an hour the scene
would deteriorate into low-level roundtable sniping, a
schadenfreude skit where the only common spirit would be glee
over someone's lost grant or retracted paper. The temporary
descent of otherwise intelligent, decent people. He had been
a part of it and now the thought of them – under-socialized
and overwrought, unfettered and myopic; academics on the
loose – appalled him. Patrick had imagined business would be
different – maybe only more honestly, openly crude – but
now he wasn't so sure.

He waved a goodnight at the barman and got up to feel the
full, gravitational effects of the alcohol. An empty elevator led
to an empty hallway, conduits to a room he didn't recognize
when he turned on the light. He opened his computer to feel
the brunt of Edwin's wrath. He. Had. Messages. Too many to
count. His partners in Boston accounted for the bulk of them,
of course, testing his promise of accessibility, correctly
predicting he'd do a "Helen Keller" and turn off all his wireless
devices – he could just imagine how it would be if he hadn't:
text messages continually scrolling across the display like a
hysterical stock ticker. No, it was saner to maintain radio
silence; let his messages land and deal with them all at the end
of the day. But, as if to punish him for his lack of response,

each of his partners had sent him multiple e-mails. This was their plan, he realized, a strategy of constant digital harassment. It probably wasn't even *a* plan but three identical plans, each hatched around the same time, responding to the same stresses. Even though the other founding board members of Neuronaut all came from different backgrounds, Patrick had noted that there was something about their business school education that caused them to come out with identical responses to any problem. And not a collective response either. These three budding masters of the universe were definitely not "one plan-one mind" or "all on the same page" or whatever cliché they used this week; you could put these three in separate soundproof rooms for six months and they would still emerge ending each other's sentences with a frightening certainty. It was as though any differences in intelligence or culture or gender – Marc-André was ostensibly French and Jessica was at least genetically a female – had been shimmed away by their MBA training, giving the impression that they'd instead graduated from a military academy or a theological college. He liked to think that Bancroft could see this too, and Patrick imagined Bancroft – whose pedigree in business was simply that of a man who made money wherever he went – as more of a throwback, a gentleman privateer in the midst of an army of corporate automatons.

He scrolled down past the messages:

11.12	from: Stallins, Jessica j.stallins@neuronaut.com
	re: Urgent. Time Sensitive.
11.12	from: Dumont, M-A ma.dumont@neuronaut.com
	re: Urgent. Brain question.

11.12	from: Dumont, M-A ma.dumont@neuronaut.com
	re: Urgent reply needed. Brain question.
11.12	from: Gopal, Sanjay s.gopal@neuronaut.com
	re: communication, lack of, serious
11.12	from: Bancroft, Jeremy js.bancroft@neuronaut.com
	re: The Hague
11.12	from: Zaks, Steve s.zaks@neuronaut.com
	re: Urgent. Re: Valuation model

And so on. Twenty-one messages, most concerning the uproar that the marketing arm of Globomart was making about the studies not being as conclusive as in the previous campaign. They were demanding to know why. "Tell them that we're still evaluating the data," Patrick typed. "Talk to Sanjay." Simple. The second question was "The Olafson brothers want to know – what are Talairach coordinates again?" and it took him a minute to come up with an answer that was accurate and Globomart-appropriate, respectful enough for Lyle and Henrik, but not too patronizing. "It's a 3-D map for the brain, lets you know where you are in the brain with reference to certain landmarks. Like a GPS for the brain. Tell them that. You should be asking Sanjay," he wrote again. Sanjay's message was, of course, that no one was talking to him.

His colleagues had been, from the start, in a state of constant perplexity about the science, and he didn't know whether this offended him – they should know *something* about the basic premise of what they did and if they didn't it reflected poorly on him as a teacher – or gave him that sense of power that allowed him to do things like disappear just as their biggest project was entering a critical juncture.

Bancroft's message was refreshingly different. Human, actually. He sent his best wishes and hoped that things would go well and mentioned that the Gemeentemuseum had a Kandinsky exhibit that he should check out if he could, but that he should still answer his e-mails at least once or twice a day. Point made. Thanks, he replied. He looked through the other messages, hoping for one from Heather. Anything. He'd settle for an accusation or even one of those cryptic quasi-girlfriend haiku pronouncements. But nothing. The screen blinked through a familiar sequence as the computer shut down.

He'd been too tired to unpack completely the night before, so he spent the next ten minutes transferring his clothes to a sleek chest of drawers, pleased to accomplish something tangible before the day ended. On his bedside table he placed the two books he'd brought along – *The Angel of Lepaterique*, Elyse Brenman's primer for what was about to come under discussion, and *Moby-Dick*, a book of Marta's that Hernan had sent to him after her death, the only memento he had of the Garcías. In the last few weeks, aside from what he needed to read for work, he'd read little else. Packing the books was a reflexive act, but seeing them now, companion guides to the Garcías' decline, made him wish he were the type of person who preferred the comforts of a fat airport novel.

He washed, and swallowed a Valium and a capsule of his antidepressant's generic equivalent (the benefits package at Neuronaut hadn't yet caught up with its stock price) and then went to bed, where he tossed for another hour, the sheets roped like a python holding him some distance short of sleep. Finally, five time zones away from a normal night's rest, he turned on the television. The news was an endless loop of coverage of a funeral service for a Dutch politician gunned down the week before in Amsterdam by some North African on a jihad with hints of ties to a larger organization. *This* he had heard about, even in Boston. News like this from Europe made the radar now; no matter what your opinion was, there was something in the story to bolster any bias. The funeral was followed by footage of uniformed men breaking down doors with a truncheon, and police cars – making that uniquely European whee-oh, whee-oh siren sound – careening through darkened streets. Then the square-jawed Dutch anchorman appeared and even though Patrick couldn't pick up a word of it, it wasn't difficult to derive the rest: arrests have been made, clash of cultures, fundamentalism versus a modern sensibility, tolerance sorely tested, etc. It all trailed into an ellipsis that ended most sentences now. He changed the channel, hoping that the taped replay of a soccer game between two Dutch club teams chasing the ball around would usher him off to sleep, but the action on the pitch was strangely compelling and even the television commercials had that odd quality he'd noticed in other cultures of being kitschy and riveting at the same time. He turned out the lights after PSV Eindhoven finished off Groningen and in the dark felt only worry gathering around him like a greatcoat of Den Haag fog, a weariness that he knew would not be eased by sleep.

TWO

–

The indictment against Hernan García was laid out on the tribunal's Web site, a discovery Patrick had found both helpful and heart-rending. The information was there for anyone to find. Patrick had clicked on "case information sheet," and scrolled down to GARCÍA DE LA CRUZ, Hernan Eduardo – IT-03-8/1. Another click and, off in the corner, a window had appeared with a summary of the case:

THE ACCUSED

HERNAN GARCÍA DE LA CRUZ

BORN ON 14 JULY 1940 IN TEGUCIGALPA, HONDURAS

VOLUNTARY SURRENDER: 4 JUNE 2005

TRANSFERRED TO ITCH: 6 JUNE 2005

INITIAL APPEARANCE: 22 JUNE 2005

FURTHER APPEARANCES: PENDING

OCTOBER 2005, PLEADED "NOT GUILTY" TO ALL COUNTS

SENTENCING JUDGMENT: PENDING

The factual allegations followed, in trade-manual language, and then the charges:

THE INDICTMENT CHARGES HERNAN GARCÍA DE LA CRUZ ON THE
BASIS OF HIS INDIVIDUAL CRIMINAL RESPONSIBILITY (ARTICLE 4
(2)) OF THE STATUTE OF THE TRIBUNAL WITH:
   TWELVE COUNTS OF CRIMES AGAINST HUMANITY (ARTICLE 7 –
   PERSECUTIONS ON POLITICAL, RACIAL, AND RELIGIOUS GROUNDS;
   TORTURE, INHUMANE ACTS).

The indictment was modest in tone and detail. The facts of Hernan's involvement were related in far greater detail in *The Angel of Lepaterique*, which in turn owed much to an investigation by the *Baltimore Sun* published in the mid-nineties. The newspaper uncovered details of events that occurred in Honduras more than a decade before, breaking the story of state-sponsored, CIA-backed torture, tracking down and interviewing victims and their alleged torturers who had fled to North America in hope of anonymity and a new life.

It was shortly after the *Sun* report that a Montreal journalist named Elyse Brenman stumbled onto the story of Hernan García, a local grocer who would come to be one of the faces of the trial. The account began innocuously, as a dispute between García and a customer who wanted to buy a lottery ticket along with his groceries. García informed the customer that his store did not sell lottery tickets on principle. This drew a sarcastic response from the customer, which led to a spirited verbal exchange that took place in Spanish, as the customer, like García, was also from Honduras. It was during this argument that the customer stopped short, not as some admission of rhetorical defeat, but because he suddenly recognized García. Perhaps it had been a gesture, or tone of voice, but the man later said it was a word García used – *rídiculo* – and the way he said it, that cued his memory. The customer left the Garcías' store immediately, but came back the next day after a sleepless night, wanting to confirm that this sanctimonious grocer was the same man he'd crossed paths with fifteen years earlier, under very different circumstances. A call to the local newspaper followed, and because the receptionist who answered the phone thought the story was little more than an argument between two people in a grocery store, the customer was referred to the Community News Desk. It was Elyse who'd answered the phone.

It was eventually alleged that between 1981 and 1983 Hernan García spent a cumulative total of six weeks away from his family in Tegucigalpa and his post as professor of medicine at the National Autonomous University. Until Elyse's inquiries revealed his whereabouts during that time, many, including his family, believed he had been away on university business or academic meetings. When formerly classified documents were made publicly available by the Honduran government, it became clear that Hernan García de la Cruz had been one of many involved in the activities of what had come to be known as Battalion 316, a covert operation head-quartered in the small town of Lepaterique, not twenty miles west of Tegucigalpa. It was here, from 1981 to 1983, that Hernan García was accused of participating in the torture of subversives undergoing interrogation.

Patrick first read the details in Elyse Brenman's articles in the newspaper, archived and mailed to him by his mother. At that time, he remembered dismissing the accusations; it all seemed so ludicrous, the names of covert organizations and places piling up like the details of a bad spy novel. But then *The Angel of Lepaterique* came out in the spring of 2001 and Patrick had to admit that she'd done something more than simply libel a friend. She'd done something larger, more ambitious and impressive, framing the allegations in a well-researched and compelling history of Honduras. He'd read the book in a single, fevered weekend.

She laid the groundwork in the first chapter, explaining that with the Reagan administration waging war against leftist insurgents in El Salvador and the Sandinista government in Nicaragua, Honduras became a convenient base of covert operations. The CIA understood that it needed a willing local presence; this was more than amply provided in the person of General Gustavo Álvarez, chief of the Honduran armed forces.

It was Álvarez, a name Patrick would come across again, in another setting, who created and directed Battalion 316, using American counter-insurgency experts and the Argentine 601st Intelligence Battalion to train Honduran forces in how to deal with communist subversives. Álvarez's brutal techniques were already well known, Elyse continued on page 17 of *The Angel*:

> In briefings and interviews, then-U.S. ambassador to Honduras Jack Binns made numerous complaints about human rights abuses by the Honduran military. In the fall of 1981, Binns, an appointee of the Carter administration, was recalled to make way for the appointment of John Negroponte. Before leaving Tegucigalpa, Binns took pains to warn Washington of a possible link between death squad activity and Álvarez.
>
> Negroponte's relationship with Álvarez was significantly more cordial: Binns's concerns were dismissed, military aid to Honduras

(under the jurisdiction of Álvarez) increased from $4 million a year in 1981 to $77.4 million a year in 1985, and U.S. administration support for a regional peace initiative for Nicaragua dissolved as Honduras became the training ground and logistical base for the anti-Sandinista Nicaraguan Democratic Force (FDN).

What followed in Honduras during these years were summary arrests of union leaders, journalists, political figures, and sympathizers. For years, bodies would be found dumped in fields or along rivers, some bearing evidence of torture, much of which could be traced back to the activities of Battalion 316 and General Álvarez. In contrast to Binns's assertion that Álvarez was modelling a campaign against subversives based on Argentina's "dirty war," Ambassador Negroponte's opinion of General Álvarez remained highly positive, lauding him (in recently declassified state department "back-channel" memos from October 1983) for his "commitment to constitutional government." This was also the prevailing opinion of the Reagan administration that, in 1983, awarded General Álvarez the Legion of Merit for "encouraging the success of democratic processes in Honduras."

Elyse went on to tell the stories of the survivors, those who'd kept quiet for years about what had happened to them. After talking to that customer in Hernan's store, she was introduced to others, each new voice lending weight to the story. These histories formed the basis of the twelve indictments issued against García de la Cruz, as he was then known.

The charges against Hernan were clear. He was the physician present during interrogations, and while it was disputed whether he physically participated in torture, it was Hernan whom the torturers consulted, it was Hernan who revived the patients after the electric shocks made them lose consciousness.

Electrocution was the method of choice in the Lepaterique secret jail known as INDUMIL, a Battalion 316 installation, where electrodes were attached to the genitals of suspected communists and shocks were given with increasing frequency and intensity as the interrogation proceeded. What wasn't immediately clear was why a civilian physician had been recruited to Battalion 316 when so many military personnel with medical training were available. It was Elyse, in the course of her research, who came up with the answer in the form of a memo, also made public by the Honduran government in 1994, issued from Álvarez himself to a subcommander at Lepaterique requesting that "more skilled medical personnel be recruited" to oversee the health of the detainees during interrogations, as they were "expiring prior to potential useful tactical disclosures." The Honduran military was still struggling along the learning curve of techniques adopted from their Argentine tutors and decided that it needed the specific skills of a cardiologist in resuscitating those who developed near-fatal arrhythmias after their initial electrocutions. García was their man.

There were other hypotheses for Hernan's participation: a sense of patriotic duty in the all-out war against the communists, the suggestion being that, despite having no previously declared political stance, his time training in America had sensitized him to the dangers of communism and cemented his trust in any policy supported by the United States. There were theories half-heartedly put forward by Elyse, ones that didn't particularly relate to Hernan as much as seem like a laundry list of sociopathic rationalizations: the desire for career advancement, class hatred, pursuit of vendettas, and personal depravity.

After Patrick first heard the accusations from Elyse in a small room at Caltech in the summer of 1998, when they were no more than absurdities, he clung to the most harmless explanations, that the allegations were trumped up or that it was all nothing more than a case of mistaken identity. But as the months passed and Elyse's articles appeared and no rebuttal came, Patrick was finally forced to consider that Hernan could have been present during such acts; yet this admission was always qualified by the belief that Hernan must have been coerced or tortured himself. Hernan had to have been a victim too.

After a year at Caltech, he'd accepted a faculty position back in Boston, and it was there, in the autumn of 2000, that he heard the news that Hernan's wife, Marta, had died. Patrick had been away for ten days in Portugal – a vacation grafted onto the tail end of a meeting, the young academic's standard mode of travel – and returned home to hear his mother's voice on his answering machine. One message among many, right after the reminder that his car was due for servicing. His mother said there had been an accident, and she gave him the slim details she knew, but Patrick wouldn't remember any of them. All he could think about was Marta. Already dead a week. Already buried. What had he been doing on that day the week before? Was that the day he skipped a plenary session to do some sightseeing in Lisbon? For some reason, he was obsessed with trying to remember what he'd eaten that day, hoping it hadn't been something he'd enjoyed, wanting it to be anything other than a local delicacy savoured at the very moment his friend lay dying. Then came the thought of Marta's children and Hernan, weathering through a life that had become absurd in its clustering of grief. The funeral had come and gone, and embarrassed about the reason he'd missed it, he'd sent a card to Hernan instead of calling.

He'd listened to his mother's message again and again. She had been uncharacteristically vague about what had happened, and it wasn't until a few days later, when the newspaper clipping she sent finally arrived, that he understood why. The article was one of those matter-of-fact page three summations filled with the details of murders and drownings and other violent misadventures of the last news day. Below the fold he saw her name. Marta García, age fifty-seven, wife of the NDG resident under investigation for possible war crimes, had been killed in a car accident. Single vehicle. Seat belt unused. The concrete support of an overpass and an icy road at night cited as contributing factors. An investigation was ongoing.

The next spring, with the publication of *The Angel of Lepaterique*, Patrick was faced with the final, definitive assault on the Garcías. There was no surprise in the attack on Hernan – most of the allegations had been made in the newspaper reports. But in addition to what was expected about Hernan, Elyse had speculated about the nature of Hernan and Marta's relationship, going so far as to claim that Marta's death had been no accident, but was instead the deliberate act of a woman who knew the truth, a confirmation of the charges against her husband. But the bulk of *The Angel of Lepaterique* was focused on Hernan, making it clear that the man present in the interrogation rooms at Lepaterique had been him, positively identified, his presence documented and corroborated and in no visible way coerced. Unlike so many Hondurans who had disappeared into the grasp of Battalion 316, there was never any evidence that Hernan had been kidnapped. Marta had filed no report with the police after that first absence in 1981. He left and came back three days later, nine days after Álvarez's initial memo was drafted.

But Hernan García also had his supporters, who didn't deny he was present at Lepaterique but argued that instead of committing barbarous acts he had tried to save countless lives amid the most atrocious, coercive conditions imaginable. There were dissenting witnesses to support this notion – two former detainees and two military personnel who attested that Hernan's actions during the interrogations were more consistent with someone wanting to give aid. Another witness claimed it was Hernan's voice she heard shouting "Enough" during one of her interrogations. There had also been a groundswell of dissenting opinion in America that, on days when Patrick felt hopeless, could be psychologically reconfigured into support for Hernan. A well-known right-wing American radio personality had, in the midst of his daily invective, taken up Hernan García as his *cause célèbre*: a man falsely imprisoned on trumped-up charges to be tried in a court that had no authority, a situation that no American would countenance, but one that the weak-kneed folks up in Canuckistan would bend over backwards for. In *his* eyes, he said to his audience (syndicated to 112 stations nationwide, local numbers in the Arbitron '05 report showing a 5.1 share in one of America's biggest markets, and pistol-whipping competitors in the prized 25-to-44 demographic), Hernan García was a patriot and a victim of revisionist history – after all, hadn't President Reagan awarded the Legion of Merit to the head guy involved in all this? Was this how we repaid our compatriots who fought the war on communism? Was this how we treated a man who had served in a war on terror before we even knew what a war on terror was? As the trial started, Hernan's name began speckling the blogosphere – most sources regarding his silence as a noble gesture, as a tacit refusal to acknowledge the authority of the tribunal – and a detailed daily recap of the trial's progress appeared, where the case against him was dissected and mocked by a thousand echoing voices and the whole process dismissed as little more than a liberal-guilt show trial. What followed from these new ethereal supporters was an alternative narrative of Hernan García to refute the one put forward by Elyse Brenman, García as hero and healer, successful immigrant small-business owner, now a convenient victim offered up on the altar of internationalism and political correctness. Patrick watched uneasily as Hernan was championed in this manner, a Dreyfus for the neo-cons. It was a relief, in a way, the political antidote to *The Angel of Lepaterique*, and Patrick supposed he would have welcomed it had those involved not been completely indifferent to Hernan the person, and their motivations not been tainted by ideology and a reflexive bias against Elyse Brenman's version. As the trial approached, noise from both sides of the argument rose in unison: there were candlelight vigils for the victims of Lepaterique at college campuses throughout New England and news that the Democratic Voice, a think-tank specializing in Latin America policy-making, had offered support to the Garcías and were sending a representative to Holland to observe the proceedings – "simply to ensure fairness."

Marcello di Costini, with his client mute in the defendant's chair, had the dissenting witnesses on the stand for the better part of two weeks prior to Patrick's arrival in Den Haag, trying dervishly to spin their words into a larger narrative worthy of competing against the chorus of damning testimony. Several witnesses had gone so far as to attest that the conditions in the camp improved after Hernan had been brought there to replace the military's doctors. Marcello spoke to Patrick on the phone after one particularly good day of testimony, excited and for the first time sounding optimistic, proudly telling Patrick that he had finally been able to advance the notion that Hernan was a man caught in terrible circumstances, a man whose instincts were to heal, whose intent was good.

But if that was Hernan's intent, it was lost on many of the witnesses who were now on the stand. The majority of witnesses called said that Hernan García de la Cruz worked to prolong their misery, that unconsciousness was a relief of which he repeatedly deprived them. They swore that the first thing they saw as they regained consciousness was Hernan García's face, that they looked into his eyes and saw nothing human there.

Patrick had clung to the mock-heroic fantasy for months himself, thinking it impossible for a man to do the things Hernan had been accused of and then carry on with a normal life. Then he read profiles of the physicians stationed in Auschwitz and learned of the common delusion among them: how the routine of selecting certain prisoners for death was perversely transformed in their minds into the act of saving others. Under the necessary conditions, any action could be rationalized as necessary, as inevitable, as morally justified. Men like Hernan had done terrible things and gone back to their quiet lives as husbands and fathers and physicians. Perhaps Hernan was deluded, Patrick thought, caught up in a situation that didn't permit judgment, that paralyzed judgment.

But this was a matter of more than sincerity, more than what Hernan García believed he was doing. The tribunal was about what he had done.

And he was accused of doing terrible things.

Half of the next morning's session was all Patrick could take. Again, no García in the courtroom. But the trial carried on and the testimony continued, intensifying even, making him wonder if Hernan was absent because he could not bear to hear what was being said against him. The facts arrived and were assembled into a wall of truth. Another witness, a thin man in his sixties with a face like hammered copper and thickets of white hair, took the stand and gave his account of events between November 1982 and April 1983. He had been a teacher and a grass-roots organizer in San Pedro Sula, where he had been picked up on a warrant for sedition. He had been beaten and revived, then more soundly beaten. He spoke about what was done to him after he could no longer talk. A mask made out of an inner tube had been tied around his head. Patrick recognized scattered Spanish words: *cabeza* and *capucha*. The union organizer's testimony was disembodied further by its transmission through the voice of a female translator, a voice of gentle determination now describing, in first person, in smooth and impeccable English, the abuse his penis and scrotum were subjected to.

Patrick became aware of Elyse Brenman again; though she was as nondescript as ever, something today was different, something from her buzzed in his peripheral vision like a bulb that demanded replacement. Patrick tried to ignore it but gave in and looked over to see Elyse staring straight at him. Then, of course, she waved. He stood up, fumbling with the cord of his earphones and shrugging his jacket on, all one continuous, incompetent motion. The gallery spectators and guards registered his departure, casting disapproving glances as he edged along the row and climbed the stairs to the door.

Outside the tribunal building, he was immersed in light and air and relief and felt the urge to walk, anywhere, just away from the glass walls and industrial-carpet smell of the tribunal. He reached the fountain in front of the Congress Centrum when he heard his name being called.

"Dr. Lazerenko."

He turned and saw Elyse Brenman. She was trotting from the tribunal building toward him. Another wave, golden-retriever friendly.

"Patrick, hello, I saw you in the gallery. I didn't know you'd be here."

"Likewise."

Elyse Brenman smiled as she approached. It was her default facial expression, one that she likely learned to deploy from her first day as a reporter. Her demeanour softened people. Patrick knew first-hand how difficult it would be for someone who didn't know Elyse's purpose to slam a door on that friendly face. It had worked for her faultlessly when she'd first appeared at the Cognitive Neuroscience Department office at Caltech in 1998 and asked for him. A cold call, the paradoxical stealth of Elyse Brenman. The departmental secretary, a fearsome lady in her sixties widely treasured for her ability to be a Berlin Wall of administrative hostility to unexpected visitors and their queries, turned out to be a true Berlin Wall and collapsed under the weight of Elyse Brenman's charm. The secretary phoned Patrick in his new post-doc's office – a fluorescent-lit converted utility room the size of a confessional – and said that he had a visitor. Elyse was ushered in and at first Patrick assumed she was a student in one of the labs he was teaching. She quickly corrected that impression by pulling a notebook and a tape recorder out of her backpack and introducing herself as a reporter who needed to talk to him about Hernan García.

Elyse summarized what she knew, and what she was about to report in a series of articles. And so his first experience with Elyse was of a miscalculation followed by a visceral sense of alarm, causing his hands to dampen and his heart to make that thin-air, no-ropes climb into his throat.

With Elyse sitting there in his office that first time, he remembered being momentarily speechless, then having individual words appear and clot together, not having enough meaning to emerge, until finally he stuttered out a plea of ignorance of anything about Hernan García's former life. It was true, he had worked for him but he was only a teenager then and knew as little as any worker would know about their employer. And yet, Elyse countered, not all employees date the boss's daughter. With that she launched into a dozen other questions before Patrick realized that he didn't have to talk to her, that he could pick up a phone and call security and it would be over. But that would provoke her, and he decided, to his credit, that to get rid of Elyse Brenman he would have to prove he was no use to her. That he had no story to tell. So Patrick Lazerenko rhapsodized the vague details of his adolescence in Montreal, of growing up in NDG and working for the Garcías in their store, Le Dépanneur Mondial. Banalities, dull summers of stoner glory, a splash of teenage angst. It worked: Elyse Brenman turned off her tape recorder. He had no way of knowing that Elyse would reappear in his life – a message left on his machine, an e-mail asking how he was doing – every six months or so, certain that he wasn't telling her everything, that he was some sort of cog in the evil empire of Hernan García and was holding out on her in some way, hoping that the accrued weight of guilt would convince him to speak to her more truthfully.

But their first meeting ended civilly enough. Elyse thanked him and closed the door, leaving him in that small office, the light humming, his body aching in such a way that he could believe the confrontation had been, at least in part, physical.

He'd been at Caltech for little more than a month after finishing four years of a residency in Boston, and he thought, if anything, the succession of American place names would have given him a soothing distance from Montreal and the Garcías' problems. But even in America, where international news was treated with indifference or, at best, with an almost patronizing anthropological curiosity, it became impossible to avoid the story Elyse eventually broke. Patrick had never been a great sleeper, and his habit of keeping the television on an all-news station was rewarded with the occasional television image of Hernan trapped in that stock pose of categorical denial, shielding himself from a camera. Elyse's story led to more coverage, a television crew camped out on the sidewalk in front of the Garcías' store, other images appearing: photos of the victims – including a picture that he would come to know in too much detail – and the accusers who were marshalling opinion and demanding justice. He could only watch and call his mother for more details from Elyse's newspaper reports.

And after hearing all the crimes that his friend had been accused of committing, Patrick Lazerenko did what ended up troubling him for the next seven years. He did nothing.

It didn't start out as nothing. It started out as a calm assessment of the facts, taking one's time to figure out what was obviously a complicated situation. Hernan would understand, he wouldn't want anyone just jumping to his defence as a point of personal loyalty. No. He would demand that the case be analyzed. But there were so many facts, so many allegations. Then it came to seem that too much time had passed, that to call now would be to patronize Hernan or admit failure for not calling in the first place.

He concentrated on his own life: getting back to Boston after Caltech, accepting a faculty position and creating the infrastructure of a research program. He wrote grants and went to meetings and worked at developing that necessary reputation as someone on the rise, someone who could publish citable papers, manage a lab full of post-docs, and, in the words of his former departmental chairman, "develop the necessary public-private partnerships that would see us into the next century." All of this was understandable, he reassured himself, and he became a bystander as the Garcías came under siege.

He wished that his inaction could be chalked up to the dedication of a young faculty member feeling the pressures of being freshly tenure-tracked, that he was too occupied with starting a career and developing a reputation as a researcher to care about the allegations, but the truth was that during that time he collected every piece of information about Hernan's case. He couldn't avoid buying *The Angel of Lepaterique* when it finally came out a couple of years after that first visit from Elyse, and when its spine split from use he bought a second copy. He wasn't alone; the book spent the better part of two calendar years squatting in various locations on the best-seller list. *The Angel of Lepaterique* won awards and thoughtful appreciation, and the indictment levied in the book was probably the cause of a Royal Commission investigating how refugee status was granted. The book, which read like a grand narrative of infamy, changed everything for Patrick too. Elyse was not content for the book to be just a recitation of García's actions in the context of Honduran history. *The Angel* was also a journal of the family's flight from Honduras and arrival in Canada, a history of lies and delusions and fear. It was also a story heavy with personal details and psychological analysis of the Garcías' lives and, to a degree, his own. In it were portraits of family and married life whose intimate tone shocked Patrick. How had she known these things? It was here that Elyse brought together the photos of the victims, here that Patrick had the first chance to see the only existing photo of José-Maria Fernandez, the most famous detainee at Lepaterique, a young man whose story Elyse found so compelling, and so similar to Patrick's – both of them coming into contact with Hernan García at a critical moment in their lives – that she twinned them throughout her book. It was while searching through the sixteen-page index to the book that he had first found his name mentioned, as a prelude to being summarily analyzed. The sight of his name, not as the senior author of a paper or being cited for the work he'd done, but among the others embroiled in this secret history, brought a shock of recognition as sudden and disorienting as a physical blow:

Lazerenko, Patrick: Dépanneur Mondial, 216–17; José-Maria Fernandez and, 230, 231, 252–54; Celia García and, 229–31, 248–50; medical school, 231; protegé of Hernan, 228, 229–30.

He took the book with him everywhere, even when he visited Tegucigalpa on the way back from a vacation in Costa Rica. He spent two unsatisfying days there, wandering like a faithless pilgrim through the streets of the Colonia Palmira neighbourhood where the Garcías had lived. He held *The Angel* open in front of him, hopeful of finding inaccuracies and mistakes that would discredit its premise. But it didn't help. Not a bit. The allegations against Hernan outlined in the book were like anti-matter, altering the rules of the universe as he knew it. Evil was introduced and made real. Evil not as the adjective that he'd always imagined it, but as the noun, the big dark cloud of human doom. Then there was the Fernandez reference, the assertion made by Elyse that this particular victim of Lepaterique had a special significance to Hernan, and, by extension, Patrick. There was no way he could talk to Hernan after that.

In the middle of the Churchillplein, Patrick felt the fight-or-flight thing again, the Pavlovian Elyse Brenman reaction that he had apparently been hard-wired for. He turned from Elyse without a word and walked away. Elyse's footsteps rang out on the plaza pavement. She was following. Trot to canter. A full-fledged arm-swinging sprint was next in the chain of embarrassing adult movements.

"Can we talk?" she asked, pulling up beside him.

"I'm going into town."

Elyse pointed ahead of them to a tram stop.

"I was headed that way too. We can take the Number 10."

Patrick didn't want to go into town, it had just seemed the best way to dodge Elyse. But she had a habit of making evasion difficult through affability and pure helpfulness. He

45
–

had learned that among journalists, this made Elyse fairly unusual. Less than a year ago, travelling to Boston in another effort to convince him to be interviewed for an upcoming article, she crashed a dinner Heather and he were having at a restaurant – introducing herself right there at the table, flirting with him in that asexual, joking way that she knew wouldn't make Heather uncomfortable, enough so that it was only natural for Heather to suggest that she pull up a chair so they could all have a chat before the food arrived. To Patrick's surprise, Elyse didn't mention the case at all, choosing only to intimate that she and Patrick were childhood friends from the old neighbourhood in Montreal, just two kids from NDG who'd made good, and that this crossing of paths was nothing more than a coincidence. At first he didn't know if Elyse had actually deluded herself into thinking that they were friends. There was no way he was going to bring up the subject of Hernan García in front of Heather, and he sensed that once Elyse knew this it was as though something between them changed, as though she took pleasure in enlisting him in some sort of game, that it was them against Heather in a bit of a con. He didn't let on anything – he barely said a word as the two women spoke – more out of mortification than willingness to play along with any charade. Elyse talked with Heather about global warming and vacation spots and the latest minivan crash-test data. It was like watching a dare. When Heather wasn't looking, Elyse would turn to him and smile, and he couldn't figure out if he was chilled or excited. All he could think about was why she would be doing this. Was it done to show him that they were somehow in this together, bound up in lies? Maybe she was just telling him that she was there, insidious and in no hurry. She kept talking to Heather, and he realized he had no idea about her. And if he'd been impressed by her restraint in not grilling him about Hernan, it was more than balanced by the creepiness of her knowing where they were eating and what time they had reservations.

He should have shooed her off, he thought. Right then and there he should have come clean with Heather about who Elyse was and explained the entire García situation. In the end he was rescued by the waiter's arrival with the food and the fact the table was too small to hold another place setting.

Heather raved about Elyse, of course. She had never met any friends of his, from Boston or Montreal or anyplace else for that matter, and the fact that he was even capable of having friends, much less fascinating journalist friends – non-threatening female ones at that – who thought enough of him to abandon part of their own evening to reminisce, impressed her. Why hadn't he told her about Elyse before? she asked in the car on the way home. She thought Elyse was *fan*tastic, that was the word she used, with the accent on the first syllable, the American way to say it. She said Elyse reminded her of her sister, a grad student at Northwestern, except for her sister always being stoned, that is.

Patrick used to think that it was only annoying to have someone so pleasant dog him, that Elyse's manner must be an obstacle to her advancing in her trade. He would even admit to feeling sorry for Elyse for having a personality so seemingly at odds with the job she had to do. But it became clear to him that over time people like Elyse gained your confidence and insinuated themselves into your life until your story became their story. And then it was everyone's story.

Just then, as if to justify Patrick's bias, she produced tokens for the Number 10 tram – one for him, which she dropped into his inexplicably opening hand – and pointed out the stop, and before he could come up with a plausible alternative excuse to get away from her they were heading south together into the city centre.

"Where are you going?" she asked.

"I haven't decided."

"I've been here for weeks. The trams are the best way to get around."

Patrick found a seat as the tram gave a metallic shout and pulled away from Churchillplein. Elyse sat beside him and said nothing. Her silence made him squirm as he imagined her biding her time purposefully, as someone capable of using nonchalance as some form of long-term tactic, trying to elicit a silence as fraudulent as that spiel in the restaurant. This is crazy, he told himself, calm down. He tried to remember Elyse that first day she came to interview him, wanting to conjure up an image of her being disorganized and inexperienced, but he couldn't recall her as anything other than competent. Focused. Even as an inexperienced reporter covering the purgatorial beat of the Community News Desk, she had been smart enough to sense that the call from that customer who'd recognized Hernan was something big. And when the newspaper tried to get one of their more senior feature writers to take the story over, Elyse had supposedly made a stink and held onto her scoop with both hands. And while she would have probably been a good reporter even without ever having met the Garcías, she wouldn't have been famous. The story of Hernan García had been more than a great story for Elyse, it had become award-winning, career-making. She had ridden it for years, parlaying the investigation and subsequent allegations, the sad arc of the García family – Marta's death,

Hernan's estrangement from his son, the near failure of the store – into a series of articles that had appeared in increasingly prominent magazines and had metastasized into *The Angel*. Elyse had been transformed into a journalist, flying to Tegucigalpa to research the details of her subject's past life and now setting up shop in Den Haag for long enough to become familiar with the tram lines and the local points of interest. They had that in common, Patrick thought. They both owed Hernan García everything.

They crossed an avenue, passing a building Elyse told him was the Gemeentemuseum. He chose not to look back at the museum, more intent on the succession of bare plazas and tidy Dutch streets rolling past. The sky had been steadily darkening but at one point the clouds thinned and it appeared as though the sun would break through, but it never did. Throughout the ride, squalls from the North Sea dropped rain at regular intervals, speckling the tram windows and making Den Haag pass by all the more indistinctly.

Elyse followed him off the tram near the Binnerhof just as it began to rain more heavily, chasing people off the streets, holding newspapers over their heads. Elyse had remembered to bring an umbrella, which she opened after pausing dramatically to register his umbrella-deficient state. The umbrella was big enough, typically, and she was only too happy to share.

"You hungry?" Elyse asked, taking great pains to position the umbrella exactly between them.

"No," he said, and regretted sounding so petulant.

At that moment a wave of fatigue crested over him. Perhaps it was the jet lag or sitting in the gallery hearing the testimony or tramping around the city in the rain like an idiot, but he felt ankled by a sudden, shuddering fatigue, something definitely not physiologic but deeper, a weariness, a narcoleptic ache to close the eyes.

The street narrowed and the facades of buildings darkened with stains of water and soot. They stood watching traffic pass. Wordlessly. It was a dream, a recollection of a street from moments before.

He caught a glimpse of a street sign that read "Frederikstraat" and he felt the need to say the word aloud – *Frederikstraat* – to hear the sound, as if saying the name could give him a better sense of where he was.

"Frederikstraat," he said. It made no difference.

"What?" Elyse asked.

"Nothing," he replied.

"Let's get something to eat."

He was too tired to refuse. He needed to sit down. Elyse found a Javanese café just entering the lunch rush, and they were seated at a table near the clatter of the kitchen. Patrick ordered the bami goreng along with a beer. Elyse asked for something he wasn't familiar with and then filled the silence with an elaborate ethno-cultural history of the dish.

The hectic sway of the restaurant ebbed, and his fatigue passed with it. He studied the pattern on the tablecloth, unwilling to look up at her, aware that she was watching him. When he finally looked up, he found her studying the wine list.

In a world full of people now very interested in Hernan's life, the woman sitting across from him probably knew more about it than anyone. More than family, more than he. She had built a career amassing the details of Hernan's life before Canada, constructing that plausible, abhorrent reality, and had seen Hernan through a different set of biases than family loyalty or ideology or pure defensiveness. Elyse knew the facts;

everything he knew of Hernan was coloured by friendship. No wonder he hated her.

"I thought he'd be in the courtroom," Patrick said finally, as the waiter brought their food. She paused until the waiter left the table. Her eyebrows tented and she stirred her bowl of curry with her fork.

"He has been, but he's been sick," Elyse said.

"What's wrong?"

"I don't know. He won't talk to me, of course, and neither will Celia or Roberto."

"So they're here?" Patrick said. He knew they were here. He'd been searching through the gallery for Celia's face when he'd spotted Elyse. A dubious consolation prize. "Is he getting medical treatment?"

"I'd say so. Although I imagine it's hard to give a cardiologist advice about his own health."

"I can try to speak with his doctors."

"There's a little thing called doctor-patient confidentiality," she replied, smiling.

Eventually, the plates were cleared away and he began grudgingly to appreciate Elyse's company. It was a relief to talk to anyone after three days of travel and hotel rooms. Elyse told him how she'd tried to make the most of all the weeks in Den Haag, how she'd visited every museum and then made her way through the B-list stuff like the amusement park where the city of Den Haag was reproduced in miniature, and he was amused by this thought, the image of Elyse towering over the city, inadvertently terrorizing a good part of coastal Holland. But Elyse said after a while a sense of indigenous Den Haag claustrophobia had set in and she had recently started fleeing the city for a regular weekend of respite in Amsterdam.

Patrick admitted to a certain curiosity about how she worked, now that she didn't need to write for a newspaper. The success of the book had freed her. She worked when she wanted to. And when she was working she was on the road a lot, she said. She missed Montreal, missed her boat.

"A boat?" he said, a tone of genuine surprise asserting itself before envy could arrive. A boat. Affluence squared. The confluence of money and stretches of leisure time. He'd never had both simultaneously.

She brought out a photo of herself on her sailboat on Lake Champlain. Bright interlocking pentagons of lens flare trailed off into the Vermont summer sky. It looked like a warm day. A perfect happiness. He wondered who took the picture. Elyse was in a bikini top with some sort of sarong-like skirt around her legs. And while he smiled and nodded appreciatively as he held the photo, he could feel himself grow irritated at being unable to look away from her tanned legs and her boat, unable to get thoughts of the boyfriend holding the camera out of his mind and he held his breath against the feeling of jealousy billowing, categories of jealousy compounding. He handed the photo back. Elyse asked if Heather and he were getting serious, and he told her he didn't have a clue where things were going. It was a pleasure to tell a journalist the truth. She paused, and Patrick dreaded that she was going to offer him advice.

"I see that your company's doing well," Elyse said, changing course. "I read about it in *Business Weekly*."

He nodded and was prepared to leave it at that. The one rule he had learned during his brief career in business was that information was a commodity. His lawyers had pointed out that he had been celebrated and sued and made rich, all because of information, and if they were at the table, they would tell Patrick not to say a word about Neuronaut or his research or the Globomart work. But the lawyers were far away. They hadn't been alone for three days or seen the photo of Elyse relaxing on her boat.

"We're pleased. Thirty-five employees, thirty-six if you count one of my former post-docs we just hired. We have our own machine, an MRI machine," he said, and gestured with his hands trying to convey the *bigness* of the machine, "and in a few months we'll be having our second annual general meeting."

"Congratulations. It's like the nineties again. Technology types like you getting rich."

He enjoyed the envy in Elyse's voice. *Technology types.* "Except we actually have a service to offer."

"I heard someone was trying to buy you out before the IPO."

"That's old news."

"It's just that I'm freelancing," she said, pausing. Patrick wondered what else Elyse thought about besides ruining Hernan García's life or side-swiping his own. "I've been reading about the work you're doing. Neuroeconomics is a fascinating field." He watched her mouth move, as though it were easier to understand her that way than by only having her words to go by. "I was thinking of maybe writing a feature on it. The technology and applications, the personalities. It could be very good for your company, good for you. I mean, you being here, at the trial, that can't be good for Neuronaut or your clients." Elyse played with her crumpled napkin. Information was a commodity, he reminded himself. He tried to think of speaking to Elyse as a form of conversational tennis, just keep a rally going. Say nothing, he told himself, or just keep talking. Platitude, platitude, generalization.

"It's an exciting field to be in right now."

"What exactly are you working on?"

"I can't say."

"You are *so* paranoid, Patrick," Elyse said, easing into a conspiratorial smile. "You don't have to say. It would take me ten minutes to find out, if I wanted to."

"Is that supposed to reassure me or threaten me?"

"Neither. Asking you is a courtesy. Everything can be off the record, okay?" Elyse was clearly relishing his discomfort. "This is a conversation between friends in a restaurant. If I want to interview you, I'll let you know. So what are you up to?"

Patrick recalled a phrase from his company's Web site, a description that soothed and puzzled prospective clients and investors in that way that only technospeak could. "We've developed a prediction-valuation model. The way the brain compares the value of future acts or stimuli, how economic decisions are made. We're able to see what parts of the brain are activated during these decisions."

"Just economic?"

"We're interested in economic decisions."

"I heard that you're working for Globomart."

"Well, no. Not really. We don't 'work' for anyone. They're one of many clients, but we have – "

"What do you do for them?"

"Basically, it's an advanced form of market research," Patrick said. He wouldn't say more. He'd made that mistake at a party recently, explaining his work to the boyfriend of one of Heather's co-workers/friends, Josh or something similarly soulful. Patrick had had a couple of beers and been cornered by Josh on a back patio where all the party's significant others were quarantined, and when the chit-chat ended and his "market research" explanation for what he did drew a stare, he'd felt the need to elaborate, saying that Globomart, like any big corporation, spent hundreds of millions of dollars on advertising, so they wanted to develop a strategy first. And it was natural that they'd want to test their strategy before they fully invested in a product or an ad campaign. His job, he said to Josh, was to use a brain-imaging machine to determine how the brain responded to whatever: a product, an environment, an advertisement; looking for a pattern of response that correlated with eventual "success" for the client.

Josh said nothing, choosing instead to frown performatively, which segued into more explicit outrage, as though he'd been forced to listen to Robert McNamara gush about the efficiencies of incendiary bombing. "He should have introduced himself as a consumer activist," Patrick had complained to Heather as they left, the trumpet of Josh's raised, righteous voice ushering them out. Of all the things said, Patrick remembered the "crypto-fascist mind-control theorist" insult most distinctly, mentally cataloguing it to cross-reference with the threatening letters he'd received.

Elyse spoke in vague terms about coming to Neuronaut headquarters in Cambridge when all of this was over. She wanted to sit down with the team and get a feel for what neuroeconomics was all about. *Yeah, right*, he thought and nodded, wondering where he could get her picture to better warn security that she might show up. She'd like to see Heather again too, she said, maybe have dinner. The waiter brought another beer to the table. Patrick didn't remember ordering it.

"I heard one of your big fans from the Democratic Voice is coming," he said, taking his time pouring the beer into a glass, enjoying the theatricality of turning the tables on Elyse. But Elyse just shrugged, as though he'd described an extended forecast of rain.

"I'd be disappointed if they weren't here," Elyse said. "I'm happy they're here. I find being on the other side of an issue from the Democratic Voice reassuring. I mean, everyone knows their agenda" – her voice descended to a practised, reason-enumerating drone – "protect American corporate interests, maintain and protect puppet dictatorships friendly to said American corporate interests, reframe the debate so that anyone who opposes them looks like a Marxist dupe. Am I missing anything? And it's not like they dispute the facts. They're lining up behind what Hernan did, behind everything that happened in Honduras. They'll probably be there when they try those soldiers for what went on at Abu Ghraib and Guantanamo."

"They say they just want a fair trial for Hernan."

"They say a lot of things."

Patrick wanted to ask her what she meant but was too occupied by the enormous head of foam that had dribbled over the side of the glass and onto his hand and the table. As he mopped up the suds, Elyse leaned over to him: "Why do you think Hernan won't meet with them?"

"I don't know, Elyse. I haven't talked to him either."

"C'mon, Patrick, you must know something. Why else are you here?"

Patrick went cold. "We've been through this. You know everything I know. More."

"He was practising medicine in the back of his store, Patrick. Did that just slip your mind? All those years you were there, you knew it. How do you think I felt having someone else break that story, knowing you hadn't told me? Well, I think you have more you're hiding."

"Believe me, I don't."

"You have choices, Patrick."

"Pardon me?"

"You can tell me anything, you know that, right? That way you'd at least have some control over how it came out."

. "What do you mean?"

"It's just that I've heard that you might be subpoenaed." Elyse's expression was neutral, a sky of imperial greys. "I'll let you in on a little secret: everybody knows everyone else's business here. It's common knowledge that di Costini was talking to you in Boston. I've heard rumours that the prosecutors are interested in speaking to you too. Now that you're here, I wanted you to know."

"Thanks," Patrick said, as calmly as possible, as he felt the physiologic reaction to a threat engaging inside him. He knew the circuitry: pathways converging on his amygdala that, in response, fired like an automatic weapon, a heartbeat pattering after, spent shell casings bouncing off the floor. He'd never considered being called to testify against Hernan, never thought that coming to Den Haag would make issuing a subpoena such a simple task. He'd been a fool to come. He imagined Elyse watching him for any sign, sneaking a look at his pupils or checking his brow for that first sheen of perspiration. Wondering how much he knew and what could be proved. And then, as if making a compromise to another physiologic reaction, the sense of panic passed. Elyse was just another person across the table. *Nothing will happen*, he repeated to himself. "Would you like dessert, Elyse?" he said, and felt the moisture on his upper lip.

THREE

–

Big bright sun outside the restaurant and Patrick stared up like a tourist taking in a special attraction. The wet Frederikstraat glistened and gave that odd sensation of something clean and filthy at the same time, which to Patrick seemed a pretty good civic motto for any place, even Den Haag.

The topic of a subpoena had ended the meal, and they'd waited in uncomfortable silence for the waiter to arrive with the check. After that, Patrick excused himself and, without further explanation, got up to leave. Not one to take offence, Elyse announced that she too had other business – trams to ride, threats to make, he thought – and added, to his back as he walked away from her, that she was ending her afternoon with a meeting with someone at the tribunal.

He tried to flag down a cab on Frederikstraat, but they blew by him like he was waving a meat cleaver. It was nothing personal, he was assured by the cab driver at a taxi stand in front of a hotel two blocks away, no roadside pickups – that was just taxi policy. He sank into the seat and minutes later he was deposited at the entrance of the Metropole, where Pieter the concierge, Edwin's shift replacement, made a scene.

"Dr. Lazerenko, there are *people* who are *wanting* to talk to you *all* day," he pleaded, almost breaking into tears at having met the man who had been the source of his grief, the serial MBA threats he had endured, all those identical shouting American voices. Patrick understood that hotel culture must have a tolerance for clients like the one he had become: frightful, messy mysteries, importance gauged by the depth of complication they left behind them, forgiven only because they also trailed certain rewards in their wake. And sure enough, when Patrick promised he'd attend to the messages immediately and thanked Pieter for his attention with a requisite gratuity, the clerk dipped his head as if to acknowledge this understanding. It was wonderful, cleansing them both, like a UN guilt-for-cash exchange program. Then came the elevator ride of mirrors and silence followed by the exquisite calm of a thickly carpeted hallway outside a newly made-up room, and for a moment Den Haag was nothing more than a theme park of business-class adventures where no one had been hurt and no one was accused of anything more than not answering their messages. He found a mint on the bed.

He called Neuronaut and spoke to Steve and Jessica, needing to reassure both of them that he wasn't dead or in rehab somewhere (although he suspected doubts lingered about the rehab denial), and then Marc-André got on the line, telling him that Sanjay had taken the Globomart data and barricaded himself in his office, causing an increasingly worried Bancroft to check up on the young man every half-hour. The employees, beginning to sense the pressure of the spiralling Globomart mess, had done the logical thing and established an

office pool – the Sanjaywatch – estimating the date of his resignation, offering a triple payout if Sanjay did anything more
rash than quitting. Marc-André said he'd put his money
down on Thursday, noon, immolation. Oh, and, by the way,
he added, Barry Olafson (Lyle's son – or was it Henrik's?), a
Globomart senior vp, had called from Medina to tell Bancroft
they'd have to postpone their marketing launch if they
didn't have an analysis they could use by the end of this week.
The resulting sequence of events – botched advertising
campaign, disappointing fiscal fourth quarter, a failure to
meet earnings, massive layoffs, the squashing of Neuronaut
like a bug – were implied in the way that Barry Olafson had
calmly said, "The marketing launch will not be postponed.
We trust that is understood."

Patrick listened to Marc-André and wondered if every
future success would, by necessity, lead to moments like this,
the never-ending crisis of raised expectations. It was enough to
make a person want to explore the healing qualities of
systematic failure. Neuronaut was officially a victim of its own
success, having its first big corporate victory advising
Globomart with its last campaign – a huge re-orientation of its
marketing strategy into something the company christened
"Values" – that had featured unprecedented saturation
advertising and had resulted in a spike in sales and profits. The
campaign ended up airing commercials that Patrick found, all
in all, fairly compelling and creepy in that Leni Riefenstahl
sort of way. Prior to this, Globomart had spent billions on
advertising with only the vaguest idea that its marketing
worked, the assumption based on the observation that the
company continued to crush its competitors and produce
profits along the lines of the gross domestic product of Spain.

Neuronaut hadn't told Globomart what to do, so much as confirm for the company that the theme of a certain campaign had a profound, measurable, and reproducible effect on the brains of consumers Globomart was targeting. As a result, Globomart felt confident about immediately doubling its advertising budget, in the end achieving spectacular success. Neuronaut's results, which had showed decreased activation in a part of the frontal lobe associated with complex decision making when a person was exposed to certain types of advertising, was the marketing equivalent of the smart bomb. Or the dumb bomb, as Patrick liked to say when the people from Globomart weren't around.

And now Globomart had made the commitment to dominate the world's retail landscape more completely, more scientifically. It had ponied up a budget for neuroscience research that dwarfed half the universities in the country. After the success of the Values campaign, Globomart wanted – demanded – proof that every dollar they spent had *effect*.

The problem was that none of the data for the new campaign made any sense to them.

"Globomart is upset because the imaging tests aren't showing any difference between the various themes they have to choose from," Marc-André said. "Nothing is clear like it was in Values. Globomart wants Values, just like they had before."

"They don't understand the technology, we're talking about percentages of difference. There's no guarantee there'll be a difference between the choices anyway," Patrick replied, before telling Marc-André that the data could be modelled in different ways, that he and Sanjay had run up against these sorts of problems before. "Sanjay will get it done."

A grunt, emitted in Boston, travelled three thousand miles into space and bounced back to earth, where it was relayed from a tower in central Den Haag to be heard by Patrick the moment before Marc-André ended the call.

It was late in the court day when Patrick got back to the tribunal. The crowd had partially dispersed – there must have been more lurid proceedings in another courtroom – but it was still a respectable showing. He took his place among the other congregants and fiddled with the cords and the earpieces, something that made him feel grumpy and old. It wasn't until later that Patrick looked up to see Hernan García in the dock, blue shirt and erect posture, hair and moustache greyed to the point where he bore an ungodly resemblance to Omar Sharif. The defendant sat motionless, apparently listening, although there was no way an observer could tell for sure. It was riveting to see him now, making Patrick worry that even though he'd accepted Hernan's guilt, he had somehow re-invented him over the last five years as a more heroic figure, that in his mind someone could grow in stature even through pure infamy.

Then García moved, brought a hand to his eyes to wipe something away, and Patrick saw him differently. It had taken a moment, but he had found the man who was his friend and who, at one time, he would never have believed could be a part of this. And he was in a cage.

He had met Hernan García on May 24, 1986, at a little before eleven in the evening. Patrick was sixteen and had been downtown with friends, part of the crowds celebrating the Canadiens' Stanley Cup victory. The whole city was out, whooping down St. Catherine Street from the Forum to downtown. The crowds stopped traffic, and as the revellers streamed by, the cars had no choice but to join in with their horns. It was before the era when overturning cars became part of the expected civic response during post-championship celebrations, and the cops were smiling and high-fiving too. Patrick didn't care for hockey. If pressed he could probably name a few of the players, but he was sixteen and the spectacle of so many people in the streets was irresistible. So he was a fan for a night.

Later, he went to a party in a semi-finished basement where he gathered among a group of teenagers bullied into a corner by a pool table. When they ran out of beer, Patrick offered to go to the *dépanneur* to get more. He rushed because he knew it was illegal for *dépanneurs* to sell alcohol after eleven – owners slapped padlocks the size of a fist on the coolers at the stroke of the hour. To Patrick this was a typical adult law, arbitrary and stupid; the only effect it had was to make teenage drinkers like himself acutely aware of the minutes before closing. He began to jog.

By the time he reached Monkland Avenue, he was sprinting. Still, six blocks away from the nearest dep, lungs on fire and beginning to doubt he could reach it in time, Patrick came across a newly opened store on the corner of Marcil. He checked his watch, two minutes to spare, and decided it was the right time to support this new business. He opened the door of Le Dépanneur Mondial to that nasty aural itch of wind chimes, and was met by the intense stare of a dark-skinned woman who managed to smile, seemingly against her will. A thick book was cleaved open in front of her. She had a pencil, and Patrick could see she was underlining or writing on the pages. Patrick smiled back at her, gave her a thumbs up, and said, "Go Habs," to her bewilderment. Then he began to stalk the store for the beer aisle. His first recollection of

Le Dépanneur Mondial was the eye-aching glare off the clean floors, much too clean for a real dep, something he chalked up to the newness of the place, knowing that in six months it would be scuffed, pissed on, and beer doused into a more recognizable shade of *dépanneur* grey. What struck him next was that the store didn't seem to have recognizable food in it. The shelves were well stocked and clearly marked but the shapes and colours and smells were different. The labels were strange and even the fruits and vegetables looked disguised. Then it dawned on him. It was an immigrant *dépanneur*: noodles from somebody else's country and spices that would wring tears from your eyes. He would have been curious but he needed beer and that was the one thing he couldn't find. Patrick did a quick perimeter search and then came back to the counter lady.

"Beer?"

"No." She shook her head placidly, the punchline to a joke he hadn't told.

"Beer, or wine?" He pointed at his watch to remind her that he had been there before the padlocks were due to go on.

"Her-*nan!*" she shouted into a back room, and a man materialized, six foot two and athletic-looking for a guy stepping out of the back room of a dep. He crossed his arms and leaned toward the woman.

"What is it?"

"He wants beer."

The *dépanneur* owner turned to Patrick.

"We don't have beer."

"But you're a dep. Every dep has beer."

"We don't carry beer."

"You should have to put up a sign," he said as he looked at his watch and shook his head. "Shit, now it's past eleven.

Thanks a fucking lot. I don't know where you come from, but in this country, if you don't sell beer, you put up a sign."

This altercation, which embarrassed Patrick whenever he recalled it later in his life, was best thought of as a geopolitical conflict. The geography involved was his neighbourhood – Notre-Dame-de-Grâce, a district of Montreal with correspondingly high densities of *dépanneurs* and teenagers, its 160 square blocks a testing ground for new and innovative forms of dep owner abuse, the alkali flats of smart-assing. Throughout his adolescence Patrick – endowed with a temper and a taste for the darkest vocabulary – spat profanity at French Canadians and Anglos alike and generally took pleasure in browbeating men and women of all colours and creeds who dared to serve behind the cash registers of neighbourhood corner stores. Once, he had made a Korean dep man cry and shouted at his angry, more resilient wife when he returned the next day to see if he could make him cry again.

The man looked calmly at Patrick. "Are you mildly mentally retarded?" he asked.

Just "retarded" would have provoked Patrick, but the addition of *mildly mentally* knocked him off balance with its sincere curiosity, as if concern were being offered along with a rebuke. "No," Patrick said, already cursing himself for having answered.

"How old are you?" the *dépanneur* owner asked. The lady at the cash sat motionless, letting him go to work. She looked like she had seen this show before and didn't mind it at all.

"What?"

"You are too young for beer."

"That's none of your business."

"It is my business, indeed. Let's see your ID."

Patrick was on his way out when the dep owner said this, but he turned back.

"You can't card me if you're not selling me beer."

"It's my store."

"This isn't fucking Pakistan or wherever."

The dep owner pointed to bags of rice. "It's Spanish you see all around you. We are not from Pakistan, you idiot."

"Fuck you."

"Good night."

When Patrick returned later it was with a spray can and plans to redecorate for the new Pakistani grocer. He found the back of the store in the lane and felt the exhilaration that the young and angry and slightly drunk know so well, a buzz amplified by shaking a spray can, that infectious rattle tocking away as a wall is sized up and claimed. Then came the hiss of the spray and any tagger will tell you that that alone is a trip, a serpent muse calling out, even if it isn't art, just profanity dripping down a wall. It was better than art; it was you imposing yourself on a white wall. Sovereignty and revenge in one vaguely creative act.

Patrick's bliss was halted by the sudden thud of a hand clamping onto his right shoulder while another slapped his forearm, knocking the spray can to the ground. He spun away and ran, hearing footsteps pounding down the back lane behind him. It was likely the owner of the dep, making Patrick think he was home free since a city block was all anybody over forty was good for. But five strides later, he had the sick feeling that his pursuer was gaining. At the end of the lane near the corner, Patrick felt a hand on his jacket, this time pushing him forward. He flailed and lost his balance, lurching into some bags of trash but finding enough concrete to take some skin off his forearms. The man hauled Patrick out of the garbage and he braced for a fight but found he was too tired and embarrassed to take a swing at anyone. They both just stood there, bent over, unable to speak. In the light of the streetlamps Patrick saw the man shake and sweat and try to catch his breath and for a moment he thought about bolting again, but the *dépanneur* owner was a big guy and angry as hell and even though he was breathing hard he had already run Patrick down once and could probably do it again. He looked at Patrick and muttered, "I should call the cops" over and over between breaths until Patrick finally said, "So call the fucking cops," but the guy was already marching him around the corner, which was freaking Patrick out, thinking he was in for some rough justice right there on Monkland. He was relieved when the guy only grabbed his wallet. He assumed the man would take whatever money he had – which wasn't much – and call it even. But the man he would come to know as Hernan García just stood there, keeping Patrick collared on the sidewalk and going through his wallet. A couple of good citizens passed them and said nothing. And while it was now, all these years later, painfully clear to Patrick why Hernan had wanted to avoid contact with police at all costs, his decision that night to deal with the matter himself – perpetrator in hand, past midnight – seemed far more ominous than a brush with the law.

But back then, Hernan García let go of the younger man, gave him his wallet, and straightened him up.

"Hingston. Where's Hingston Street?" he asked.

And in keeping with the general mood of surprise and bafflement, Patrick pointed without hesitation in the direction of the street where he lived.

His parents met Hernan García on the porch of their house a few minutes later when they answered the door to his bailiff-like poundings. They had probably been awake at that hour but even so opened the door with the understandably aggrieved look that seems appropriate when some stranger is banging on your door past midnight. There was some shouting between Hernan and Patrick's father, Roger – Patrick was reminded of a nature show's classic two-bear encounter: the two rogues swiping at each other, the bark and roar before someone ambles away. Patrick's mother, Veronica, who had popped her head out like a prairie dog inspecting the air, vanished from the doorway, ostensibly to say a rosary and call the police. Then Roger – T-shirted, mountainous, and Popeye-armed, and yet causing no apparent alarm in Hernan – looked over at his son and, seeing him, obviously decided that Hernan must have had a legitimate complaint. Roger did a wonderful homage to a concerned parent as Hernan introduced himself and then described the encounter in the alley. Patrick knew that as the culprit, caught and collared there on the porch, his fate was sealed and punishment was clearly coming. And yet his father seemed to take Hernan's earnestness as a cue to pretend that he hadn't made up his mind about his son's guilt or innocence, that they'd discuss this in full because they were all enlightened people. Patrick would have preferred the standard Roger treatment: nod at the accusation, tell the accuser that he would handle it, and yell at the kid to get inside the goddamn house. But it had been different that night; there was a polite discussion, some thoughtful nodding and excessive wrinkling of the brow, as if Patrick were six and had taken somebody's Lego. Then Roger took a stage pause, looked his son in the eye (what was this, an after-school special?), and asked Patrick if what *Mr. García* said was true and *waited* for his son's reply. *As if.* Patrick was incapable of responding in the same spirit of improvisational theatre, choosing to nod yes and then forced to say the word when finally goaded. Hernan García listened to it all, quiet enough that Patrick thought he too was going to nod, satisfied, and walk away. But Hernan wasn't finished.

"There is still the matter of the cost of damages."

Roger, impressively, kept his composure even through this, not slamming the door or telling Hernan to piss off and call the cops already. He listened to this stranger on his porch and agreed that in lieu of immediate payment, the debt could be worked off in Hernan's store. Patrick was incredulous. It wasn't that Roger was keen on compromise or alternative forms of restitution. No, he agreed because, in Patrick's eyes, it wouldn't cost him time or effort or hard cash. It was hardly fair, but still, it was better than the cops or a back-alley curb stomping by a wronged dep guy. Both men ponied up the decorum for a solemn, friendly handshake, the last act in that night's theatre of the absurd. As he was turning to go, García had told Patrick to show up for work at seven on Saturday morning.

Patrick slowly turned his head and surveyed the crowd. Most were watching Hernan. This was why people came. García then leaned to one side and his right elbow flexed and although Patrick couldn't see his hands it was clear he was fishing something out of his pocket. He brought a small pump up to his mouth, an inhaler with reddish-pink liquid inside. Even from a distance, Patrick could tell it was nitrospray. García held his hand in front of his face, the thumb and forefinger pinched together around the inhaler, as though he were taking a photo of the gallery. His face changed: a grimace, the slightest puckering of lips, and then – Patrick could swear, from sixty feet away he was certain – a look of surprise. Patrick was alarmed and suddenly became conscious of his own heart, of the pains he'd never felt before. But in a moment it was over. The inhaler disappeared and García's face returned to its default setting. Minutes passed in this way, his expression still, a placidity unimaginable outside sleep or cults. Patrick was relieved when Hernan's brow finally furrowed, followed by the slightest elevation of his gaze. Hernan was looking out at the crowd. Patrick followed, mentally crawling into Hernan's chair and scanning along with him, trying to guess what he was seeing. This process fascinated him, in a professional way; he couldn't think of any other act so intimate and yet speculative as imagining what another person saw, projecting into someone's head and then out again. Hernan scanned past the prosecution table and up three or four lower rows of seats that were never occupied. A woman sat alone but he passed over her. Up again to the sixth row and over to the right where a young man and woman sat. There. These were the faces he had sought out. It was Roberto and Celia. Patrick was certain García must see them too.

.This first glimpse of them almost drew Patrick from his chair but he stayed seated, instead slowly altering his posture, a ship listing to starboard, to get a better look at García's family, at Celia specifically. Celia and Roberto stood out from the others in the gallery so clearly that he was astonished he hadn't seen them before. Roberto sat with his arms crossed, as always, as though restrained by an invisible straitjacket, his indignation barely held in check. It was immediately evident to Patrick – after more than ten years, across an auditorium, in another country – that he'd lost weight. Celia sat beside him. She was beautiful. The words came to him, as though some independent observer had broadcast it over the PA in his head. Though he knew it was trite to be suddenly struck by the beauty of a person he had always considered beautiful, it was an alarming experience to see her. He saw Celia in profile, her black hair gathered into a thick ponytail. Her eyes periodically darted down from the scene in front of her to her lap, where she was writing in her notebook.

Patrick understood he was a poor witness to history. He was the sort of person who took some consolation in thinking that, human nature being what it was, during the Nuremberg trials people undoubtedly doodled in the margins of their notebooks or dozed off or daydreamed about loved ones far removed from the atrocities under discussion. But Patrick's particular disgrace came when, during the testimony of witness C-144, Celia looked over at him and they made eye contact for the first time in more than a decade. C-144 was forgotten, all the shocks and trauma and meaningless pain, lost. The words dissolved into a hum of consecutive sounds, buccal, lingual, glottal. He saw Celia. The physical reaction was as clichéd as one would expect when one's insides are hosed down with adrenalin, when every good memory is compressed and released into one moment of remembrance and all of it is coupled to the heartbeat like the repetitive slamming of a door. *I loved her.*

This experience, of course, is never complete without the trough that follows the swell. He felt sweaty and shaky and for a moment the room seemed dimly cloud-covered as he remembered that this woman that he'd lived with for three years, staring back at him now, was someone he had already disappointed and injured, someone who likely considered him to have been one of the major mistakes in her life. As an accompaniment to watching Celia, Patrick heard the testimony from C-144 – "Once you regained consciousness, did you see him then?" – followed by the sound of C-144 shuffling in his seat, noises (the chair, his joints, a sigh) audible through the microphone, untranslated. Witness C-144 continued, describing what he'd seen, what he thought he'd seen when he came to in that interrogation room in Lepaterique and Patrick thought, *Yes, this is a disgrace.* But he couldn't look away – why was the brain like that? Able to slip loose of the reins of a more serious issue for a glimpse at something else?

Celia held his gaze for a moment more and in that epoch he wondered if there was a sadder statement than *I loved her.* The severance it implied. The loss and constant accounting of the loss. He'd lost her. Celia's face showed no anger, no surprise. They were little more than strangers now. She gently tilted her head toward the proceedings as if to admonish him for taking his attention away from what was important.

He was ill. His first bet was the bami goreng or the beer stirred up by adrenalin. The room drew tighter around him and he felt a swell of nausea. He got to his feet, not caring what the guards or the other voyeurs thought, and shuffled back down the row to the aisle. He found a washroom and threw open a stall door, certain he was going to be sick, but it passed, leaving him sweating and winded, sitting on a toilet in Den Haag, studying the freshly scrubbed surfaces of the stall. Patrick ran his hand through his hair and it emerged damp, a Den Haag shower. His throat was tight and he was still short of breath; it was only when he managed to get a couple of tablets of Valium out of the bottle in his pocket and into his mouth that he felt the pressure fade away. He sat and breathed and waited for the pills to do their business, soaking his synapses in that feeling that passed for relief. In the lower corner of the stall's door, an area that had escaped the cleaners' scrubbing brush, handwritten words were faintly visible. He bent forward to take a look, wondering what type of graffiti a place like this attracted, expecting feverish political indictments or blood libels with an ethnic spin, but he could only make out a telephone number and, three inches to the right, the word *moordenaar*.

Twenty minutes passed before he could stand up, and when he did he was able to take only tentative, newborn calf steps past the stall door, then a quick stagger toward the sink before he felt cold water on his face. "I am better," he said to the faucet, to the water spilling off his face and down his wrists to wet the sleeves of his shirt. *I'm better. I am.*

Once out into the corridor, Patrick began to feel stronger. People were passing through the foyer, heading to the exits. It was quiet and dreamlike, surprising him, pleasing him. He floated out into the crowd, a balloon of him filled with benzodiazepine bliss, messages of distress falling from him like ballast.

The crowd dispersed onto the Churchillplein, swallowed by space. He looked around the plaza past the fountain and saw Celia and Roberto walking away. Nina – that must be her, little Nina outfitted in an adult frame – was with them now. Patrick shouted out "Hey" in an embarrassing broken croak, the voice of someone who hasn't spoken to anyone for hours, a voice that caused quite a few heads to turn. Roberto stopped and looked at him, a Serengeti stare, a calculation of space and velocity and a certain type of hunger, all of which caused Patrick to freeze in his gazelle tracks; but that lasted for a brief second before passing into a haze of memory. *These were my friends.* His stoner calm returned and he approached them. The Valium whispered a tuneless hymn of brotherhood and peace into his ear. He could see Celia. She was holding a child, a young boy who had buried his head under her chin. She was walking toward him. Roberto was beside her, several paces ahead. She had a son. He tried to read the look on her face, to see any sign of emotion, his eyes riveted to the details of her eyes and mouth, taking in every gesture in that way humans are wired for. But nothing came easily; with every step closer her features became more distinct, but she was still inscrutable. Her face. Celia's face, changed now into an adult face, a Modigliani of sadness and beauty. It was the last thing he remembered, this intense effort to decipher Celia García's expression, before he saw a flash of movement shear in from the right and a vision of sky, spinning, dusky.

FOUR

Celia smiling at him through a window that he still needed to clean. Evening. At seven o'clock she installed herself on the balcony with her easel, surveying the view down Lorne Crescent. She kneaded the pigment out of her brush with a rag, looking away from him and back to the scene in front of her.

He was pleased Celia brought her paints; the smell of her oils and turpentine filled the room, masking the stink that he noticed for the first time seconds after the janitor dropped the keys into his hand at the door. Hours later, he was still inside the apartment, scrubbing the sink and hoping that this and running the water would take care of the odour. He washed his hands and reached for a bag of plums, tore open the plastic bag and, holding two plums in each hand, washed them in the sink that still smelled. The give of the plastic and the deep crimson plum skin. The fruit was the only colour in an apartment filled with still-unopened cardboard boxes, a few with his belongings from home, others with pieces of entry-level Swedish furniture waiting to be Allen-keyed into existence.

He heard shouting in the distance but it didn't disturb him. This was where he lived now and so it counted as ambiance, as neighbourhood. He had moved not just to be out of his mother's house or closer to the hospital but specifically for voices, talking, laughing, even shouting. He felt guilty leaving his mother alone in their old house but they had lived in a silence that mutually acknowledged he was already on his way. He lived in the student ghetto now, twenty square blocks of studios and three-storey walk-ups, a neighbourhood of balconies and student apartments polished and worn with use, a patina of serial tenancy. The walls were freshly layered with that skim-milky wash that greets new tenants, veined more thickly around corners and over the electrical outlet plates.

He opened the door to the balcony and, to his delight after the anaemic pall of his apartment, entered a world that could not contain its colour. The eastern slope of the mountain rose from the rooftops to take a deep verdant bite of the sky. Who could blame its appetite? It was an evening of soft scattered clouds, flanks bruised with shades of yellow, shades of blue. Celia sat, working. His plums belonged out here. Windows were open. He heard music along with voices.

Below them, pickup trucks jammed with personal belongings and mattresses wedged on end weaved between other trucks pulled up at angles to the curb to better unload. It was the first of July, moving day in Montreal, the only jurisdiction in the world with the inexplicable rule that leases should all end on the same day. It was a day of heroic friends and physical exhaustion and curbside drama, a windfall for movers and pizza deliverymen. Everyone he knew had spent at least one moving day dealing with unconnected phones and cardboard boxes and the competing physics of walk-ups and sofas. Moving was a shared experience, a tribal event that renewed and reset the neighbourhood. It was a rare day when people from other countries, provinces, and neighbourhoods took to the streets in migration. Forget the calendar, this was the real New Year's Day.

He sat down on one of the lawn chairs and dried off the plums. Celia was using broad brush strokes to cover the upper parts of the small canvas in front of her, trying to capture the light of the evening sky while there was still time. "Good luck," he wanted to say but didn't, knowing the way it would sound.

He heard voices, louder, making what Celia was saying unintelligible and with this he felt a surge of panic. He looked over the balcony and then pulled himself back to the fruit resting on his lap, cradled in a crumpled paper towel.

All day long it had been building. It was the most unusual feeling, a simultaneous emptiness and fullness, and the only way he could explain it was to say it felt like the hunger for what he assumed his life was going to become. He wanted the future to arrive, a desire not based on any hardship he'd endured, not because he felt he was due this future, but simply that he thought it was going to be as beautiful as the mountain and the plums and Celia recording it all. It was an intense optimism, amplified now under this sky, a desire that frightened and consoled him, a succession of feelings that he knew were the first conceits of an adult life.

The sky ran through its riot of evening colours, finally ceding to a deep shade of purple. Their eyes stung with the day's last light. Celia put down her brush and he stood up to see what she had done. He had always taken pleasure in being the first to see each new work, but she reminded him that he could only ever be the second. He was the boyfriend. And while she tolerated his sneaking around for a peek, maybe even condoned it, she let him know that she didn't particularly need his approval. She was the artist. He looked at the painting. In an hour, she had easily captured the movement of the street below, the lines of the neighbourhood and the looming swell of mountain. It was her sky that stopped him. It wasn't just a skilled representation but an exploration of sky, all possible skies, made plausible in front of him. He could tell her any number of things, all of which would sound facile and wouldn't properly convey what he felt. So he said nothing, instead choosing to stare dumbly at the street settling into shadows and at the illuminated cross on Mount Royal. What he could not say, could not even understand at the time, was that Celia's sky saddened him in a vague and shameful way, hinting of a future of beauty and promise that he had no hand in.

Then, more voices, barking and guttural, rising to a tunnelling roar but Celia didn't react. He couldn't understand what they were saying. Everything around him darkened except for the lights from the cross on the mountain, which amplified and coalesced into a single point that grew until everything disappeared into its luminous centre. A voice, closer. Smaller than the god-voice he'd imagined as a kid.

"Can you hear me?"

Patrick awoke in another Dutch room. Regaining consciousness had turned out to be an underwater experience, the pull of unfathomable currents and a variety of blurred lights: natural, fluorescent, the point of a penlight boring through his skull as he surfaced to find a doctor in the tribunal's infirmary examining him. The right side of his head felt tense, and when he was asked to follow the doctor's finger with his eyes, he experienced an ocular pain equivalent to having an arm twisted behind his back.

"What happened?" he mumbled to the doctor. He was a complete coward when it came to any pain but *this* pain was unprecedented, an accessory heart beating against his right cheekbone. He touched his face, a move that elicited a tender, admonishing "No, no" from the doctor.

"Roberto hit you," a voice said behind him. He swivelled his head around on the bed's pillow, a manoeuvre that bent and twisted his facial discomfort.

"Celia?"

"I'm so sorry. I didn't think he would do something like that."

He couldn't see her. She was sitting off in a corner of the room made more obscure by the way he was lying and his swollen eye. Patrick felt uneasy turning his head any further – Celia or not – a wariness that seemed justified as one end of the room began to sink. He tried to grip the bed sheets but they were taut and thin with over-laundering.

"Hello, Mopito," another voice said, similar but less recognizable than Celia's.

"Nina?"

"Yes," the voice replied, a tone of satisfaction evident, even through the haze.

He heard Nina say something to Celia and then the sound of a door opening and closing. Someone had left.

The infirmary's doctor, a trim, pleasant man in his forties who introduced himself as Dr. Bolodis, proceeded to run through a fairly thorough exam and then suggested Patrick go

to the hospital for X-rays. Patrick acknowledged his advice –
slipping in the fact that he was a doctor too – and then
thanked him in that overly polite way that let a fellow professional know his recommendations would be immediately
disregarded but that it wasn't a reflection of his opinion of
the other man's expertise. A tribunal doctor probably didn't
treat many people who were free to do what they wanted.

"Where's Roberto now?"

"He's been detained. I don't know if that means he's been
arrested."

The doctor, under his white coat of industriousness, was
listening in on their conversation and had gone so far as to
accompany certain remarks with a smirk or a grimace (Patrick
couldn't tell which – both his eyes and head still felt partly
unyoked). He told Patrick he could rest in the infirmary as
long as he wanted. The doctor then nodded politely, this
much Patrick could discern, and left. Neither he nor Celia
said a thing. Only silence as the room undulated. Patrick
wondered if he could have sensed Celia was there behind him
without her having said something. Doubtful. He was never
any good with presences. He remembered her saying that. Or
was it absences? He wished she would say something.

Patrick heard movement, the ruffling of clothes and then
the murmur of a child, still in sleep.

"Is that your son?"

"Yes. His name is Paul."

"How old?"

"Two."

For many years Patrick had imagined a moment like this
between them, meeting again years later with their lives so
decidedly adult and separate and complete without each other.

The two of them would stand there – probably in the rain, yes, rain felt right – and shake their heads in that world-weary manner. And even though they were in a city in Europe where one could safely assume it was raining or about to, and he was cradling his contused head and she was holding her child (something he hadn't foreseen), well, it just wasn't meeting the standard of how he thought it would be, and he wasn't sure whether it was a shortcoming inherent to the moment itself or his expectation. Either way, something seemed very B-movie. Patrick wanted to sit up. He wanted to go.

He tried to stand and with only the slightest effort to roll onto his side the room swayed and rotated. He stopped and the sensation didn't worsen so he restarted, slowly regaining the vertical. At the end he was perspiring and wished the doctor hadn't gone, but after a minute or two he was closer to feeling better. He looked around for Celia, turning his whole body in the slowly spinning room. She and her son floated by, sitting in a corner. He tried to focus on her but it was difficult. Her son was sleeping in her arms. Teetering in front of her, Patrick remembered that her father was sitting in a holding cell waiting for transport and now her brother was probably in handcuffs somewhere. The boy she held looked to be the only man in her life who wasn't making things difficult for her. Patrick was able to focus on her face and was surprised to see no sign of the expected anxiety or despair. In fact, Patrick had trouble deciphering her expression, except to say it was something other than stoicism. Something more impressive. Calm but intent, not the face of a martyr, but a look he'd seen worn by tradesmen, plumbers contemplating the extent of a job. A shitload of work.

"We need to get Roberto out."

He didn't even ask why Roberto had hit him, which was fairly instructive about where that relationship stood. Maybe that's why the pain of his face, which was now trying to become a bigger face, swelling to close over his right eye, was, after the initial shock, sort of manageable. In a way, he could understand Roberto's anger. Patrick had avoided contact with the García family for years, through the allegations levelled against Hernan and through Marta's death. It wasn't just indifference, it was betrayal. On the plaza, Patrick was a representation of every person who had walked away from the García family, showing up too late with an empty gesture of support.

And now Roberto was being detained. Patrick knew he wouldn't be much good as a witness, but he understood that wasn't the reason he'd been enlisted to help. He tried to imagine what the police would ask him, their questions becoming his own: why had he continued to walk toward an advancing Roberto, how had he not managed to see the fist coming? He'd been watching Celia. Or maybe he hadn't seen Roberto coming because that was easier than seeing him coming. Maybe it was the Valium or just guilt he had wanted absolved. It didn't matter to Patrick, he was raised a Catholic and trading guilt for pain was a fairly standard currency conversion.

He tried not to look at Celia as they made their way out of the infirmary and walked down the underground corridors they hoped would lead them out. Patrick drew alarmed reactions from passing staff. He suspected they were more familiar with theories of violence and forensic data than with a specimen like his mottled face. The tribunal personnel offered solicitous and vague directions how to get out of the lower levels of the building. It took them another ten minutes before they were outside. Celia was still holding Paul, and though

Patrick couldn't be certain, it seemed the boy was still asleep. She made no noise and he followed her across the plaza for the second time.

"Where are they holding Roberto?"

"At a precinct station two blocks from here. Nina's there right now," Celia said without turning. Fifty yards farther across the plaza, aware he was being marched over on an errand, that his forgiveness and consent to help were assumed, he stopped.

"Maybe he needs to cool off for a while."

She turned and stood silently for a second or two. Paul was in her arms, awake but quiet. He played with a length of her hair. He looked like her.

"I need Roberto with us, Patrick," she said without emotion. It was the quality of her appeal, the complete pragmatism, that made him nod and walk after her.

It took the better part of an hour speaking to a Dutch police inspector to get the charges against Roberto dropped, during which time Patrick lied repeatedly – the bruises were sustained in a fall after a relatively minor scuffle. Patrick's fault entirely. Clumsy, clumsy. He appealed to her to understand the cultural propensity of North Americans to physicalize their conflicts. He mentioned, in passing, that he was a doctor (a tactic he used selectively with the general public – it often backfired in retail situations, acting like a 20 per cent surcharge). Patrick even played the war card, mentioning that he was originally Canadian, which he hoped still carried some weight in a part of Europe liberated from the Nazis by a bunch of people he never knew but who held the same passport. The police inspector said she would have to consider the matter further and asked Patrick to wait in the lobby of the station for her answer.

He met Celia and Nina in the lobby and told them that nothing had been decided about Roberto, that they'd have to wait, which caused the García sisters to fume and glare in tandem. He couldn't help but take their reaction personally; he felt like reminding them that he'd done more than his fair share, and they should remember it was their brother, after all, who was responsible for this mess. But he knew better than to tamper with anybody's indignation. They trundled Paul off to the ladies' washroom, and Patrick was glad to see them go.

Somewhere, he supposed, there must be a record of it. He had only a shadowy recollection of the event, little else beyond shouting and a glimpse of the plaza through a thicket of moving legs. But somewhere, in a vault, on a disc or a hard drive there was most probably a record of a grainy rectangle of plaza captured by a surveillance camera into which he strides and then suddenly lurches away from another body, wheeling across the frame. He falls to the concrete, Roberto looming above, the two of them there for a moment before the arrival of others. He didn't want to see it. By the time the police inspector got to see it, if she ever did, it would all be a memory, like the bruise might be. They had another advantage in trying to get Roberto released. The police were quite visibly in full crisis mode following the murder of the politician van der Hoeven. A punch-up in a plaza must seem little more than a nuisance.

He sat on the wooden bench and closed his eyes. His head ran through cycles of pain, and as it intensified, thoughts began to buzz like the light from the lobby's failing fluorescent tubes. He'd never imagined joining that fraternity of those who'd taken one in the head. Through the strobing he didn't see the typical icons of injury – no football players shaking off their concussions, no reeling heavyweights or flashes of Dealey Plaza – no, he saw Phineas Gage.

Phineas Gage, railway foreman, worked on the Burlington and Northern Line in the 1850s, surveying and helping to construct a railway through the schist of central Vermont. The hills of granite did not yield easily, and a great deal of blasting was needed. One morning in June 1856, Gage was at work, using a twenty-pound metal tamping rod to prepare a hole for an explosive charge when, because of an error in the sequence of loading the charge, an unforeseen explosion occurred. Everyone in the crew reflexively ducked and, after a pause, looked over to see their foreman lying on his back, without his hat on. The gunpowder was still in the air and whatever stillness existed was broken by the tamping rod clanging to earth fifty yards away. Witnesses described Gage as never losing consciousness, but no one was sure. When they reached him, he was moaning and trying to sit up. One man fainted and another had to turn away so as not to vomit on their foreman.

The tamping rod – which he had slammed into a hole that had already been set with explosive – had been shot straight through the left eye socket and exited through a gaping hole on the left side of his head at the upper edge of his forehead. Gage was taken by wagon to the nearest doctor where it was presumed he would die quickly.

But Gage did not die. Amazingly, he did not bleed to death nor did this man with two holes in his head, each the size of a billiard ball, succumb to infection or any other complication thought to be inevitable. It was with some wonder that weeks after his accident, his doctor felt it was safe to say that he thought his patient would survive. After months it was apparent that Gage could walk and talk, fairly normally. He would never work again, but he was alive.

But his survival was not the only significant outcome to the accident. In the most famous of many epitaphs of Phineas Gage, his physician, John Harlow, wrote that while his recovery was miraculous, an effect of the injury was that "Gage was no longer Gage." Gage had survived, but his behaviour had changed. The pious and industrious foreman was now dis-inhibited and unable to complete the simplest of tasks. He was undependable and shiftless. He became an offensive, lecherous man, one whom people cautioned women to avoid. Gage, of course, seemed unconcerned by any of it and ended his days as a drunken drifter.

Gage was the starting point, the living experiment that showed that the brain did not just control movement or perception but played a role in complex behaviour, per-sonality, and temperament. The rod blew Gage's prefrontal cortex into the Vermont sky. In that annihilating moment, knowledge was advanced, and Patrick's field of expertise was baptised. There was much he owed to Phineas Gage.

Patrick was still sitting on the bench in the lobby of the police station waiting for Celia and Nina to come out of the washroom with Paul when he felt two hands on his shoulders. He opened his eyes to see Roberto and instinctively closed his good eye, opening it again to find Roberto sitting next to him on the bench. Patrick expected him to fidget, for the impulsiveness that fed the attack to be subdivided into a hundred smaller tics and twitches, but he was motionless and cool. And anything but repentant or thankful. Aside from the fatigue stamped on his face, he looked like a world champ resting between rounds. It made Patrick sorry he had come to help him.

"Hello, Mopito."

"I did it for your sisters," Patrick said, studying the pattern of tiles on the floor.

"They're going to drop the charges, I guess."

"I figured that out."

Patrick was suddenly overcome by the need to ask Roberto if he was angry at his father, resentful for having to come all the way to Europe only to hear his father's story again. Was this what the punch was for? The thoughts tumbled together, racing around while he experienced third-person alarm at almost saying the words. He felt drunk and perversely giddy despite the half-moon face of ache, which made him wonder if his frontal lobe was contused by the punch and further disinhibitions were on their way. A fate like Gage. Maybe Lazerenko was no longer Lazerenko, which he felt wasn't so bad an outcome, given the situation. Patrick tried to focus on someone other than Roberto, anyone.

"I'm sorry about your dad."

"Why should you care, Mopito?"

"Cut the *mopito* shit, please."

"Okay," Roberto replied, suddenly standing up and leaving Patrick alone on the bench. It surprised Patrick how quickly he walked away, disappearing through the doors at the end of the hallway.

Celia and Nina eventually returned from the washroom with Paul in tow, his face streaked with tears. Patrick looked at the boy. This was the life of a child, sudden, off-screen eruptions that didn't warrant an explanation. Celia apologized for the way they'd reacted earlier, and she and Paul sat down on the bench with Patrick. Nina remained standing, scanning the hallways for her brother. Patrick was going to tell them about Roberto's release, but something held him back. Instead, he rose to properly say hello to Nina, not knowing whether to shake her hand or embrace her but in the end Patrick did the stuttering two-cheek kiss that most clearly identified an exiled Montrealer. On the second kiss, Nina reached around to kiss him somewhere on the angle of his right jaw, a gesture that seemed shockingly intimate until he realized that she was doing it to avoid the swollen cheekbone. Patrick remembered Nina as a shy eleven-year-old. She was a person as new to him as Paul. She resembled her mother more than Celia did and seemed less affected by everything that was happening around her. Patrick shook Paul's hand with more formality than was necessary between a two-year-old and a guy with a big black eye. To his surprise, the little boy didn't seem to be bothered by the look of the swollen face and Patrick wondered if Paul had seen his uncle swing at him, if that would lessen or heighten any reaction he had now. Paul started writhing to get off Celia's lap and, once he was on the ground, began to run the marble hallways. Celia's good mood returned and Patrick wanted to take it in, not ashamed to use whatever credit he had earned as the wronged-party/reluctant hero to get her to sit there a while longer, to look at her while her son clomped up and down the corridor, swerving between Dutch police officials. Nina went to rein him in.

"I didn't think you'd come," Celia said.

"I hadn't planned on it." Paul ran by. Patrick thought for a moment that he could detect the sound of the boy's footsteps rising in pitch, a mini-Doppler effect, but he knew it was impossible. "I wanted to hear what he has to say."

She looked at him as though every word were a ploy.

"People have made up their minds. Besides, he's not talking."

"You were all very important to me," Patrick said, immediately regretting having said it. Celia did the right thing, he thought, by not responding. They both watched Nina and Paul idling at the far end of the corridor.

"Nina doesn't talk about the trial," Celia said. "She doesn't want to go. She's glad to have Paul to watch during the day. So if you think he's guilty, please keep it to yourself."

"What do you and Roberto think?"

Celia fixed him with a look of such sadness. Grace and despair residing on a face at the same moment. Nina and Paul jogged by, holding hands.

"I wonder when Roberto will be released," Celia said, craning her neck to look down into the lobby.

"I don't know," he answered, as she turned back from the lobby. Celia looked at him and he thought she could tell he was lying, but he realized he was imagining this. That was the way it used to be. Now she just looked away. But it didn't disappoint him. He wanted to sit. Just five minutes more, then he would tell her. He had earned this much.

FIVE

Reverberations. A limited form of seismic activity, enough to make a chandelier sway. It was dark now and he felt dizzy as they crossed an intersection, the empty space like a hole he needed to avoid. Once they got to a sidewalk, something about the comfort of parallel lines cordoning him in, perhaps, he felt steadier. Celia and Nina and Paul were to his left and it required a surprising amount of concentration to stay at the same pace. The discomfort seemed an adequate karmic repayment for having misled them, having kept them waiting at the police station. He had settled on a smaller lie to redeem the larger deception, finally telling them that while they'd been in the washroom, he'd caught a glimpse of someone leaving the building who (and he'd pointed to his head as he said this, implying the cloud of his concussion and the need for understanding), in retrospect, might have looked like Roberto.

He staggered along, a zombie walking toward daybreak. He almost put out his hands to steady himself. Each footstep hurt, tugging at a part of him he couldn't immediately identify. Celia turned around to find him with one hand to his forehead.

"Are you okay to be walking?"

He answered back with a grimace and a minimalist nod.

"Maybe we should go to the hospital."

"I'd rather not," he said, but he was thinking the same thing. He wanted to ask Celia if Roberto had hit him only once. Maybe he'd banged his head on the concrete of the plaza. As he recalled the tribunal doctor advising him to get medical attention, a textbook chapter of head trauma opened to him: worst-case scenarios of depressed skull fractures and subdural clots collecting, molasses thick, swollen brain squeezing out of the skull's tight cap like cookie dough. You were fine for six hours, until the pressure mounted and you died in your sleep. Or if you were lucky, you'd get a shaved head and a burr hole, followed by months of windmill-watching while you rehabbed somewhere in the Dutch countryside. And as he thought this, he felt Gage shadowing him, stumbling along in tandem disrepair.

The four of them carried on along the streets of Den Haag and thoughts of Gage faded. He was not Gage. He would be okay. Patrick touched his head as if to assure himself that the skull was still there, and it was, the scalp feeling parboiled and tender. The burden of conversation – generic chat about the rain or the hotels they were staying in – was shared equally, each of the adults taking their turn, the interval of silence widening as topics were used up.

"So how's Boston?" Nina asked, old enough, he thought, to recognize conversational pauses for the terror they brought.

"Boston's great."

"We read about your research," Nina said, smirking, "the pornography research."

Celia turned to her sister, and Patrick could feel an exchange between the two women, the pulse of energy thrown off by what he assumed was a castigating glance.

"Yeah, that got a lot of press," he said. Patrick had mastered a response to the sniggering questions about his research. Sheepish acknowledgement was the standard tone he adopted in hopes of ending the discussion. It often failed. But here it worked. Perhaps Nina felt she owed him this courtesy.

"We heard you started your own business."

"That's right."

"But you still do research?"

"Well, yes. It's just a change of location."

"Who are you doing the research for?"

"Companies."

"Like who?" Nina asked, and Patrick couldn't help but notice the familiar tone of questioning, the cheerful, never-ending inquisitiveness. Perhaps Elyse Brenman wasn't just an aggravation, but a type of personality that Nina had also grown into. An army of Elyses, with follow-up questions. He was certain Nina was playing dumb. He'd heard from Elyse that Nina had finished a business degree and was running Le Dépanneur Mondial. If so, then Nina had got her business education in the shadow of the Globomart phenomenon, studying – with admiration and dread, the dual sentiments evoked by any leviathan – the tactics used to dominate retail. She knew exactly who he worked for. He felt he had a licence, a reason, to be vague.

"I work with a lot of different companies."

After a few more minutes of sparring, Nina let it go. He was surprised he didn't have to explain the technical details of his research to them, but he reasoned they already knew about that too.

"Do you ever see patients?" Celia asked. This sounded like an honest question and it caught Patrick off guard.

"No. But even back when I was with the university, I wasn't actively practising."

"Don't you miss being a doctor?"

"I'm still a doctor."

"I meant as more than a title."

Jesus, he thought, someone should be ringing a goddamn bell for the end of the round. They walked on in silence and Patrick tried to hide his growing annoyance with the Garcías, but he could feel his mood curdling with every step. He understood what Celia was getting at. She was letting him know what she thought of him, the insinuation he wasn't a "real doctor" and, in that way, could never know what her father had gone through. He didn't see patients – so what? Because he didn't write prescriptions he should suspend judgment?

At one point during his medical training, Patrick had finally acknowledged he was not the type of doctor who could deal with someone like Gage, the rages, the endless explanations to his increasingly horrified family. The hollow pep talks to a man no longer able to listen to anyone. He didn't miss any part of clinical neurology, a part of his life he'd happily confined to four years of residency, a specialty that a friend once described as the study of brain catastrophes, paid upfront or mortgaged out.

In truth, he was a doctor but not really a doctor. At one time Patrick thought that he would be quite a good doctor and he supposed he could have been – he had pictured the type so clearly: competent, up on the latest developments and willing to tweak the reigning controversy with a prescient insight, a good teacher, not a prick, carrying it all off with some sort of humility that passed for grace. But it just didn't happen, or rather, it happened differently. It wasn't as though he'd planned a career in research. A year into his neurology residency in Boston, he'd become involved in research that used a new imaging technique, which came to revolutionize brain research. At first, he didn't know the technique was cutting edge – everything was new to him and the technique simply had an appealing logic. Then everything seemed to fall into place. It turned out Patrick had all the qualities that lend themselves to a successful career in scientific research. He was dogged. He was able to work long hours. He had enough imagination to formulate the next, necessary question and yet not so much imagination as to be distracted by the unnecessary questions. The first paper he ever co-authored was published in a leading journal and while his supervisor, a slightly paranoid Ph.D. named Ed Phipps, was ecstatic, it was viewed by all to be something akin to a minor lottery win. But then six papers followed in the next two years, each publication causing a departmental buzz, together constituting a run of success that drew a congratulatory letter from the then-chairman. Phipps's ecstasy evolved into bafflement – he'd never had a post-doc publish like this – and then into collegial wariness, as it became clear that with each paper the work was becoming as much Patrick's as his own. From student to protegé to equal with a suddenness that bruised egos; at that point Patrick was introduced to how contused his supervisor had become: he was asked to leave the laboratory. After finishing his residency (barely scraping through the board exams), he was told in no uncertain terms by Phipps that he should "go away" for further training. So he had gone to Caltech for eighteen months before coming back to take over his supervisor's job when Phipps didn't get tenure. For a year or two, Patrick would see his old boss at meetings in places like Toulouse or Aberdeen, always able to sense Phipps's stare like a rifle's laser-sighting device from across a half-empty convention hall. But that's life.

And so it happened that even though he was trained and certified as a neurologist, he had never really practised. His first university appointment was in the department of psychology, not in the faculty of medicine. This was a mutual acknowledgement that his value was as a researcher and that he wasn't going to put on a white coat and start ministering to people. He had a medical licence but this was to keep his credentials up for the purpose of writing grants, the way some people kept an unused driver's licence in their wallet for photo ID.

In his research, Patrick used a technique called functional magnetic resonance imaging to measure the minute differences in blood flow between different parts of the brain that occurred when subjects did certain mental or physical tasks. This change in blood flow made the affected part of the brain appear to "light up" and areas of the brain could be "mapped" accordingly. Initially the tasks examined in this way were relatively simple: look at the blinking light, move your index finger, and so on. Then language became big, everyone had studies examining word generation, syntax, and grammar structures. After that, working more and more with neuropsychologists, he became involved in research on generation of language and this led to projects studying more complicated responses, such as arousal, and specifically arousal to certain complex stimuli. This was, as the press (and many in his department) dubbed it, his "blue period" when he "single-handedly gave scientific credance (sic) to the depravity that pornography encompasses" (that little gem came in a threatening letter he found taped to the mailbox of his apartment and addressed to *Patrick Lazerenko–Smut Doctor*). It was, of course, less titillating than that: he had subjects – usually university students who participated without complaint or a hint of embarrassment – watch selected "vignettes" while being scanned, showing how their right occipital, cingulate, and then frontal lobes lit up in a sequential pattern that was the brain equivalent of arousal.

His new chairman, a recruit from another university visibly harried by the demands of fundraising and budget cuts, invited Patrick into his office for lunch and a discussion. Patrick remembered the view from the office as he sat down, the expensive slice of green quadrangle rationed out to the upper-floor offices. A secretary brought two salads, and as he speared a small forest of broccoli – "Good source of folate," his luncheon partner said – the chairman admitted to Patrick that he found having a non-psychologist in the department to be an "invigorating" experience. The chairman said this in a way that implied he was not the sort of man who enjoyed such invigoration. The former chair, then deep into his last term, had made a controversial decision to hire Patrick, and he had championed the young researcher almost as a rebuke to the grumblers in the department who questioned his authority. Now, regime change had come, and the mood for many in the department had deteriorated into one of frank paranoia. The new chairman tried to dispel this atmosphere with a series of private lunchtime talks with his faculty. And as they ate, the new chairman explained how he wanted the best for Patrick and, in that vein, wouldn't it be more efficient for all involved if they thought about having his appointment – and salary support and office space requirements – transferred to another department? This was followed several days later by a "personal note" from the chairman, something to the effect that no decisions had been made but that he should try to "keep his work in the news." In this spirit he accepted an invitation to a televised round-table discussion of pornography where he was one of a number of pundits. He spent the program like a reluctant punchline, trying to hide between a baby-faced Internet pornographer with a Russian accent and a very troubled-looking priest. After a while, Patrick grew frustrated with the sniggering and began to refuse interviews. That didn't please the chairman.

All this coincided with a drop-off in his publications, due to what Patrick would call a "re-orienting" of his research. The grants dipped too, which set off an alarm in the chairman's office. And then Marc-André called. He had seen Patrick on television, knew something about the brain imaging work he was doing, and was interested in, as he put it, *applications* for the work. Patrick was leery, but agreed to meet for lunch.

It was a coincidence, that's how Patrick thought of it later. He was never one to believe in coordinated door openings and closures but there was Marc-André, talking about neuroeconomics, the newly coined study of the processes behind economic and consumer decisions, without knowing that Patrick had already written a proposal to study what parts of the brain were activated in states where decisions were made with competing goals. "We're organisms driving toward not just some *thing*, but many things, constantly evaluating multiple variables and shuffling our desires," Patrick remembered saying to the growing grin of Marc-André as he explained the research. Patrick told him he wanted to know how that happened and what part of the brain was responsible for that shuffling. The biological basis for all the utilitarian choices that needed to be made. Marc-André finished Patrick's sentence by saying he couldn't think of a big player in the world of business that wasn't asking the same question. And willing to pay handsomely for an answer.

So Patrick had the option of continuing to do research in his university – waiting for his turn on the machine to do the necessary functional MRI studies, dealing with the infighting in a department where his career was on a death watch, scrambling for grants and hanging on – or, as Marc-André said after the food arrived, he could establish his own company and control everything. Marc-André gave Patrick what he now knew was a standard business-school presentation: a neo-Marxist analysis delivered over lunch in an expensive Thai restaurant. And during this particular Marxist-Thai fusion meal, Marc-André reminded Patrick that he did not own the means of production, that he would be a worker forever crouched in the great field of science. To remain in that state required Patrick to accept a false consciousness. Patrick didn't know Marc-André at this time, so he was very impressed.

It didn't turn out to be that simple. In resigning his position at the university and founding Neuronaut, Patrick discovered that he'd traded the collared tensions of an academic department for the open warfare of a lawsuit, where, in the university's deposition, he was portrayed as little more than a not-yet-tenured thief. The judge saw it differently.

Now, he was rich.

It turned out that Patrick had set his sail at high, high tide. Neuronaut went public with an initial offering whose success stunned even the MBAS. He had become a salesman, explaining the technique in terms that anyone with ambition and a chequebook could understand. He spent a disorienting season in countless meetings, luring Jeremy Bancroft away from another biotech start-up to act as Neuronaut's first CEO, poaching psychometricians from various psychology departments, and trying to set up the first free-standing functional brain-imaging centre in the United States, all accompanied by the beep, beep, beeping of the Brinks truck backing up to the door. And it wasn't like he'd been doing poorly before; it's just that what he made as a junior faculty member at a prestigious university was less than what now periodically fell out of the crevices of his sofa. He was rich enough that he was uncertain of his worth at any one time. For Patrick, wealth was best understood in terms of degrees of freedom. He was free to pay his team of intellectual property lawyers. He was free to have his own laboratory. He was free to go.

Personally, it had been necessary to retool. Becoming suddenly wealthy in America was a consciousness-raising experience, perhaps inferior only to becoming famous or publicly battling cancer, and Patrick recognized the responsibilities that went along with this newfound status. He stepped away from rental life in Brookline with the speed of an evacuee, and anyone who wanted the furniture remnants of that life was welcome to it. He took his computer and his books and some clothes and, like switching sectors in post-World War II Berlin, he migrated over to a new life. He purchased a condo in Kendall Square, appreciating the irony of living in a brand spanking new building constructed to look like a period terra cotta-clad warehouse converted into condos.

"Is this Chicago style?" guests would ask as they admired the prominent overhang through one of the two smaller double-hung sash Chicago-style windows.

"You have a good eye," he would reply, handing them a glass of Pinot Noir that ached, ached.

He thought that he liked his apartment. The Chicago style was very popular. Minimalist, modern, American. Ornament subordinated to an overall structural theme. Yes, he was drawn to this terra cotta cliffside, its fraudulent history, its height.

A lifestyle change followed his new address. He wanted simplicity, he told himself as he cycled to work on a bike that cost more than his first year at the provincially subsidized medical school he had attended. He owned a black Saab 9-5 – the regimental sedan of the technocrati – that slept in the caverns of a garage under the condo, but he didn't drive it. Simplicity. He had space now, beautiful space. He took off his shoes so as not to hear footsteps like mortar rounds sounding off the cherry-wood floors in the main room. The ceilings were high and the windows big enough, and the only outside disturbance to his peace was the occasional rimshot of birds meeting their terminal reflections.

The apartment was empty for the longest time until Heather convinced him to have it decorated, convinced him to let her "prepare" the rooms. Now his furniture was sculpture, his rugs tapestries, and his kitchen an anteroom to the larger cathedral of asceticism. He would have liked it to stay museum-bare, gallery-bare. When guests nodded admiringly at the furniture, he could still tell them of his misgiving about certain pieces, his curatorial restlessness. They appreciated it.

It could be said that everything had gone well, that having no limitations and becoming wealthy had made him feel renewed and re-energized but he found he couldn't shake a sense of exhaustion. He attributed it to holdover fatigue, a lingering after-effect of the petty, narcissistic atmosphere of academia, and then, over time, he reasoned it was the stress of starting a business and that eventually he'd feel that energy again, that unfettered curiosity amped up by entrepreneurial ambition. But he felt nothing other than nagged by his partners, even Bancroft. He felt lost.

In the last year his insomnia had worsened. He woke up earlier and yet was always tired. Typical stuff. It wasn't difficult to see what was going on. He had the chance to speak to a psychotherapist but really, how can you be talked out of a serotonin problem? A physical thing, a serotonin thing. He decided on the pharmaceuticals because they made the most sense to him. And he had felt a little better recently, more able to face people at the office and able to come to Den Haag. Perhaps the war crimes trial of a friend in the middle of a Den Haag autumn was too stern a test for any medication. It made him feel like a test pilot, brave and doomed, his fate only partly under his control; *let's see what this baby can do. Take before meals.*

But this helped – here, walking on a Den Haag sidewalk with the García sisters and Paul, he felt something. Maybe it was the aggravation of their questions. Or just strolling in the warm Dutch November twilight. His face hurt, drooped with pain, but he felt better. Maybe it was the punch, Roberto's gift of a mini-lobotomy. But more probably, it was the Garcías. Getting pissed off, after all, was a very human emotion.

Across Johan de Wittlaan, Patrick heard voices rise and then the thud of a ball being struck. People in a park. A makeshift playing field, the grass a dull yellow under the streetlights. Nothing unusual about a game of six-a-side soccer, except that the players were speaking Spanish and one of them, now on the ball, was Roberto. Patrick didn't say anything to Celia or Nina, instead slowing his pace, falling behind to watch. One of the men on the sideline was a white-haired man whom Patrick recognized as the union organizer from San Pedro Sula. He had been on the witness stand earlier in the day. People shouted and laughed, they knew each other, they were Hondurans. So this was where they went after the trial, Patrick thought, suddenly alarmed at Roberto's recklessness for playing on a field with some of his father's accusers. His victims. Roberto chipped the ball ahead and another man, in his twenties, judging from his pace, latched onto the lofted pass and nudged it between the two shoes that served as goalposts. Half the players lifted their arms and gave a shout and Celia and Nina looked over. They must have seen Roberto too, but they said nothing, and walked on.

The Garcías told him they were staying at a *pension* a few blocks down the road from the strip of hotels where the Metropole stood. It hadn't occurred to Patrick that Den Haag continued past the Metropole, and the thought of houses and pets and people cooking food and scratching themselves out there was slightly unsettling. Once at the Metropole, they idled on the sidewalk for a while, the events of the day and ten years of silences weighing on them. Patrick didn't want to go back to the hotel room. He didn't want to be alone, a realization that would make anyone lonelier, more panicky. He offered to get some milk from room service for Paul if they wanted to come up. They agreed to come in, still wary, looking up at the towering Metropole as though they had been asked to scale the facade. Patrick asked Celia if she wanted him to carry Paul, and after she paused, he qualified the offer by saying she must be tired. Celia then passed Paul over, slowly, as if to allow maximum time for the child to react to this stranger. But there was no eruption. Paul settled into Patrick's arms and they carried on through the revolving doors. They walked unaccosted through the lobby, the Dutch respectful of what they assumed must be a sleeping child and so he was spared the frantic clerk waving him down as they crossed to the bank of elevators. The child was light in his arms. His brown eyes studied Patrick, and he tilted his head from side to side to survey the swollen eye and compare it to its unpunched cousin. Patrick could only guess at what the boy saw, the before-and-after effect.

Despite the scrutiny and the headache worsening with exertion, Patrick felt taller, stronger. He considered that carrying Paul, carrying any child, must confer an ennobling effect. He imagined he skulked less with the child in his arms. With a child, he was not a man with a bruised and beaten face but simply a man carrying a child. Anyone would look at them and surmise that Patrick got this bruise defending the boy, rescuing him. Paul could be his son. Yes, Patrick would give his life for him. The small boy touched the swollen ridge of Patrick's cheekbone, not a ridge any more but a hillock inflating into a butte, and Patrick tried not to wince, not to react in any way that would alarm the child. He couldn't help but wonder who Paul's father was. He saw only Celia in the boy.

In the panelled mirrors of the elevator, Patrick was presented with multiple views of his face that he felt striking him like a second punch. No discoloration in the yellow light but the entire right side looked deformed, a stuck-on prosthesis from a bad movie. He tried to turn away from reflections of himself, but it was impossible.

When they got to the room, everyone spent a few respectful minutes in front of the view of Den Haag from sixteen floors up. The streetlights were on, and a half-galaxy of stars scattered on the flood plain until they were extinguished by the North Sea. From her bag, Celia extracted plastic bags of sandwiches and carrot sticks, passing them out to Nina and Paul, who accepted them wordlessly. Patrick called room service for milk and they sat down. Paul climbed onto the bed with a sandwich clamped in his mouth.

After finishing his meal, Paul began bouncing tentatively on the mattress, negotiating the surface like an astronaut. The García sisters looked lost, and the room seemed smaller to Patrick than it had earlier that morning. Nina, sworn enemy of silences, picked up the remote and snapped the television on. Whatever pleasure he had in inviting them up dissolved into the admission that having them there felt like nothing more than an embarrassing foray into nostalgia, memory burdened with need. But it was human need, he thought, as Paul bounced beside his aunt and Celia stared out into the twilight, and he did need the Garcías now, as much as he had needed them then.

SIX

That first day Patrick showed up at Le Dépanneur Mondial, García was waiting for him at the front door. He unlocked it and, after letting Patrick in, gave him a sheet listing all the tasks his young ward would do that day. It was a contract. Patrick was to read it and García waited until it was signed. They went first to the back alley where Patrick whitewashed over the aborted spray-painted message. He swept and then scrubbed the aisles. He replaced light bulbs and washed counters. García showed him how to "face" items on a shelf of canned goods and then told him to do the whole store. This was before nine. Once the Dépanneur Mondial opened, customers began to drift in, and by mid-morning there was a constant crowd. Some people sat at one of the two small tables the Garcías had set up near the newsstand at the front of the store, drinking concentrated coffee from small cups and reading their papers. Many were people who Patrick recognized from other deps, new customers here now, thumbing the fresh produce and chatting to Marta García, who again and again lifted her eyes to keep track of Patrick, as she would do throughout the day.

At eleven that first morning, Roberto backed through the front door, pulling a dolly piled high with boxes. He was a year older than Patrick but clearly a different species: much taller and already growing a moustache that made him appear even more like his father. He wheeled the dolly around with a professional indifference to the safety of others, purposely weaving toward Patrick to make him jump out of the way. Not a word of acknowledgement, which told Patrick that Roberto must have known why he was there, what he'd done to his father's store, Roberto's store. Patrick's fists clenched as he passed, but nothing happened. The door chimes sounded again and this time it was a young woman, carrying another box of what looked like bananas. The young woman leaned over the counter to kiss her mother. Roberto shouted something in Spanish to his father, who turned to Patrick.

"They left another six boxes of plantains out front."

Patrick said nothing, watching the girl. She had the blackest hair he had ever seen. She wore a dress with flowers on it. This was Celia García.

"Go get the plantains."

"What are plantains?"

"They are a type of fruit. To you they would look like bananas, except for the fact that they are in boxes that look like boxes. Go."

Patrick remembered passing Celia. He had often thought about that moment. He would have loved to be able to say that he saw his future walk out in front of him, or that he'd heard music or had goosebumps. But his first memory of her was a solitary sensation. Synapses formed at that moment, a new circuit was created, and Celia García was fused into him. Just the sight of her in a hotel room activated a sleeper cell of memory, entraining other synapses, long dormant, now powering up. A network of Celia.

Nina ran through the television channels with Celia and Patrick watching from the corner. She settled on an English-language news channel and he saw Celia hover closer to her younger sister. The news everywhere was mostly bad and here it was worse: sirens throughout the city and word of more citizens brought in for questioning, some of them in Den Haag, all in the wake of the politician's murder in Amsterdam. Any news aside from Hernan's problem would be a diversion, he supposed, but not this. Celia, preferring not to have Paul watch Muslims marched off to police precincts or have another viewing of the politician's body covered by a sheet, took the remote and changed the channel to something else. She handed the controls to Nina and then threw up her arms in frustration as her sister promptly turned back to the news program.

"What was going on there?" Nina asked, staring at the television.

"Someone was killed by an extremist," Celia whispered, even though Paul was rolling on the bed, oblivious.

"What for?"

Celia looked at her, obviously not wanting to explain the geopolitics of the situation in front of her son. Patrick sat down on the bed. He'd seen this montage, the stock footage of the politician, the police staring at the sheeted body, unaccustomed to this sort of thing.

"It's about head scarves," he said. "I was watching it last night. The politician wanted to ban head scarves in school, I think."

The covered body disappeared. Nina pressed the remote repeatedly until she found something for Paul, settling on an animated show that featured exploding underwater animals of some kind. She and Paul sat back on the bed and watched. Celia browsed through the basket of delicacies sitting on the minibar, fondling the punitively priced cashews and glancing over in his direction. He didn't have the heart to tell her to take what she wanted, that Neuronaut had a corporate account with the hotel chain that made cashews seem like nothing more than, well, cashews. She took a bottle of water from the basket and sat down by the window with that view of Den Haag.

"How's your father been holding up?"

"He's all right, I guess. It's been difficult for us, his silence."

"I thought he'd at least talk to you."

"Not to us, or di Costini. Certainly not to the tribunal."

"Do you know why?"

"No."

"I saw him use some medication." Patrick made the gesture, pinching the empty air before his slightly open mouth, the internationally recognized sign for someone using a medication inhaler.

"He's doing all right," she said dismissively.

Nina and Paul had turned up the volume enough that he could fire a pistol without much notice. Patrick grimaced and leaned in to speak to Celia.

"Jesus, Celia, could you give it a rest? It's me."

"Not a word from you. Seven years since this started, not a word."

"I'm here now. That should mean something."

Celia's face drew tight. "I had to get di Costini involved to get you here. It's been seven years for my father" – she made a sweeping gesture with her hand, as if blaming all of coastal Holland, blaming the tides – "and in all that time, no calls from you. Nothing."

One of the characters on the television screamed, and the room filled with the shrieking, metallic sound of a circular saw and Paul's laughter. Celia leaned in this time: "You've already made up your mind."

He said no but it didn't matter; she'd already turned to look out the window.

The ring tone of a cell phone, difficult to discern at first but rearranging itself into a tinny digital chorus of "These Boots Are Made for Walking," sprinkled onto the noise coming from the television. Celia and Patrick turned to see Nina stand up from the bed, rummaging through her purse. She flipped open a phone.

"*Oui, âllo?*" Nina said, as she plugged her free ear for a moment and then, grimacing with the insufficiency of the action, reached for the remote control and muted the room into a vacuum of deep-space silence. As Patrick watched from across the room, Nina aged ten years. She spoke, and it was evident that she wasn't talking to a friend or even an acquaintance. Chiding and hectoring, she spat out a termination to the conversation and snapped the phone shut. She barely had time to glower when the phone rang again. The tone of her voice changed; maybe this time she was speaking as the superior to the poor slave-wager she had just finished haranguing. In thirty seconds, frank disgust, incredulity, bemusement, and then ironic concern found a way onto her face. It was a wonder to Patrick the way the facial muscles arranged themselves in the same way even though the conversation involved someone who had no way to appreciate it. Even her free hand gestured to the back wall of the hotel room, culminating in what could plausibly be the sign-language equivalent to "You'll never work in this town again."

With a discreet beep, she closed the phone again, looking like someone who very much missed the satisfactions of an era when a phone could be slammed into its cradle. *Our little girl is all grown up*, Patrick thought.

"We'll be getting our produce from Laurendeau. As. Of. Today," she said in a way that would sound perfectly natural coming from the mouth of a pharaoh. As if to acknowledge that the news meant nothing to either Patrick or Celia, Nina turned away: "Excuse me, I have to make a few more calls."

"Wow. So she *is* running the store."

"Since last year."

"And Roberto?"

"There were some problems. He's still at the store. But Nina's the boss."

Six phone calls later, a contract was agreed to and a GPS-tracked truck carrying crates of iceberg lettuce and California seedless grapes had been diverted to Montreal. Someone at the store would be there to accept the delivery that night at eleven. The next morning there would be fresh produce available at Le Dépanneur Mondial.

"Jesus, she should be on Hernan's defence team."

"Di Costini won't take her calls. It drives him crazy that some Garcías talk so much while others won't talk at all."

Nina put the phone away and sat back down on the bed.
She yawned and patted the bed for Paul to come over and sit with her.

"Do you believe he's guilty?"

"He's pleaded not guilty," Celia said.

"That's not an answer."

"Did you speak with di Costini?"

"Yes. A lot."

"And?" Celia said, turning up the volume on the television again so Paul would be distracted.

"It's not like an insanity defence. There isn't precedence for it in trials like this. It's hard to argue Hernan has an abnormal brain when he's shown excellent moral reason and judgment all his life except for the six weeks in question."

He said this matter-of-factly; it was an argument he'd repeated to di Costini over and over again. But looking at Celia, her lips pursing into a grimace, it must have been her last, faint hope. She fixed him with her red-rimmed eyes.

"Do *you* think he's guilty?"

Patrick paused. "I think he did the things they say he did." Celia put her head in her hands. She glanced over to Nina and Paul, both in another time zone of thought. Patrick touched her shoulder and leaned over: "But he could have been coerced, he could have been tortured himself. Nobody knows. Did he ever say anything?"

"Nothing."

"And he won't see you?"

Celia lifted her head and said, "No."

He was afraid that she would start crying then and there, but she maintained herself, likely because Paul and Nina were only five feet away. Patrick noticed the vermilion of her lower lip blanch, and the muscle near the angle of her jaw flicker, and understood he was seeing a person accustomed to maintaining composure through pure will.

Celia rose and told Paul he needed to go to bed. He had been staying up later since they got to Den Haag, she explained. Patrick offered to walk them back to their *pension* or to call a cab but they declined. Celia collected Paul and shepherded him toward the door, but little Paul's head was still turned and eyes fixed on the screen. Patrick turned off the squalling television and said goodnight, watching the three of them pad down the hallway. He was ashamed of the relief he felt once the door was closed. The room was quiet with the television off, and he spent fifteen minutes examining himself in the mirror. His right eye, visible only when he tenderly separated the swollen lids, was bloodshot. But he could still see from it. The cheekbone was red and tight with the bruising and shouted out disapproval as he tried to wash it.

He thought it was unfair of Celia to chastise him about not calling; it wasn't as though he hadn't agonized about speaking to Hernan most days for the last seven years. The urge to call had been, of course, strongest right at the start – yes, he *had* wanted to declare solidarity with him, to express his incredulity at the charges. But he hadn't called. And then, of course, Marta had died and it was as if her death was a more explicable disaster, one for which he had a ready-made response. He wrote to Hernan, yes, he had contacted him then, but how could he raise the issue of the allegations as his friend was burying his wife?

Even so, there *had* been contact in the last five years, but perhaps Celia didn't know about the worn-out, annotated copy of *Moby-Dick* that Hernan had sent to him weeks after the funeral, Marta's copy, the margins festooned with notes. Along with the book, Hernan had included a letter – perfunctory, not a word about the accusations he was facing – saying that Marta wanted him to have this particular book. No other explanation. It was an act, an object, that mystified Patrick at the time.

It was a failure of belief, he eventually thought. His belief. If he truly had faith in Hernan, that would have trumped any accusation. But that wasn't fair; after all, Hernan was the one who taught him to objectively assess the world and to consider the evidence, who taught him that dispassion was more worthy of an educated man than blind loyalty, and it became a mantra to him that he repeated over and over again as he made up his mind about the new life of Hernan García. Evidence was stronger than faith. He didn't call. But still, he could have called – Celia was right about that. He could have called even if he doubted Hernan's story (*Hernan's* story? *Hernan* offered no story, he offered silence). And if he had called Hernan? Or Celia, for that matter? Well, what he would have said was another issue altogether. He could imagine the agony of silences in that conversation. How did a person make up small talk about accusations of torture? Of murder?

The sad fact was that one of the reasons he refused to give Elyse Brenman an interview was that everything he had to say about the situation sounded simplistic and false. He could go on the record and say Hernan was "a good man" or that

Hernan had "the highest ethical standards" but he had nothing that could convince anyone that Hernan was innocent in the face of accusations and witnesses and mounting evidence. Good character was no longer a defence against such charges. People had grown accustomed to normal, apparently healthy minds committing depraved acts, inured to the recurring televised puzzlement of neighbours and friends as a backyard gravesite was dug up and another monster in their midst was revealed.

Elyse probably wouldn't have believed it if Patrick had told her how much he had learned in a week of working with Hernan, about honest effort and consideration, about how to do a job for the sake of it, the beauty of it, even if it were only moving plantains on a dolly. He assumed she wouldn't understand the feeling he had in the store, how Marta García's fretful gaze dissolved after that first day, becoming a smile that was modestly held in check for the most part, brought to full bloom when her children or Hernan appeared. By week's end Patrick had earned her smile – how important that was to him, how he felt like an ass for the way he had behaved to her, to anyone behind a counter, minding their business in every sense. How could he explain to anyone what the Garcías would come to mean to him, the friendship they showed a person who had tried to cause them harm? He thought at first that they were afraid of him in some way, that they considered him another bewildering item in the cost of their admission to this country, that they accepted him because of some weakness they sensed in themselves. But they were so unlike anyone he had met. They were so happy together. They weren't weak and they didn't need anyone, certainly not Patrick. He needed them.

Patrick could have told Elyse about the men and women who came to the store for Hernan's advice and opinions, people who didn't care that he wasn't a doctor any more. Hernan tended to them when no one else did. Would anyone know how heroic that was to the teenager who witnessed it? It was too difficult to explain how complicated heroism was, how the same act became something new when it was viewed later.

Elyse wouldn't have been interested in the effort the Garcías put into Le Dépanneur Mondial. Details about Hernan being up at five o'clock to receive the day's fresh bread, or the Mozart that he always made sure could be heard throughout the store, or the fact that Le Dépanneur Mondial would not sell alcohol or cigarettes or lottery tickets – the economic cornerstone of the dépanneur industry, those details would only confuse her readers. Her readers weren't told of the irony of his discovery that day in Le Dépanneur Mondial, that Hernan had been found out because he'd refused to sell lottery tickets. Because of principle and the willingness to defend his principle, Hernan was in Den Haag. Elyse's readers wouldn't appreciate the irony of the lottery ticket that never existed. Her readers would know only that a former victim came face to face with a man he regarded as his torturer. Indignation needed to be carefully crafted and could not admit such things as irony. There was so much Patrick couldn't tell her.

SEVEN

–

At the end of his week of work, Patrick sat down with Hernan
and they went over what Hernan felt he was owed and the
value of the jobs Patrick had done around the store.
Calculations complete, Hernan said they were even and
smiled, holding out his hand to shake as a way to seal their
contract. Patrick told him then and there how much he had
enjoyed working at Le Dépanneur Mondial and if Hernan
would allow it, he wanted to be kept on. The only jobs he had
had before were delivering newspapers and a couple of purgatorial shifts bussing tables at one of the interchangeable
franchise restaurants down by the highway. Up to that point,
work had been nothing more than the soul-crushing exchange
of time and effort for money, something his father and others
disappeared to do every morning, something foreign and
vaguely risible. But that had changed for him in one week at
Le Dépanneur Mondial. He couldn't explain it to Hernan or
years later to Celia, and so he surely couldn't expect Elyse to
understand – but he found himself invested in his work,

feeling for the first time in his life the impulse to do something for more than just the money. He immediately recognized the oddity of it, the simple, almost hokey conviction that mopping the floor of a *dépanneur* had meaning in and of itself. At first, there were the satisfactions of extra money and, if he was honest, a chance to see Celia. But it was also about working with Hernan García. He didn't fully understand it until years later, when he was taking a course in psychology and saw the standard stock photo of ducklings following in a line behind the Austrian psychologist Konrad Lorenz. The photo was the standard accompaniment to a discussion of imprinting, the explanation for intense attachment that occurred in the wild (in Lorenz's case the ducks became attached to his bright yellow rubber boots). Aside from the stimulus of the yellow boots, imprinting required an animal to be in a "critical period," a time when the neural connections that led to attachment could be made. The attachment hadn't been about the place alone, it had been about Patrick. He had been ready for it. Business at Le Dépanneur Mondial was good, but it clearly wasn't so busy that they required another person around the store, and Patrick suspected that the decision to keep him on may have ended up costing Hernan. But Hernan never hesitated. Patrick was hired as Le Dépanneur Mondial's first stock boy, and aside from Madame Lefebvre, who handled the evening cash for ninety minutes every night so the Garcías could all sit down to dinner together, and Jimmy Padopoulos, who did odd jobs around the store, he was the only other outsider at the start.

And so Patrick continued his summer as Hernan García's shadow, following him from the first dawn deliveries and watching as he and the other Garcías negotiated the day through to its end. He would have his jobs to do, the menial tasks that, during the course of a day, would bring him into moments of contact with Marta or Roberto or Celia, but he worked with Hernan, it was Hernan to whom he looked for direction and example. Patrick had never known how many details needed to be attended to in the running of a typical grocery store – he'd assumed that the busiest part of the day was hassling teenage customers like himself or attempting to close the overstuffed cash register tray – and the truth shamed him for the way he had treated people behind the counters. Hernan was in motion for eighteen hours a day, never rushing, never seeming to exert himself, and it became clear that without his continual interventions the appearance of a well-run store would quickly dissolve into that of a listing ship, taking on water and bound for a reef. By watching him, Patrick became aware of how much expertise and practice went into making work look effortless.

Patrick had never seen anyone who wore such utter competence so lightly. Among the people he knew, any partial aptitude – car repair, sports trivia, the ability to operate a hash pipe under even mildly adverse conditions – was an occasion for sustained bragging and the basis for a reputation. But Hernan did his job quietly, almost secretly, it seemed. But at all times, he had the command of a general in the field, able to keep a running tally of inventory, expiry dates, and deliveries, as well as knowing how to troubleshoot the ventilation or the electrical or the refrigeration system – all without arrogance or impatience, especially when dealing with an employee who lacked any of these skills. Hernan did things the right way. The windows were washed and the floors were megawatt bright and no one could ever recall seeing a burned-out bulb in Le Dépanneur Mondial. Patrick remembered the inordinate, adolescent pride he had in the place. It was the cleanest, best-stocked, best-run store in NDG; not as much a dépanneur as a full-service specialty grocery store at a time when that kind of store was rare in Montreal. In every way, the store reflected Hernan. But it was more than that. He was good to his customers, honest enough to tell them when the mangoes were a little off or taking them seriously when they came back with a product that failed the test of coming from Le Dépanneur Mondial. It was fairness, not fairness as some policy plastered on the wall to keep the customers unaware that they were being more systematically cheated. It was simply a person being fair, and it must have had a cost, a cost that could be balanced against the benefits of customer loyalty, but Patrick felt that it was a calculation that Hernan chose not to make. To a teenage boy, this was decent and heroic. Patrick tried to explain it to his friends only to see them roll their eyes as they reacted to one of their own extolling the virtues of hard work like some babbling Junior Achievement convert, happy in his newfound nirvana of buckets and pails and fresh produce.

Because Hernan knew the ins and outs of running a store and managing an inventory so thoroughly, Patrick simply assumed that the García family had been grocers for generations before coming to Canada. This was their lifeblood, he thought, nonetheless impressed at the success that the Garcías had in bringing something new and good to his neighbourhood. Which is why it came as such a shock to Patrick to learn from one of the customers that Hernan had been a doctor before coming to Montreal. It was Marta who finally confirmed it after Patrick started asking questions about the clientele who cornered Hernan in the back aisles of the store. Patrick would watch, pretending to stock items on a nearby shelf as a whispered conversation would take place and someone would invariably point to an affected area. The Hispanic population of NDG had already become devoted patrons of Le Dépanneur Mondial, but now families would show up with plastic bags full of their undecipherable medications, asking Hernan for advice, what should be taken, what could be thrown out. Hernan could have dismissed them with a wave of his hand but he listened and looked through their medications before telling them to ask their doctor about this pill or that pill. He wasn't a doctor any more, he would say, as a way of giving them a chance to turn and leave. They always stayed.

Memories of a summer twenty years before disappeared as he turned on the light in his bathroom. Not really a doctor any more, he had that much in common with Hernan. Patrick took a Tylenol, the contents of a couple of those little bottles in the minibar, and followed it up with a Valium. He lay down on the bed. His antidepressant could wait until morning. The phone on his bedside table pulsed with a red light that signalled awaiting voice mail, but the prospect of having to *listen* to his partners' messages, their grievances made more urgent, more authentic for having been weighted with the inflections of a human voice (plaintive, pleading, reproachful, all, he knew, calculated for maximal effect) was enough to scare him off. Beyond that his only other thought, strangely enough, was of Heather. It was the confusion of seeing Celia again – memories of tenderness and old emotions complicated by her obvious lack of regard for him – that made him think of someone who hated him less. He had never told Heather about Celia per se. What he felt for Celia had been merged into the more general sentiment he had for the García family – memories recounted warmly, but infrequently. But any mention of the Garcías had been a mistake, allowing Heather enough material to psychoanalyze his need for another family – for lionizing the Garcías, as she put it – when he already had a perfectly good family.

And while his affection for the Garcías was enough to make Heather suspect he'd had a Dickensian upbringing of gruel and periodic beatings, this wasn't true at all. The reason he wasn't especially close to his own family was, paradoxically, biological. Patrick Lazerenko was, as people tended to say in that era, a surprise. His mother was forty-two when he was born and his father forty-five, and although he felt they loved him and tried to communicate that love, he could never get over the feeling that to them he was the equivalent of a second mortgage taken out very much against their will. Things were better now. He spoke to his mother and was on good terms with his two much older sisters – both mortally embarrassed teenagers when their mother became visibly pregnant in the spring of 1970. He was aware of situations like this where the "surprise" anomaly baby rejuvenated the aging parents and was doted on by older siblings, but Patrick supposed he would have found a way to chafe against that too.

Roger and Veronica. Hard-working people who probably deserved better than some smart-ass son entering puberty as they were thinking about winding down their working lives. And while they never said anything, he knew. *He* was what was keeping them from a Florida condo or tooling around the hillbillier parts of America in some apocalyptically big motorhome. He was loved, but he was on the clock. It was different at the Garcías'.

That first summer at Le Dépanneur Mondial he saw the Garcías' clientele grow and began to recognize the cycles of patronage: daily shoppers seeking fresh produce, others doing their weekly marketing, and the monthly shoppers − pensioners or young women with strollers holding one too many babies − appearing in the days after the cheques arrived. Hernan would get him to bag and deliver these monthly orders; any tips were to be refused, a general policy of Le Dépanneur Mondial. It was a sum Hernan promised he would make up later. And for those who couldn't afford it, Patrick would soon learn that Le Dépanneur Mondial was more than a store. Through the years, more than one neighbour of Le Dépanneur Mondial would compliment Hernan on the cleanliness and general lack of stink in the alley behind the store, not knowing that the stink usually came from dumpsters full of food thrown out and left to rot. The dumpsters behind Le Dépanneur Mondial rarely saw food, unless it was spoiled on delivery, and this was because Hernan combed the store every night before closing, culling items he knew would not sell before they spoiled, creating parcels of food − day-old bread, cartons of milk skidding toward their expiry dates, canned goods shunted to the back of the shelves − all of which Patrick or Roberto or Celia would deliver to addresses Hernan wrote down on the back of an envelope. The instructions were explicit. Leave the parcel outside the door. Knock once. Leave immediately. He began to understand as he rode through the alleys of NDG during the nights of that first summer, heading to the next delivery, that Hernan García was different.

The rudiments of cleaning and stocking the store came easily, and with time he became more familiar with the names and shapes of products. But most of the time, he watched the Garcías. They were newcomers without extended family or any Honduran community to soften their landing in Montreal. All they had was each other and they knew that to be the central fact of their existence. Night after night in Le Dépanneur Mondial, he watched as the Garcías passed time in the store. Celia would get out a sketchbook and sit at the small counter they had near the front window, watching the scene on the sidewalk, imagining what she would later draw. He remembered Nina playing behind the counter. Marta García would turn often to check on them, a gesture that was for the most part unnecessary except to continually restate that claim they all had in each other. Then Roberto would burst in and every face would brighten and they would all speak at once – shout – in Spanish, as if his enthusiasm ignited them. It was natural that Roberto, with his fearlessness and gregarious nature, had become their source of reconnaissance in the neighbourhood. It was his job to scout out the swimming pool or the playgrounds and ensure they were safe for his sisters. It was likely along those lines that he felt it necessary to pin Patrick on his back against a shipment of potatoes in the storage room. They wrestled for the second or two it took Roberto to flip Patrick around and pretzel him into a more painful hold.

"Don't look at my sister, *perrito*," Roberto said with an authority known to those who had the truth and a definite physical advantage on their side. Patrick, his face wedged between sacks of potatoes, was in no position to deny the charge. "Just a warning. My dad doesn't see these things." Roberto leaned against him, the twisting force of the headlock now more painful than the accusation. "I do." Then Roberto loosened his grip, allowing Patrick to struggle free. He offered Patrick a hand. This was ignored as Patrick made a show of getting to his feet under his own steam.

In the weeks since he'd started at the store, Patrick hadn't said a word to Celia outside of conversation made necessary by working in the same place. But he watched her. Felt the excitement as the store opened and another day in which he might see her began. He loved her and it must have showed – Roberto knew, any teenage boy would know. That summer Patrick found himself wondering whether Celia understood English, as she seemed so completely inured to his presence in the store. Undaunted, he attempted sonnets and learned rudimentary Spanish just at the thought of one day being better able to express himself to her. He refused to think about her when he masturbated, and, in the bizarre, emblematic way of sixteen-year-old boys, that was love. He lingered around her whenever possible, making sure she knew how hard he was working for her father, for her, and with time Patrick imagined she noticed him as someone notices the arrival of good weather, the gradual acknowledgement that something surprising and pleasant has happened and could be counted on to happen again. Patrick did all of this only to overhear her speak on the phone, in perfect English, with a new friend, and say that she was in the store and had to be alert as she was alone with "the vandal."

Before, a humiliation like that would have sent him, spray can in hand, to wreak havoc on the walls of Le Dépanneur Mondial, but now her judgment only had the effect of sanctifying his infatuation, spurring him to redouble his efforts to be worthy of her.

Even with Roberto's threats and Celia's indifference, Patrick still felt at home at Le Dépanneur Mondial. Marta García was mysterious, her attentions always divided between the book in front of her and the other world with its hazards and complications. And although she smiled at him, in those first few weeks Patrick knew she still had her suspicions, even more so after he asked to stay on and became part of the growing non-García staff contingent. And if the atmosphere in those early days ranged from indifference to low-grade hostility, Patrick reasoned it wasn't anything he couldn't live with, but he knew that something drastic would have to change for anyone but Hernan and Nina to like him. So when Gerry Delaney, a well-known small-time (meaning largely unsuccessful) criminal, showed up in Le Dépanneur Mondial late on a Tuesday night in August with his hands in his pockets and a furtive look in his eyes, Patrick's first impulse wasn't to call the cops but to watch and wait, sensing this could be an ideal opportunity for character rehabilitation. He crouched down behind some shelves and glided closer to the cash, the Pro-matic industrial mop like a javelin in his hands. The first, skittish strains of the overture from *The Marriage of Figaro* sang out from the speakers. Patrick poked his head up to see Gerry loitering around the front of the store, waiting for the final customer to leave. When the chimes above the door finally died down, Delaney looked up and subtly manoeuvred himself to the register, where

Celia's attention was focused on a magazine she was leafing through. His jacket pocket bulged, a non-specific shape and size; a ruse, Patrick assumed, as Delaney had a reputation in the neighbourhood for big talk and see-through bluffs. But then his two hands fluttered and in a surprisingly deft motion, he pulled a black ski mask over his face. The act was an unexpected kick-start: countless biologic cylinders fired simultaneously, throwing Patrick forward like a man electrified. The mask energized Gerry Delaney too, turning him from zigzagging crab to a truer predator, lunging at the counter and shouting at Celia to empty the cash. Patrick remembered Celia's face, that terrible fright and what it aroused in him, a feeling outside of anything he'd felt before, not just the need to intervene or to seem a hero to her, but the snarling, primordial need to defend family.

The Pro-matic industrial mop is rightly famous for its solid design. It weighs in at more than thirteen pounds, bone-dry, right out of the manufacturer's wrapping. Add another couple of pounds for soaked-up water, and raising the mop above one's head is a formidable task. But in those first few moments the mop was a butterfly net in Patrick's hands; the true heft and momentum of the mop became apparent only in mid-flight, as he was propelled forward, trying to hang on to the suds-soaked battle-axe aimed at Gerry Delaney's masked head.

"You could have *killed* him," Hernan said later, when he sat Patrick down and read him the riot act in the wake of the mop-swinging incident. After the way the story was featured in all the papers – a photo of Celia and Patrick staring into the camera from behind the shattered counter with the accompanying story of a young hero acting to prevent a robbery of the store he himself had once vandalized, all under the headline "Forget the cops, grab the mop!" – Hernan's anger caught him by surprise. Hernan made it clear how upset he was about the risks Patrick had taken. Gerry, it turned out, *did* have a gun and for once, according to the cops, had managed to load it correctly. Celia could have been shot. "You could have been hurt," Hernan said. Only years later did Patrick understand how Hernan must have dreaded the publicity, the cops and reporters crawling around Le Dépanneur Mondial, taking down everybody's names. He *could* have killed Gerry Delaney too. The mop head did land, stoving in the counter with a wicked, splintering force, but it missed Delaney by a mile. It shocked the assailant, though, and as he recoiled, he slipped on the trail of soapy water the mop head had left on the floor and he fell, breaking his left hip. Patrick remembered Celia's scream twinning up with Gerry's alto yelp, calling out against Mozart's overture to *Figaro*, and then sirens, sirens, sirens. In someone else's fantasy, Patrick would be cool in the aftermath, he would have walked over to Celia and taken her in his arms but, in reality, Patrick was scared and shaking and instead, he turned his attention to Gerry. He knelt down to hold Gerry's clammy hand, hoping it would make the injured man stop screaming until the ambulance arrived.

And while the true mechanics of heroism were, in his case, distressingly banal, even inadvertent, they were dutifully ignored by all. He was a hero, celebrated by the community and, more importantly, by the Garcías, and allowed to revel in that tight-lipped, aw-shucks modesty that all heroes exude. Once Hernan got over being angry, he found it impossible to suppress a smile every time he looked at Patrick. Marta began calling him by his full name, Michael Patrick. Roberto let his wariness slacken and, along with Nina, started calling Patrick "Mop." So did Celia, which hurt a bit. But Patrick preferred it to what she had called him before.

By his second month at the store, he had assumed all the duties of stocking and cleaning up, inheriting most of the other jobs that Roberto balked at. He felt increasingly comfortable handling customers' questions about the produce, occasionally venturing an opinion on the quality of the mangoes, and in a pinch, he'd even be called on to operate the cash. And when the day was over and the front door of Le Dépanneur Mondial was locked, he ran deliveries on a ridiculously antiquated bike with a seat so uncomfortable he preferred to stand on the pedals and pump up and down the streets of NDG like a Tour de France *domestique*.

But above all, he was an anthropologist dropped into Le Dépanneur Mondial, permitted for a time to observe the Garcías and all their rituals. They weren't a perfect family, which made them more fascinating to watch; in their moments of raised voices and slammed doors, during the times when Hernan and Marta García didn't get along or when Roberto seemed to take pleasure in testing his father, Patrick only came to see them as more authentic, and more authentically happy. He understood that even though Marta was bored working in the store, the book she kept with her was not a mere diversion but a source of pleasure, her concentration returning to it as soon as the door closed on a customer.

With time, the Garcías began to reveal themselves. Hernan, who would go about his work and not say anything for hours, began asking Patrick questions about his family or about school. And, perhaps understanding that his teenage employee was less inclined to ask questions, volunteered facts about his own life. He confirmed what Marta had already confided in Patrick; he had been a doctor, a cardiologist, before coming to Canada. Years later, Patrick would ask himself why Hernan would choose this bit of personal information to tell him. It couldn't have been boastfulness; Patrick suspected Hernan knew how much he admired him already, nor did he need to prove his credentials to a sixteen-year-old in order to give advice to the arthritics and asthmatics who frequented Le Dépanneur Mondial. The only answer that made sense to Patrick, at the time as well as retrospectively, was that as some people enjoyed discussing sports or politics or the weather, Hernan García truly loved to talk about medicine.

Patrick's medical education – not just the acquisition of facts but the realization that he was an able and eager student, the first dangerous primings of an autodidact's pump – began that summer under the auspices of Hernan García. While only one of the refrigerated sections in the store was dedicated to meat, this did not stop Le Dépanneur Mondial from occasionally taking delivery of a beef heart, an organ immediately commandeered by Hernan and taken into the back for an impromptu anatomy lesson. Celia and Roberto, perhaps having witnessed these back room demonstrations too many times before, would find other things to do when this occurred, relieved their father had another potential pupil to call on. And while Patrick wanted nothing more than to impress Hernan, he became squeamish and dizzy at the thought of watching a dissection – the high school ritual of splayed frogs and rats came to mind, anything worth learning lost amid the hilarity of jocks hiding animal parts around the classroom. But he composed himself, hammering down any qualms, suppressing the nausea that seemed to arrive from nowhere. When Hernan peeled back the pink butcher's paper and exposed the heart on a table in the back, he swallowed hard and stared at the bloody mass, unblinking. Hernan took the heart in one of his hands and felt its heft. Patrick shifted his weight from one foot to the other. It occurred to Patrick that the back room was an odd place to conduct this sort of business, dark and cavernous, adding creepiness to the encounter. Hernan must have sensed this, and told him that the first anatomic dissections of humans were carried out in secrecy, in rooms much like the one they were in, as the act was forbidden by church law. "It was considered an indignity," he said, "but over the centuries dissection has become part of what every doctor has to do. It is tradition." Patrick remembered the authoritative first cut in the dissection of the organ, the thick, deeply red flesh sliced open to reveal the chambers of the heart and the stringy webs around the edges of what Hernan explained were the valves. Hernan would describe the orderly lub-dubbing of valves in the heart as a choreographed action of door closings, of ushering a crowd through the rooms of a house. The tone of his voice lifted and his arms acquired extra gestures to ease his points home. "Do you understand?" Hernan would ask in such a way that no one could ever doubt his sincerity.

And, as is the case for any hungry self-learner, what Patrick was not given, he took. This meant, in addition to asking Hernan more and more about signs and symptoms, diseases and cures, he took to spying on Hernan, observing how he dealt with the customers who came for advice, how he would sit and say nothing as their sagas of swollen ankles and sore backs were laid out before him. When he had something to say he leaned in and lowered his voice, then leaned back and invariably nodded when the response came.

Hernan had endless patience, perhaps because he knew it was often all he could offer.

"Do you miss medicine?"

The question caught Hernan off guard – they were in the back of Le Dépanneur Mondial, installing new fluorescent bulbs in the refrigerated produce shelves. Hernan was speechless. For a moment Patrick thought he had pushed too far, but then he could see that Hernan was considering his answer. Rather than being angry at what could have been seen as an impertinent question, he seemed surprised that anyone would ask it at all. Holding the long, fragile tube in his hands, he looked at Patrick with an expression on his face that was legible even to an emotionally illiterate sixteen-year-old.

"I miss it terribly," Hernan said, and then leaned over to place the bulb in its socket.

Patrick had never heard anyone speak about their working life, current or former, with any sentiment other than resignation or outright dread. When he had his medical school interview years later, he was asked the standard question of when he first thought about pursuing a career in medicine. Patrick chose to tell the interviewers gathered around the table that he had come to the decision slowly – skipping any mention of Hernan and the back room anatomy lessons – believing that the interviewers would view a description of a reasoned, deliberative process more positively than the story of an epiphany in a refrigerated produce unit. But that was the first instance, when something about Hernan's dignity and honesty and the sense of loss that he conveyed made Patrick consider what he wanted to be.

In August of that summer Patrick's parents announced that they were going away to a rented cabin up north. Having had thirty summers' worth of family holidays, first with his two older sisters and then with Patrick, his parents were now weary of any vacation requiring much in the way of planning or activity. Both parents had hinted broadly that an ideal vacation for them meant that Roger would fish and Veronica would play solitaire in a different kitchenette for three weeks. And that was okay with Patrick; he was of the opinion common to teenagers and their parents that extended family trips were a variation on a hostage-taking, with each party assuming themselves, at different times, to be the victim. And in that spirit, his parents' vacation plans were presented to Patrick on the understanding that, while he was invited, he probably wouldn't want to take them up on the offer. He was given the phone number of the cabin for emergencies. Everyone was relieved and no one's feelings were hurt.

When the Garcías found out, they weren't so much appalled as incredulous that a sixteen-year-old could be left alone for three weeks. Their concern struck Patrick as charming and old-fashioned, and probably best explained as a Latin American close-knit family thing, a new-immigrant-family-paranoia reaction. Hernan and Marta voiced their worry for Patrick's health and safety. "How will you eat?" Marta had asked as he mopped the floor near the cash register. She was even more shocked when Patrick shrugged in response. Roberto regarded him with newfound respect. Patrick had absolute freedom – even if it was temporary, even if it was likely to be wasted – something that would elude him until he was out of his parents' house. Celia was steadfast in her indifference, but Patrick hoped that she secretly shared her parents' alarm and pity. He did play it up, too, doing little to dispel their notion of his abandonment, happily accepting their invitation to dinner. He was sure they would think less of him had he told them how relieved he was not to spend three weeks pickling in the boredom of a cabin in St. Donat.

Dinner, Hernan explained, as he gave Patrick a piece of paper with their home address on it, was the most important time of the Garcías' day, the only time when all of them would be together outside Le Dépanneur Mondial. It was a rare ninety minutes, a gap in the day when they trusted the operation of the store to Madame Lefebvre.

The night of the dinner, he took a shower so long it ended only when the first lashings of cold water signalled an empty hot water tank. While picking through a pile of clothes on his bedroom floor for the cleanest he could find, he had inaugural thoughts about cologne but finding that his choice was limited to an ancient, unopened bottle of Brut in Roger's medicine cabinet, he thought better of it. On his way over to the Garcías', a typical red-brick duplex near the south end of Harvard Avenue, a couple of blocks from the store and not really all that far from his house, Patrick stopped and bought a cake to present to Marta, which he thought would be the sophisticated thing to do.

Patrick expected crossing the threshold of the Garcías' house would be memorable. He imagined foreign-sounding music greeting him as he entered, a melody rising, a prelude to what awaited. The Garcías lived here. It would be special. The house would be fragrant with flowers that had been gathered and arranged as a centrepiece on the table, the varieties a mystery to him, a sunburst of petals and thick stems bound with string to steady them into a huge earthen vase. He knew it, he'd been able to see it so clearly as he climbed the steps to their front door. He'd be dizzy from the colour, heady with expectation of the meal and eating with the Garcías. He rang the bell.

Marta greeted him at the door. She looked pleased and puzzled as he handed her the box. And then she disappeared, leaving him standing at the doorway to stumble over the pairs of shoes scattered about. He waited, and after no one appeared, he took a couple of steps into the house to find it remarkable in its resemblance to his own. No music, not even the Mozart that accompanied every working minute at the store. The walls of the entryway were bare and there were still cardboard boxes visible at the end of the hallway. He took another step and leaned around a corner to look into the living room, still suspecting that something exotic must lie just beyond. Again, another room. White walls and furniture similar to what he'd just left at home. Nothing special, really. Nothing even different. No colourful decorations, nothing that distinguished the Garcías from any other family on the block. It was a home like his own. He thought he would find something typically Honduran, but was uncertain what that meant, not knowing anything Honduran except for the Garcías themselves. He thought he could hear someone down the hallway, but there was still no one in sight. It was hot in the house, and the air was still, and, like in his house on hot days, you could smell the faint scent of wet towels. When he looked down, Nina was at his feet.

Marta returned after putting the cake away to find that Nina had taken Patrick by the hand and was leading him on a tour of the front room. A small group of dolls was assembled on the couch and Nina introduced each one in that way specific to five-year-olds, citing their elaborate names followed by their accompanying emotional frailties, a roll call of dolly psychopathology. Nina then left the support group on the couch to show Patrick the "whale stuff." Patrick assumed he was on his way to more stuffed animals with bulging eyes and hopefully less dramatic psychological problems and was surprised to be brought before a bookcase. He didn't recognize the objects on a single shelf in front of him, except that they were obviously on display, arranged in that particular way that suggested someone valued them. Propped against the back of the shelf were two black-and-white photographs, the edges ragged with age, each showing a clutch of houses running the length of a dock. "Nantucket 1853." "Gloucester 1855." There was no clue to what time of year the photos were taken, but the blue-tinged seas looked frigid. Five sharp-ended spears lay at one end of the shelf, gathered together like arrows ready for use. Fragmented pieces of what appeared to be yellowed bone crowded the shelf in front of the photos. Patrick wondered why Hernan had collected these things. As he peered closer, he saw the bone was covered in intricate carvings of ships and whales. He reached in and picked up one of the carvings, examining the tiny grooves darkened with grime.

"Scrimshaw," Marta said over his shoulder.

"Is this yours?" he asked, and Marta nodded. "What's all this stuff for?" Patrick said as he looked more closely at the pieces. On the bone in front of him a spear lanced the flank of a breeching whale. Even though it was rendered in miniature, it effectively conveyed the theme of a battle to the death.

"For? For nothing, for me," Marta replied, picking up what he had recognized was part of a harpoon. She gripped the spear as though she were acknowledging its heft and considering how far she could throw it if she had to. "It is history, Michael Patrick, history, a way of life that is gone.

"I studied Melville," Marta added, as if in explanation, and he tried not to look blank-faced. "You know, *Moby-Dick*. *Billy Budd*." She smiled and put the harpoon tip down. Nina played with another piece of whalebone until Marta asked her to stop.

"Come to the kitchen," Marta said, and Patrick followed with Nina like a little satellite, a moon of a moon.

The smells in the Garcías' kitchen – a pungent cloud rising from a pan of chopped peppers and onions – were the first sign of anything different from his parents' house. He sat on a stool beside the stove and watched Marta coax the meal into existence.

"You are how old, Michael Patrick?"

"Sixteen."

"Do you have brothers and sisters?"

"Two sisters. Older. Way older."

"Sisters," Marta said, scraping rice off the inside of a pot with a wooden spoon. She rapped the spoon firmly against the pot's edge. "So what is it that you like to do?"

"Pardon me?"

"What do you do when you're not at the store?" Marta's gaze bounced from the pots and saucepans to Patrick. He tried to speak to her when she was facing him but she always turned away too quickly. He wasn't sure he was being heard.

"I don't know. I just sort of hang out."

"You have friends."

"Yes."

"What do you like in school?"

He shrugged involuntarily, and he felt Marta watching him, watching the shrug. He shifted on the stool and then he said something that surprised him for its honesty and, later, for its accuracy: "I like science. I like, you know, how things work."

Marta nodded as she stirred a large pot that bubbled on one of the stove's back elements. Patrick felt no better. *Science.* He heard noises from the back of the house and Celia appeared from behind a door. Her hands were buried in an old cloth and the jagged odour of turpentine cut through the other smells in the kitchen. Marta turned to her.

"*Vaya afuera y lávese las manos. Nina está aquí.*"

Celia turned and left without a word. Marta didn't explain what she'd said, and with the silence Patrick felt increasingly self-conscious. Marta moved a lid from one saucepan to another. For a moment he considered bolting, leaving the stool upturned and the pots on the boil and cake behind for them all to laugh at. He'd brought a *cake*, for christsake. It was a step away from a bouquet of dandelions or a sitcom quality compliment: *My, you look lovely in that apron, Mrs. García.*

He felt more comfortable when Hernan and Roberto arrived from the store. Roberto pinned him with a stare as hostile as it was familiar, a reassuring source of gravity in the house, holding him down. Nina ferried between the counter and the table, depositing a fistful of cutlery on each placemat that Marta arranged into a table setting. Nina then sat down in her chair, looking over at Patrick in what he thought was an invitation to sit beside her. Marta and Hernan were occupied with carrying dishes of food to the table, Hernan pausing several times to call for Celia.

Patrick took the seat beside Nina, who smiled and promptly got up, wandering away from the table. Hernan chased after her, trying to shepherd the girl back, cajoling her. With Marta still at the stove and Roberto and Celia nowhere to be seen, Patrick was now the only one seated at the table. He felt someone tap him on the shoulder.

"That's not your place, Mopito," Roberto said. "Up."

As Patrick prepared to get up, a hand came to rest on his other shoulder, preventing him from rising.

"Roberto," Hernan said curtly, "Patrick is our guest, he can sit where he wants."

"That's *your* place."

"It doesn't matter."

Facing away from them, Patrick listened, unable to tell how the exchange ended. Marta seemed not to notice and brought the last dish to the table. One by one the Garcías sat down around him, Celia the last to come to the table, without a word or a glance.

Marta said grace and then Spanish phrases volleyed across the table as the steaming dishes were passed around. Patrick couldn't understand a word but after a while, listening to the percussion and rhythms of the García family conversation, he convinced himself that he could follow what was being said: the excitable, teasing inflection in Roberto's voice, Celia calmly rebutting him, Hernan and Maria reining them both in. Nina smiled and surveyed Patrick for the alien that he was.

On the other side of Patrick sat Hernan, who would lean over to translate a particular phrase or explain a dish. A plate of *carne asada* appeared and along with it Patrick was given a short history of Honduran cattle farming. He bit into a tortilla, anticipating a taste he thought he knew but instead experienced the earthier tang of what Hernan explained was the taste of flour made from corn instead of wheat. But the tastes and the sounds and the smells came too quickly and without ceasing; the exotic soon became unintelligible and Patrick found himself feeling increasingly apart. He was a stranger here. He watched and ate.

Hernan must have sensed this, as he made every effort to steer the conversation toward topics that would include their guest. He asked Patrick about his parents' vacation, reacting as if the potbellied hills of the lower Laurentians were the Andes themselves, expressing an admiration for anyone fit and adventurous enough to attempt a mountain holiday. Hernan spoke of a trip he and Marta had taken with the children when Roberto and Celia were small, a journey by station wagon across the eastern states that ended up on the beaches of the Jersey shore. And while the beaches weren't much compared to what they had in Honduras, it had been a trip they'd always remembered.

"We did it for the ocean. I needed to see the ocean," Marta said.

"You lived in the States?" Patrick asked, turning to Hernan.

Hernan paused as he wiped his mouth with a napkin. He nodded. "Detroit," Hernan said. "For a few years. I was working. Celia was born there."

Hernan changed the topic to an update on Gerry Delaney: hip stable after an operation; legal prognosis less optimistic. Discussion of the robbery, and Patrick's involvement in foiling it, drew Roberto forward, smirking: "You didn't tell us, Mopito, that you knew this guy Delaney."

"He's from the neighbourhood, everyone knows him."

"But you knew he was a criminal."

Patrick fumbled for words, but before anything could emerge, Hernan interceded. "*Roberto –* "

"It's just that I was surprised a guy like that would know when Celia would be alone in the store."

"She wasn't alone in the store. Michael Patrick was there," Marta answered.

"Where were *you* that night?" Hernan asked Roberto, and Marta placed her hand on her husband's forearm.

"Yeah, yeah. We were lucky he was there," Roberto said, pretending to back off, "lucky he had his *mop*."

It was near the end of dinner when the phone rang and Hernan excused himself to answer it. Celia was, as usual, in a world all her own, and Marta was occupied with cleaning up Nina. Roberto, in what Patrick thought at the time was an unexpected but welcomed gesture of reconciliation, offered him the last green vegetable on the platter. In the spirit of camaraderie, Patrick popped it in his mouth and bit down hard. The sensation was immediate, foreign, and incendiary. By the time Hernan returned, Patrick's mouth was ablaze, his eyes leaking as though a canister of tear gas had been lobbed into his lap. Coughing and choking as he downed a tumbler of water, Patrick pushed back from the table and ran to the hallway, desperate for a bathroom. Finding it, he kicked the door shut and spun open the cold water tap, trying not to retch as he gulped and spat. Even with his head in the sink and the water a torrent in his ears, he could still hear Hernan shouting.

When he returned to the table, red-faced, the hair at the front of his head still damp, he was met by the Garcías all sitting silently around the table. Order had been restored. Hernan patted him on the back and said plainly: "That was a jalapeño." Roberto then apologized.

"Cake?" said Marta.

At the end of the table sat Celia. All evening he had tried not to watch her, to concentrate on what Hernan or Marta said, but she would appear at the edge of his vision and he would have to look. Now embarrassed, he avoided her eyes. She and Roberto were engaged in another argument – he was animated and loud, while she was trying to affect a look of boredom. Patrick turned in the other direction, wanting anything else to concentrate on, studiously watching Marta slicing the cake, fingering the pleats in the tablecloth. Finally, he glanced up as he passed a plate around Nina to Celia. And that's when it happened. She looked at Patrick and smiled. The memory of that smile was encoded deep within his temporal lobes, spliced with the lingering autonomic throb it produced, filed away with other landmarks, those moments when life seems to blossom ridiculously into something more beautiful than can be imagined. A second. Two. No one else noticed. No, that was wrong. Roberto noticed.

"Did you bake this yourself, Mopito?" Roberto asked, Hernan glaring at him as he said it.

"Yes," Patrick said flatly, knowing it was probably the only answer that would shut him up. At this, a corner of his vision cracked open like a door onto daylight. Celia smiled again. He remembered the Garcías like this, a composite of retrieved sensation: tears in his eyes from the jalapeños, the sweet taste of cake in his mouth, Celia smiling.

EIGHT

—

Patrick sat up and swayed in Den Haag's early morning daylight. Grey outside, grey on the far wall of the room. The Garcías he loved seemed to exist only in memory. The room floated as he passed through it to the bathroom. There, he dug through his toiletries for more Tylenol. Next, a container that spilled out blue and white capsules, little armoured bugs of better mood, of improved sleep. The right side of his face was a bloated bruise, demanding that he touch the skin for verification, but he resisted, letting the eye rest, preserved in the bunker of his face. He showered in the darkened room.

Patrick's computer and cell phone told him he was the most popular man in all of Holland. He had more e-mail. His business associates, having given up on calling the hotel and having to go through Edwin or Pieter, were storming the beaches with wave after wave of message, direct to his cell phone.

"Hello? Do you hear me? Hello?"

"I just wanted to let you know that one Barry Olafson is

planning on coming. That's right, Olafson *fils*. The hatchetboy."

"Sanjay is fucking it up."

Marc-André summed it up in his most recent e-mail. Neuronaut's analysis of the new Globomart campaign was definitely stalled, and even with Sanjay pulling a series of all-nighters remodelling the data, none of the ads or visual cues were eliciting anything close to the results from the Values campaign. This meant that Globomart, which had such faith in Neuronaut that it didn't have a Plan B, was, for the first time in its corporate history, faced with postponing the start date of its new advertising campaign, which was the retail equivalent of scrubbing a space shuttle launch during the final countdown. Mere rumours of the decision were already creeping onto the business pages, with its stock expected to take the predictable tumble – and Neuronaut's right after it – and Barry Olafson had indeed flown from the Globomart world headquarters in Medina, Minnesota, to Boston to meet with Bancroft, a meeting that featured some high-amplitude finger-pointing at the meeting and Barry Olafson's request to meet the "guy whose bright fucking idea this all was." This, Marc-André said, was doubly noteworthy as it was the first time anyone from Medina, Minnesota, had used profanity. In Patrick's absence, Sanjay was offered up as the technical spokesman and he tried to handle the situation, but Olafson and his entourage left after tossing him back like a worked-over goat carcass. Then Marc-André got personal:

You've completely deserted us in a crisis where you are to blame.

I won't take the fall for this, you coward.

Bancroft should be bringing you back in shackles.

Patrick would have been angry had it not been for what he discerned as honest emotion. But it was typical of them all to overreact. He typed in a response:

> If it can be fixed, I'll fix it. Tell Sanjay to send me the data. I'll analyze it here. I need the data.

Then he put his laptop on the desk in the room, swearing that, other than corresponding with Sanjay, he would not use it for the rest of his time in Den Haag. Yes, a vow of silence. The ascetic in his hotel suite. Ted Kaczynski does Europe. He decided to clear all his messages, snuff the red light once and for all, and then unplug the phone. He keyed in the codes and heard that polite Dutch voice – a woman's this time, thin and bland as a slice of Edam – telling him he had two new messages.

"This is Marcello di Costini calling for you, Professor Lazerenko. Patrick, if we could meet tomorrow morning around nine, at my office, M-218 at the tribunal building. You will have to bring your passport. Ciao."

Patrick replayed Marcello's message while searching for a pen to write down the office number. Then he rifled through the contents of his briefcase for the folder that held the notes and references that Marcello had asked to see.

Marcello, in a manner so pleasant and collegial that Patrick only vaguely felt like an underachieving grad student, had asked him to review the entire literature relating to the neurobiology of criminal behaviour and guilt. He was still convinced that there was some biological explanation that they were not exploiting (*pursuing* was the word he used, but essentially he was trolling for loopholes based on some form of physical evidence, something to counterbalance the reams of photographs and depositions that implicated Hernan). Patrick had warned him that such defences had been advanced before but they rarely succeed. Even juries in the States, con- ditioned by an endless number of television shows to regard forensic evidence as unimpeachable truth, smelled something not quite right about a neuroscience defence. They could sense the loophole and they wouldn't buy it.

Message two followed di Costini, surprising Patrick.

"Hello, Mop. Roberto here. I just want to say I'm sorry for hitting you. I hope you understand why I had to do it. But it's done. I hope you're not hurt, anyway."

Despite the assaults that had book-ended their relationship, Patrick had never felt Roberto was his enemy. They were never friends, though. Patrick would be the first to admit that when they met that summer in 1986, he was jealous of Roberto. As a teenager Roberto García had had an almost pathological confidence and ease with people. He was new in the neigh-bourhood, new in the country, for God's sakes, and within a month, it was *his*: he had dozens of friends and was going out with this incredible girl from Westmount who looked hypnotized when she was in the same room as him. He was an invading army of charisma, blitzkrieging from barbecues to pool parties to clubs downtown. Remarkably, he did all this without abandoning his life in the shop and as part of the Garcías. His friends would come into the store and say hi to Hernan or Marta and he'd be wearing an apron and holding a mop and he'd be totally comfortable. It was as though just being Roberto trumped everything.

Then, suddenly, it was over between Roberto and Jennifer from Westmount. While Roberto seemed indifferent, Patrick watched, worried, having just established an entire cosmology based on his charisma. He was reassured days later when Roberto appeared with Isabelle, a film studies major who went to Concordia. Hernan and Marta were unimpressed. The fact that their seventeen-year-old son was seeing an austere-looking university student who wore black and watched Fassbinder movies for *fun*, seemed not to trouble, or even interest, them. To a feral teenage boy such as Patrick, this was more than impressive. This was climbing Everest without oxygen.

But that sort of charisma had a shelf life to it. It was a supernova thing, glowing most intensely in high school and college but it demanded a person go out and have an interesting life or they receded into the shadows of that memory. Roberto talked about travelling, but the store seemed to keep him grounded in NDG. In there somewhere, he had registered for a semester or two of management studies, but it didn't stick. So he stayed in the store and everything else kept moving. Patrick heard he got married and even had a child but that he and his wife had split up after Hernan's problems started and Marta died. Elyse had told him that, her voice trailing off and employing a look of wry disappointment to imply her opinion of cause and effect at work there.

Elyse had also been the one to tell Patrick that Roberto had taken over running Le Dépanneur Mondial by himself after Hernan's arrest, buying the property next door and expanding the store against the advice of just about everyone. He'd hired staff and for a time became one of the bigger independents in town, although there were so few now that that wasn't saying much. He overextended himself and came close to losing the place to the bank a while ago, but they had survived. Since then, Nina had been in charge – *Nina!* Forever still a child in his mind, now finished a business degree and exercising authority enough to pry her brother's hands off the wheel of Le Dépanneur Mondial. Patrick had seen the store when he'd been in Montreal for his niece's wedding the year before. At first he thought about going in but reconsidered, leery about bumping into Roberto when he'd made no attempts at contact for years. Even though it was more of a supermarket now, the sign still read "Le Dépanneur Mondial." After looking through the windows to make sure Roberto wasn't there, he'd decided to go in. Patrick had walked up and down the aisles, wanting that inescapable sense of place to swell inside him. He needed to feel better, to see those clean floors and smell fresh mangoes and get lost in those aisles. But almost everything inside had changed, and he felt pathetic standing there, pretending to look for something on the shelves. He wandered around for a while and then bought a pack of gum, paying the young cashier and walking out.

It was a little after eight in the morning, but outside it was still so dark and hazy that the streetlights of Den Haag remained on. Patrick dressed, the slow and deliberate act of an aching body. He put his folder of notes back into his briefcase. As he was about to leave, scanning the room for the credit card–sized room key, the room's phone rang.

"Hello?"

"Dr. Lazerenko?"

"Speaking."

"My name is Anders Lindbergh. I'm calling from the tribunal."

NINE

—

Marcello had yet to arrive, so Patrick was ushered into his office by his secretary. The office was pretty much what he expected, space used in that way familiar to anyone experienced with European hotel rooms or airplane washrooms. His desk was well-organized, no atrocity so unwieldy that it couldn't be contained in a file folder. Patrick noticed a couple of bound law journals sitting in various places around the room. He was used to the American style of having rows of them stacked high on bookshelves, forming an imposing gold leaf and Moroccan leather wall-of-law. Impossible to breach, expensive to scale.

On the opposite side of the room hung a framed photo from a newspaper, dated in the nineties, showing Marcello in action, assisting in one of those big organized crime trials that Patrick had read about, the type with half the town behind bars in the back of the courtroom like a Mafia zoo exhibit. Patrick leaned forward for a peek at the framed photos that sat facing the other way on Marcello's desk. He turned the photos around for a better look. Patrick presumed these to be family photos: two children, not yet teenagers but already with that look of precocious competence, as though slowing only to pose for the photo before getting back to composing their operas or sight-translating some Latin. It was difficult to describe his wife's physical beauty, except to say that she looked just as attractive without Botticelli's clamshell wakeboarding her onto the beach. Marcello swept in and took off his jacket in one fluid movement, as though he were shedding a cape. He smiled, apologized for being late and Patrick realized that being in Marcello di Costini's presence would forever make him feel like he was wearing white socks. Marcello's forehead, up to now engaged in battle with his cheekbones and chin for structural supremacy of his chiselled looks, broke ranks and wrinkled into a look of puzzled concern.

"It's nice to finally meet you. What happened to your face?"

"Long story."

"No, really, have you been to a doctor?"

Patrick brought a hand to his cheek. He had momentarily forgotten about it, although he should have figured how bad it looked by the way the tribunal guards had scrutinized his passport. And while it hurt, Marcello looked at him like he'd had a farm accident.

"I'm pretty sure I saw a doctor. Here."

Marcello nodded, understanding when to cut short a line of questioning that was clearly heading out to deep space.

"Thanks for coming. How long have you been in town?"

"I got in a couple of nights ago. I've been in and out of the courtroom, mostly out."

"You missed the excitement last week – we finally made some progress. Two witnesses admitted that Hernan helped them, and we were able to cast doubts on some unhelpful testimony."

"But still, there's, what, a dozen who will testify that he tortured them?"

"I will do what I can with that. You know how memory is, how it can be shown to be less than completely accurate." Marcello stalled for a second, a voice deflating, and Patrick found it hard to discern whether he was lost in thought or just tired. "I thought we would go over a few things . . ."

"Someone named Anders Lindbergh called me."

Marcello looked up from a file folder that Patrick was shocked to see had the name "LAZERENKO, P" on it. Marcello's expression had frozen. Then, as if a button has been pressed and a gear engaged, his face moved again.

"What did Mr. Lindbergh have to say, Patrick?"

"He said he wanted to speak to me in person."

"That *shit*," Marcello spat. It was a refreshing curse, a little hiss and flare of emotion, a hint that he had a bit of the brawler in him.

"I'm supposed to see him at noon."

"Cocksucker."

"Can I refuse to meet with him? Should I?"

Marcello didn't answer at first, occupied with what Patrick imagined was pure strategic alarm. Patrick was relieved to see evidence of it on someone else's face; it was an expression he imagined he wore as he listened to Lindbergh's invitation.

"No, no," Marcello said, leaning forward and raising his hands, "don't make him think that you have anything to hide."

"I don't know how the tribunal works. Can he subpoena me?"

"Technically, yes. They can subpoena anyone. Usually it's different, if you are a hostile witness, there's extradition and other matters before they can even get you to the tribunal," Marcello explained. He was holding the file so tightly that his nails blanched white. "But you're here. That's a problem."

"It's no problem, I can leave tonight – "

"Patrick. Don't think like that. They haven't issued subpoenas. You haven't even met with them. You don't think he's going to ask you about, you know, any possible biological defence?"

Ah yes, *the biological defence*. Patrick felt for the briefcase sitting at his feet, knowing it was full of notes he had written on free will and neurological correlates of diminished responsibility. Full of what Marcello hoped was an anthology of freshly minted loopholes.

"I don't think so. I think he wants to ask me about Hernan."

"About what, precisely?"

"I suppose if I know anything incriminating."

Marcello nodded. Those muscles must have got a lot of use. "And why do you have that feeling?"

With that, Marcello gave him the look – one Patrick imagined Anders Lindbergh would also deploy when they met later – a polished, gunmetal stare-down that some of the nastier personalities of the genocidal era have faced. Tyrants. Warlords. *Lazerenko, P.* Patrick imagined his file nestled in the same cabinet with the others.

"Hernan didn't give up practising medicine when he got to Canada."

Marcello put the file down and rubbed the back of his neck, "Yes, yes. Oh, this fucking case." He reached into a drawer and brought out a pad of lined paper at the same time he produced a bulky fountain pen. He readied himself: "And you saw this, you saw him treat patients."

"Yes. They came to him in the store."

"They came to *him*?"

"Yes. New immigrants, maybe some illegals, too."

"But you don't know for sure they were illegal immigrants."

"No."

"Then don't say that. Did he mistreat them? Did he give them drugs?"

"I don't think so."

Marcello looked straight at Patrick. "Let me rephrase the question: Can you say with absolute certainty that you never saw Hernan hurt anyone?"

"That was twenty years ago," Patrick said, and Marcello leaned forward. "I don't know. I didn't know what I was looking at."

"Oh, Christ," Marcello muttered and kept scribbling. "Look, Patrick, you were young, what I am hearing is doubt. Doubt is on our side." He looked up from his pad. "So how did these people pay Hernan?"

"Hernan did it for free."

Marcello snorted and put the pen down. "This does not worry me. This is maybe a little reckless, that's all they could argue. Just say what you said to me. You didn't know what you were looking at. You were young. Besides, I think this is a decoy. Something to throw a little scare into you. I don't think they will ask you about Hernan. Now, for the real business at hand." Marcello took the elastic band off the oversized folder. Across the table, Patrick recognized some of the items he'd referenced for Marcello.

"I have looked for precedent," Marcello said, flipping through the pile of papers, journal articles, photocopies of textbook chapters, extricating the ones he had tagged with a yellow Post-it note, "and of course, there is none. The normal brain scan didn't help us. Okay, yes," Marcello said, and paused. "Here is my premise: Hernan is a good man. You know that, of course. We both know that. Hernan has been implicated in some terrible situations, and let's say, for argument, that he actually committed these acts. Let's say I want to prove that he was incapacitated in some way during the time he was at Lepaterique. I have no psychiatric explanation, so I would like to explore trying to explain his incapacity in terms of abnormal brain function. The scans you use at Neuronaut, the functional scans – "

"Functional magnetic resonance."

"Yes, could these scans show that Hernan's brain responds differently, atypically, in certain situations?"

"And this difference would mean he wasn't criminally responsible?"

"Yes," Marcello said, leaning forward, clearly excited, as though his pupil was now able to conjugate a verb properly.

"So the court would allow he wasn't responsible for his actions."

"Well, yes. Of course. Look, Patrick, let's for a moment think about the judges in this case. They're fair people. They're reasonable. I know most outsiders think that all the judges do is weigh the evidence for and against. But these people want to understand. They want a verdict to make sense, to themselves, at least. I want to appeal to that. The acts that Hernan is charged with are abhorrent, a good man with a normally operating brain would not act this way. I am not talking about clearing Hernan, I'm talking about something that will mitigate the guilt. Most of the people I deal with, there is a history of hate. Something suppressed until it explodes. But not with Hernan. I read that book on him, with all the theories, and I know the details. He's had a psychiatric assessment. He's not a sociopath, he's not an ideologue. But one day he appears at Lepaterique and participates in torture. He's not defending himself and yet he refuses to accept guilt." Marcello looked at Patrick with an expectancy that lapsed into disappointment. "I'm not explaining myself. Correct me if I'm wrong. With your business, Patrick, you use the technology to understand why people make decisions."

"Well, I – "

"So how do we demonstrate the decision-making process is faulty in this man. I mean, can we?"

"I don't think so. That's what I wanted to tell you. I don't have the faintest idea why people make the decisions they do, the research isn't about that. I study what part of the brain is activated by certain stimuli and how that relates to pre-dictable behaviour. There's not a lot of 'why' in it."

"Okay, okay. No 'why,' but then 'how.' I want to know 'how.' I see Hernan in that room: above all, he is a doctor and even then he has competing goals, first, keep the person alive; second, do not let them suffer. What impulse does Hernan listen to? Maybe he was beaten himself, or deprived of water, maybe they threatened his family. These are competing goals, a situation just like the ones you study, no? And the behaviour is the torture."

"But I deal with experimental conditions," Patrick said, conscious of trying not to disappoint Marcello, "not an actual event that occurred twenty-five years ago. You can't just propose a situation like that."

"We can simulate, can we not?" Marcello flipped through papers and pulled something out of the pile. "There's a company in Amsterdam that does contract work, very much like your own company. I thought perhaps we could stage a simulation, see if this causes some response in Hernan that's different from controls." Marcello handed Patrick the papers that advertised the services of a company called Cervoscan. He tried not to appear pessimistic, but Marcello was sounding like a grad student whose thesis plans have collapsed, grasping at ideas to help salvage the data he'd cobbled together.

"Who's going to pay for all this?" Patrick asked, knowing that a functional MRI study was a strictly à la carte proposition; that time in the scanner ran in the range of a couple of thousand dollars an hour, and interpretation would be extra. A lot more extra. Another mortgage on Le Dépanneur Mondial for Nina to work off. Then Marcello smiled and introduced Patrick to the true meaning of demure.

"That's not important."

"Tell me," Patrick insisted, but Marcello was silent, assessing Patrick in a way that frustrated him more than the lawyer's evasiveness. "I've come three thousand miles because you've asked me to, I'm facing a subpoena, I – "

"Enough. It's a group called the Democratic Voice," Marcello said. "They've been very active in – "

"I know who they are. Do the Garcías know about this?"

"It was the Garcías who introduced Oliveira to *me*," Marcello said, and, registering what appeared to be Patrick's partial recognition of the name, continued: "Caesar Oliveira, he represents the Democratic Voice. He's been in Den Haag since the start of the trial."

"And this man, Oliveira, he's going to pay for a scan. You're okay with that?"

"Why not? What choice do I have? You have to realize the situation, Patrick. Lindbergh came into this case with a room full of witnesses, eager to testify. I have a client who won't even talk to me. It was the Democratic Voice – an investigator hired by them, anyway – who tracked down both our witnesses. And it was Oliveira who showed me this – " Marcello pulled out a journal article that Patrick had seen recently. It was a study showing subjects being imaged while in the act of deceiving others and it claimed to show increased activity in certain brain areas, the caudate, anterior cingulate gyrus, and the thalamus – that were not active during truthful responses. The study caused a rash of speculation that an infallible method of lie detection was around the corner. Even Bancroft got excited, proposing that Neuronaut should consider developing a protocol for lie detection. Marc-André loved the idea, said they should apply for matching funds from Homeland Security and install a Neuronaut scanner in every airport, right next to the baggage X-ray machine and the metal detector. Too unproven, too contentious, Patrick had said, and used his veto for the first time.

"This is completely different from what we've been discussing, Marcello. This is about lie detection. Plain and simple. The Democratic Voice brought you this paper?"

"Yes. Oliveira has been doing his homework. He found the lab in Amsterdam, too."

"Please don't take this the wrong way, Marcello, but it seems like the Democratic Voice is calling the shots."

"No, no. Not at all. They are helping, certainly. And to tell you the truth, I am interested in all options to prove my client's innocence. You are telling me it isn't feasible to examine whether Hernan feels responsible – "

"Don't say *feels*," Patrick said, cringing.

"Okay, it's not feasible to examine whether his brain responds normally when confronting a moral dilemma. Well then, is it feasible to do a test to see if he is lying?"

Patrick held up the paper, impressed and disturbed that someone else was combing the research literature on Hernan's behalf. "This 'lie-detection paper' is an experiment, too. Tightly controlled conditions, not people being interrogated. Hypothetically, even if he passes – "

"*If?* You don't think he'll pass the test?"

Patrick lifted his hand, refusing to add another card to this shaky house. "Where's the precedent?" he said to Marcello. "There must be rules of admissibility."

"But this is where you come in. If we did any test, even this lie detection protocol, you'd be invaluable. You're an expert on the technology. You've done consulting work for some of the biggest corporations in the world. Your opinion would be valued by the court. You wouldn't have to weigh in on the results, just the validity of the science."

Patrick had enough experience in academic departments and the business world to know when he was being asked to use science as a weapon. He knew he should take it as a compliment. Patrick worked in an area of science that had recently promised answers to the most basic questions of human behaviour and yet was a daunting mystery to most. The world of knowledge was being prefixed with his specialty: neuromarketing, neurophilosophy, neuroethics.

Any new religion needed its priests. He understood. To Marcello it must have been obvious: Patrick had sold himself before, for Globomart or whatever company could pay the bills; this was another proposal. For a moment Patrick felt the desire to reach over the desk and choke the lawyer, see his handsome face purple a little.

"I don't do forensic work."

"You have expertise. You're interested in these types of questions; I've read your work."

"That was before. And what I was interested in, well, it wasn't meant to be applied in this way. And besides, I *know* the man. They wouldn't allow me to give expert testimony in his defence."

"Again, listen to me: not to testify. Write a brief. A technical opinion."

"Is this what Hernan wants?"

"He's not talking."

"But you ran this by him. He knows that we're talking about this."

"Yes. Yes. Of course," Marcello said, and nodded, a well-oiled movement. A precision even Patrick could appreciate.

For someone not permanently employed at the tribunal and in possession of one of those laminated all-access passes, getting from the office level of the building to the tribunal level was somewhat more complicated than emigrating to Afghanistan. Patrick's attempt caused so much alarm and grimacing among the security personnel that in the end it would have been easier for him to leave the building and re-enter through the same entrance, as though he were rebooting a clunky computer. In the end, he gave up. The day's proceedings were due to begin at 1:30, and with his high-noon meeting with Anders Lindbergh still a couple of hours away, he had time to kill. Den Haag was beginning to make him think of time in that way.

The mid-morning curtains of cloud and fog had been drawn back, revealing the otherworldly buzz of Dutch sunshine. He shook out a couple of tablets from a bottle of Tylenol he had stashed in his coat pocket and started off to the southwest down Johan de Wittlaan. He had to concentrate to remember that it was Friday, counting the number of sleeps he'd had, backwards to the last normal day, early in the week, five time zones ago in Boston. What followed was predictable, a conditioned response: guilt. A pang over turning off the phone and provoking anxiety attacks in his partners, reacting like frightened children, none of them trusting that Sanjay would send the data if he couldn't solve the problem himself. They had imprinted on him as surely as if he'd been Lorenz trotting about in his yellow wellies, and now that he was gone he imagined them scuttling around the office in noisy disarray. He also thought about money. Although he didn't admit it, he thought a lot about money. And now that the Globomart project seemed to be skidding into disaster, he felt a fleeting panic at the thought of having nothing again. As if to acknowledge the terror of this thought, and his embarrassment at having it, he turned his mind to other matters. There was, for instance, the larger issue of Hernan.

He hadn't left Marcello's office on particularly good terms with the lawyer, unable to hide his anger at feeling duped in order to get him to the trial. *Come to Den Haag! Let's talk about culpability!* Marcello even seemed offended that Patrick would leave without shaking his hand. On the way to the elevators,

Patrick had tried to remember the expression that would describe the way in which he'd been manipulated. He was terrible at these things, always confused by the plot of movies about cons and scams, never able to guess who had the upper hand. He'd got out of the tribunal building and put the meeting behind him when the phrase "bait and switch" came to mind.

Even if he did everything Marcello asked, endorsed the idea that the technology could be used as a lie detector, there wasn't a chance of it holding up in court. The prosecution would call their own people, with no reason to exaggerate any technological claims. Patrick could imagine someone like his former lab supervisor Ed Phipps springing to the stand, refuting every claim Marcello wanted Patrick to make, running all his photocopied articles through the shredder. Patrick would lose all credibility, and not just in the tribunal.

Then, as if to stake her claim, came thoughts of Heather, who, if she was thinking of him at all, was likely re-assigning him to that category of mistakes to be put behind her. Patrick hadn't called her, and she would say that this is pure *him*, making a decision through sustained avoidance. Then he thought about his mother, for no particular reason except that it seemed to be the logical way to complete his trifecta of guilt.

He walked as fast as he could without provoking the right side of his face. After twenty minutes, he felt the threshold precisely, tightrope-walking at a pace where he could barely feel the little accessory heartbeat under his right eye. The boulevards that led away from Johan de Wittlaan had a freshly evacuated emptiness to them and he was happy for it, glad there weren't many on the sidewalks, only a few whose understandable stares he had to duck.

Patrick stopped at a corner where the street sign read "Carnegieplein." Across the street a perfect green hedge-wall guarded a building with an elegant tower. Then, for the first time since he'd been in Den Haag, he walked with purpose toward some feature of the city rather than just passing the surroundings. Patrick discovered a breach in the great wall of shrubbery and the hedge entrance opened up to a formal garden, kept in the manner one would expect in a city filled with institutional money. It was a short walk to the building; he had never been good with styles of architecture and this one eluded him too, except to say that it was beautiful and if a building had a soul, then this one's was much less troubled than the tribunal building or the Congress Centrum. He realized that his impression could be wrong, and for all he knew he could be walking toward the front door of the North Korean Embassy, in which case the sight of a rifle was likely trained on his forehead, but he decided he wanted to see the damn building and, armed with a tourist's sly immunity, he marched up to the front door. A wall plaque announced that Patrick had arrived at the front entrance of the Vredespaleis, or Peace Palace. The building was open and he was feeling emboldened by not already being stopped by any security personnel. Sequestered on Bermuda for a weekend conference, he had once wandered around the parliament buildings in Hamilton for an hour before coming face to face with a man who eventually introduced himself as the prime minister. Patrick had explained who he was and lied that he was lost. Nice guy, the prime minister. Looked a bit tired. And although he grimaced when others give him travel tips, he highly recommended just meandering through interesting places until told to go away. Of course, this mode of sightseeing would get you killed in certain parts of the world, and so it had to be applied with some discretion.

The foyer was impressive, not too heavily marbled, although each footstep echoed. He kept walking, a good clip, like he knew where he was going but still prepared to deploy a tourist's arsenal of excuses should he be questioned. Patrick saw a sign for the International Court of Justice and thought this could be Bermuda all over again, that he would open a door and find himself in chambers with the justices as they worried over the details of a fishing dispute.

But then a tiny blond woman stepped out from nowhere. She just stood there, dressed in a Peace Palace blazer, which made her look small and young, precociously competent, an adolescent superhero. Patrick smiled his pained smile that was supposed to declare "I know where I'm going, kiddo," and he started walking about as fast as a person can without breaking into a run.

She lifted her hand and, seeing the beginning of the act, Patrick flinched, foreseeing a Taser or a canister from which she'd empty a blast of pepper spray into his face. But the hand was empty, and the woman smiled. Not really a smile but a sexless grimace favoured by those trained to deal with large crowds.

"Are you here for the ten o'clock tour?" she asked.

"Yes, I am. I was told to meet here."

Her name was Birgita and on a November Friday morning at ten o'clock, Patrick lied his way into being her only charge. And while he was disappointed to have his wanderings curtailed, this was tempered by the pleasant thought of being the only one on a tour, avoiding that sense of the herd that defined the typical tour dynamic. They talked for a while before setting off – Patrick told her he was Canadian (although, for a tour of the Mecca of internationalism, simply not being American was probably more valuable than being Canadian), and, as he was the only person present, Patrick gave her the option of calling the whole thing off, which she refused in a way that told him the gesture already endeared him to her. She pointed to the side of her face and asked him what happened. Patrick told her he had been assaulted and solemnly gave her enough vague details that she was able to construct a plausible history of an altercation with some Dutch skinhead. Birgita dropped the Peace Palace-approved repertoire of underwhelmed postures, settling into what he felt was a more natural friendliness as she told him the provenance of the place.

The building was constructed on land donated by Czar Nicholas and the plan was to have every nation send representative building materials or furnishings, which resulted in, according to Birgita's diplomatic assessment, an unfortunate pastiche. To Patrick, the place looked like a *fin-de-siècle* Pier 1 showroom. Now, she assured Patrick, most of the tchotchkes were safely catalogued and kept in a locked vault with all the other physical evidence of crimes against humanity, but the place was still garish enough to evoke a certain *schadenfreude dekorativ*. Birgita laughed, and so did he. His face hurt. So what. The main hall was impressive though, and as the Gilded Age grandeur vaulted and arched above them, Birgita told him that the Peace Palace was finished just as the world arranged to meet for four years of limb-shearing annihilation in the mud fields of Europe. Apparently the point of the place was lost on most.

By mutual consent, they skipped the tour of the museum and the Peace Palace's new wing. Instead they had a coffee.

Patrick realized that at this point things could become awkward – they were strangers after all. But they had already spent time together in that no-risk way that most people find intoxicating. Secondly, caffeine is a wondrous drug and whole economies don't run on it just for the taste. Urged on, they talked. Birgita told him she was doing her degree in public policy. She liked working in Den Haag, she said, the park around the palace was beautiful and the job looked good on her resumé. She smiled and Patrick couldn't help but notice how his first impression of her had been altered. At first she had seemed so small and young and animated by the blazer's sanctioning threat, but now, as she told him a few details of her life – about the books she read and how she liked to go to the beaches in nearby Kijkduin or Scheveningen, even if they were, in her words, kitschy-touristic – she seemed taller and looked, more appropriately, like a woman in her mid-twenties. A person appeared. And yet, for all the authenticity these details brought to her, Patrick was aware that this reappraisal was not just objective. Example: her close-cropped blond hair, which before seemed sexless and juvenile, was now stylish. She became human to the degree he allowed her to be. It was a repulsive thought, as much as it excited him. He looked at the pendant around her neck, how it nestled in the hollow right above the sternum and between the thin, twin straps of her sternocleidomastoid muscles. He thought she could be lonely but that maybe he was just projecting his own loneliness onto her, the first stranger with whom he'd spoken at any length in the last week, with whom he'd made any real connection. He didn't know if she was happy, but hoped she was. This was probably a projection, too.

One thing was certain, he couldn't imagine talking to someone like this in the States. Mutual fear and imagined pathologies would have kept them firmly on the tour, on time. Away from the dangers of coffee and talk.

She asked Patrick what he did for a living and he told her he was a doctor and a researcher and then she asked why he was in Den Haag and he told her about Hernan, not feeling the need to lie or embellish. She didn't appear to make any new appraisal of him after hearing any of what he said. Instead, she drank her coffee. He watched the grounds settle in the bottom of his own cup and felt guilty for saying he'd been mugged by one of her countrymen.

They said goodbye and Patrick gave her his card from Neuronaut. He asked for directions to the Metropole, even though he was already fairly certain how to get back. But he felt no embarrassment – after all, he was a tourist in this city.

"Do you know Johan de Wittlaan Boulevard?" she asked, pointing.

"Yes," he said, "I think I know that one."

TEN

–

This was his memory of it –

One Saturday morning Patrick arrived at work to find Hernan loading up his Ford Taurus with supplies from Le Dépanneur Mondial. Marta García looked on in silence as her husband stuffed dry goods into the trunk. Patrick stood there, next to her, watching him bring over box after box to the curb. He remembered her face, muscles tightened into a hard-held mask of spousal tolerance.

"You can manage?" Hernan said to Marta. He was leaning into the trunk of the car, pulling intently at something.

"I can manage, Roberto will be here. And Madame Lefebvre," she replied. Hernan looked at Patrick, and said, "You're coming."

Even though he didn't understand what was going on, Patrick gave himself credit for intuiting the curbside dynamics that were at play on that late-August morning in 1986 – he looked over at Marta García for her permission. She thrust her head toward the car.

"Go. Roberto doesn't want to."

Patrick got in the car. It was perhaps a measure of just how bored he was with his life – or how much he trusted Hernan – that he would get in the car like that without asking where they were going. But he bounded into the back seat like a golden retriever. Then, to Patrick's surprise and undying gratitude, Celia came out of the store carrying a cooler and sat in the front seat beside her father. It was four days since she had smiled at Patrick at dinner and the memory had been mentally replayed to the point where he wondered if it had been his invention in the first place.

As they drove toward the Mercier Bridge, Hernan addressed Patrick, intermittently meeting his eyes in the rear-view mirror.

"You're not curious where we're going?" Hernan asked, and Patrick shrugged, meaning it in the best possible way. "Have you ever met anyone from Mexico?" he continued.

"Sure, I mean *you* guys are Mexicans, aren't you?"

Hernan and Celia looked at each other. Hernan shook his head and Celia laughed.

"But, besides *us*, Patrick, have you met any?"

"No."

"Then today is a big day for you."

They drove through fields quilted in crops, navigating progressively smaller roads, until they approached the American border. Hernan turned off on a side road and followed it until it led them to a field within sight of the Adirondacks. They pulled into a parking lot beside a very large building with a curved roof that looked like corrugated tin cut lengthwise and turned on its side, something Hernan told him later was a Quonset hut. In front of the hut sat a large rock painted with the words "Viva Mexico," and a flagpole from which a Mexican flag hung limply. Two broken-down-looking school buses were parked beside the hut.

"What's this?" Patrick asked, leaning forward, trying to get a better look and using the opportunity to smell Celia's hair.

"It's work," Hernan said, bringing the car to a stop beside one of the buses. "Let's go."

Patrick helped unload groceries from the trunk of the car and brought them into the hut, his eyes aching and blinded as they adjusted from the brightness outside. He could barely make out Hernan in front of him and had to concentrate on his ghostly, shifting image as he was led to a makeshift kitchen. It was brighter there, and for the first time Patrick could see that he had been led through a dormitory of more than a hundred empty cots arranged in rows. Several cots at the far end of the building were occupied by sleeping men. They were met by an older man who had obviously been waiting for Hernan. He had a weathered face and a small, compact body. The man did not appear pleased. He and Hernan shook hands and spoke for a short time in Spanish. After that the man helped Celia and Patrick load the perishables into the refrigerator. More than just being allowed to tag along, Patrick was pleased to help. Charitable acts were, at that time, still a novelty to him – and to do all of this with Celia, to have the chance to bond with her in such a wholesome, magnanimous, asexual way, was producing a kind of mid-morning euphoria in him, but all of this was held in check by his impression of the dour stranger. By this time Patrick liked to think he was familiar with the expats who gathered around the coffee counter at Le Dépanneur Mondial. He was accustomed to the rhythms of their speech, even in Spanish; he was certain he could fish out the emotion in the voices of people enjoying each other's company or tell when a conversation became contentious. So when Hernan and this man spoke, even Patrick sensed there was something less than unconditional gratitude being expressed. This unease was compounded by what Patrick swore were flickers of resentfulness beneath the man's mask of stoic resolve. He didn't know what to make of it. Years later, he would learn that humans are wired for faces: a nice little portion of the parietal lobes were committed to parsing facial expressions, decoding the slightest nascent snarl or elevation of a brow. Then, it was only ominous to Patrick. He reasoned it was a territorial thing, a man who didn't want an outsider like Hernan bringing in provisions. Maybe this was how a man having to accept a gift of food looked.

While the two men continued to talk, Patrick helped Celia put the rest of the groceries away in the kitchen. She worked without enthusiasm and sulked whenever Hernan asked anything else of her. When Patrick told her she looked bored, she denied it, admitting only to being upset at having to come out to this place. She had never liked it and this was her third visit with Hernan in the last six weeks. Her mother couldn't go because of the store. Roberto always refused and Nina was too young. At that moment, Patrick heard Hernan's voice again, raised, clashing with the voice of the other man.

"Who is this guy?" Patrick asked.

His name was Aguirre, Celia explained. He was from Guatemala. And although he supervised the fieldwork, Hernan had told her he was much more than a foreman. He was in charge of arranging everything: the hiring in Mexico, obtaining the temporary work visas, the lodging and food.

Until that moment, Patrick had been unaware of the foreigners crouching in farmers' fields at certain times of the summer for different harvests. But Celia had been out with Hernan before, and she knew who did what: Sikhs for lettuce, Haitians for green beans, the Mexicans arriving in August to harvest sweet corn. The school buses would drop the workers off at the fields before dawn and bring them back to the dormitory at nightfall. In a couple of weeks they would decamp and move on to another harvest, other fields.

"What's your dad got to do with it?"

"He says he's helping them," Celia said quietly, but loudly enough that Patrick could detect some shame in her voice.

From the kitchen, they listened as the argument between Hernan and Aguirre continued. Celia whispered to Patrick that the delivery man who brought plantains to Le Dépanneur Mondial had told her father that there had been a dispute over whether the cost of food was included in the contract that Aguirre had negotiated, and while this was being settled, the workers were caught between jurisdictions, and, without anyone to represent them, they were going hungry. The church was organizing a food drive, Celia said, but Hernan said it was crazy to rely on the church, a case of canned chickpeas or cling peaches that would arrive in September. Hernan said they needed something fresh, now. Celia was worried because this was an unannounced visit to bring provisions – and clearly Aguirre wasn't pleased. Hernan suddenly came into the kitchen to find the two of them finished their work and listening to his conversation. He told Celia to take Patrick out back while he finished speaking with Señor Aguirre, and as they left, Patrick heard Hernan close and lock the dock behind them.

The morning, which had been uncomfortably hot, now seemed a faint, fresh memory. Heat lines swayed like a distant crop over the asphalt of the parking lot. It had been a dry summer, a fact a person could forget in the city. Here, the world was divided into places with water and places without. The grass around the compound grew in sparse yellow tufts and the ground was hard packed and lined by thin fissures. Fields of green corduroy stretched out into a vast, distant country, unimaginably fertile, veined by irrigation pipes, worked by another nation. At the edge of the parking lot, faced by a wall of cornstalks, Celia took off her shoes, putting her bare feet into the lush grass that rimmed the cornfield. Patrick tried not to look at them.

"It's nice out here," he said, turning to find her staring intently at a leaf that she held in her hand, pulling it apart along the parallel yellow-ridged veins, slowly, as if she was unzipping the plant. Then she gave a surprisingly forceful tug that shook the stalk and shuddered loose an ear of corn.

"It's okay," Celia García replied, starting on another leaf.

He wished he could remember that their conversation was deep and witty and soulful, that he told her everything about himself, how he thought she was beautiful and that he loved her, but none of that happened. He pretended to be as bored as she obviously was. They just stood there and talked about nothing and slowly destroyed a cornstalk or two.

Hernan had told them to be back at the dormitory by noon, the time when the buses that picked up the field crews were due to return. Patrick and Celia went back to the dormitory to find sixty or so men milling around the entrance to the building waiting for the front door to be unlocked. A couple of the men stepped out of the crowd to look more closely through one of the dormitory's front windows. Another knocked on the door, to no reply. Finally, Aguirre unlocked the door and came out with a folding chair held flat under his arm. He put the chair down, opened it, and took a step up onto the seat. Patrick and Celia stood among the workers, watching Aguirre, his head barely above the crowd, balancing on the chair. He addressed the crowd, speaking slowly, solemnly, and even in Spanish Patrick could understand that this was an oration of sorts, he was making an appeal to the crowd. Patrick asked Celia what Aguirre was saying.

"Trying to save his ass."

At one point, the crowd emitted a collective groan, and as the workers turned to each other even Patrick could pick up on a sense of grievance only partially redressed. Aguirre lifted his hand to silence the crowd and the gesture succeeded. He was working hard and it was paying off, he was beginning to earn scattered clusters of applause. Apparently heartened by this, Aguirre's voice rose in pitch and he became more animated as he finished his speech. Then he got off the chair to lead everyone in for lunch and everybody clapped.

The men sat down to eat in the dining hall of the dormitory building, an area partitioned from the sleeping quarters. They started eating with what seemed to Patrick was less a sense of pleasure than relief. For ten minutes the building was voiceless. Patrick sat on a bench with Hernan and Celia, and from their end of the table he watched the rows of men eating, shoulder to shoulder, heads bobbing as food was scooped up. Hernan could see Patrick observing the men, and leaned over to him to explain that the workers were chosen exclusively from the area around Mexico City – all married men with families who wired home their wages and caused no trouble.

In a low voice, Hernan listed the indignities suffered by the workers: a wage that would insult a teenager, harsh bosses and ceaseless haggling about the details of the contract, plus not the rumour of a benefit even though they paid into un-employment insurance and pension plans and, still, if you asked them, Hernan said, they would reply to a man that this was good work and they felt lucky to be here. He offered no explanation about Aguirre, and Patrick was confused whether the man worked for the growers or the workers or himself. He thought about Hernan and Aguirre behind the locked door of the dormitory and wondered if the reason for the locked door had been some sort of confrontation between Aguirre and Hernan. Whatever the case, Hernan was not about to share the details with his daughter or his employee.

The workers finished eating and filed back onto the buses, which disappeared in their own dust storm. After the clatter of lunch, the main room was quiet again, empty except for a few men who remained, lying on cots in the dormitory building. Hernan looked over at them and then turned to Patrick. "Come," he said.

With a nod to Aguirre, Hernan led Patrick to a room in the back of the dormitory. Aside from the kitchen and some showers and washrooms at the back of the building, this seemed to be the only truly private space. Hernan placed on the table the small black bag he'd been carrying. The leather was worn and the bag's hinged opening was permanently splayed, wide enough for Patrick to see it held a tangle of medical instruments. Celia hesitated by the doorway, watching her father.

A migrant worker, a young man in work clothes with his arm in a sling, appeared and Hernan waved him in. Celia gave a snort of disgust and left without explanation. Hernan untied the knot of the rudimentary sling – made up of plaid material that looked like it came from the remnants of another work shirt – and spoke to the young man in Spanish, then summarized for Patrick.

"He dislocated it a week ago, but it seems to be doing fine," Hernan said as he moved the man's arm through its range of motion, pausing when his patient winced. Although Hernan hadn't reacted to Celia's departure, he must have sensed Patrick's confusion: "They don't have access to medical care. Usually, it's included in the contract but this year there's been a problem. I help out from time to time."

"And the food too?"

"The food is usually more dependable." Hernan frowned. "But they need the work, and so they have to take the risk." Hernan put the man's arm back in the sling, offered a professional parting smile, and sent him off with a pat on his good shoulder. "They're lucky they have the dormitory."

Patrick stayed for the next five patients, among them a sprained ankle, a bad back, and a chronic cough for which Hernan wore a mask and made Patrick wear one too. And while Hernan was describing what he was looking for as he examined each man, Patrick found it difficult to keep his eyes on the patients. He was really watching Hernan. Patrick studied him as he performed his tasks with care and confidence. Patrick saw how the patients responded to him, how even when he had done nothing more than listen to their chests or look in their throats, they felt better. His presence had meant something, it had been enough. In the back room of that dormitory, Patrick began to appreciate that this wasn't just a job for Hernan. This *was* Hernan. He knew why Hernan missed medicine so much, how the work and the man were not two separate things but fed off each other, and as Hernan ushered the last patient out of the room, Patrick understood why Hernan had come out in the middle of a field to tend to these people, and why he'd chosen to bring Patrick along.

An hour passed before thoughts of Celia returned, and Patrick excused himself to go outside to look for her, finding her at one of the picnic tables behind the dormitory. She had brought along some watercolour paints and a tablet of paper and to Patrick looked to be engrossed in painting the corn-field in front of her, but as he approached she started speaking without looking up to see who it was.

"He's not a doctor any more, you know. It's wrong, what he's doing."

"He said they don't have anyone else."

"So that allows him to break the law?"

Patrick was dumbfounded. Legal or not, Hernan's work was necessary, vital. Would she prefer a father who operated a crane at the port all day? That was legal. Would she prefer he sit and do nothing when there were people who needed him? How could she not see what type of man her father was? Patrick felt a burst of anger at how easily she passed judgment as she dabbed at her watercolour paints and turned her back on the dormitory. "There's more to your father than just that grocery store," Patrick said fiercely, and turned to go back in. Try to help maybe.

Inside, Hernan was examining the last patient. Instead of having the man come to the back room, Hernan leaned over the cot where he lay. He helped the man sit up and just this act seemed to provoke a breathless grimace. Patrick hadn't had much experience with sick people, but this man's pale, moon-like face made an impression. He had only ever seen lips that colour on someone who had been enjoying a grape Popsicle. Hernan asked the man to breathe and in response he took a few shallow, unpromising breaths. Hernan then laid him down and studied the side of his neck, where a vein appeared and grew in prominence until it looked like a worm nibbling at the man's ear. Hernan placed the pad of his index finger firmly against one of the man's swollen feet and lifted it to reveal an indentation. He then knelt down beside the man and showed him the stethoscope. The man nodded and mustered a smile through his panting breaths. Both of them glanced at Patrick, who had advanced enough to announce his interest in watching.

Under the man's T-shirt Hernan held the head of the stethoscope and was inching his way toward the man's throat, listening intently, softly naming or describing something with each stop, as though he were a train conductor and this was his line. "Mitral valve," he said, and closed his eyes. "Aortic valve." In this way Hernan catalogued the parts of another person's heart, listening to it thumping away in the dark. "S3," he said, and gave a soft "tsk." The sick man stared up at the ceiling and Patrick wondered if he was thinking of his family.

And when Patrick looked back at Hernan for a clue to what was happening, he was certain he saw a man caught in reverie, soothed as though he were listening to music or the singing voice of one of his daughters.

Hernan thanked the sick man, packed up his gear in his little black bag, and stood up. Patrick followed him out of the dormitory and into the soul-crushing early afternoon heat. Celia had disappeared.

"What's wrong with him?" Patrick asked, hurrying to keep up with Hernan's long strides.

"Heart failure."

"Did he have a heart attack?"

"Maybe, once. More likely an infection. Chagas disease."

"But he's going to be all right, right?"

"He's going to die."

"He's going to die," Patrick repeated. He had never heard these words said in real life. He imagined the news of someone dying would be accompanied by shouting and sirens and an effort whose urgency would justify the declaration. But Hernan just kept walking, his pace unwavering. More than any frantic response, Hernan's behaviour heightened the panic swelling in Patrick. The heat pressed down on him and he felt weak. Hernan was searching for something in the car, the trunk open like a disbelieving mouth.

"Are they going to call an ambulance?"

"He'll die on the way if he doesn't die before they get here."

"But we should call one anyway."

"He doesn't have insurance, and even if he did I don't know if he'd want to go to hospital here. He's dying. He has a bad heart and it's been that way for years probably." Hernan shook his head. "They don't have to pass a physical. If they did, he wouldn't have been allowed to come north." Patrick remembered the competing desires of wanting to run, somewhere, and wanting to go to the toilet. "I'll help him," Hernan said, noticing Patrick's alarm. "Don't worry, I'll help him. Stay here."

With that, Hernan walked away from Patrick there in the parking lot, opened the door to the Quonset hut, and disappeared inside. Patrick hovered outside for another quarter-hour, hyperventilating in the heat. Waiting.

Years later, it was still unclear to Patrick why he'd returned to the dormitory, if it was curiosity or the need to prove to himself that he wasn't afraid, but he went in through the back, so that Hernan would not see him. He crept through the kitchen, and from there he saw Hernan sitting on a stool pulled up to the sick man's cot. Hernan was bent over slightly, supporting the man's head. There was a movement of hands: Hernan's reaching for something, the patient's fluttering from his head to his chest in a way that Patrick recognized was the sign of the cross. Hernan appeared to be saying something to the sick man, but Patrick couldn't hear any of it. He witnessed the agony dissolve from the man's face. When Hernan let his head rest on the small vinyl pillow, Patrick understood that he was dead.

By the time Hernan had gathered his things and left through the front door, Patrick was already outside with Celia. Hernan said nothing except to call for them to get into the car. They were going home.

They stopped at a *bar laitier* just outside St. Remi where Hernan offered to buy ice cream. There was no space on the terrace so they sat inside the little canteen and ate their ice creams in silence. Celia got up to use the washroom, and in an effort not to speak to Hernan, Patrick peered around the room: a little theme park of wood panelling and Arborite furniture. In the corner, a large sunburned man enthusiastically humped and slapped a misbehaving pinball machine.

Celia came back from the washroom and the sunburned guy gave up on the pinball machine. By dinner they were back in

Montreal. Patrick felt stunned by the day's sun exposure and everything else he had seen and stumbled home without a word to Celia or Hernan.

This was memory. But what *was* memory? Over a hundred years ago Ebbinghaus showed that details degrade within seconds. Studies showed that eyewitness testimony – including that of a sixteen-year-old boy (or even that of the Hondurans who were listened to with reverent awe at the tribunal) – was disturbingly unreliable.

He knew too well that the larger items, moments with emotional heft or novelty, were retained, burned into more permanent memories that then served as points around which a more dubious narrative was constructed. That was the moment when memory began to fail, where bias, suggestibility, and misattribution clouded the truth.

An example: he remembered Hernan listening to the sick man's heart, looking up and saying "S3," a term used to describe a heart sound present in patients with heart failure. Looking back, Patrick was fairly certain there was no way he could have remembered Hernan saying that. People just don't recall arbitrary terms that they have never heard of. Patrick would have had no idea what an S3 was until medical school – five years after that moment in the dormitory. More plausibly, he reasoned, the memory had been recreated and rehearsed with the knowledge he acquired later to make sense of the situation, creating something compelling: a man lay dying, Hernan attended to his failing heart, diagnosed him properly, and served him humanely. Yes, Patrick had decided, watching all of this, he would be a doctor too.

Patrick was certain he remembered some other things that were real. The big guy and the pinball machine. The heat and the odd claustrophobia of being outside but surrounded by fields. He remembered Celia.

All the other details had been arranged and recounted in his mind so many times that they seemed part of a story he'd always known, its truth implied. But in the last seven years, from the moment Patrick met Elyse, he'd been forced to revise that history, focusing on one moment, a moment that he now worried Anders Lindbergh suspected and needed to know more about. What had Hernan carried from the trunk of the car to the bedside of the dying man? Patrick remembered something being cupped in Hernan's hand as he walked by. For the longest time, this object was unimportant. Patrick assumed it could have been any of a hundred objects a doctor could be expected to carry during a day of work. A bundled tourniquet. Some gauze. A bottle of Tylenol or aspirin, anything. But Patrick hadn't seen the object clearly, not seen enough that he could say for certain what it was. Or wasn't. And so the memory was revised and the object altered. Had it been a vial of potassium chloride, a single shot to stun and stop the heart? Could he have seen an ampoule of morphine in Hernan's hand? Or was it something else, similarly effective? He once wished he had the answer, but now he knew better than that.

The scene that followed made perfect sense. Hernan, seeing a man gasping for breath, a man for whom he could do nothing, chose to relieve his suffering. The morphine, if it was morphine, depressed the respiratory centres in the brain stem that controlled breathing, easing the air hunger. It was used in the care of the dying, and in the medical profession's nervousness about euthanasia, the dose was carefully calculated to ease pain without obviously hastening death.

But in the dormitory in the middle of a field, with his patient panting through dusky lips, what calculations had Hernan made? Had he made the decision, not to let the thought of death limit the relief he would provide? Minutes after Hernan went to the bedside, the man had died. Patrick remembered Hernan holding the man's head, the way he had since seen a father hold his son's head, whispering encouragement during a swimming lesson as the child floated on his back, kicking at the water. What did Hernan say? Did Hernan tell him he was about to die?

Anders Lindbergh lacked the air of solemn vindication Patrick imagined for a chief counsel for the prosecution who was winning his case. Lindbergh looked tired. Or bored. Maybe the drama of the case, if there was ever any, was done. Without drama, Patrick imagined the job became one that involved a series of formalities. Get the witnesses to Den Haag, record the data, and have the justices pronounce. Any interesting job could be reduced to a series of bureaucratic functions, and Lindbergh appeared to be a man content with being a well-referenced concierge of justice.

This was a bias, and it was likely wrong, but it was based in part on the fact that in the two minutes Patrick had known him, Lindbergh succeeded in giving off an aura of a man perpetually trying to stifle a yawn. His lips were drawn, barely meeting to keep his teeth hidden. At first Patrick had to consider whether Lindbergh was grimacing, if the chief counsel was in terrible pain.

Lindbergh's office was larger than Marcello's, or so it seemed, although Lindbergh moved with an economy that could create a false impression. Patrick searched the office for something of scale, a bookcase or a window, and these elements seemed similar to those in Marcello's office. He was becoming too familiar with these offices.

Patrick knew Elyse had probably interviewed Lindbergh in the course of researching her latest article. The climax, really, of her story. And although he didn't seem like the sort of person who could carry the story, maybe Elyse had found something fascinating about Lindbergh, a childhood trauma or personal tragedy, a thin wedge of personality she'd use to split open the story. More likely, she had gathered a hundred factoids about the man, which she would scatter throughout the feature to flesh out the barrister as she went along.

"Firstly, welcome to Den Haag, Dr. Lazerenko," Lindbergh said, his hands folded on a tidy desk. "Mr. McKenzie, my associate, should be here any moment. He has asked to sit in on the meeting. I hope you don't mind." Patrick was shaking his head just as the door opened behind him. Lindbergh stood and Patrick pushed himself out of his chair. "James, this is Dr. Patrick Lazerenko," Lindbergh said and swept a hand toward Patrick. By the time Patrick had got to his feet, McKenzie was already in his face, a snapping-turtle handshake making the violation of personal space complete. McKenzie was tall and athletic-looking, probably the type who enjoyed regularly beating people at games of squash.

"It's a pleasure to meet you, Patrick. Elyse Brenman has told me a lot about you," McKenzie said and sat down in the chair next to Patrick, across the desk from Lindbergh. *Ah-layze.* He spoke with an accent that Patrick guessed came from South Africa or New Zealand. Just the mention of Elyse and McKenzie's wide, almost lurid grin led Patrick to consider that he was the person who'd taken that picture of Elyse on the sailboat. This epiphany discouraged Patrick and started a parade of other mysterious and equally unpalatable mental states, jealousy for whatever sort of relationship this man had with Elyse, embarrassment for being jealous, outrage at himself and amazement for concocting all of this out of nothing, all in the moment it took to shake hands.

"What happened to your face?"

"I was assaulted."

"Here, at the tribunal?" McKenzie asked, flatly enough to make it sound not without precedent.

"No. Outside. I was mugged." McKenzie winced in commiseration.

"I like your work," McKenzie said, and Patrick dreaded having to smirk his way through another tired recounting of the "porno studies" before McKenzie and Lindbergh got down to whatever good lawyer/bad lawyer shtick they had planned. But then he fired an aside at Lindbergh. "Dr. Lazerenko once delivered a paper called 'The Neural Basis of Utilitarianism.' Very interesting. But that was the last of his publications," McKenzie continued, talking to Lindbergh in a way Patrick understood to be staged. "After that, our friend left academia and went to work for the dark side."

"I moved on," Patrick added.

"You sued your department."

"I had to. To be able to pursue my own research."

McKenzie smiled in a way that reminded Patrick of nature programs. Stalking calm. "They were preventing you in some way?"

"Departmental politics can be complicated."

"Is that why you were suspended?"

"That was appealed and overturned."

"I'm aware of that."

"Then why did you ask why I was suspended?"

"I know the details, but the context can be different." There was a pause as McKenzie surveyed him. "Has Mr. di Costini spoken with you?"

"Yes."

"May I ask about what?"

"Don't you have to disclose evidence to each other?"

"If the contents of those discussions aren't going to be used as evidence, no. And Mr. di Costini hasn't declared."

"Well, I guess it doesn't matter."

Lindbergh stepped into the fray. "Please, this is informal. Not a deposition, even. So please, I suggest we all relax. I should give you some background information, some context, as you say. Mr. McKenzie and I have worked on this dossier for more than four years, and in that time I've spoken to many people who've known Mr. García de la Cruz, from his time in Honduras and after. I asked you here because I think it is valuable to hear the entire story. It was my understanding that you were not in contact with the Garcías for years, so you can imagine my surprise when you arrived at the proceedings, unannounced. Here is an opportunity I cannot pass up, I said to myself. I must speak with this young man who knew García."

"I don't know what I can tell you. I knew him after Honduras." Patrick frowned. He could have used a glass of water. "I was a teenager. I worked with him for a couple of years. I dated his daughter."

"And you have a high opinion of him."

"Hernan is a good man."

"Yes. Yes. The verb tense is much appreciated. More specifically though, he made an impact on you."

"I'm sorry, I don't follow you."

"It's not unusual for such a man to be a role model for an impressionable youngster," Lindbergh said, never making eye contact, the weight of his gaze like a finger on Patrick's Adam's apple. "That's my point, Dr. Lazerenko, you didn't become a greengrocer, now, did you? No, you became a physician. And if he mentored you in this way, if he confided in you, admitted certain things, well, those are details the tribunal would naturally be interested in."

"Hernan never spoke about Honduras, if that's what you're asking."

The fingers on Lindbergh's right hand made a flicking movement, cleaning invisible crumbs off his desk. "Let us for a moment put aside the facts of the case. I would like to know your opinion. When you worked with him, did you think of him as a doctor?"

"Not really. I knew he'd been a doctor before, though."

"How did you know that?"

"I heard. I heard things around the store."

Lindbergh lifted his index finger. "Dr. Lazerenko, we know about the people who came to see him. I suspect you thought of him as a doctor because he thought of himself as a doctor. *Doctors are like that*," Lindbergh stage-whispered. "They hold on to that identity. I understand that. That's ego. He had ego enough to think he could practise medicine. He offered medical counsel, he saw patients in the back room of his *store*," Lindbergh said in mock horror. "That isn't the urge to help. That is more than simple ego. That is a doctor revelling in his power, above all things. We thought you would have some insights into that."

Not for the first time, Patrick wondered about Aguirre, if the man was still alive, twenty years after that day in the fields. Maybe he'd seen him already and not recognized him among the other witnesses at the tribunal. It occurred to Patrick that Aguirre could have not only witnessed everything that happened that day, but perhaps even seen Patrick watching events unfold. Belatedly, he thought having a lawyer present would have been a good idea. It was seven in the morning in Boston. He looked at his watch and wondered whether someone from the firm Neuronaut retained was available to help him through the nuances of international subpoenas. Marcello had been less than helpful.

"I don't think I can help you," Patrick said, summoning what he hoped was a look of helpless disappointment. Patrick felt Lindbergh examining him. He wanted Lindbergh to say something. But instead of words, Lindbergh smiled, his face smooth save for a vertical crease forming on the lower part of his forehead, the smallest fault line on a visage of lawyerly equanimity. It disappeared. Patrick stood up: "If you don't have anything more to ask me, I'd like to go."

McKenzie and Lindbergh offered their hands. McKenzie softened his grip, and Lindbergh bared his tiny Scandinavian teeth into what Patrick understood to be a smile. The goodbyes were perfectly pleasant and indefinite.

ELEVEN

Patrick left the building again, well aware that his pass to the administrative floors conflicted with his pass to the public galleries of Courtroom One. The guards were amused, and one of them gave him a half-wave as he ceremonially exited and turned around to once again present his passport.

On one of the benches outside the courtroom, Celia and Roberto sat eating sandwiches half-wrapped in foil. The approach to the foyer in front of Courtroom One was from the side, and they didn't see Patrick as he arrived. Patrick stopped and hung close to the wall and watched them eat for a moment. It was oddly intimate and was beginning to feel a touch voyeuristic when he noticed a third person standing with them, someone he didn't recognize. The man was dressed in a suit, looking immune to the fatigue that branded family and friends of the trial's participants. Was he a crank who had recognized the Garcías, insinuating himself with small talk until he had a chance to become a bigger nuisance? Their conversation appeared to be amicable. It occurred to

Patrick that this was Celia's husband, freshly flown in from wherever to lend support. The inevitable comparison to himself ensued; the man was thankfully shorter. He was better dressed and looked confident in his suit. A man for whom wearing an expensive suit was not a special occasion. He was Celia's husband, though there was nothing intimate about the scene. Seeing them all together made Patrick feel alone. But the man bent to shake Celia's hand and Roberto's after that, a series of gestures that seemed to reset all possibilities and gave Patrick a pulse of undiluted glee. The man was an acquaintance. A well-wisher. Patrick waited until the man walked past and down the stairs to the building's lobby before approaching the Garcías.

Celia reacted first; caught in mid-bite, she raised her eyebrows in acknowledgement. Roberto lifted a hand and kept eating. She turned to her brother and said something that drew a curt response. The only word Patrick heard from her was "Now." Roberto stood abruptly, extended his hand and mumbled "Sorry" through a mouthful of food. Patrick had shaken quite a few hands already today but he didn't mind another. It was worth it just to see the family dynamic in action.

"He apologized already," Patrick said to Celia.

"I heard. A phone message. Very commendable," Celia said, not hiding her sarcasm from Roberto.

"Did you speak with di Costini?"

"Yes."

"And?"

"We talked about different approaches," Patrick said, hoping that would be enough. But Celia wanted more. Watching her made him remember the stress of having to speak to the families of seriously ill patients, how they would parse whatever was said for any hint of hope. Hope was then amplified into certainty, which was the weapon they would beat you with when things went wrong. "I don't think it's going to help. The work I do is all experimental. I don't think the court would accept using it even if we could apply it to the case in some way." Patrick sat down. "It's just that he's not saying anything. I mean, all the technology in the world isn't going to exonerate someone who refuses to defend himself."

"We can't make him talk," Celia said, and at this Roberto snorted in disgust. Celia fixed her brother with a withering glance, a clear warning about breaking rank. Roberto accepted her wordless rebuke without further reaction. More evidence of the apparent re-ordering of authority in the García family, it made Patrick want to change the subject.

"So who was that guy you were talking to?" Patrick asked. Roberto looked away and started eating his sandwich again, apparently happy to cede this duty to Celia.

"Just someone we know."

Roberto kept his eyes averted. Patrick could hear Celia breathing heavily through her nose.

"That was Caesar Oliveira from the Democratic Voice. They're a group who've been helping us."

Patrick turned his head to scan the foyer, trying to affect a tone of neutrality. "Di Costini told me about them. I knew they were here, but I didn't know they were *here*."

"Oh, they're everywhere, Mopito," Roberto said, just loud enough to be heard. Celia acted as if he'd said nothing.

A few of the tribunal's regulars congregated in front of Courtroom One's gallery doors. Though the gallery was never full, they jockeyed to get nearer to the door as the security officer produced his key. The urge built to say something nasty

to them, tell them to get a life, but Patrick thought better of
it. Celia packed up what was left of lunch and noticed Patrick
eyeing the uneaten sandwiches.

"Are you hungry?"

"I haven't eaten today."

"Here," she said, unwrapping one and handing it to him.
Roberto got up, saying he was going to find seats.

The sandwich was made with one of those heavy flat
"brodts" that did nothing to dispel the rumours that baking
with yeast was illegal in some parts of Europe. Trying to chew
the bread was like enduring another beating. Patrick passed
on the second half.

"Where's Nina and Paul? Do they ever come to the trial?"
Patrick asked, flipping megaton crumbs off his lap.

"They're at the park," she said. "There's no way I'd let Paul
see any of this and Nina's too pissed off to sit through it."

He wondered again about Paul's father, where the man was
as Celia ate her sandwich and Paul played somewhere in a
Dutch city park with his aunt. The father would be here if he
was still with her, whoever he was. He'd be here, Patrick
thought. *I'm here.*

Celia stowed the leftovers in a plastic bag. She hadn't
changed in that way, had never been the sort of person to put
up a fuss about where she was eating. A proper meal meant
only that you sat and ate what you liked with people you
liked. A restaurant, a picnic table, a bench somewhere, these
were all simply changes in venue. She had been just as
undiscerning about the food they'd eaten together. None of
it had mattered, which he remembered thinking was unusual
at the time, as in other parts of her life – her art or the
way she organized the physical space of their apartment –

she had definite opinions and was exacting in their pursuit.

They'd eaten hundreds of meals together, surrounded by family or strangers in a cafeteria somewhere. Others, alone. The meals weren't memorable, and other than the fact that he'd shared them with Celia, he could only remember the physical spaces – the Garcías' kitchen, the back porch of his mother's house on Hingston, a balcony over Lorne Crescent. He'd choked once, and remembered the small punch in his throat when a peanut had gone down the wrong way. Celia saved his life with the Heimlich manoeuvre that time, wrapping her arms around him and hoisting with a vigour and effectiveness that impressed him almost as much as the return of oxygen to his lungs. Yes. Of all the food he'd eaten with her, he remembered the peanut. And he didn't even get to swallow it.

She was gathering the rest of her belongings and getting ready to head inside to a seat with Roberto, a place where Patrick figured he'd not be welcomed by either. But standing there, he felt rumbles of emotion like distant geophysical events. It must have been the concussion and its effects: dis-inhibition, emotional incontinence, lack of self-reference. Don't cry for christsake. The sight of her putting away the uneaten sandwiches and stuffing her sweater into a bag made him want to tell her to stay. In this nondescript foyer he felt an infantile need to grab her and sit down again. *We don't need to say anything*, he thought, *just stay here with me*. But she readied herself to move. She was going, and every gesture of departure set off tripwires of memory.

It was Hernan and Marta's twentieth anniversary, and they had decided to take a rare night off, leaving for dinner earlier that evening. Neither Madame Lefebvre nor Jimmy Padopoulos could work that night, so prior to setting off, the Garcías had convened with the children in the store and gone through what amounted to a briefing session about how the evening would go: Roberto was in charge, and a babysitter had been arranged for Nina. After closing the store, Celia and Roberto would go home and relieve the babysitter, Mrs. Robitaille from down the street. After that Roberto was free. Celia crossed her arms and groaned at the implication. The phone number of the restaurant was tacked to the board behind the counter. With that, the Garcías had escaped, smiling madly at the thought of their liberation.

Roberto lasted an hour before he announced he was leaving. He had a new girl and was in his Outremont phase now – methodically working his way through the districts of his new city like a census taker with only one question on his mind – and that night he had a party to go to. Celia threatened to call the restaurant, and even Patrick recognized the futility in the gesture. Roberto smiled and walked out as she held the phone receiver poised by her ear. He wasn't stopping. Still, she put the phone down only when he was out of sight.

Usually Patrick would have gone home at nine, but he stayed that night until Le Dépanneur Mondial closed. He was bored, his parents were only coming back at the end of the week, and he had nowhere in particular to go. The thought of an evening with Celia, even with her mood soured with anger at her brother, was still promising.

Less than a week had passed since they'd spent that afternoon together with Hernan at the migrant workers' dormitory, and in that time, neither of them had spoken of it. It was understandable for Celia, he reasoned – the visits bored her and she had been visibly angry at her father. But it was different for him. He had arrived home stunned from all that he had seen, fully expecting he would have nightmares, the terror of the sick man's moment of death replayed endlessly. But he had awoken the next morning after a night of sound sleep with an unquestionable sense of well-being. Eventually, he understood that he didn't feel this way in spite of what he'd been through, but because of it. That day with Hernan – tending to the workers, watching him argue with Aguirre so that the food they brought would be accepted – had been an immersion in the adult world. His first real test. Hernan had trusted him enough to bring him along, and when Hernan had tended to a dying man, he'd seen that. Patrick had been there and seen a man die. A body completely still, one arm hanging off the edge of the cot. That initial sense of shock at what he'd seen became something else; it was the wisdom of life and death. And Hernan had allowed it to happen. And now, Patrick walked the aisles of Le Dépanneur Mondial a different person, a man really, revelling in the glow of the newly initiated.

He thought it was impossible that Celia wouldn't see the change in him too, and perhaps it was that sense of confidence that gave him the courage to speak to her. They talked about music or movies or the start of school – she was starting at the same school as Patrick that fall. It was meaningless talk, talk as a way of not saying anything. These conversations – conducted in the purest dialect of adolescence: halting, punctuated with his grunts of feigned indifference – were about nothing, and yet he would go home and replay the transcript of all that was said, cringe at every idiot phrase, relish every joke that made her laugh. But that night, after Roberto's mutiny, she was in no mood to talk. She stood behind the cash – where he detected a new Celia vibe, one of delicious glowering – and refused to even acknowledge the boy with the mop in front of her. They had closed up the store and were standing on the sidewalk outside Le Dépanneur Mondial when she spoke to him, seemingly for the first time since Roberto left.

"Walk me home?"

He tried not to nod too avidly, hoping a show of concern for her safety getting home would mask any sign of euphoria. Very likely, it was a beautiful night, moonlight sifting through the canopy of trees, but Patrick was blind as he walked beside her, forcing himself to relax but feeling as nonchalant as a one-man band. At her front door, her only words were "Wait here."

She disappeared into her house and left him there. Wait for what? A tip? A sign from God?

After a short lifetime of fuming and confusion, Patrick saw Mrs. Robitaille come to the door. She waved to Celia and picked her way carefully down the front stairs. Reflexively, Patrick stepped behind a tree until Mrs. Robitaille was past.

Another lifetime, longer, before Celia appeared at the doorway, waving him in.

He smelled sex. He was doused and set on fire by the very act of her *waving*. She could have waved him over a cliff and he would have zombie-walked into thin air. Marshalling all his restraint so as not to bound up the front stairs of Celia García's house, he followed. Inside, the duplex was quiet, lights lowered, empty except for the two of them and Nina who slept in a back bedroom. Celia held her finger to her mouth, as though he needed a reminder. Down a darkened hallway, he heard the whoosh and thud of a clothes washer filling.

They walked through the kitchen, past the table where they sat two weeks before and she had smiled at him. I'll be quiet, he promised, I'll be very quiet. His brief restaurant career finally came to good use and he was instantly aware of how much time they had until her parents returned, able to calculate with NASA-like precision the minute-by-minute timeline of an average couple in their forties out to dinner. Seating, menus, and ordering: twelve to fifteen minutes. Appetizers: fifteen to twenty minutes. Main course: forty-five to sixty minutes. Dessert and coffee: twenty to thirty minutes. Final bill: fifteen minutes. French restaurant: add one half hour. Anniversary: tack on another thirty minutes. They should already be home by now, but if they made arrangements for a sitter maybe they would stay out a bit later.

He was a small-scale seismic event of adrenalin and testosterone. If she had known, she would have run and locked the door behind her, but she kept walking, now past the kitchen and down the other hallway that led to the back of the house. She was in front of him. Total Celia immersion. He saw and smelled her, heard her footsteps. He imagined her bra and panties, the inventory of first sightings. They'd have to be quiet. They reached the end of the back hallway and the door that he assumed led to her bedroom. He wanted touch. He wanted taste. But she opened the door to the back balcony, turned on the outside light, and stepped outside. He couldn't wait. He reached out, touching her shoulder. She turned.

"Yes?" she said, looking at Patrick as though he'd just tapped her on the shoulder to return a glove she had unknowingly dropped. He didn't understand. It was stark disappointment, like someone had turned on the lights to reveal a cinderblock room. She smiled and tilted her head toward something sitting in the corner of the balcony.

"I have to paint out here. Nina has asthma," she said, and lifted a canvas up, surveying it before turning it around for him.

Patrick was speechless, presented with the canvas and the utter obliviousness of its artist. His first impulse was to pitch the canvas into the leafy darkness below the Garcías' back balcony and walk out the door. But he didn't. He held the picture in his hands and tried to keep from shaking. To defuse his anger at the injustice of the moment, he reminded himself how a little sensitivity and self-control demonstrated now could reap rewards in the future. This didn't work – he still felt like a car in a skid – and so he imagined Hernan and Marta arriving and the competent beating from Roberto that he had probably avoided, and these thoughts helped him regain his composure.

Above, shadflies were engaged in mad, barrelling flight around the balcony's light bulb. Yellow light fell like sprinkler mist. It was hard to appreciate the colours of the painting. The first details he made out were the vertical lines and a figure among them. The figure's hands were lifted to chest level, separating and pushing away stalks of corn. The figure was him.

"Can I take this inside?" he asked.

He heard the clack of the frame as she put the picture flat on the kitchen table and switched on the overhead light. The canvas came alive with colour. It was beautiful. The densely green fields, the detail of his hands. But what he examined most closely was how she had painted his face. There, before him, emerging from the cornstalks, wearing his clothes and inhabiting his body, was a face that he didn't want to recognize. He scanned the other details but returned to his face, finding again that it showed a person he didn't want to be. It portrayed him as a child. An expression of petulance. That was how she saw him. He was a child to her, a cranky boy in a field. Redemption came in the thought that he was not this boy she could capture so easily. *This was before*, he told himself, painted before he'd witnessed the man in the dormitory. Now everything was different.

Celia was watching him, waiting for the first words of praise, he thought. Patrick knew he could have reacted in many ways. Years later, he felt ashamed for not being more magnanimous and telling her he was honoured to hold a thing of such beauty, that he was without words, impressed at her skill and creativity. It was true, after all. But he could not say these things. She thought he was a child, she had shown him that, and what followed seemed natural, inevitable. He had shrugged and handed the painting back to her.

"I have to go," he said, and he left.

Patrick followed Celia into the public gallery of the courtroom where they parted, mumbling like a couple of teenagers about him sitting over here and her sitting toward the front with Roberto. The tribunal reconvening, Patrick was now able to recognize the players. Lindbergh and McKenzie sat across from Marcello and Ing Song Park, the only lawyer of the group he hadn't met (so far, but the day was still young). A court official entered and Hernan followed, in steps easy enough to convince Patrick that Hernan's legs were not shackled. He'd somehow expected this, as though the tribunal would be less than credible without leg irons. Hernan wore his plain blue shirt, and Patrick wondered whether that was tribunal issue as well or just a habit of the accused. Hernan stepped into the small glass cage and settled himself in the chair, briefly glancing down, appearing to be thinking or praying, and then dispelling any doubts by lifting the fiddly little earpiece and plugging it into the side of his head. Why did he need to listen, or even be here, if he wasn't going to speak in his own defence? Why did he need translation at all? Patrick supposed Hernan was like anyone, occupying himself. Trying to get through days that presented him with a schedule divided between boredom and vilification.

A man in his forties took the stand, stated his name, and the questioning began. He was a professor at UC Davis. He had been a student at the National Autonomous University when he was arrested two decades before. It was explained to him after the arrest that they were looking for his cousin, who was suspected of being a Communist. When he told the two officers he didn't know where his cousin was or anything he was involved with, one of the officers hit him in the face with enough force to knock him over. He described his vision being blurred, the stinging pain and then the metallic taste in his mouth. The witness remembered pursing his lips to breathe out and seeing a red mist. With his hands secured behind his back, he could not staunch the flow of blood from his broken nose. The front of his shirt turned red.

McKenzie asked him if he'd been alone when he'd been arrested and he said yes. But during his days at Lepaterique, he'd seen glimpses of others as he was moved from one interrogation room to another. McKenzie asked him the names of those he'd recognized but the witness said he couldn't recall. During his confinement he'd seen many faces, but wasn't sure whose were hallucinations.

The witness then reported how the interrogation intensified. New people appeared in the room. He was blindfolded but could hear smatterings of English being spoken. The university professor told the court that the beatings were made worse by the regime used between interrogations. Prisoners were kept awake for days on end, or forced to stand for hours with the rubber mask, the *capucha*, on their heads and made to endure near-asphyxiation. Not sleeping was the worst, the university professor said plainly, as though he were describing a food he once used to dislike.

When he could not give his captors any useful information, they moved on to other means involving a different team. He remembered only the electrodes being placed and, at first, the mildest of the shocks. The rest was pain and fear and movement of people around him. McKenzie asked if this was where the university professor first encountered the doctor, and the university professor said yes. Is this man in the room with us now? McKenzie asked. Yes, he is, the man responded. Indicate for the court. The university professor raised his hand, as if indicating directions to a fellow traveller who had become lost, and said, "Hernan García de la Cruz." He pointed directly at Hernan in the glass dock. It made Patrick want to cry. Pointing was a vector, a directional force, a hurricane heading ashore or a hawk bearing down on its prey. Words, even accusatory ones, were scalar. Words floated in the air. The pointing was unnecessary, but there is an undeniable hunger for it, an act that accomplished what all those words fell short of. The university professor lowered his hand, away from Hernan. After this pistol shot, Patrick imagined a spider-web fracture pattern in the fronting glass panel of Hernan's cage. But it remained smooth, the bottom of a well from which Hernan stared, unflinching.

Instead it was Celia who responded. Throughout all of this, Patrick's attention had been split between Celia and Hernan.

Hernan was a sphinx behind the glass; Celia, a repertoire of gestures as coping mechanisms: a hand brought to the brow was denial; intent scribbling as sublimation; a rare despairing glance in Patrick's direction (another vector, emotive force to be determined). She put her elbows on her knees and held her head in her hands.

McKenzie asked the witness how he knew that the accused was a physician, and the university professor replied that Hernan had tended to him. When asked to elaborate, the university professor said that when he awoke it was Hernan over him, involved in some hurried activity that he presumed to be medically related. Once, he awoke with an intravenous line in his arm and the accused was tending to that. The witness reported that initially he thought Hernan was helping him. But each awakening became a resurfacing into pain, and after a day of torture, after repeatedly awakening from unconsciousness to find Hernan hovering above him, the doctor became inseparable from the pain. He remembered asking Hernan to stop hurting him. He remembered getting no response.

Marcello's questions centred on acts. It was not a crime against humanity to make sure that someone was well-hydrated, he argued. The witness described duress and lapses of consciousness, was this an adequate state of mind to facilitate recall of remote events? How could anyone know what Hernan did to this man except for others in the room at that time? Can we trust those accused torturers, men trained and committed to acts of violence? Hernan was there, true. Presence alone did not necessarily make a doctor into a torturer.

More than most, Patrick was aware that people in his profession had been known to do some very bad things. But then again, if a group had an ethical code dating back twenty-five centuries, it probably meant that it had been necessary for at least that long. In these past seven years, he had become a student of those moments when doctors transgressed in the most abhorrent ways. He tried to keep this interest to himself, sparing his acquaintances, who he doubted, even with their worldliness and anthropological detachment from evil, could have stomached the material. But Heather had discovered the books eventually. Having her find the books stowed away in a cabinet had been the worst possible outcome, making the cache all the more illicit in her mind and multiplying her disgust. She told him what she thought of the books and let him infer her revised opinion of him.

The history of doctors and torture was voluminous and detailed and he had read it all cloaked in twin moods of horror and fascination. Of all the seismic events in the moral imagination, Auschwitz still made the ground shake most profoundly. And there, as at other times, he found it was the doctors who epitomized the descent; the most highly educated and respected group of a technologically advanced, previously civilized society effectively renouncing its oath and devouring itself. It was the doctors who were the experimenters and selectors at the camps, who performed their tasks under the mantles of science and healing. And among the more easily understood monsters described in the death camps, Patrick had been kept awake nights pondering the disturbing story of Ernst B., an Auschwitz physician commended by prisoners for his kindness and humanity in the camps, while at the same time being fully committed to the ideology that led to their creation. Ernst B. had been a gentleman, a man capable of committing heinous acts and inspiring warm sentiment from his victims, fully able to live two lives, of proving to Patrick that something like this could be done, had been done.

And while Auschwitz was the standard for his profession's depravity, it was not the sole appearance. The doctors were there, on hand for Japanese atrocities in China. They were there in Cambodia, sweating like masons behind a wall of stacked skulls. They were there in the Soviet Union, establishing their own little gulag of a psychiatric system, because any difference became more explicable, more acceptable, as a pathology. (Ironically, Marcello wanted him to do something similar for Hernan, except that the diagnosis would come with an extended day pass.) And with each instance, the commonalities became clear: physicians caught up in the swell of a larger impulse, a mass movement or sentiment or state of emergency that made all the old rules seem obsolete. Expertise was divorced from morality, honing itself in predictable, terrible ways. Even more predictable were the ways in which perpetrators dealt with the accusations when they were called to account for their crimes years later; they would explain themselves in one of three ways: they were simply acting on orders, implying that war or civil emergency suspended their ethical responsibilities; others spoke of their experience as though it had been a dream, one they could not yet comprehend. The last group killed themselves. Whether they had come to a fuller understanding was debatable.

It would be reassuring to think of these horrific moments as nothing more than past chapters in the history of medicine, like surgery before anaesthesia or antisepsis. But they became persistent, dogged reminders, footnotes appending themselves and forcing Patrick to look down at the smaller print.

The first pictures Patrick saw of the broadcast of a captured Saddam Hussein – the surprised, tousled look of a bus terminal indigent – were not of him simply sitting there; they were of his medical exam. The tyrant opened his mouth, and instead of defiance streaming out, a tongue depressor poked in. *Say ahh, Satan.* Of course it was more than a medical exam; the edge of the tongue depressor scraped the inside of the mouth, capturing a fine layer of the monster for a definitive identification.

It was startling because it was familiar. It was a quaint act of submission, captured on tape and disseminated worldwide. No one Patrick knew had any response to this exhibition other than glee that the monster had been caught, and while Patrick would deny a finer moral sensitivity (if a tongue depressor shoved into his gob was as bad as Hussein got, he'd be infinitely better off than the luckiest of his victims), he couldn't keep his eyes off the doctor performing the exam. Performing the exam, that was the word. Who was this guy with the tongue depressor? Patrick knew that if he tried to talk to his more liberal acquaintances about this being an abuse of power, that the broadcast of a simple medical exam was a gross breach of ethics, they would smile at him indulgently and think that he should get a life. And it wasn't that far a drive in a pickup truck to find others who would return such talk with a look of wordless revulsion reserved for a blood enemy. No, Patrick kept quiet. He didn't need to be called naive or sanctimonious or just dismissed as an ACLU headcase who should care more about the troops in harm's way than about some clapped-out despot getting a free army physical. But the broadcast of Hussein being examined bothered him because either no one was thinking about it or somebody was thinking about it, very hard, and allowed the exam to be broadcast anyway.

There were rules, of course. The Declaration of Tokyo, which he had never known about until he became aware of Hernan's situation, stated clearly that the physician shall not "countenance, condone or participate in the practice of torture" and then went on to state that the physician "shall not be present during any procedure during which torture or any other form of inhuman or degrading treatment is used or threatened."

In this light, Hernan was guilty. If he wasn't tortured as a way of coercing his participation, then his presence alone, for whatever reason, constituted a violation of the Declaration of Tokyo. All the mitigating circumstances, all the rationalizations were nothing compared to the fact that he was present in the room. And yet violating the Declaration of Tokyo was not enough to convict; for international law to be satisfied, witnesses were needed who would say that he was involved in the act.

After twenty more minutes of questioning and cross-examination, Celia stood and shuffled sideways to the aisle. Roberto glanced at her, then returned to the activities in front of him. Patrick shifted, bracing his feet against the base of the seat in front and sliding up ever so slowly, trying to avoid attracting Roberto's attention. Always evading him. A minute passed of what seemed like a hydraulic process, his thighs aching as he finally got to his feet and slipped out of the gallery.

He expected Celia to be sitting there, crumpled and tearful just past the doors of Courtroom One, but the benches in the foyer were empty. He walked to the stairwell and leaned so far over the railing that one of the security guards adjusted his stance, giving him a bouncer vibe. But she wasn't down there either. The hallways were quiet. She was gone.

He fought the impulse to give the guard the finger, felt the muscles in his hand tighten to stop the digit in question from extending because that was the key step, the launch code for the rest of the gesture. To lack control would be to set off another sequence of events; he would be collared and frog-marched and kicked out of the tribunal. Patrick clenched his fist and waited for the guard to turn the corner. He scanned the foyer for Celia again, but saw no one. He wanted the guard to come back, felt the need to go through the motions of self-restraint again, maybe things would come out differently. As he thought this, he found himself walking, pacing really, making zoo-lion laps of the foyer, feeling his hostility toward the guard become something larger and hotter, the shaping of an indignity. Patrick walked down the stairs to the exit and explained to the entry guards that he needed to get some air. One guard, who was younger than most at the tribunal and had seen Patrick's comings and goings, joked that they were about to install a turnstile for him. But he needed to be outside. He decided he didn't want to be caught waiting for Celia García. Not again. No, he'd keep moving and if she wanted to talk with him, then she'd have to catch up to him or watch him leave. He was outside now, heading toward the large reflecting pool in front of the Congress Centrum and just walking made him feel better, clearing the air of the tribunal gallery from his lungs and giving him respite from the Garcías and their complicated goddamned lives.

Patrick sat on a bench beside the reflecting pool, watching the fountain gurgle and froth. A bus stopped in front of the

Congress Centrum. After a short pneumatic hiss, a door swung open and from it, a line of people debarked, heading straight for the doors of the Congress Centrum, all carrying cloth bags emblazoned with a mysterious symbol. Below the symbol, Patrick could make out the words "The Hague 2005." Patrick wondered what sort of group would choose to have a convention in Den Haag in November, what set of chronically lowered expectations would make this place seem alluring.

The movement of the fountain spume nauseated Patrick. The energy he'd had was spent fuel now, and he felt the need to close his eyes, there, beside the fountain. What was he doing here? What did these people want from him? He'd jeopardized his company and reputation to come here, and for what? A concussion and a subpoena. Hernan was saying nothing, making no effort to defend himself. But that made no difference to Celia. Celia. Faithful, stubborn Celia could not be swayed from trying to free her father, and Patrick had done exactly what she wanted. He was nothing to her except a way to free Hernan. The thought fanned his every vindictive instinct, made him want to catch the next flight back to Boston, or tell Celia that he hadn't called in the past seven years not because he was circumspect or lazy but because he was ashamed of them all, that they had lied to him and done terrible things and refused to face the truth. But he wouldn't say any of it. He knew he would always do what Celia wanted him to do.

When she had shown him that painting all those years ago and he had feigned indifference, Patrick had felt a little pearl of pleasure, the type of which he'd not yet known with Celia. The look on her face – the incomprehension, the need to rethink him as a given – had been an odd new drug, potent, transforming. In her house that night, Patrick had sensed a person's pride and understood how it needed to be fed and how it could be starved. If he had to argue it out, he'd say that it wasn't pettiness as much as restoring the balance of power. She already had more than he, a family that may have argued and disappointed her, but a family that cared. And now, seeing the painting, it was clear that she was in possession of a technical prowess. She had talent and a vision, and in the painting it all came together.

In the years since, Patrick had come to understand that a bigger man would have put aside his disappointment and been pleased to be the first person to see such a painting, to have been in such a work, but he had not been that man. Not that night. He wanted Celia, not to be an object she worked into the scenery. She offered the painting to him, and he declined. She had been shocked by his response, he could tell. But in the end he relented and when she handed the canvas over, he had thanked her coldly and walked off into the night with it. Under the trees on that August night, he remembered smelling the pigments of the paint. It was still wet. He carried it home and put it up on the wall of his bedroom and stared at it until he fell asleep.

They didn't speak after that. He knew that Celia had every right to be upset with him, upset with herself that she had given her painting to a simple lout who couldn't appreciate it. He'd figured that she'd steam for a while and then get over it. It would be awkward for a few weeks, he'd have to duck around corners to avoid coming face to face with her, but it would evaporate into something that they'd laugh about later. But Celia would not talk to him, would not look at him. He was nothing. He was how the mop got manoeuvred around the floor, a noise at the back of Le Dépanneur Mondial. At first it almost made him laugh: okay, okay, the silent treatment. A bit primitive but it beat screaming. But it went on, and intensified, as if she had sealed the doors and opened the valves on the freezers until the windows frosted up and his fingertips turned a shade of deep-winter blue. He would have preferred the screaming.

But then his regular life intervened. His parents returned from their holiday and school started, odd for either to be a source of such relief. He saw Celia less frequently, an occasional evening at Le Dépanneur Mondial or passing in the hallways of school. He was happy to be back in school, and told himself that he didn't care that she was there too, that Celia would be just another new kid in class. He was absorbed back into his circle of friends and wanted nothing more than for the months he spent working at Le Dépanneur Mondial to seem foreign and fleeting, like a summer camp suntan that would fade. He didn't even have the satisfaction of seeing her relegated to that lowest-caste status of new-kid-at-school either. Instead, she had violated every known law of human adolescent interaction and become popular in school. This was genetic, a chromosomal charisma, Patrick was coming to understand, as Roberto García's younger sister continued to exert a part of her personality that he had assumed didn't exist. She was smart and had enough confidence to be cleverly disdainful of the ruling-girl cliques (a double victory in the *realpolitik* of high school: once defeated, this tribe was submissive, all other witnesses to regime change flock to receive the victor as a liberating hero). Celia had triumphed. He was being left behind. It was then that he thought about quitting.

If Patrick remembered anything about that autumn, other than the ascension of Celia García to the top rung of the school's social ladder, it was the panic he had felt. NDG had always been his home, and he had never wanted to live anywhere else, but now he was overwhelmed with the thought he would never leave NDG. Celia brought into full focus his fear that the people he admired and envied would grow and achieve and leave. If he didn't change, he would be stuck. And he couldn't tolerate that happening in front of Celia García.

Even though Patrick loved Le Dépanneur Mondial, he felt he needed to stop working there. He found Hernan in the storeroom one afternoon and stammered through the usual things about school starting and needing to devote himself to his studies, but it was tough to convince even himself. Hernan, no doubt aware of Patrick's recent restlessness around his daughter, rightly seemed to sense the impulsiveness of the decision and the reasons behind it, and offered a compromise. In the end, Patrick was dissuaded from quitting and, instead, wound up working fewer hours on selected days, able to insinuate himself into the schedule without crossing Celia's path.

His new shifts coincided with Marta's time alone in the store. At first they were quiet around each other, each attending to their own tasks and passing their time together in silence. But over that year, a sense of companionship grew. It was through Marta that he learned the nuances of chat and gossip, both foreign dialects to a sixteen-year-old boy.

Sometimes Marta would mention *the family* but never Celia by name, as though understanding the needs of someone trying to break a habit. And he liked to think that he gave something to her in return, that he became her confidante during those shifts. She had a family, like him, but, like him, she was alone. And so it all seemed a part of that kinship when Marta admitted to him that she wished to go back to school when her children were older, or when, shocked that he had never read Melville, she pledged to get him a copy of his complete works. Patrick had been around people whose energy or good humour was infectious, but with Marta, he was surprised to find that another person's curiosity could be just as affecting. Despite being uninterested in politics, to his surprise he spent countless shifts watching the televised Iran-Contra hearings with her on the little black-and-white portable behind the counter, as she gave him a history of the politics in the region and described the roles played by the central characters. And while she never stated her political beliefs to Patrick, it was clear through her frowns and comments that she was upset with the revelations of the trial. She practically hissed when Oliver North took his oath before testifying. More revealing later for Patrick was her desire to conceal from Hernan her interest in the hearings. He became a co-conspirator, warning her when Hernan or a customer came into the store so that the television could be switched to a *novella* or another program more appropriate for the wife of a local merchant.

When he met up with old high school friends years later, they would point to that time with wonder and disbelief. "You changed," they'd say in that way that wasn't always meant to be an accusation. He tried to explain it, always stopping short of crediting the Garcías. But he was never the same because of them. He had an awareness of the world and an idea of what role he could play, courtesy of Hernan; from

Marta he'd received unexpected friendship and the knowledge that he belonged in some way to that tribe of loners, the curious, the bored. This explanation suggested only a positive impulse, the guiding mentor, success as a result of a quest for personal improvement. But Patrick understood how much more complicated the Garcías' effect on him was, that the source of motivation in his life had been far less noble. The real legacy of those early years, measuring himself against the Garcías, suffering through disappointments with Celia, was that he felt unworthy. He understood himself to be inferior. How could you explain that to people? It was an inescapable feeling, and not one for which he blamed the Garcías, but it was something he promised himself would change.

He cloistered himself and began to read. He applied himself, viewing every book, every fact and principle as the next necessary step in the razing of an inferior intellect, a purging of ignorance. The transformation didn't go unnoticed: anyone seriously applying themselves in high school automatically becomes the object of scrutiny. He was suddenly considered different and reclusive and, by virtue of being more difficult to classify in the taxonomy of high school, vaguely threatening. There he was, lumped in with his school's queer pioneers, proto-goths, and Dungeons & Dragons players, all happily set aside from the social hierarchies of school because of their indifference to them. If this had been the world of the early twenty-first century, his sudden detour would have red-flagged him to a team of school psychologists who would then break down the door to intervene and "risk stratify" him, but it was the eighties and people were still fairly relaxed about ninety-degree turns in behaviour as long as it didn't involve drugs.

His grades, which hadn't been bad to begin with, improved dramatically, a change that perplexed his teachers for a semester until they found more important things to be perplexed about. He achieved and was grimly satisfied. And, as with any achievement that occurs within the confines of adolescence, the desire to escape replaced the fear of being trapped. His parents' house, even Le Dépanneur Mondial, all of NDG in fact, seemed to be a fenced-in place where he now saw people walking the grid of streets in an agitated trance. But now it had become an escapable place. It was then that he felt the desire to leave, not as panic but as a pleasurable ache in the stomach. Eighteen months later he was able to quit Le Dépanneur Mondial for more substantive reasons than hurt feelings.

Patrick was still sitting on the bench, eyes closed to the mid-afternoon sun, when he felt someone shake his shoulder. He prepared himself to get up, expecting to face a security guard just doing his job, but it was Celia standing in front of him.

"I saw you leave," Patrick said.

"I needed a break."

He was going to ask her where she'd been, tell her that he'd been looking for her, but he stopped himself. He was sore, and shifted his weight on the bench. It was different from the benches outside the courtroom, but they were equally uncomfortable, sharing a design that numbed legs and prompted movement after a certain amount of time. He was going to tell her he was leaving Den Haag. He couldn't help Hernan, he'd say, and she would just have to take it. But when he looked at her he didn't see what he'd expected, a visage held like a shield, the look of a lieutenant called upon to enforce order in a disintegrating situation. Celia looked like a daughter contemplating loss. She sat down on the edge of the bench.

"Your mum didn't know you were coming here."

"You spoke to my mum?"

"I run into her. Same neighbourhood. Same shops. She looks well."

"Indestructible."

"She talks about you a lot."

"Oh yeah? Was she able to tell you what I do?"

"She doesn't know, really. But she's proud of you."

Patrick's mother wouldn't speak to him for months after he told her that he wasn't intending to practise medicine. The pornography research era was another low point; this time she admitted to him that she'd begun to actively disavow any knowledge of his work, not through a sense of shame but just because it was all too complicated to explain to people. Becoming wealthy had rehabilitated him somewhat – the Caribbean cruise he'd sent her on for her birthday was more easily explained than the work that financed it.

He and his mother had grown closer in the last few years, both of them realizing how much they were a version of each other, especially in their darker moments. A wariness so often mistaken for indifference, a tendency to lose patience and hold grudges, a temper like a tire-fire, building slowly but burning hard. Now his mother left a weekly message, always at a time she knew he wasn't home, always accusing him of call-screening. He'd retaliate with calls of his own, trying to gently goad her into some red-necked declaration by discussing the latest common outrage, but she refused to be baited. And he was certain that while they were talking, she knew, they both knew, that this amounted to a particular type of fondness and that it would do fine.

He had come to recognize that his mother was a certain kind of Montrealer. Five generations off the boat from Queenstown, two generations removed from the Irish ghettos of Griffintown, and she was officially enclaved. The neighbourhood of NDG had been transformed around her into one of the more cosmopolitan places in the world, a fact seen by her as little more than a series of continued assaults on her concept of what Montreal used to be. In her mind, the arrivals aggravated the departures. Friends were gone: dead, or to Toronto. The churches emptied out on her. Even the priests disappeared. Since Patrick's father died, she hadn't withered as much as crystallized into an archetype. Happily. She was unmoved by society's repeated attempts to encourage her to learn French, convert to metric, stop smoking, treat people with different pigments or religions as equals, oppose the seal hunt, recycle, get more calcium in her diet, or embrace gay rights. Decades' worth of grime had collected on the unadjusted dial of her little transistor radio, testament to her only connection to the outside world: a reactionary, staunchly Anglo-Montreal outfit that echoed her sentiments and where the morning show personalities served longer, and with more clout, than most popes.

Nothing was going to get her to change. Instead, she carried forward, buoyed by twin currents of nostalgia and paranoia (maybe this was genetic, a bequest from her immigrant ancestors), remembering the summer of 1967 as both the high point in her city's life and the moment when she first saw the slide to what it would become. It wasn't so much intolerance as indifference. She delighted in telling Patrick that if Quebec separated from Canada, she would just send her taxes to a different place, and if they ran the gay pride parade down the street, well, she had curtains and knew how to draw 'em. She just didn't care, which she liked to remind Patrick was the most honest form of tolerance that existed.

But she was never indifferent to the Garcías. She was always, in her ironic way, wary of them, immigrants – "And what sort of immigrants from Latin America don't go to church?" she liked to ask – with their own store and strange foods and language and with a daughter distracting her son from making something of himself. Her attitude toward Celia had softened considerably in recent years. Maybe it was Marta's death, he thought. She'd even bought one of Celia's paintings. Classic.

"My mother always liked you," Patrick said, deadpan, casting a line onto that still surface. The line tightened. She smiled a little and Patrick's legs began to tingle.

TWELVE

–

Patrick returned alone to the gallery in Courtroom Number One. None of the other spectators seemed to notice his re-appearance, which made him worry that he had become a regular. The crowd had thinned out, the justices yawned more frequently and less discreetly; yes, Friday afternoon was a global concept, ratified in the tribunal. Patrick watched Roberto sit motionless in his seat two rows ahead and wondered if his eyes were closed. He scanned the crowd to see every posture slumped except for that of Elyse Brenman. As usual, Elyse was busy, ruinously vigilant.

Although Elyse had been clear in apportioning guilt, Patrick had never asked her what she really thought of Hernan. If she thought he was sick or deluded or simply another man caught up in events. He'd read that journalists who had profiled people accused of terrible crimes sometimes ended up with ambivalent feelings toward their subjects, and he wondered if searching for that redeeming quality was part of a larger protective mechanism a person needed to have in order to spend months with a monster. Perhaps ambivalence was simply the inevitable result of creating a character complex enough to be worth writing about.

As he studied Elyse, Patrick realized that most of what he knew about Hernan García's life before 1986 hadn't come from the man himself. It had come from what Elyse had written or what Marta García had told him. And if Elyse, in her telling, could not admit Hernan having any human worth, then it was these memories of Marta that had offered redemption. Reminders of decency and warmth. An assertion of a personality beyond what had been alleged. Until recently, it was their versions of the man that Patrick had weighed, the veracity of their contradictory testimony he had been judging. Hernan rested in the prisoner's dock, and Patrick wondered what had to happen for a life to double on itself, for separate trajectories to form and diverge, and if living this lie took as great a toll as another having to discover it.

The son of a surgeon and a prominent family in Tegucigalpa, Hernan García de la Cruz passed through the medical school of the National Autonomous University with expected ease. To his father's chagrin – chagrin was not the right word, Marta García would say when relating the story, *horror* was more precise – Hernan decided that surgery was not his love and instead travelled to the United States for his residency in internal medicine and fellowship in cardiology. Marta, whom he had met at university, accompanied him to Detroit with their infant son, Roberto. (The details of this era in their lives always seemed to Patrick to be clouded in a category nestled between mystery and scandal; there was a wedding, a decision to travel abroad, and Roberto's arrival. The chronology of events was never clear, and the children sensed it – whenever this period was discussed, Roberto and Celia would grin wickedly at each other until their mother chastised them.) She finished her masters in American literature – a thesis entitled "Colonialism and Catharsis in *Moby-Dick*" – as her husband was becoming one of the first experts in the art of performing coronary angiograms. They were both pursuing their interests in the American heart, she would say.

Hernan himself described learning this skill to Patrick one day at Le Dépanneur Mondial. Even though angiograms had become fairly routine tests in the intervening years, for Patrick it was something new and exotic, and it wasn't difficult for Hernan to impart the risk and sense of excitement that accompanied threading a catheter up the aorta, past the aortic valve and into the left ventricle of a patient's beating heart. Hernan and his colleagues would watch the tip of the catheter advance on the monitor, all of them enveloped in that tense silence people describe as hushed. The procedure was performed under X-ray guidance, so the gazes of all those involved were directed toward a monitor placed above the patient and away from what their hands were actually, materially doing, a dissociation Patrick had often thought about since, given the accusations against Hernan. The catheter would be introduced through an artery in the patient's leg and snaked up, inch by inch, through the aorta until it reached the great arch of the vessel, beyond which lay the heart. Hernan would describe the physical sensation of pressure against which he had to advance the catheter. He told Patrick that he imagined the whole procedure as a conflict to be entered into, that one had to advance slowly, had to indulge the weight of opposition and proceed by stealth.

Once inside the heart, they would release a small amount of contrast dye, which emerged from the tip of the catheter looking like a puff of smoke on the monitors. They would watch as the inner contours of each chamber were defined in this cloud. From there, they would pull the catheter back and inject dye into the coronary arteries, which would appear seconds later, forking like bolts of lightning, exposing areas of narrowing along their lengths.

The arteries were important, of course, but, according to Hernan they were little more than conduits, so after gaining proficiency in the procedure, he became bored with this aspect of the test. Instead, he became fascinated by the inner contours of the heart's chambers. He would retrieve the film loops of the procedures and spend hours studying the planes and niches, the subtle irregularities around the base of a malfunctioning valve. At times, during procedures, the catheter's tip would inadvertently touch the wall of the patient's heart and occasionally, depending on the location of the point of contact, produce irregular electrical activity – arrhythmias. The heart would skip a beat or two before returning to normal or it would stumble and trip into a rapid and unstable rhythm that would require urgent action. This was the start of Hernan's interest in the electrical wiring of the heart, and the origin of his hypothesis that if normal rhythms could be tripped into abnormal ones by small physical insults like the tickling of a catheter tip, then perhaps the reverse was also possible.

Hernan extended his fellowship in Detroit for another three years, starting up his hospital's first electrophysiology lab where he studied patients with potentially lethal arrhythmias. Here, in a room just down the hall from the angiogram suite, he applied electrodes to determine the origin of the heart's abnormal electrical activity and proposed to destroy the tissue that provoked these short circuits.

The hospital administration was less than impressed. Arrhythmias weren't a major concern in comparison with the busloads of well-insured patients with coronary artery disease who needed his services to diagnose them prior to their operations. Besides, there was the question of liability. Mistakes could be made in the procedure. Hernan could not argue with this, he had experienced for himself the way a rhythm could disorganize – the chaotic descent from sinus tach to v. tach to v. fib, the heart fluttering like a moth's wings. He was a decade ahead of himself, before chaos theory and higher quality electrophysiological testing revolutionized the procedure. Patrick could see him, though, hunched over in that darkened angiography suite, taking time to study the currents of electricity in the heart, working alone on his own Manhattan Project. A few papers came of it and can be found in the literature. Too theoretical to be seminal, they were curiosities now. Patrick saw a reprint of an original article dating back to 1977 that Hernan had authored in *The Journal of Investigative Cardiology* offered on an online auction house. Bids were up over two hundred dollars, rising fast as his trial approached.

Elyse Brenman covered the Garcías' Detroit experience well in her book, tracking down Hernan's departmental colleagues from that time for their take on the man who would gain such notoriety later. One of his contemporaries, a Dr. Stanley Feinbaum, recalled Hernan's participation at the resuscitation of cardiac arrests in the hospital. In Elyse's hands Hernan's dedication became something more sinister.

"There were a number of times when other doctors wanted to call off treatment and Hernan would step in and take over. If there was a heart rhythm, he'd just keep going, pumping in intravenous fluids, making the orderlies continue CPR until they were exhausted, using the defibrillator over and over again, even trying to insert a pacemaker during the arrest, which was pretty audacious back in the seventies. It was like he was trying to coax the heart back to life. Hernan's arrests would last ninety minutes and they were, I have to admit, unnerving to witness. And the orderlies hated Hernan. Hated him."

In other parts of the book, Elyse provided a fairly credible (although occasionally heavy-handed) analysis of the socio-cultural and historical framework of Honduras as a context to Hernan's actions in Detroit and then back in Tegucigalpa.

She did go predictably far at times, hypothesizing that Hernan was just another raw export from this banana republic shipped off to America, inculcated into all the myths of the American dream, and then sent back to become an imperialist tool of oppression. It was an analysis Patrick didn't completely buy, one that ignored the Garcías as anything other than educated pawns, denying them a capacity to think or feel. A colonial critique of a colonial critique. Patrick remembered Marta García telling him about moving to Detroit in the early seventies, how surprised she was to arrive, heavy with Celia, Roberto in diapers, to find a city in a state of ruin familiar to her from Tegucigalpa. They lived in a suburb of Detroit called Hamtramck, a nice enough place but without much of a Latin American community, and there they had learned to be that self-sufficient family Patrick met in Montreal fifteen years later. It was Marta García who told him about Hernan's experiences in Detroit, recounting the years with clear nostalgia as she and Patrick worked their shifts together in Le Dépanneur Mondial. In the early seventies, Detroit was a city not just reeling from race riots and the descent from prosperity to poverty and disarray, but a place clearly recognizing that the completeness of its descent had become its new civic image. Despite this, Marta García seemed to cherish the years they spent there: the backyard of the small place they rented, Celia's birth that first summer, the work she and Hernan were pursuing. This wasn't to say they viewed their American experience uncritically but rather they both realized that this was their necessary journey, one known to anyone from a country such as theirs, a journey fraught with hardships and isolation but one that they endured as a family, and from which they would emerge as something more. As for Hernan, his opinions of a city still raw from its newly declared racial divisions and a country embroiled in the staggering last months of the Vietnam War were kept private.

It was during an evening shift shared with Marta that he had first seen some of the Detroit photos. She knew he was curious about Hernan, and during a lull she pulled out a shoebox of photos that she had brought with her that day. They were the typical snapshots of a young family in 1970s America: birthday parties, picnics in Veterans' Park, Roberto and Hernan crouched in front of a car – the grille or the side panel, nobody ever posed in front of a rear bumper – faces squinting in Greektown sunshine. There was one particular photo where Celia sat trapped in a pram, scowling at the camera, as though knowing in advance that a future boyfriend would view the picture. Beside Celia stood Roberto, squinting under the bill of a Tigers' cap, holding a baseball bat at such an angle that one could almost hear Marta warning him to be careful around the fontanelles of his little sister.

It was on one of these nights of shuffling through pictures that Marta García showed Patrick a particular photo of Hernan. In the photo, Hernan appeared almost surprised by the camera. Behind him stood a diorama of urban disaster, a fantastic, perplexing scene that Patrick had no reference for at the time but which became recognizable to him years later as the typical backdrop to the televised nightly sermon of foreign correspondents who reported from places of chaos. Grozny, Sarejevo, Baghdad. As Patrick held the photo, Marta told him that in the midst of his medical residency, Hernan decided to volunteer in a free clinic located in a Detroit neighbourhood freshly infamous for its razed buildings and abandonment by police. Part of the regular routine at the clinic was to be held up at gunpoint by somebody looking for drugs. Hernan would come home and, once Celia and Roberto were asleep and the house was quiet, lie in bed next to her and tell her about the most recent robbery, at whom the gun had been pointed, and how close it had come to catastrophe. Several times, it had been Hernan facing the gun. If only for the immediacy and the point of view, Patrick would have preferred to have heard the story from Hernan, but Hernan himself never spoke of it. And it hadn't mattered; after Marta's description, he'd been able to stage the scene in his mind, replaying it until it became his stock footage of heroism and dedication. It was strange, but if there was anything he could talk to Hernan about now, he would ask him what he would think about when the pistol – more ominous in Patrick's imaginings for being held in trembling, desperate hands – was lifted to his own face. Did he feel surprise or hatred? Pity? Patrick imagined him standing there as the gun was lifted, using his voice to calm the person down, trying to keep the other staff from doing something stupid. In an act of cognitive reconstruction Patrick saw him doing all this, not in some clinic in the charred core of Detroit, but from behind the counter of Le Dépanneur Mondial. No wonder Hernan looked so surprised in the photo, he thought it would be a gun and not a camera. "Not even the children know this," Marta García told him as she took the photo back and placed it in the box. He almost told Elyse about the clinic. But he didn't. She could easily have interpreted it in any number of other ways, the crucial moment in the Angel's education: the sickening feeling of helplessness before a criminal, the source of his rage at the underclass, the first necessary step designating them as the *other* before the hard business began.

The university professor had left the stand and another witness was being questioned by Lindbergh. This man was barely in his forties and given the arithmetic, he must have been a teenager when he first came into contact with Battalion 316. This was the particular shame of having to watch the proceedings, this calculation of ages and timelines. At an age when Patrick was embroiled in the melodrama of whether Celia García loved him, this man before him was being beaten with a rubber hose for his political beliefs. Patrick wondered if he even *had* political beliefs. He believed in the scientific method and the dependent variable, in quantification and reproducibility. More recently, he had come to believe in good corporate governance and the power of the quarterly report. Yes, he thought, he believed in something. But he doubted he'd take a beating with a rubber hose for any of it.

Fifteen minutes into his testimony, after the description of the morning he was taken into custody, the witness was asked by Lindbergh to give the names of those arrested with him. Without pausing, he leaned toward the microphone and listed the five names. Patrick recognized only one, José-Maria Fernandez, a student Elyse had memorialized in her book. The name of Fernandez was like a roadside shrine in a devout country. It generally brought things to a halt. Lindbergh was no exception, veering off into questioning about Fernandez, what the witness had seen done to him, the last time Fernandez was seen alive by any of them. Lindbergh asked the witness how they found Fernandez, and the man calmly responded that they found his body several weeks later in a banana field outside of Tegucigalpa.

The words of the witnesses who had already testified were powerful enough, but, like any trial, it was usually one victim's story that rose above the others to encapsulate the act committed. Elyse Brenman understood this and was the first to use the story and the sole surviving image of José-Maria Fernandez in that way. September 3, 1981, became the reference point from which his story was told. From this date, when Fernandez had his photo taken for his student ID, his story cleaved, backwards to describe his life as son and student and alleged communist sympathizer, and forward to his arrest and interrogation in Lepaterique and his death on June 28, 1983.

Fernandez was the youngest of a family of five and worked making deliveries in his father's truck when he was not studying at the National Autonomous University, where he was registered in the faculty of medicine. Of all the victims of Battalion 316, of all the *desaparecido* or those who lived to tell about them, there was no instance other than this of a detainee already knowing one of their captors. Elyse pursued the connection doggedly, hoping to uncover the drama of Hernan coming face to face with a protegé. But it was more random than that. They were not friends nor particularly close. Just one course brought Hernan and Fernandez together. Elyse even found the course: introductory cardiac physiology. She went so far as to tabulate the hours the two men spent in seminars together and retrieved Fernandez's exam papers to see what comments Hernan had written in the margins. Several witnesses confirmed that while receiving medical attention after an interrogation at Lepaterique, Fernandez came face to face with Hernan García. The doctor did not recognize his former student (the young man having sustained facial injuries), and so it was the student who recognized the teacher. According to Elyse's book, the young man may have even at first assumed that his professor had been arrested on the same charges and was being subjected to similar treatment. Elyse ventured that for a moment the younger man may have felt relief that there was someone he knew sharing this ordeal. From that point, Elyse could not say what José-Maria felt next, whether once he understood his professor was working with his captors he felt angry or abandoned, or whether the terror and pain he felt shut out any other sensation. What José-Maria Fernandez felt was a matter for speculation. But two facts were known: José-Maria Fernandez died forty-eight hours after arriving at Lepaterique, and Hernan García de la Cruz left the compound shortly thereafter and did not return.

José-Maria Fernandez had become famous to North Americans in that very Latin American way; his black-and-white picture, *à la Ché*, speckled by layers of photocopying from an already grainy newsprint image, was all that remained of him. It became a central image in the case. The photo often shared the television screen with footage of Hernan handcuffed and moving from one holding cell to another or with stock photos of the field where Fernandez's body was found. Fernandez's photo was only one of many such photos from Latin America in the 1980s. His story was neither more tragic nor poignant than any other, but for various reasons it resonated. Hernan's actions could be explained in the larger political context and his victims categorized as opponents of the regime, but for the true weight of the accusation, a victim with a name was needed.

Patrick had read accounts of people who had covered the tribunals for Rwanda and the former Yugoslavia. These were hardened journalists, men and women who had catalogued the machete-shorn limbs and shallow, self-dug graves and seen every permutation of horrific behaviour; they would be the last to sentimentalize the tribunal's proceedings. Yet they all reported that among the atrocious acts discussed and admitted to, they felt a presence in the courtroom. Perhaps this was nothing more than liberal guilt or a shared sense of belated responsibility, but when Fernandez's name was mentioned, Patrick could sense such a presence, concentrating, almost condensing into a mist to sit on his skin.

The heightened drama invoked by Fernandez's name was defused by the lateness of the day. It was almost four o'clock now, and the proceedings were losing speed. Not even Fernandez could change that. As one of the justices was speaking, Hernan García dipped his head and brought his right hand up to his face. A bright red container was visible through his fingers. He cupped his hand in front of his mouth. Amid the summing-up and gathering of belongings and the barristers closing their cases, Patrick suspected few people noticed it. Hernan raised his head, and Patrick saw him more fully, the wider-eyed state, the pallor, evident even across the gallery, through the glass. Hernan teetered for a moment and an arm extended to brace against the glass wall of the defendant's booth. The heel of Hernan's hand pressed against the glass surface, producing a pale, featureless island of flesh. Patrick had edged to the lip of his chair, and he looked around to see who else was watching. Roberto was stretching, eyes closed, apparently unaware. Patrick then looked over to Elyse Brenman. Her eyes were fixed on Hernan.

Patrick got to his feet quickly and then froze, stalled in that moment of uncertainty over what was happening, unsure of what he should do. He almost pointed to the kiosk where Hernan wavered, ashen-faced. Then, as quickly as Hernan's colour drained, it returned. Hernan steadied. By getting up so quickly among a crowd whose preparations to leave were of the same glacial pace as the proceedings, Patrick had attracted more attention to himself than to Hernan's condition. People stared, always eager to try deciphering the alarm on someone else's face. Reduced to just another gallery oddball, Patrick sat down again. He turned around to see Elyse staring at him, registering everything.

The proceedings were adjourned, and Hernan was led away. Surprisingly, he looked solid on his feet. Elyse remained in her seat, fervently massaging the keyboard of her laptop. A few rows ahead, Roberto sat forward, rubbed his eyes, and stared at the tribunal's empty courtroom and the defendant's dock. Then he turned around to find Patrick in a field of empty seats. They acknowledged each other, a fellowship of stragglers.

Roberto gathered his coat and two-stepped out of his row,

coming up the steps toward Patrick, who was still freshly sore enough that this was a menacing sight. Roberto must have realized it too because he seemed to relax, a posture slackening from threat to non-threat as he got near.

"Jesus, your face *is* messed up."

Patrick had been sitting so the damaged parts hadn't pulsed or throbbed in a while. "It doesn't feel so bad."

Roberto checked his watch. He surveyed the gallery and saw Elyse in the far corner, pounding out another non-fiction award-winner.

"Man, that girl is everywhere I look," he said, a little too loudly for it to have been just for Patrick's benefit. "Can't get enough blood from the Garcías."

Together, Roberto and Patrick walked out of the tribunal building. The sun had disappeared behind some Belgian clouds and the sky looked fluorescent-lit, as though it were about to start flickering. Patrick thought about Hernan and his episode of what must have been chest pain. He should be getting medical attention now. Patrick tried to remember where the examination room was at the tribunal, that labyrinth of hallways that led to the doctor, but after a day and a resolving concussion, his memory of that was bundled in gauze. The most he recalled was the room he awoke in, Celia waiting there, leaning against the wall.

"Has Hernan been ill?" Patrick asked.

Roberto turned, considering the question as he pulled a cell phone out of one pocket and his wallet from another. He stared back in a distracted way, then sat down on one of the benches outside the tribunal building. Patrick joined him.

"He sees a doctor here," Roberto said as he lay down the phone. He pried open his wallet and thumbed through currency notes and scraps of paper, looking for something. He pulled out a business card, then opened his phone. "Celia wanted him to see another doctor, someone who didn't work for the tribunal. But my father refused, of course. Nothing my father can't handle."

Roberto dialled a number and put the card down on the bench. Patrick saw that it was the business card for the *pension* in Den Haag where they were staying. It wasn't difficult to pocket the card without Roberto noticing, his attention focused on the long tonal blips Patrick could faintly overhear. Patrick had no qualms about taking it. Nina came on the phone and immediately Roberto was on his heels, backing away from what Patrick assumed was a barrage of questions. He listened to Roberto try to answer, the telegraphic speech of a person begging to end a conversation.

"I don't know, Nina, maybe she's still at the meeting. Yup. Okay. Bye." With that, Roberto closed the phone. "Celia hasn't checked in. She doesn't believe in cell phones." He was obviously relieved to be speaking to someone other than Nina.

"She's meeting with Oliveira," Patrick said. Roberto understood it wasn't a question. He nodded.

"She's been discussing 'our options' with the Democratic Voice. As though we had options."

"You don't sound too happy about them."

"They're here, whether I like it or not." Roberto was looking around the ground by the bench, then patted his pockets until he gave a small shrug. "So, Celia tells me you do this brain research thing."

"Yeah."

"Can you tell me how his brain works?"

"No. Can you?"

"Not a clue. But I don't need some brain scan to tell me he fucking did it." Patrick knew better than to interject when someone's engines were revving, but nothing more happened. Roberto seemed surprised at having made his admission.

"Did he say anything to you?"

"Us? No. We're just his family. We get to find out like everybody else." Roberto pulled his jacket more tightly around him. "My father is still a child in some ways, you know? Years, we've had to face this shit. It would have been easier if he had admitted it at the start. But he honestly believes he's done nothing wrong." A group of six people in business suits and carrying briefcases walked past them, organized into a tightly packed cluster of movement, like a flock of indigenous birds. It distracted even Roberto for a moment. "And now he won't even talk about it. Won't talk at all. It doesn't surprise me. He's always been in his own little world."

"Some people see it another way."

"Oh yeah? Who?"

"Your sisters." Roberto fixed him with a caustic stare, forcing Patrick to dig deeper. "And he has his supporters at the Democratic Voice – "

"They have their own reasons for being here. Listen to the people who are testifying, the real victims, and you'll hear what the Democratic Voice is all about."

"I don't think Celia feels the same way."

"What the fuck do you know about Celia?" Roberto said angrily. "All she can see is that they're helping. She's actually happy after she speaks to Oliveira, at least for a couple of hours. And it kills me because I know what they stand for and I know they're playing her, but what am I going to do? She has hope, even if it's totally blind. She can't even admit what he's done.

I wish the Democratic Voice and these *witnesses* they found and all these people who support my father could see what he did to our family. I wish they could see what it did to my mother. If he had admitted it, just said he'd made a terrible mistake, she could have dealt with it. I'm sure of it. She loved him. But he never admitted anything. He never explained himself to her. That's what killed her."

Roberto looked so old now. Watching him, it wasn't hard for Patrick to imagine how anger, fed and fanned and stoked, wasn't that much different from a ball of malignant cells or a blood clot when it came to claiming someone. The Roberto he knew was dead, his charisma nothing more than a headstone. Making his excuses, Patrick got up to leave. Roberto asked him where he was going and it was easy for Patrick to fashion a quick lie. Roberto would be angry if he knew where Patrick was going. He was angry enough.

On his way back toward the tribunal, he met Elyse marching across the plaza. To avoid having to speak to her, he was prepared to do anything – duck under her gaze like a guilty child or turn and run – but, quite unusually, she didn't break stride. Elyse offered up only the smallest wave and she continued to walk past. Patrick turned his head to follow Elyse, his surprise turning to alarm as he saw her heading toward where Roberto sat on the bench. There was a time when he would have stopped to watch, indulged in the joy of the fracas that was sure to follow, but he hadn't the heart or the time and so kept walking.

The guards couldn't hide their amusement at Patrick's reappearance at the tribunal building's main entrance. It was Friday, late in the day for a government building, no matter how tight the security, and Patrick got the feeling they were entertained by him and his exits and re-entries. He was like a space shuttle that wouldn't explode.

A guard who had already leafed through the pages of his passport several times that day now looked at him with puzzlement. "Where to now, Dr. Lazerenko? We're getting to being closed."

"I need to speak to your medical personnel. Dr. Bolodis, I think."

"For the face?"

"Yes, the face is giving me trouble."

Somewhere in the tribunal building a pager went off, and like all pagers that go off at twenty to five on a Friday, it must have stung on the beltline like the passing of a kidney stone. When the doctor arrived at the desk, though, he appeared placid, as if he had been idling in an alcove somewhere for just such a deployment. His serenity could have been a Dutch thing or a UN thing or a pharmacological thing; whatever the explanation, Patrick was impressed.

"Hello again, Dr. Lazerenko. How can I help you?"

Bolodis didn't look at all familiar from the previous morning. Prosopagnosia, loss of ability to recognize faces. No, more likely to be just part of the overall amnesia after the concussion.

"I'm sorry, I don't recognize you. We met yesterday?"

Bolodis smiled and nodded. "Yes, I am Bolodis. I treated you after the altercation." He was a little older than Patrick. European thin and wearing a linen suit a bit too tight and worn enough that the material around his elbow had organized itself into corrugations, like the bendable part of a drinking straw. He wore his hair gelled and combed back, gathered into little furrows and ridges that reminded Patrick of the pomaded hair of his Ukrainian uncles.

Bolodis regarded him the way Patrick imagined he had looked at patients with brains in varying states of disarray, estimating the wreckage before setting to work. Work wary. Brain wary. In full view of the guards, Bolodis lifted his hand to Patrick's face, put his middle finger just under the angle of Patrick's jaw and examined the contusion closely. It was something only a doctor would have the nerve to do, a gesture at once intimate and distanced, a public act that drew no attention from the guards at their kiosk.

"You didn't go to the hospital."

"No."

A fraternal grimace. Patrick knew he understood.

"Follow me, Dr. Lazerenko."

Bolodis led him down a stairway – they had been downstairs, that much he remembered – and from the first hallway the familiarity of place emerged, previously laid-down tracks rolled out with each corner turned, and he was able to recall the entire maze of corridors that ended in the medical office and the infirmary. The lights were still on and the screen saver on Bolodis's computer flashed a medley of UN-approved Den Haag architectural cheesecake photos: the Vredespaleis, the Grote Kerk, and even the tribunal building got a glamour shot, photographed next to a reflecting pool to make it look like a twelfth-century castle rising from its moat. Bolodis extended his hand and Patrick sat up on the examining table.

"Bolodis. That doesn't sound Dutch."

"It's not. I'm from Latvia. Riga," Bolodis said, and opened a file. "I came in 1994, a few years after the Soviet Union fell."

"Do you ever think of going back?"

He looked up at Patrick. "Why do you ask that?"

"No reason. It just seems that with the new freedoms . . ."

"I could have stayed," Bolodis answered, shrugging like the thought was a wet coat he wanted to shed. "You're American?"

"I work there. I'm naturalized."

Bolodis pulled a piece of loose paper out of Patrick's chart: "We make a photocopy of the passports of anyone seen here, and I couldn't help but notice you are an American citizen, but you still have a Canadian passport."

"I kept it. Some places you have to show your passport to get in."

"I gave up my Latvian status." Patrick nodded. "Why are you here at the tribunal?"

"I knew Hernan García when I was young. I grew up in Montreal and worked for him then. The two women – "

"Celia and Nina, his daughters. Yes, I know," Bolodis added, sitting on the desk opposite the examination table. "Well, let's have a look at you." Bolodis got up and washed his hands. He snapped on a pair of latex gloves and asked Patrick to open his mouth, his fingers on the skin over the joint to determine how the jaw was opening. He pulled a penlight out of his breast pocket and clicked it into a knifepoint of light. Bolodis held the light in front of Patrick's face, swinging it from one eye to the other. Blindness followed, the intermittent, sequential blindness between the bright lights. The light was painfully intense, and impossibly had the sound of a bonfire when it came near.

"Do you have headaches?" he asked.

"Some. More last night."

"Follow my finger. Are you dizzy?"

"When I move quickly."

"Dizzy like spinning or dizzy like being on a boat?"

"Like a boat."

Bolodis brushed the tips of his index fingers over the skin on Patrick's forehead. The cheeks and chin were tested next: "Do you feel this?" Patrick nodded. "Close your eyes, please. That hurts?"

"Yes."

"Now please open your mouth."

The doctor shone the light into Patrick's throat. When he had finished, Patrick asked him how many doctors worked at the tribunal.

Bolodis clicked off the penlight. "I am the only one. If you'd like to see another – "

"No, no," Patrick replied, and Bolodis disengaged, leaning back on his desk, as though expecting what was coming next. "I didn't come for me. I came because I wanted to speak to Hernan's doctor. I'm worried about him." Bolodis nodded. He crossed his arms and brought one hand, fingers curled into a loosely held fist, to his mouth. It looked as though he needed to cough.

"What exactly are you worried about?"

"His health."

"Tell me what you're worried about. Exactly."

"He's sick. He's obviously having angina. Every time I see him, he's using his nitrospray. Today, I thought he was having a heart attack."

Bolodis paused. To Patrick, he was a man thinking of job security and working conditions in Riga. "I can't tell you anything. His medical information is confidential. Please understand." Bolodis took a piece of gauze and dabbed it against Patrick's swollen lower eyelid. Despite the delicacy of the act, Patrick winced. From what he could see, the gauze was moist but not discoloured.

"No infection," Bolodis said, happy to get back to the routine of minor trauma. "These are tears."

"I'm a doctor, I'm a friend of the family."

"So much more the reason for discretion."

"Can I see him then, to ask him if he's okay?"

"You know he's refusing visits. That is his right. Would it reassure you to know that we're aware of every detainee's medical history? The fact that he is taking medication in front of you should put your mind at ease, I would hope. And please let me remind you that we have never had a case of someone suffering at our hands . . ."

"It's not that – "

"You don't practise, do you, Dr. Lazerenko?"

"What does that have to do with anything?"

"And he is a cardiologist – "

"*Was* a cardiologist."

"Yes, yes. He was a cardiologist, Dr. Lazerenko, please remember that. Perhaps he has insights into his own condition that his friends or his family don't have. Turn your head." There was a pause and Bolodis pointed to his own ear when he saw the puzzled look on Patrick's face. "I have to look inside." The exam was painful and made Patrick want to yawn. "You do research," Bolodis said as he examined the other side, as though he had discovered this fact looking into Patrick's ear.

"Yes."

"I read about it. After you left I did a literature search on you. I read about your research." Always a non sequitur. He never knew whether to say "Thanks" or "Sorry" when what he usually meant was "I don't care." "It was very interesting," Bolodis said earnestly. "I like to think about these questions too." A broader version of the smile appeared, which was then revised into something cloudier: "Is that why you're here?"

"I'm sorry?"

"Your research. I read that it hopes to explain certain behaviours."

Patrick shook his head. "I'm here for personal reasons. Besides, I don't do that kind of research any more."

"I mean, I can see it, you know. The brain determines our mental states, how we feel, and brain function is subject to physical laws; it's determined."

"Sure."

"So, where is his free will? How can he be guilty? How can anybody be guilty?" Patrick was glad Bolodis added the last part, it made it easier not to have to answer him. Bolodis paused, then said, "I've met a fair number of unusual people at the tribunal. You can't help but think. You get a lot of time to think."

"Do you see Hernan regularly?"

"Yes."

"Every day?"

"Most days. Yes. Every day."

"He talks to you, doesn't he?"

"Of course he does. I'm his doctor."

"No, he *talks* to you. Not just about his medical condition."

"Confidentiality, Dr. Lazerenko. A physician should respect that."

"I think he's unwell."

"I can't discuss this."

"Why does Hernan think I'm here? Is it because of the research? Because that's not what I do."

"What *do* you do, Dr. Lazerenko?"

Patrick sighed. "I study how people make certain decisions with their money. Period. I look at situations and variables in order to help make marketing decisions. Who told you I was a researcher in the first place? Did I tell you that when I was here before?"

Bolodis shook his head: "No. Celia told me." He put the file down on the desk, and as his arm extended, Patrick saw the creases of the elbow of his linen suit open up.

"He should know how he's affecting his family by not talking."

"I'm sure he's aware," Bolodis said flatly, and jettisoned the latex gloves into the container next to the examining table.

Bolodis smiled but Patrick understood it was anything but a smile; it was a default mechanism, professionally applied but still a Soviet-bloc–grade obfuscational device. He would prefer open disdain. He had grown used to disdain – in the world of business it had become one of the indicators that he was doing his job well. The smile was like a handshake held too long, a breach of decorum, more flagrant for it being used among people who had some sort of shared experience. But he and Bolodis were not the same. To Bolodis he was a lapsed colleague, a theoretical thinker, a mercenary, a pain in the ass on a Friday afternoon. But he shouldn't be so harsh, he thought, a smile could mean so many things: tolerance, beneficence, sympathy – samplers of goodwill, sentiments lasting long enough to get him out of the office.

"I think you're fit to go, Dr. Lazerenko."

–

THIRTEEN

The village has been captured by enemy soldiers with orders
to kill all civilians. A group of townspeople have sought refuge
in the hayloft of an abandoned barn. They can hear the
soldiers outside; the soldiers are coming toward the barn. At
that moment, a woman's infant daughter begins to cry. She
covers the child's mouth to block the sound. If she removes
her hand from the child's mouth, the soldiers will be alerted
and will kill the woman, her child, and all the townspeople. To
save herself and the others, she must kill her child.

The story was a thought experiment, and it preoccupied
Patrick as he walked the deserted streets of Den Haag. The
crying baby dilemma was meant to highlight the conflict
between group welfare and personal moral conviction.
The emotional response, the abhorrence associated with the
thought of killing one's child was forced to compete with
the abstract understanding that the child would die under
either circumstance and that many lives could be saved by
committing this act.

It was a terrible thing to contemplate. Something visceral occurred, Patrick had felt it. He'd watched as the faces of his undergrad students furrowed, as though for the first time, while considering this dilemma. They'd answer slowly, toeing their way along the process as though they heard ice creaking.

What is the right thing to do? How do we decide what is right? Philosophers had the question to themselves for centuries. Utilitarianism versus deontology. John Stuart Mill against Kant in the ultimate cage match. And after three centuries without a resolution from the philosophers, neuroscientists had begun eyeing the dilemma – specifically, what part of the brain was activated in a decision-making process and if relatively greater activity in certain parts of the brain reflected a more utilitarian response.

Even though Neuronaut didn't study these sorts of problems, Patrick had thought of this dilemma a lot in the last two years. He had watched from the corporate sidelines as the research of his former colleagues progressed without him. At one time, he had wanted to do the experiments himself, to define a neural basis of conflict in moral judgments, to understand how they are resolved. He wanted to know what happened in the brains of the Nazi doctors to allow them to continue with their day. He wanted to know what sort of brain activity, what deft imbalance between competing regions made it possible for Hernan García to participate in the torture and killings of civilians, in the death of José-Maria Fernandez, a boy he'd taught. A boy he'd known.

Of course, Patrick didn't do this experiment. He was busy getting a prospectus together and figuring what parts of Globomart's new promotional campaign were maximally activating temporal lobe structures. But the study, which used functional magnetic resonance scans to study the brains of subjects as they considered the "crying baby dilemma" was done, and done well, and showed that parts of the brain – the anterior cingulate cortex and dorsolateral prefrontal cortex – were activated during the moral angst that came with these dilemmas, and when the decision was made to pursue the utilitarian route, to smother the child, the dorsolateral prefrontal cortex was even more strongly activated.

He didn't want to think about Hernan practising that pragmatism, killing for a larger cause. It was once a solace for Patrick to think that Hernan made the decision to trade the lives of those held at Battalion 316 for those of his family. And even then, he hoped Hernan had felt anguish, hoped for a moment of moral hesitation when the reflexes of everyday life were stripped away and one's actions had to be considered. But even if he was coerced, Hernan had come to the conclusion that someone's death made sense. It was easier to think about the brain malfunctioning, and that is how he needed to think of Hernan now, that his dorsolateral prefrontal cortex was activated at a crucial moment, resolving the conflict. In some ways it absolved him. It made the smothering of a child easier to contemplate. Evil was unfathomable, but Patrick knew how to measure blood flow.

This was Den Haag at dusk. This was the sea.

He had come to the very edge of Holland, in Scheveningen, the place that Birgita had told him about. He thought it would be a bus journey away but it was really nothing more than the northeast corner of Den Haag. Scheveningen was a beach town, infamous and deserted and so close to Den Haag that he'd walked there without particularly intending to. In the early evening light it was beautiful, even more abandoned than the city just to the south. In the guidebook he bought at one of the few open stores, he learned that Scheveningen, other than being the North Sea version of Daytona Beach (with everything, positive and negative, that that entailed), held a special place in the psyche of the Dutch as the proper pronunciation of its name – Skay-veninguh – was so difficult to German speakers that it was used as a shibboleth, a test by the Dutch to identify enemy spies during the war.

"Skay-veninguh," he said, loudly and ineptly enough for any bystander to cast a suspicious glance, but he was alone. Ahead there was a boardwalk that led to a pavilion on a pier, all of it stilted above a sea the colour of slate. He was an invading army of one. The city was his.

Patrick turned a corner and walked down another street and this confirmed the emptiness, an almost pathological emptiness. It was the sort of abandonment that reminded him of evacuation from some impending civil catastrophe. He expected to look through windows to see pots bubbling on stoves or doors swinging on their hinges. Maybe a flood was coming, the rising waters even now overwhelming the vaunted system of dykes and canals, leaving scant hours until they were all waist-deep in North Sea. Maybe the evacuation orders had been issued in Dutch, and the foreigners, stumbling through Skay-veninguh in every sense, had been left behind to fend for themselves. "Skay-veninguh," he repeated to himself, lacking even the conviction of a proper spy. He had been found out, consigned to a Dutch rooftop in the coming flood, wind-whipped and waving for rescue.

He told himself that if he had been alone on an empty beach the solitude would have been tolerable, even pleasant, but wandering the streets of a ghost town filled him with dread. He wasn't used to seeing everything closed, everything was 24/7 back home, and he understood in that very North American way that only the sight of a functioning retail establishment was going to reassure him now. He grew so desperate that he almost retraced his steps to the shop where he had bought his guidebook. It took him another ten minutes to find a restaurant that didn't look boarded up on one of the side streets off the Strandweg. He was further relieved to find the door unlocked, and he ventured inside, coming face to face with two restaurant workers who regarded him with a look of astonishment and shock, as though he'd emerged from the foam after having swum over from Norway.

They were apologetic for only having sandwiches, but it was fine, Patrick told them. The meal in the dining room, with its huge diorama window fronting the coast, calmed him down. By the time they brought Patrick a cup of coffee and the bill, Scheveningen had again become just another off-season beach town, one of a fraternity of forlorn places. The sky deepened and then the sky was black. No stars, but the lights of the coast extended to the right and left and that was enough for him.

It was cooler by the time he left, and he could smell the sea now. The pier disappeared except for a small skeleton of lights that outlined where the pavilion would be. He could go back to the Metropole, but he thought about his cell phone and laptop and whatever concierge was on duty, all waiting for him. No, right now the empty streets of Scheveningen were what he needed. Shop windows full of beach gear, bicycle rental places boarded up; even though it wasn't yet seven o'clock, nightfall had normalized the streets for him and he was able to imagine it was three in the morning. As he passed the shop windows, he could see the flesh over his cheek sagging now like low-lying Dutch evening clouds, a right eye still swollen to the point that it looked like he was winking. Patrick stopped and peered into a darkened shop window. He opened his mouth, and the skin over the swollen cheek stretched. His eye opened slightly. Past the reflection he saw that the shop was a gallery, with paintings stacked on the floor against the back wall. Two paintings still hung in the window – seascapes, with more compositional skill than typically seen in tourist-grade oils – asserting a more-than-seaside-town-gallery aspiration for the establishment. It was natural that he thought of Celia at moments like this. Art from the sidewalk, inadvertent, brought back memories of a moment like this on a different street fifteen years earlier. It was how he had found his way back into the Garcías' lives.

It was 1991. He had barely seen any of the Garcías and hadn't talked to Celia at all in the four years since he'd quit Le Dépanneur Mondial. After a year dodging Celia at the store and at school, he had been relieved to escape to the anonymity of a different CEGEP. He had friends and girlfriends and a life and Celia García was demoted to just another person he knew from his old neighbourhood. He was accepted into medical school after CEGEP (something routinely done in Quebec, if only for the extreme social experimentation of graduating twenty-three-year-old doctors) and became immersed in books, treading water with the other overachievers. In late September of his first year, walking through the downtown early on a Friday evening after a day of gorging himself on another thousand facts of biochemistry, he stopped on the sidewalk and turned his head sharply to the right. He still thought about that response; the flare, perhaps reaching the occipital lobes, tripping through substations in the temporal lobes, retrieving a visual memory, comparing, triggering other associations. Not a decision to turn, but a response to something only partially understood and then the decision created later. He stopped. He was stopped. Through the window he saw something familiar among other paintings at a student exhibition. Patrick saw himself, emerging from a field of corn. He went into the gallery.

The exhibition space, a building belonging to the other English university in the city, was already full. Half the crowd – obviously family – was dressed up for the event and milled nervously, never straying far from the work of various offspring, while the other half, younger, whom he assumed to be the artists themselves or friends of the artists, were dressed less formally but with more eccentric precision. He was the rarity, the walk-in business, likely the only one. He strolled through the aisles of art, making his way to the wall that had been visible from the window.

He looked at the painting again and had to remind himself that he hadn't given it back, that this was a copy of the one that hung in his bedroom. Artist: Celia García. It was exactly like his. It was him in the painting, titled *Unknown boy in cornfield #2*. It was him pushing back those stalks.

She had four other paintings there. Stunning paintings. Patrick saw a rendering of the inside of the Garcías' house, distorted and yet still recognizable, a point of view that he could imagine only as coming from inside the aquarium that sat in her parents' living room. Another showed her parents, American Gothic-style, standing in front of Le Dépanneur Mondial. Hernan and Marta, gaunt and stoic, clutching a mop and carafe of coffee respectively. There was a portrait of a man about Patrick's age in which she captured something intimate, a knowing smirk, that made Patrick feel the stab of a butter knife somewhere in his ego. Of course, there was *Unknown boy in a cornfield #2*, which was unsettling and impressive in its own right. Patrick's favourite was one whose point of view could have been his for the summer he worked at Le Dépanneur Mondial, impressionistic banks of colour on either side of a produce aisle.

"My professor doesn't like that one," Celia said, having crept up on him. She whispered: "She doesn't like any of them really, they're all devoid of a personal style, all 'imitative.'"

Patrick stared straight ahead at the painting, into a churning sea of yellow that he thought must be mangoes. "That's why they're being exhibited, I suppose. Setting an example."

"No, seriously. She hasn't said so, but I get the feeling she wants me to discover my inner *La-tee-na*. You know – folksier style, crucifixes and skeletons, the new Frida Kahlo. That's how I'll get to be a great Canadian painter."

He turned toward her. She had her arms crossed – all the students identifiable as artists stood with their arms crossed, as though sentries against the marauding philistines. But she smiled at him. She was taller than when he had last seen her, and she wore her hair pulled back and gathered into a thick cord that hung down her back.

He didn't know what he was supposed to say to someone he hadn't seen for three years. A summary of what he'd done in the intervening time maybe. He had imagined just this sort of situation, hoping whatever he had accomplished would impress her, surprise her. In these fantasies she was always the same, the Celia he'd known from the store, from that day they'd walked home together. But he was surrounded by evidence that she had changed too. Art was no longer a hobby for her. She had become an artist, and it intimidated as much as it impressed him. As much as he tried to think of himself as different, as an older or more accomplished version of himself, it was still just a version. And she knew the other versions.

"Hi," he said, holding out his right hand, "I'm Patrick Lazerenko."

"Nice to meet you," she replied.

He had arrived late. Hernan and Marta had come and gone earlier, and he had missed Roberto by a scant five minutes. The gallery emptied but he loitered, pretending to develop a taste for the work of the nearby exhibitors. Finally, he asked Celia if she wanted to go out for something to eat. Patrick didn't notice much about the meal – all his neurons were committing themselves to various Celia-related details. She laughed differently, the nasal snort was gone, and instead she pursed her lips. She was more comfortable in English now, pausing less as she spoke and, unless she wanted to make a point, the Spanish words had disappeared from her con-versation. She spoke about art and her ambitions, sounding confident but not arrogant, a neat trick for someone in university. At one point, Celia mentioned a guy's name and the soup turned sour, but Patrick managed to carry on with some measure of composure. She wanted to know about medical school, and he told her it was, up to that point, a morass of facts that he had difficulty imagining would have any application. "We're learning about the brain," he remembered saying to her, then regretting it as the words made him sound like a grade school child eager to impress with his knowledge of the alphabet.

There he was, over some meal listening to her talk about her family, explaining to him how she'd finally decided on pursuing a career in art, seeing her smile and laugh. Both he and Celia still lived at home, not six blocks from each other. They laughed at that, but neither one of them could figure out why. And through it all, Patrick felt like a grey-raincoated dissident finding himself on the other side of the wall, enjoying an inexplicable day of freedom and wondrous excess.

They rode home on a nearly-empty bus and didn't say much to each other. They'd talked all night, after all, and so were reduced to the residue of conversation, to chit-chat – how Monkland Avenue was coming back to life and what it would mean for Le Dépanneur Mondial. But the ease, the pleasure they both had in each other's company, impressed him. The silences were like a lovely snaking song, full of subtle, irresistible grooves and hooks, mirrored in the rolling motion of the bus. He was counting stops until theirs arrived. Three. Two. One. We'll be friends, he thought. We are friends. He said goodnight to her and tried not to have his face drawn into the smile of a sidewalk cult recruiter. The night ended, quietly and definitively, like a door closing.

A couple walked by on the sidewalk behind Patrick as he stood at the window, the reflected flare of a red windbreaker in the window registering only by the time they passed. He listened to their footsteps already abbreviating into the night. Patrick fished out the card that Roberto had used to call the *pension* and saw that the address was listed as Geestbrugweg, fifteen blocks away, according to his map of Den Haag. He turned away from the gallery and began the walk back into town.

Along the Strandweg, the buildings dropped away, and in the dark interval between the street lights he got a slow, cycling sense of the depth of night. The lights of a tanker hung suspended in the North Sea. He picked up the pace, enough to get his head pounding and feel a little sick to his stomach.

One morning, a few weeks after running into Celia at the art exhibit, Patrick had sat down for breakfast and watched as his father suddenly reached out with his right hand. Patrick's mother was looking for something in the cupboard; he remembered this, he heard the door close with that cupboard door sound. The radio was on. For some reason his eyes were on his father's hand as it froze there in the mid-breakfast air, and he had the impression his father was trying to ward something off. He watched the right hand drop slowly and then grip the edge of the table. His father had massive hands, the base of his thumb muscled thick as a chicken leg, and he squeezed the table so tightly that the thumbnail blanched. Patrick watched in fascination, as though he could only make sense of the man piece by piece, following the forearm up to the sleeve of his T-shirt and then finally arriving at his fixed and ashen face. He called out to his mother.

His mother dialled 911 while Patrick eased his father to the floor – *eased*, that was a joke, he remembered easing him like a lumberjack eases a redwood. Patrick started doing something that approximated CPR. His father's lips were already cool and bluish, and he had stopped breathing. He knew he should remember something personal from his father's last moments, he should, by rights, have had a flood of memories, some expression of devotion to him, but all he remembered was thinking: "This is a man dying." Then he felt panic and the cold burden of futility, the sense that he was trying to overturn some unstoppable physical fact. *This is a man dying.* They took him to hospital in the calamity of sirens and frantic, chore-ographed action, but he was dead. Patrick and his mother sat in the hallway in the emergency department, watching the doors open and seal up again like great tectonic plates. Patrick was in sweat pants, he remembered the cord dangling, and his mother was still in her dressing gown underneath her overcoat when a doctor came out and told them he had died.

An aneurysm had formed on his aorta. The doctor suspected that it had enlarged gradually, the vessel's wall thinning under the pressure until it burst. The doctor, who had up to this point been holding his hands together in a seminarian pose, suddenly extended the fingers of both hands into the gesture of explosion, a little supernova. In case they hadn't understood.

His mother didn't cry. Not a tear. Not the second cousin of a tear, as she would say. She looked like a person who'd been promised a ride on a wet day and had been forced to walk. Deep disappointment in an aorta. She looked at her son, with what Patrick imagined was that same air of disappointment, as if in the first months of the first year of medical school they should have taught him what to do when the biggest artery in the body ruptured. Patrick was mute, watching the doctor's hands resume their marsupial lives deep in the pockets of a lab coat. The doctor turned and walked away.

The next few days were full of well-dressed people saying fairly predictable things to him, kind things, telling him he was a good son. Lying, he felt. In that mood, the constant parade of condolence-givers – all with that beatific, gas-pained look on their faces, all having the same pronouncement of him – seemed to be little more than an organized prank, an ironic indictment of his failings.

After the funeral mass came the cemetery and its hillside stubbled with gravestones and a big hole in the ground, big enough to stare into and see the bottom of miry clay and small pools of water. He remembered the graveside: his sisters and their husbands and kids shifting gears through various Kübler-Ross stages to suit their individual terrains of grief, and his mother, more composed than anyone in the immediate family, a person more than pleased to tell the good Dr. Kübler-Ross to *feck off* with her stages and just let her be. And he felt plainly stupid at not understanding until then how death changed things, that death was not only possible but inevitable, that death had been necessary for him to understand how much he cared for his father.

From there, it was to a receiving line in the church basement at St. Monica's, his sisters and mother ahead of him (what did that mean? Was he in charge now? No one spoke to him about *that*). He remembered the Garcías at the funeral service, how he'd never seen any of them at church before, how Marta smelled of vanilla, the traces of wariness Patrick thought he could detect on Roberto's face. A solemn, wordless bear hug from Hernan. Then Celia. Leaning over to kiss her on the cheek as she passed in line, looking at her earlobe and the tiny colourless hairs that covered her neck and for a moment not wanting to think of anything else.

The church basement wasn't enough, of course; even Patrick could sense it. If there was one rule governing the socio-cultural life of a household containing two different ethnicities, it was that the customs that survived the merger will be those that are the most trenchant clichés. In this spirit, the Lazerenkos' house harboured countless Ukrainian Easter eggs painted with orange and black geometric patterns and strategically placed Celtic paraphernalia along with the iconic Irish-Catholic devotional object: the photo of Kennedy flanked by his papal wingmen,

John xxiii and Paul vi; they listened to polka music and marched down to St. Catherine Street to watch flatbed trucks laden with drunken local radio personalities plough through the slush every St. Patrick's Day. Although he would never admit it, Patrick loved this about his family, loved this about his parents, even if he understood that in some ways the Lazerenkos knew no shame. And in that way, he knew that his mother had already decided that they would have a wake.

His mother asked to be helped up onto one of the chairs in the church basement, and from that height – her head was still barely above most of those in the gathered crowd – she announced that everyone was invited back to the house that night for a wake commencing at eight o'clock. There was an absolute, deep-sea silence, and for a moment Patrick got the impression that people were uncertain if this was some sort of aberrant grief reaction, the kind that should be indulged and ignored. But then Father Francoeur, who had been chatting with the women from the Catholic Women's League, stepped forward and said, "That is a wonderful idea, Veronica," and the crowd started talking and nodding among themselves.

It was hard to keep up with his mother after that. It was as though some long dormant genetic program had been activated. She raced home to open all the windows of the top floor to let the banshee out and unfurled the linen table cloth, her regimental banner in all things domestic. She put out the good cutlery and the Belleek china and was a dervish of the small tasks necessary to receive company. Patrick watched and knew that it wouldn't be safe to stand in her way. Platters of cold cuts and bread materialized and just after eight the doorbell started ringing. Patrick stayed downstairs with his mother and sisters and their families as long as he could. They mingled with his father's friends from the Port who told him, as a form of tribute, he supposed, that Roger Lazerenko had a great singing voice and that his father was famous for once having thrown a five-pin bowling ball onto the roof of a three-storey building from the sidewalk below. He tried to imagine the circumstance that would call for such a feat. People ate and drank, and their neighbour Mr. Lavasseur told Patrick about a real Irish wake he had been to as a child in Pointe-Saint-Charles in the forties, how in an upstairs room the body would still be present and everybody would say prayers around it before having the first drink.

All the Garcías arrived, even Marta with Nina in tow, and from the far side of the room he saw his sisters take their coats and go through the motions of introductions. He wanted the house emptied, dark and quiet as a cave. No people singing. No happy reminiscences. Grief, which he now understood to be a word describing threads of loss and fatigue being woven into a thick black cloth, made no sense in the noise. Without telling anyone, Patrick went up to his room to be alone.

It was cool in the house with the windows left partially open, and he lay down in his darkened bedroom and did nothing, satisfied to float in his gloom until sleep came. Then the door opened. He thought it was his mother or one of his sisters at first, coming to bring him back down, and it was only when she sat on the edge of the bed that he realized it was Celia.

At the time, he didn't think deep thoughts about love affirming itself in a wake-house or that they represented a life force amid all that grief. He tried not to think about his mother downstairs or his father somewhere else. He didn't care about the possibilities of banshees pausing on their way out to watch the two of them struggle out of their formal grieving attire. The thought shamed him now and then, but he could think only about the smell of Celia García's hair and the way her mouth tasted. He could think only about how much he wanted to touch her and hold her. She said, "Don't say anything," and he complied, not knowing if she wanted to stop him from saying something stupid or just to be quiet. He had nothing to say. He just wanted to listen to her breathing, loud and deep enough now that it drowned out the sound of voices rising in some as-yet unidentifiable song from the floor below. Christ, he remembered thinking, please don't let it be "Danny Boy."

Patrick walked away from the sea and back toward the lights of Den Haag. As he arrived at the Hotel Pension Henrietta on Geestbrugweg, the glow of the building's facade and the small courtyard under the streetlights gave him the impression of having experienced a shortened night, of having returned to twilight or been thrown forward into the next morning's dawn. Patrick could have got to the *pension* more quickly had he met anyone who could have given him directions, but it appeared that someone pulled the plug at five o'clock and all the citizens drained out of Den Haag.

The *pension* was a three-storey building of brown brick with a front door whose heft suggested it was designed to repel the Visigoths. Inside, it smelled like an old European house, a category unto itself. The lobby culminated in a small desk, and, as if to respect scale, a small man sat behind it. He lifted his eyes from a book when Patrick asked for the Garcías' room and, after positioning a bookmark with great ceremony, he called up. The small man gave a hooked-on-phonics approximation of Patrick's name to whoever answered. A pause followed, longer, Patrick thought, than it took to consider the name of a routine visitor. After putting the phone down, the man indicated where a visitor could wait.

Patrick sat fidgeting on the doughy sofa in the sitting room for ten minutes before getting up to look at the bookshelf. It was full of Dutch translations of well-known novels, perhaps not the most helpful collection for a house destined to be full of foreigners looking for the diversions of a good read. He pulled a book off the shelf and turned to the first page of *In de ban van de Ring*: which he thought, given the perplexed, constipated-looking dwarfs and pseudo-Celtic flourishes that defaced the cover, was probably a translation of *The Lord of the Rings*.

"What are you doing here?" Celia asked as he closed *In de ban van de Ring*. He didn't want to alarm her by saying he thought Hernan was ill. He had planned to tell Celia that he was just out walking and wanted to speak with her, but the way she appeared, bearing down on him like an angry bantamweight and backing him into a corner of the sitting room, made him adjust.

"I spoke to your father's doctor."

"Why?"

"I was worried about him. He doesn't look well to me."

"What's the doctor got to say?"

"He can't give me details, but he tried to reassure me."

"And you came to tell me that."

"No, no. I was out. I was walking around – " She pursed her lips. Jesus, he thought, a gallstone of a personality sometimes. It was like talking to his mother. It annoyed him that the most important women in his life talked to him like they were his parole officers. "I found these beaches. Scheveningen. Not far from here. I thought you might like to go."

"The beach? Are you serious?"

"Tomorrow's Saturday. What are you going to do, camp out at the empty courthouse? I thought if Nina and Paul needed to do something tomorrow, the beach would be a nice change." Nothing. Even after bringing Paul into it, leveraging an afternoon of possible happiness, she showed no sign of softening. To Patrick she looked as if she was sniffing him for some ulterior motive.

"I see," she said, her expression not relenting. He handed her the guidebook with its cover showing the pier and the beaches in summer, a pastoral fronting a boardwalk and a grand-looking hotel called the Kurhaus.

"It's not far. Close enough to walk." He pointed to the page she'd opened to, a city map showing transit connections. "There's a tram too."

"I don't know, Patrick."

"It's the low season," Patrick said, trying not to have it sound like a sales pitch. "There'll be no one there. I can come by tomorrow to take you." Celia was silent. "What?" Patrick asked.

"This," Celia said, pointing to the door, "you coming around like this, unannounced."

"What?"

"I'm not comfortable with you just imposing yourself – "

"*Imposing*? Is that what you think? If there's been any imposing, it's been your brother imposing his fist on my face, it's been your lawyer imposing on me to put my career at risk. And let's not forget the imposition of me coming all the way to Holland to be told that I'm imposing." Patrick tried to get the two parts of his jacket zipper to engage, but his hands shook too much. Celia grabbed the sleeve of his jacket.

"Patrick, I didn't mean it like that. Look, we appreciate you being here. I just meant that, personally, I'm not sure I feel comfortable with you."

He pulled his arm away from her. "Well, you don't have to go. Nina and Paul can go. Hell, send Roberto. He's a goddamn riot."

"Patrick, stop."

"I'll be here tomorrow at ten o'clock. You can do what you want. It's the *beach*, for christsake."

Twenty minutes of walking wasn't enough time or distance for his anger to subside, and he was almost sorry when his hotel came into view. He thought about walking farther, but the night was cool, a sense of November in the air, and it would get colder still. The Hotel Metropole gave off a hum that grew and blossomed as he reached the front door. The lobby was deserted and the concierge's desk was empty. He passed by the entrance to the bar, which offered a fine view of the Metropole's lobby and made him wonder if the concierge was holding court at a table inside. Patrick arrived at the bank of elevators and punched at the call button. While he waited, he walked over to the glass wall that separated the bar from the rest of the lobby. The wall was made up of several layers of tempered glass, so thick that it distorted everything on the other side into a myopic blur. It reflected well, though, and it was as he studied his own image in the glass, opening and closing his good eye, that he noticed a flickering motion from inside the bar. There was a rhythm to it, a movement like someone flapping, all of it difficult to discern through the wall of glass. As he stared at it, the movement stopped, and then started again. Patrick edged closer, the hand was really going now, and he could see it connected to a person, smaller, standing on the other side and refracted through the glass, waving from the bar. It was a woman. A scrambled channel of a woman. He ducked around the glass wall into the bar, his imagination sprinting ahead – Celia had reconsidered her ungratefulness back at the *pension* and hopped a cab, come over to the Metropole and now she wanted to talk, yes, a real heart to heart. He felt dizzy as he bounded up the two steps into the bar, regaining his balance to find her standing there, hands at her side, familiar now.

"Hello, Birgita."

–

FOURTEEN

Patrick sat up on the edge of the bed, a balancing act, and not one well-recommended after a night of too little sleep and with a hangover imposing martial law. Off to one side, a series of red lines hovering above the bedside table organized into different shapes, then numerals, and finally, a time. He should sleep but his feet were already on the floor, taking him now to the washroom and then back again. Not even a promise of morning outside. Den Haag slept in the grid of lights; administrative dreams, banker's dreams, dreams of people who wanted to go home. He couldn't remember what he dreamt, if he dreamt anything. Even though he could tell the bed was empty when he awoke, he still put out a hand, ran it over the sheets, just to make sure she wasn't there before turning on the light. The light stung when he snapped it on. The bed was empty.

After a couple of drinks in the hotel bar, Birgita had come up to the room under the mutual pretence of seeing the view. The view mustn't have been all that captivating, for he came out of the washroom to find her thumbing through his copy of *Moby-Dick* that had been sitting on the undersized desk near the window. She'd read it too, in school; it was apparently widely admired in Holland, where, he supposed, the thought of nautical catastrophe coming from something other than the sea itself was a distinct novelty. She told him she'd never seen anyone read it who wasn't doing it as part of a school assignment.

"You've made a lot of notes," she said, the pages fanning from her thumb.

"They're not mine. It belonged to a friend."

He turned on some music, and they sat and talked some more about how long Birgita was going to stay in Den Haag. She had plans to travel that were just vague enough to depress Patrick. They drank a few shrunken bottles of an unrecognizable single malt whisky (€15.50) and ate pistachios (€6.25) and rolled around in a proto-coital haze for the longest time before he got up to search the room for a switch to turn off the lights, so as not to feel like the Phantom of the Opera with his half-mangled face. Any qualms were dissolved by the scotch and a remembered list of slights and oppressors: Celia's hostility, Heather's abandonment. Even Hernan made an appearance, Fernandez in tow, then di Costini and Lindbergh, along with Roberto's fist. A Mardi Gras parade of rationalizations.

He felt he understood her – it was something he'd sensed in the bar of the Hotel Metropole, nurtured on their way up to the sixteenth floor: Birgita was lonely. Birgita – just another person putting in their time working in Den Haag, lonely enough to wander around the museums on the weekend or take in the kitsch aesthetic at Scheveningen. Lonely enough to make their way over to the bar of the Hotel Metropole on a Friday night. As lonely as he was. The loneliness wasn't sad or poignant, but it defined her to Patrick, so that when she slipped her sweater over her head, arms held up in mid-undress, making the shape of a victory V tilting one way, and then the other, she wasn't Birgita at all as much as a lonely woman undressing in front of a lonely man.

She pushed him back on the bed and giggled. They were refugees, come all the way to the same room at the Hotel Metropole in Den Haag, here to witness terrible things that normal people did. He kissed her on the neck and felt the weight of her on him and it seemed like the overture to nothing more than a few hours of comradely solace, something diverting and sustaining at the same time. He imagined trysts in the darkened recesses of London tube stations during the Blitz, the expressions of mutual need, the solidarity of loneliness.

But after that, as she swivelled her shoulders out of the last of her clothes and they were both naked for the first time, Birgita didn't look lonely any more. She smiled and the whole nature of her smile was different and although it was dark and he'd had some scotch, he could see it wasn't a look of loneliness or commiseration or even appetite. It was pity.

She was being *nice*. It angered him in the most invigorating way. He hadn't realized it at first, but thinking of Birgita as some sort of kindred spirit and having images of her lonely life spool out in front of him as she came close *was* too sad and poignant. But then the look on her face turned into an insult, and she was different now.

Birgita, touching her; all he could think about was how anger freed him. It changed the way he thought of her, his intent, his desire, and yet she was still there, oblivious to what had just happened inside him. He kissed her and searched her face for further traces of pity. He found it, or imagined it there enough that he could feel what he needed to feel. Patrick wanted to put on the light again, to see her face more clearly. But other thoughts came to him, first in slow sequence but soon a torrent. Patrick imagined Hernan in that room at Lepaterique, trying to understand what he saw when he looked into the eyes of the detainees. Fernandez's eyes. What was his intent? Was it a type of love that Hernan felt bringing them back from death, or the opposite? He had watched Hernan tend to a dying man, nothing that he'd witnessed had changed, and yet what Patrick had once found heroic now terrified him.

A stab of pain in his head made him wince. He squinted at Birgita as it passed and in the gloom she looked beautiful again, she was Birgita again, and nothing was complicated. Fernandez had vanished and any pity he'd seen on her face, if it had been there at all, was a memory. He apologized. He was a little messed up, he said.

Birgita was gone now. She must have left sometime in the night. He could see her in her apartment, making toast for herself and maybe thinking she should have stayed home last night. Maybe she would speak to her mother or one of her brothers but she wouldn't say a word about how she'd spent her evening.

He opened his computer to find remarkably few messages in his inbox. Nothing from Sanjay. One message from

Marc-André. This was good, he thought, looking at the empty space, maybe Sanjay had figured it out, after all.

11.14   from: Dumont, MA ma.dumont@neuronaut.com
          re: Urgent/ death of Neuronaut

Asshole.

Bancroft and Sanjay are gone, not even on the premises.
The nephew went back to Minnesota and now The
Olafson Brothers are coming, personally, tomorrow
at noon. It's me with the CEOs. And their lawyers. I
have nothing.

If you don't do something, I will tell Globomart
whatever I think is necessary to make them happy. I will
tell them we re-modelled the data. I will tell them you
are dead. Whatever it takes. I will not let you take us down

MAD

11.14   to: ma.dumont@neuronaut.com
          re: re: Urgent/ death of Neuronaut

Don't tell them anything until I get a chance to see
the data.

Where is the data? Where is Sanjay?

You are overreacting. And before you send another email
like this, you should remember who you're talking to.

mpl

It was like speaking to children, and the only comfort, until
now, was that his colleagues lacked the sophistication to be
devious. Over and over, he had explained to them it was a

matter of analyzing the data. The answer was there, they just needed a little time and expertise to find it. He wondered if Bancroft was trying to coax Sanjay through it, a new-age *sensei* letting his young ward find his confidence in the crisis. Patrick had been through moments like this, the crunch of time and numbers, and he was nostalgic for those times, when he had the information at his disposal and it was a matter of making sense of it. He could imagine an all-nighter, just him and the data, knowing something interesting would come of it, knowing he could make it work. Other than designing a study, it was the moment he enjoyed most. Surprisingly, he felt a few sparks of excitement thinking about the problems at Neuronaut, and fanned by the righteous indignation he felt at Marc-André's threats, it all amounted to something he hadn't felt in months. Neuronaut was his and his alone. They needed him. They were falling apart without him. He lay down on the bed, savouring the feeling, its warm narcotic ache. It was a melancholy he imagined only people who've fled could attest to, the reverie of exiled princes and runaways. He would help them, he told himself, as he closed his eyes and the Den Haag morning pressed him deeper into the bed. Yes, he would do the right thing. Once he had the data.

FIFTEEN

Patrick awoke to a room the colour of eggshells. He looked at the clock and saw it was later than he'd thought. From the vantage point of his pillow, his gaze wandered the empty room until it settled on the books on his bedside table – *Moby-Dick* on top, where Birgita had left it, as if placed there in an attempt to contain the psychic biohazard of *The Angel of Lepaterique* beneath it. He pulled out the bottom book and opened it randomly, always surprised by the density of grief inside, how every page contained its own psalm of minor catastrophes.

At approximately 9:30 on the evening of June 28, 1983, Lieutenant Hector Gonzalez called García into room 14 to attend to a detainee. It was García's first day at Lepaterique in more than three weeks, and log entries from various buildings at the INDUMIL complex suggest that it had been an exceptionally busy day. Interrogation of detainees arrested the previous night was being carried out simultaneously and García was called from one holding cell to another, often travelling between the buildings on the compound.

Hector Gonzalez – interviewed at his home in Columbia, South Carolina, five months prior to his death in 2003 – had been stationed as a guard at Lepaterique since September of 1982 and recognized García from his frequent visits.

"The doctor came in and asked the guards (JLB, AH) to move back from the prisoner and he went down to his knees to look at the man – he was a boy, really – who was lying on the floor, chained by one arm to the wall. He'd been very badly beaten. His face was swollen and bloody, and his back and arms were covered in bruises. I asked the doctor if he needed anything and he said no, but could we release the man's arm from the shackle. I looked at the interrogators and they said they didn't care but none of us had the key, so it took a few minutes to get the prisoner out.

"The doctor had his bag open and he was listening to the boy's chest. The doctor turned to me and asked me to get 'the cart' right away, so I went to building 2 where it was kept. When I got back he was pushing on the prisoner's chest and then he used the electrical paddles to shock him and I guess his heart began beating again. It took another twenty minutes for the boy to wake up and the doctor looked relieved and began packing up his equipment in that black bag of his. The interrogators were still there, I remember that. The boy, he had his hands free now, made a motion for the doctor to come closer to tell him something. He could barely speak and so the doctor put his face next to the boy's face as he whispered.

"The doctor just looked at the boy. He was shocked, you could tell. I heard the shouting. I thought it was the boy but it was the doctor. He was shouting 'Who is this man?' and 'I demand to know who he is.' And the interrogators took the doctor outside, it was a scene, really a scene. There was a scuffle because the doctor did not want to leave until he knew the boy's name. I had to leave soon after. I never saw either one again."

With this interview, a line was drawn from the boy on the floor, José-Maria Fernandez, to Patrick Lazerenko. Even though one man was already dead and the other unaware, at least at first, they had been connected for twenty years, according to Elyse Brenman. Elyse went so far as to index her hypothesis in *The Angel of Lepaterique*:

Fernandez, José-Maria: Lazerenko, M. Patrick and, 230, 231, 252–54

Patrick imagined Elyse's interest being piqued when she found out that Hernan had influenced another young man after he left Honduras, just as he could see her falling to her knees in thanks when she discovered that the young man had gone on to become a doctor. Ah, the protegé; other than the diary or sheaves of indiscriminately written correspondence, was there a more generous, unexpected gift to the biographer? The protegé as defender, as betrayer, as surrogate. Universal foil. Elyse, even he would admit, did fantastically well with this biographical device, strapping it on for a headlong rush into a psychological inquiry of the entire García clan. In her analysis, Patrick, simply put, was a project of Hernan's repentance, his way of making amends for what he realized he had done to Fernandez, little more than a child, a colleague in the making, his most personal violation of an oath. The mere facts of Patrick's life – that he worked for and befriended the Garcías, that he had fallen in love with Celia, that he had decided to become a doctor – were all preordained, according to Elyse, all Hernan's doing.

It was ingenious and psychologically nuanced and it made for compelling reading, but in this equation Patrick was nothing more than a pawn. With her formulation, Elyse

Brenman had cast doubt on many of the happier moments and relationships of his life, essentially challenging his role in it. He knew he shouldn't care. Happy is happy, and if a person had a few days, never mind a few years of happiness, it was more than several billion other people got.

Growing up disengaged from his parents, Patrick had been prone to the common childhood fantasy of imagining he'd secretly been adopted; he understood the attraction of creating an alternative life story. How it could frighten and invigorate at the same time. But it was different to have a biography imposed on you. Elyse had done that. What started out as second-rate psychologizing began to make sense to Patrick; the dead man's story had credence and soon it was part of him, inside him and declaring itself like a sore leg that still needed to be used for walking. It was enough to keep Patrick awake at night, running through an inventory of memories for examples of kindness that were now something else entirely.

I was Fernandez: it was the thought that complicated everything for Patrick. It cast doubt on Hernan's motives at the same time it explained his actions. A monster seeking forgiveness. Every act of generosity became a repayment of a debt, and Patrick was nothing in this equation except a vehicle of possible redemption, a walk-on playing the ghost of Fernandez.

Was it there, in the alley behind Le Dépanneur Mondial, that Hernan first saw the possibility in him? On that May night, was it the darkness and the threat of violence, the startled face of a boy that made Fernandez come to mind, the recognition of the debt owed? Or was it when he saw the boy was eager and impressionable, and would be deeply affected by his stories of the nobility of a life in medicine? Patrick wondered if he'd disappointed Hernan, been less of a student than Fernandez, failed in those ways expected when one is measured against a ghost. He put the book back on the bedside table.

The weekend. Two full days with no tribunal. Respite was elusive. He had wanted a break and now that it had come, the thought of not having the comfort of other people around him made him count the hours to the start of the next session. The room was silent. The entire hotel would be quiet. The Metropole was a business hotel, and once the work week was over it would be abandoned except for a skeleton staff and castaways like him. On occasions like this, without a companion or family to defuse the aura of the stranded traveller, he had been treated by the staff with particular kindness, almost solicitude, which he attributed to either their need to keep busy or his inability to disguise his loneliness. Patrick had the feeling the Metropole was different, and that except for Edwin and his deputies searching him out, he could have stayed in his room, in bed, all weekend without inquiries. He rolled onto his side and sat up.

It would be hours before North America woke up, before Sanjay would think to send him data, so he didn't bother with his computer. He didn't want to listen to music, and the television, well, the television never helped. So he dressed, poking his still tender head out of his sweater with all the élan of a drugged tortoise. Then the rest of his clothes, scattered on the ground in random hillocks after last night, none of them any less daunting than the sweater, each an affront to his desire to just lie back down and sleep. But there was a possibility that some of the Garcías were waiting for him, and so he got ready, and by the time he was out in the hallway he felt almost normal again. He should be happy. He was going to the beach.

Those first months after reading Elyse's book, he wondered why Hernan needed *him*, why he couldn't have used Roberto to fulfill his debt to Fernandez. But it was impossible to re-invent your own son for such a purpose, a burden worse than calling him junior, a feat that needed twelve disciples and some spare lumber and nails. No, it needed someone new. Patrick realized this, that he may have been nothing more than in the right place at the right time, the opportunity for Hernan to redeem himself.

But being a surrogate for José-Maria Fernandez didn't explain everything. It couldn't. Celia had loved him. Yes, Elyse had made the case that Hernan's actions could be explained by Fernandez, but not Celia's. She was his daughter, and she deferred to him, but it was crazy to think that Hernan could exert that type of influence over her, to convince her that she felt that way about Patrick. Patrick refused the thought, but it crept up on him in the darkness sometimes, abetted by a lingering sense of inferiority that shadowed every memory from adolescence. What was Celia doing there in his bedroom that night? Why did she come to him? Patrick remembered the shocking ease with which he allowed himself to forget what was going on downstairs at his father's wake, how quickly he said that he loved her. The next thought was amazement that grief could be so capsized, and that any emotion could be so beyond his control. She could kill me like this, he thought, even at the time. She could walk away and he would return to being unhappy. They lay in his bed and held each other and nothing else existed. But since Elyse's book, every memory of the Garcías had been revised, and what troubled Patrick, as much as thoughts of Hernan's motives, as much as Fernandez stalking every memory, was the memory of Celia appearing that night, appearing in his room like a second-rate adolescent fantasy. What had made her come up to his room? He wanted to believe it had been her desire that made her climb the stairs, but he was no longer sure. There had been two of them alone in a room, and everything that came from that – contact, a confession, and the explicit understanding of power – now had the possibility of meaning something else.

He and Celia had spent a few weeks that autumn meeting secretly at places downtown; he told himself they were enjoying the novelty of each other, that it was fair to keep it to themselves. But he knew they both sensed the delicacy of the situation. They talked for hours in the protective shell of public spaces. In a coffee shop on Park Avenue Celia told him how she had liked him since he had come to their house that first time for dinner, but that he'd always seemed so unhappy, an observation that stung him at first – who in their right mind would want to be with anyone they perceived as *unhappy*? – but which he took with the good humour of a man of newly reformed moods. In the library of the medical school he admitted to her that school bored him and that he didn't know if he'd made the right choice. From cafés and restaurants, they graduated to sneaking into his bedroom when his mother was out at Catholic Women's League meetings. After a month, Celia finally suggested that he come to dinner. Her parents needed to know.

He had spent three years avoiding the family and Le Dépanneur Mondial, and now he was prepared for a certain amount of wariness, even hostility from the Garcías, especially from Hernan. It was normal. No longer the stock boy. No more Mopito. Someone else entirely. The fathers of any of the other girls he'd dated might profess indifference or resignation, but they always looked upon a boyfriend as a particular species of thief. He expected no different with Hernan.

But, in the end, he felt more welcomed in the García house than before. Hernan beamed that first time Celia brought Patrick for dinner. Marta looked happy and as in command of her family as she was of the pots that steamed in the kitchen. Nina held his hand and smiled at him. He had missed them. Even Roberto seemed to declare a truce, as though acknowledging Patrick had outlasted the statute of limitations on brotherly hostility. It was almost too easy. If they had concerns about his intentions toward Celia – and they had every right to; along with being in love with her, he was deeply committed to trying to get her into bed as often as possible – they kept these concerns to themselves. No one was *that* likeable or trustworthy. He certainly wasn't.

All this was complicated by the fact of his father's death, as Patrick felt the need to recommit himself to his mother, thinking that his presence in the house, and her life, would now be vital. He imagined the house would take on an air of permanent grief, where he'd be made to feel his presence was never more than a partial, always inadequate patronage. But he was wrong. His mother proved remarkably resilient, no tears or recriminations, with a social schedule far busier than before and the Catholic Women's League and its surprisingly fractious membership eating up her time. Patrick's sisters were around more, and their children, now teenagers, one of whom could invariably be found sprawled on the couch, gave the house on Hingston the feel more of a hostel than a funeral home. In those first months, he even heard her talk of travel – the usual Irish Catholic tourist hot spots: the Vatican, Lourdes, maybe even Ireland, but they had drugs and crime and everyone was crazy with mobile phones, she said, and that would have put her in a mood. No, she was fine, he had to admit. Grief counsellors dispatched by the parish were given tea and cookies and sent on their way.

So Patrick reasoned that introducing Celia to her as his girlfriend, which he had avoided doing for months, would be far less fraught than he first considered. His mother would accept – no, embrace – this change in his life with her newfound equanimity. This was, of course, another miscalculation – he now understood that the more difficult moments in the first thirty-five years of his life were best chalked up to an unremitting dyslexia for women's moods; more proof in the look on his mother's face that first night with Celia at dinner – flickers of pained acceptance amid a larger motif of stoic resolve – suggesting that her only recourse to the appearance of this young woman, who was going to distract her son and ruin his chances, was to convene another wake.

He found respite at the Garcías. Hernan seemed to take genuine pleasure in overseeing his studies, leafing through the textbooks when Patrick wasn't using them, excited and at the same time a little depressed that medicine was continuing to advance without him in its ranks. It didn't take long for Patrick to realize that their relationship had changed in a fundamental way; they now shared an experience, and their conversations began falling into a routine of shop talk and collegial teasing that came to exclude the rest of the family. Patrick felt able to speak freely about his frustrations – he was deep into January of his first year, mired in notes about metabolic pathways and genetic disorders, and his motivations for choosing medicine seemed vague and half-hearted – and Hernan would manage to say something that reassured him. And with every admission of doubt or uncertainty, Patrick sensed he was drawing Hernan into thinking about the life he'd left behind. Maybe it was that detachment, the fact that Hernan was no longer a physician, that allowed him to speak about medicine in a way that Patrick had never heard from anyone else. His words were too modest to be a sermon, too influenced by experience and loss to be a platitude. Medicine gave you a way into someone's life with the sole purpose of doing good, and there weren't many opportunities in life to do that, Hernan would say. Immersed in a community of doctors and students, it was easy for Patrick to consider medicine as nothing more than a vast mountain of knowledge to be scaled or as a job that simultaneously challenged and frustrated, but listening to Hernan talk about it was to hear a man who espoused no religion talk about righteousness, pragmatic and applied. But he'd also discovered that having this relationship with Hernan was more complicated. There were occasions, usually when discussing a topic that had undergone major change in the years since Hernan left medicine, when Patrick happened to correct Hernan. Patrick would do it innocently, offhandedly contradicting something Hernan had said, and he found that Hernan's tone would change. Hernan would become unusually argumentative, quizzing Patrick with an uncharacteristic vigour. Then came silence. At first, Patrick didn't think of these sulks as anything more than flashes of bad mood in an otherwise stalwart character; nevertheless, he still found himself doing everything to avoid these moments, not understanding his own unease at seeing this new side to Hernan.

Down the elevator and past the sentry at the desk – not Edwin this time, someone Patrick didn't recognize – then the lobby full of echoes to the more definite assault of the outside world's noises and lights. He squinted against the daylight, glad he had only one eye that needed squeezing shut. It was cooler than the previous days, but still unseasonably warm and the sky was blue and cloudless. He worried it was just the sort of day to send the Dutch flocking to the beaches at Scheveningen.

It had been Hernan who had shown him how to examine someone, that the examination began long before the patient entered the room. Watch the way they rise from their seat, the way they carry themselves, he would say, watch how it reveals. Hernan was the one who taught him how to look in ears and hold a reflex hammer. The first heart he'd listened to after unwrapping his stethoscope was Hernan's. Hernan had told Patrick to put the earpieces in and – after twisting his hand to indicate that his protegé had put them in backwards – he took the head of the stethoscope between his two fingers and plunged it down under his shirt. "Listen," he said, his arm deep inside the shirt, his hand nearing his armpit. "The mitral valve." And Patrick heard it, the dull sound of two doors closing, the first a fraction louder. A guided tour then began, with Hernan occasionally listening himself to ensure he was in the right position before handing the earpieces back to Patrick. "Close your eyes," he said, "and try to imagine the blood moving." He tried, but the sounds were all the same, still only of doors closing. The tricuspid valve came next before Hernan moved the head of the stethoscope to an area at the base of his neck. "Now," he said, "the aortic valve." Patrick tried to look interested for Hernan's sake, as he was clearly enjoying himself. Patrick listened: lub-dub, lub-dub. Indistinguishable from the heart sounds heard elsewhere. Then, Hernan lifted a finger and mouthed the word "Listen." He clamped his lips shut and then strained forcefully, his colour changing as seconds passed. He looked at Patrick expectantly. Patrick didn't know what to make of it until he heard something different, two things really, the second heart sound become fainter, an echo of its previous self, and a whooshing sound, a low rumble that rose in pitch and intensity as though it was a truck barrelling past on the highway. He looked up at Hernan to find him pale, a shade that even then he knew meant a person was in danger of passing out. Hernan almost fell forward into him before righting himself. He slumped back into his chair, hyper-ventilating, his colour now returning, his forehead wet with perspiration. Hernan smiled as if he'd just performed a magic trick and took the head of the stethoscope out from under his shirt. Patrick remembered being mystified at the whole spectacle and embarrassed that he didn't understand the point of the demonstration.

In all the time he had known the Garcías, Patrick had tried, unsuccessfully, to get any of them to tell him what their life had been like before Le Dépanneur Mondial. No one spoke of Honduras, and other than Marta's reminiscences of Detroit, none of the Garcías had spoken about Hernan's work. And so Patrick was left to wonder why Hernan García left Tegucigalpa and his life as a doctor. He had gathered a rough under-standing of the politics of the region, and he'd learned enough to know that it was just the sort of place that people were forced to leave in the middle of the night. In that context, it wasn't difficult to imagine Hernan as a hero. A dedicated man forced to leave the job he loved for speaking out against an injustice or because he'd rubbed some generalissimo the wrong way. And so he had to leave, to protect his family, filing away a career, a vocation, as though it were just another job experience. That was why nobody spoke of it, he decided. His family understood the injustice.

In other ways, Patrick had become Hernan's confidant. As a medical student, he had reopened a world for Hernan, offering access to all that Hernan had lost. Patrick re-introduced medical textbooks to the García household, unwittingly restarted conversations that had gone silent years before. He and Hernan were now colleagues, and as someone partially indoctrinated into medical life, Patrick felt he could understand Hernan in a way that no one else could. That spring, Hernan began to tell Patrick about the people who had continued to come to Le Dépanneur Mondial looking for a medical opinion. These were snippets of conversation at first, offered with hesitation, as though testing Patrick to see how they would be received. It didn't take long for Hernan to realize that he had an eager audience. They were usually illegal immigrants, Salvadorans and Peruvians mostly, people who had heard that he could help and who would wait until the store was empty before approaching him at the cash. He related the stories to Patrick, listing the details that led him to a diagnosis as the person spoke to him from across the counter or beside the canned vegetables. He was proud, Patrick could tell, but it wasn't pride as simple boastfulness at having made a diagnosis (without any diagnostic equipment or tests), but rather something that seemed at first to be selfless: a pride in being part of people's lives, a pride in his ability to help.

The streets were movie-set empty, not even a stray Den Haagenar to add some colour as an extra. Patrick checked his watch: he was late, but there wasn't a cab in sight and to jog would be to pull the pin on what he knew would be a grenade of a headache. An empty tram glided down Johan de Wittlaan, and he thought of Birgita again, wondering how she had got back home. He thought she'd stay the night, not because he'd had any expectations of her, but because she'd fallen asleep. He'd got up in the dark to use the washroom and found her still there, sleeping beside him. He tried not to wake her. He remembered stepping over her bra on the floor, his foot brushing against the underwire. She was sleeping, breathing shallowly. He got under the covers and felt her shiver as he moved close to her. He thought she'd be there in the morning and couldn't imagine her getting up in the middle of the night to leave.

Another tram passed in the opposite direction, bound for the city centre with four or five passengers aboard. All staring straight ahead.

In reacquainting himself with the Garcías, Patrick had begun to understand the scope of Hernan's practice, how it extended beyond the aisles of the store. There had been times in those years when Patrick was at the Garcías' and someone would knock on the door, asking for Hernan by name or just requesting to see "*el doctor.*" Patrick would invariably be studying, books splayed out over the kitchen table, and he fixed his eyes on whatever page of the textbook he was reading as he tried to follow what was going on down the hallway. Then Hernan would lead them – a man or a couple, sometimes an entire family – to one of the back bedrooms and the door would close and stay shut for twenty minutes. Any other García in the house would carry on as though nothing unusual was happening, not even pausing to acknowledge the family of four traipsing through their kitchen as the visitors were led out.

And although he admired Hernan, he also had begun to feel a growing uneasiness that his mentor was acting as a doctor to these people. This was benevolence, Patrick tried to remind himself as another frightened man was ushered into a back room for a quick exam. *These people have nothing.* Hernan was the only one who cared. This was heroic, this was the righteousness that Hernan had expressed to him, the sentiment that helped Patrick through that first year of medical school. And yet, it was wrong, so clearly wrong, even to a student like Patrick.

In hindsight, Patrick's concern was understandable. With each year Patrick gained confidence in his own skills and judgment, and as he began to work with other doctors, Hernan's actions seemed increasingly questionable. Irresponsible. The argument was still there – these people needed help, but why hadn't Hernan just recertified as a doctor? It would have taken years, and even if he passed all the exams and qualified, the government would likely have assigned him to a rural practice. But still, he would have been able to help more fully, more honestly than a man practising out of a back room. Of course, he hadn't known then the reasons for Hernan's secrecy, that for Hernan, the back room was the safest place, the only place.

As terrible as all the accusations of Lepaterique were, Patrick was just as troubled by the secret practice that had taken place all those years ago in the Garcías' duplex on Harvard Street. Why had he been allowed in on that secret? What had Hernan really wanted him to see? A man doing good? A man, though he couldn't have known it, trying to make amends? Patrick, in fact, came to see Hernan not just as a person with formidable skills or heroic intentions, but as a man capable of disregarding the law and, more ominously, as someone whose life as a doctor seemed centred on need, a need as much his as his patients'. Was it a test of Patrick's loyalty? Did he think Patrick would understand?

Despite his misgivings, Patrick had never told Hernan to stop. Never warned him it was wrong and dangerous. He said nothing and Hernan trusted him. Now, all Patrick felt was anger that Hernan had not shielded him from this secret life. A friend, a true colleague, would have spared a novice. But Patrick had not been spared, and in this, Hernan had made him complicit. In a way, Hernan had already tried to make Patrick choose sides.

He walked down Johan de Wittlaan, cool in the mid-morning hotel-fed shadows. He was late and had made a mistake not taking a cab, but he continued with a pace unchanged until he reached Geestbrugweg. There, on the corner, he lifted his hand to shield his face, caught in a rare half-block of sunlight.

SIXTEEN

No one should care that he loved Celia García.

But Elyse cared. He and Celia were together for three years – thirty-eight and one-half months – duly noted by Elyse in her book. Of course, Elyse was most interested in the moment the relationship began – an event rich with inferences to Fernandez and the invisible hand of Hernan guiding the star-crossed lovers, etc. She spent a scant paragraph noting the relationship's fractious conclusion, alluding to the fact that by this time Hernan and Patrick had both "got" what they wanted from each other, and, with surrogacy no longer necessary for either man, the otherwise baseless relationship between Celia and Patrick naturally dissolved. The time in between seemed not to interest Elyse, it being happy and human and lacking the various dramatic or symbolic elements that would otherwise make it worth mentioning in her book.

But he and Celia were happy, at least at the beginning. It wasn't a lie. It was simple, ordinary love. He told himself this repeatedly, almost as if to rebut the continuous, forensic re-examination of their time together that Elyse's book had forced him into, the search for deeper reasons for why two people would willingly share the same space for any period of time. They loved each other; it was a thought that fortified him, a chance occurrence and an assertion of mutual free will in the face of Elyse's theories. No, Hernan had nothing to do with that, nothing to do with them.

The year after his father died, Patrick moved out of his mother's house to a place of his own a couple of blocks from the hospital in the student ghetto – it was Montreal in the depths of a recession. The city had emptied out like a pool after Labour Day and apartments were cheap and available. He found an apartment on the top floor of a greystone that gave evidence of having previously been a single, larger residence gyprocked into smaller rental units, each an illogical warren of rooms. All the furniture he owned filled fewer than half of the rooms, and that's when he had the idea of offering one of them to Celia for studio space.

It made sense. No canvases stacked in her room at home, no Nina coughing away, no need to rent space on some dark street on the Plateau. Not living together, just sharing space. It was his apartment, they both made that clear, but, if she had to stay over, well, that was the artist's prerogative. Again, no objection from Hernan. In the fifteen years that followed, he'd lived through his share of address changes, a succession of place-names where his mail arrived. A new locale every few years, each one convenient, provisional. But Lorne Avenue was different. He had three years there, below Elyse Brenman's radar, finding another place, besides the Garcías' house and Le Dépanneur Mondial, where he experienced moments of perfect happiness.

He could remember no dinner parties with friends, no landlord knocking on the door with the inevitable demand to turn the music down. Celia needed the same things he did – for the apartment to be quiet – and they both found the silence an unexpected bounty. There were days, with both of them working in the apartment, when they wouldn't say a word to each other for hours. A solitude without loneliness, a solitude that came to an end every evening. Was that it? Was love just another word for the rare mixture of compatibility and sex and convenience that seemed effortless? A summer camp sort of commitment, a camaraderie of similar needs and circumstance.

No, he believed it was more than that. She confided in him, telling him how she worried about her mother's moodiness or Roberto's constant fights with her father. He knew how angry she became when people made assumptions about her, how they expected the *Latina* to be fiery and volatile and how they overlooked the precision and effort in her work. No, he knew Celia. There was the smell of her when she would crawl into bed after a night of painting. She would wash but she could never get free of the scent. He would kiss her and the taste stung of solvent, the smell of pigment always there in the dark. Celia was a ritual he observed, never imagining it could be routine, never thinking it could require effort.

As much as any allegiance to Hernan, he understood it was his time with Celia that had brought him to Den Haag. But, by the time he arrived at the *pension*, Patrick was feeling a pincer grasp of panic about having to face her. He hoped she wouldn't come, but he'd presented the invitation in such a way that made it seem like a dare. She'd be coming, he knew it, if only to prove a point. He then had the sudden realization that a day at the beach with Celia was the single most ill-advised idea he'd ever come up with. Their life together was nostalgia. Now he was an imposition. He was not a solace to her, he was not a friend, he was a means to freeing her father. And he was failing at that.

A day with the Garcías, away from the distractions of the tribunal, able to channel their anger – on, say, him – was a depressing thought. And while he had been, up to that point, able to suppress any feelings of guilt about what had happened the night before, he was certain if Celia came she would be able to smell Birgita on him, that scent of betrayal particularly familiar to her. *The beach.* What was he thinking? It made him want to turn around and run back to the Metropole. Everyone was unhappy and at each other's throats and now they were all going to the beach. *Fucking. Brilliant.* Windburn and jellyfish and riptides would be the best they could hope for. At least some terrors promised silence.

When he turned the corner onto Geestbrugweg, Patrick found the García sisters already waiting on the sidewalk in front of their guest *pension.* Paul sat in a stroller, one of those technologically advanced models with metal finishes and big wheels, the type of vehicle he imagined capable, with minimal modification, of sending back images to NASA from the surface of Mars. He never thought he would see Celia push such a contraption. From behind the stroller, Celia watched him. She looked different, relaxed, actually smiling as he neared. He was a weak man, he thought, needing to remind himself of the things she'd said the night before in order not to think that this smile meant détente.

Nina was different too, and he thought it was because she wasn't playing with Paul, or that she was wearing a stylish leather jacket, almost too stylish for the beach. She had her hair pulled up. They looked more like sisters now, enough of a similarity between them to suggest that their beauty was not just an independent occurrence but a variation on a theme. Maybe the beach wouldn't be so bad after all, maybe it was just what they all needed.

"You're coming, then?"

"It's ten-thirty," Celia said.

"Yes, we've been waiting, what, *five* minutes," Nina replied.

"Sorry, I thought I'd walk."

Patrick saw Roberto, standing at the *pension* door, without a jacket on. He wore the look of a panda, a man showing the effects of not sleeping well. Wordlessly, he waved and closed the door. Nina and Celia turned away, their manner telling him not to ask questions. He would have risked a quick look back if he weren't certain that Roberto was in the window. It would have startled them both.

The Dutch sun, prodigal at mid-morning, exerted itself on their backs as they walked past the bare trees that lined the road to Scheveningen. The silence between them was comfortable. Paul sang a little song to himself and that seemed to calm everyone. Whether it was the warmth of the sun, or the camaraderie of strolling together along a road to the beach, his anxiety faded and he felt better than he had in months. Happiness like the first day of a new drug, side effects unknown. Any wariness he had about Celia seemed ridiculous, almost petty. Thoughts of Hernan and Neuronaut and the subpoena – all of it evaporated in the warm Dutch sunshine. The indiscretion with Birgita – not even that; a half-hearted, semi-drunken romp – seemed forgivable, forgettable. It was Holland, after all. For all of the mighty tasks a brain was capable of doing, nothing was as underrated as the ability to forget. He'd met amnesiacs, duly noted the beatific smiles spread across their faces.

He took a mental snapshot of the four of them, walking, smiling, and registered the moment, as if to say that this memory will be tagged in a different way, that this was more valuable to him than any future happiness, any amnesic calm.

He'd never told anyone, but he'd known a contentedness, known its coordinates, as though it were a place that could be located and homed in on and occupied. A GPS to bliss. Saturday, late afternoon, deepest February. He was in the Garcías' kitchen, his books were open on the table, and he had been studying the incredibly complicated things a kidney will do to turn everything into urine. Celia wasn't even in the room (Is that what made this so perfect? The pang?), but captured on a draft from somewhere in the house, he smelled her. The particular scent of linseed and lemon oil, the aroma of the paints she used, an occasional whiff of turpentine. He could hear her, pausing in front of what she was doing. The restless energy as she walked around the room trying to solve something. He never knew there was anything to solve in art. He just thought that people painted what they saw, spilling their talent onto canvas. Celia had shown him, the way she sweated out the composition, the precision a painting demanded at every step of its creation. He heard her sit down and return to work, a dilemma solved. He was happy.

"Are you still exhibiting?" Patrick said to her now. There was a pause that he thought meant no one asked her questions like this any more.

"Paintings? God no, that was a lifetime ago."

"But you still paint."

"I illustrate, I do mostly design work. Some photography and some design."

"You still paint," Nina said, to which Celia turned sharply.

"You do," she repeated.

"I work in an art department. I've done some book covers recently."

He wanted to see what she was painting. He imagined there would be an easel in the middle of the room, maybe the same huge wooden one it took them both to manoeuvre into the spare room of the apartment. He liked to think that he could look at her art and take something from it, that he could understand her that way still. But he wasn't sure.

Farther toward Scheveningen, they passed a series of billboards, one of them a monstrosity that was the universal identifier of Globomart, the European version of their Values campaign. He could tell Celia and Nina that he was responsible for *this*, not its conception but vetting the colour scheme (an orange taken straight from the vest of a road construction crew), the typeface (something called Garamond, which for some reason maximally stimulated the right temporal lobe, which was unexpected but good, very good), and the three strategically placed photos of ecstatic, hyperdental models. No focus groups lying their way through a day of questions, just a monitor flashing design versions and twenty normals in a magnetic resonance machine. Did the ad work? The stroller Celia pushed was a Globomart 2000 limited edition, its provenance branded on one of the aluminum struts that kept her son gliding above the ground. Of course it worked. He knew twenty brains that couldn't say otherwise, and Globomart had sent him cheques testifying to its effect. From hundreds of design permutations, he had midwifed *this*, he could say, lifting his arm up. By this time though, they'd passed the Globomart ad and were in front of another billboard for which he bore no responsibility at all.

It took twenty minutes of easy walking through the empty weekend streets of Den Haag to reach the Strandsweg, the road that ran parallel to the beach in Scheveningen. From behind a wall of houses and shops, the North Sea appeared, a gorgeous, lurid blue, as though a tanker had gone down with its cargo of dye.

"This is beautiful," Nina said, clearly surprised, surveying the empty beach. Celia pulled out a pail and shovel from a large bag she had loaded onto the stroller. The weather was unseasonably warm, but still too cold to consider swimming, and what people there were had confined themselves to the boardwalks. The beach was so deserted that the choice of where to settle paralyzed them, and so they watched the water and the gulls wheeling overhead. They could sit down on the spot or walk on with nothing but sand between them and Germany. Celia freed Paul from his stroller, and he started running across the hard-packed sand, clearly the one to decide where they would put their blankets down.

Celia hurried after her son, arms spread out, assuming that loping, prepared-for-anything stride employed by both parents of toddlers and circus spotters. "I didn't know this was so close," she said, turning back to where Patrick stood with Nina.

"I heard it's packed in the summer," he said, his voice carrying over the sand.

At this thought he recalled Birgita in a flash of guilt and regret, followed by the irrational fear that she would show up, that she was already at the beach. He felt an anticipatory awkwardness imagining the moment when he passed her with the Garcías. He'd introduce her, introduce the Garcías as his friends. Yes, he thought, we're all adults here. He'd tell the Garcías that Birgita was the one who had told him about this place. Celia was shepherding Paul into turning around and heading back toward where he and Nina stood.

"I was surprised you wanted to come along," he said as they neared.

"We needed to do something different," Celia replied. Paul stumbled and crash-landed onto the hard sand, as unforgiving as asphalt. He lifted his palms up and grimaced at his mother, who scooped him up. "Elyse Brenman has been calling."

Celia brushed the sand off Paul's hands, then set him down and looked out at the ocean. A Rothko canvas of complementary blues, sealed at the horizon. Off to the side the pavilion of the Scheveningen pier sat, an undiplomatic curatorial intrusion. The composition must have pleased Celia, though, as she took a large blanket out of the bag hanging on the stroller and unfurled it. It snapped out and hung in mid-air for a moment before floating down to the ground. This was the spot.

"She wanted to interview us. She says she wants to be able to write about it from the family's point of view," Nina offered.

"I'm so glad she cares," Celia muttered, as though to compensate for Nina's total lack of sarcasm. She dumped a bagful of cars and small plastic toys on the blanket.

"She did the same to me," Patrick said in commiseration. "When I got here, she cornered me. She's convinced I know something."

"Did you talk to her?"

"No," he replied, frowning and mentally running through

the transcript of what was said over lunch that Elyse could possibly work into a new García chapter. "It surprised me, though, how much she knew about all of us. About all of you. About your mother. You *do* know I've never spoken to her about any of you, right?"

Celia sat down on the blanket. The sun shone into her face, and she lifted a hand to shield her eyes. Nina glanced over at Celia, who did not make eye contact. Finally, seemingly harried by Nina's gaze, Celia sighed. Nina said: "Roberto spoke to her." Patrick thought he heard the name but couldn't be sure it wasn't the barking of gulls. "He agreed to be interviewed by Elyse Brenman after Mum died," Nina continued, taking off her jacket and laying it out next to the blanket. "He even gave her some of Mum's letters."

"You're *kidding*," Patrick said, trying hard to mute the glee in his voice, concentrating hard on incredulity.

Nina nodded, avid for an ear. "A lot of notes from her thesis and some letters she wrote that her sisters sent back after she died."

"Stop it," Celia said in a monotone of pure exhaustion.

"What, this should be a secret?" Nina asked, and Celia steamed silently, having no rebuttal. "C'mon, Celia, he's trying to help." Paul looked up; like Patrick, he found the sound of sharp words from these two women not directed at him a novelty. "After Mum died, Dad and Roberto didn't get along very well. Roberto talked about taking over the store. They were fighting, non-stop."

"About the store?"

"That too. But Roberto blamed him for Mum's death."

"Elyse started all that nonsense," Celia said.

"Well, it made sense to Roberto."

"Still . . . your mother's letters," Patrick said, studying a little grey toy soldier that looked like it came from the basement of his childhood. The green ones were American, the greys, German. He didn't think you could buy these any more. He remembered their standard poses. This was the one that was about to throw a grenade. Patrick looked up to see Celia and Nina staring at each other. A generation younger than his own two sisters, he nonetheless understood elements of this non-verbal exchange. The glare. The glare deflected.

"It turns out Roberto and Elyse were pretty intimate," Nina said with the seriousness that weapons-grade gossip demanded. This was too much for Celia, who got up and began brushing the sand from the knees of her pants. He remembered Celia asking him not to discuss Hernan's guilt in front of Nina; now the request seemed less ridiculous than calculating. Nina watched her sister, revving up a major huff. "Oh, sit down. Our father is in jail, for God's sake, *for torturing people*. You can't be upset about me telling stuff like this."

Patrick mentally sifted through the evidence in *The Angel of Lepaterique*. He recalled some letters being mentioned in the book, but any pleasure he derived from imagining Elyse fuming over letters full of details about the children's first steps and the weather in Tegucigalpa was muted by thoughts of the photo of Elyse on her boat and the twinge he felt as he considered Roberto taking the picture.

"But he's here with you now," Patrick said.

Nina shook her head, already a veteran of the brotherly misdeeds: "That thing with Elyse was years ago. Years. He didn't see her again after the book came out."

Celia had heard enough. As if wanting a tie-breaking vote, she grabbed Paul by the hand and tried pulling him up to his feet. Having just arrived, the boy plainly didn't want to go, and his agitation and incomprehension coalesced into tearful insubordination. Celia wasn't going to yank him up into her arms, so she was stuck there hovering over him, holding him as the boy let his body slacken, an evasive manoeuvre that to Patrick looked so effective that there must be some Darwinian significance, a survival advantage, to it. The look on Celia's face was indescribable, as she realized she was dangling a crying child, that she was in a state where such an act was defensible and understandable and unavoidable.

"Hey, maybe I should go," Patrick offered. The threat of leaving the two of them alone seemed to have the right effect: Celia stopped with the gestures of imminent departure, and Paul was released, to squirm on the blanket until he was certain no one was going to take him away. Even Nina looked contrite after the skirmish, but there was a satisfaction there too, Patrick could make it out, the thrill of mutinous impulses publicly displayed.

"Stay," Nina said.

Celia turned away from her son to face Patrick. "Do you have anything else to do?"

"No."

"Then stay. It's fine."

Patrick grabbed a miniature soccer ball from the debris field of toys emptied onto the blanket and tossed it onto the sand, gesturing to Paul to come and play. This was the extent of his peacemaking efforts, he thought: remove the innocent child from between the sniping sisters. Let them fight it out or finish off their glare-down. For the good deed, his head gave a salutary throb. Paul grabbed the ball from the sand, looked at Patrick and cocked his arm, something Patrick was ready to play along with in a limited way, more than willing to point to his head as a mitigating factor. Then the little boy looked at the ball and smiled; not an *en-passant*, thanks-for-holding-the-door-open smile either – but a sunrise of a smile, like he had never seen a ball like this or any other ball before. An ecstatic smile. To Patrick the smile was a marvel, less for what it demonstrated about the boy – he was, after all, a boy with a ball at the beach – than for what it did to him. The smile infected Patrick and he smiled too, broadly, a lunatic grin. The pain of the smile was profound and delicious and Patrick could feel it doing something to him, acting on him in some way that kept the smile on his face, a smile that Paul was now responding to with an even broader smile, a positive feedback loop, an escalation in the rictal arms race. Paul laughed, the unhinged mad scientist squeal-and-howl combo, a laugh that caused Celia to look over.

With Celia watching the two of them and smiling herself, he felt something stir, the furnace of Pavlovian response being stoked within him. He wanted to protect the boy. He wanted Celia. The boy needed a father. *He* could be the boy's father. They could all be together. *Jesus.* The blithe intensity of the feeling shocked him, it must be innate, buried deep and waiting to be trip-wired by the appropriate child-and-female stimuli. Maybe if Roberto were here, he'd feel less of the default alpha male, but Roberto was nowhere in sight and Patrick knew if he had plumage, it would be preened and fully fanned. He was thankful he had enough functioning frontal lobe to prevent him from dropping to one knee for a quick Dutch proposal or saying something even more ridiculous. Then, as quickly as it came, the sentiment passed, as if acknowledging that any resolution made on a beach carried the same weight as a Las Vegas wedding vow or a campaign promise. This was not his child, he remembered; and, well, Celia didn't like him.

They rolled the ball back and forth until Paul grabbed it and tomahawked it off the sand and down the tarmac flats of Scheveningen beach. Nina got up to chase after the ball and threw it back. The recent sweep of paternal plumage aside, Patrick was never one for children. The sole benefit of being so much younger than his sisters was being almost the same age as his nieces and nephews and therefore spared the indignities of uncledom. No sitcom attempts at babysitting, no inevitable uncle categorization as creepy rogue or charmless loser. It occurred to him that as an adult, outside the setting of a mandatory medical-school rotation in Pediatrics, he'd never actually seen a child this close up. They were fascinating. A frontal lobe still in the process of developing, not yet capable of reining in behaviour. A little Gage who would outgrow his tantrums.

Suddenly Patrick felt drained, and he sat down. It took seconds for him to remember that sitting was simply not a natural posture at the beach and he stretched out on the edge of the blanket. The sand was neither cool nor warm in the late morning sunshine. But the sun was warm on his face, and soon random, unclaimed images carouselled by him as he began to doze. A flash of Birgita's face. His old office at the university. His mother sitting at the kitchen table doing a crossword. The antidepressant he had been taking was lighter fluid to the dreams, breathing a vivid heat into them. A park in the middle of summer, municipal park green, serotonin intense. Next, the face of Hernan, draining of colour, looking at him with all the hopeless expectation of a teacher who has placed too much importance on a certain lesson being learned. Hernan was in the tribunal's booth, but Patrick was much closer than his usual seat in the gallery, next to him really, sensing something wrong. The tube of a stethoscope connected them. From that to a tunnel he remembered from Schiphol Airport, a moving sidewalk and fluorescent lights so dim it seemed the overcast sky had moved indoors to provide a more uniform distribution of weather woe. Through it all he felt the warmth, the animal comfort of warmth like a blanket pulled up over his shoulders. He shuddered awake to the sound of Nina talking. A hand to her head, cradling a phone. It used to be so comforting to listen to people talking to themselves, you knew they were crazy. Nina said goodbye in a singsong to someone half a world away. A different voice entirely. No produce being rerouted. Celia and Paul had disappeared from the blanket and were halfway to the water's edge, the child plough-horse-pulling her there.

"You clear things up with your sister?"

"Yeah, we're fine."

"So," Patrick said sitting up and trying not to make old man grunting noises, "you're running the store. I'm impressed."

"If I can turn it around, it'll be a miracle."

"I went in a while back, when I was in town. I liked the expansion."

"That was Roberto's decision, not mine. It put us in a difficult position; too big to be the friendly corner dep, still too small to have a hope of competing with the chains."

"It looked prosperous enough."

Nina smiled. "It's getting there. There was a drop in business after all this with my dad came out in the news. But the neighbourhood is doing well, that's been the most important factor."

She flipped open her phone again, checked a text message, grinned, and thumbed in a response. She closed the little clamshell and put it in her pocket.

"Celia told me that you still think Hernan is innocent," Patrick announced.

"She's projecting." *Projecting.* The last time he'd spoken to Nina alone she wore a retainer and had posters of non-threatening boy bands on her bedroom wall.

"You think?"

"You saw how she reacted just now," Nina said. "She gives this impression of being so together, but at the core, she has so much invested in him, in getting him out." Patrick squinted at her through his better eye. She was a shadow with the late morning sun behind her, haloing her. He caught a glimpse of the sun and turned away, looking into the blue sky over the pier, and the sun persisted in flashbulb footsteps across the horizon. "As for me, guilty or not, you fight. That's what upsets me most, the silence stuff. We all come over here to support him, to fight for him, and he won't even speak to *us*."

"I asked di Costini what he thought – "

"Don't mention that loser to me. Sometimes I think he's happy Dad's not speaking."

"He's trying his best."

Nina let out a sarcastic snort.

"If it weren't for Caesar Oliveira, my father would be convicted already."

"You're not worried about Oliveira?"

"Why should I be worried?"

"Roberto thinks that – "

"A person could get rich betting against my brother."

"I don't know this Oliveira, but I look at the Democratic Voice, I look at what they do, and it worries me."

Nina listened but made no effort to conceal her displeasure at what he was saying. He tried to remember what he'd read about the group, the names of former congressmen who worked for it, but the details were escaping him. "They supported using Guantanamo for interrogations, and I read they were behind those protests in Venezuela."

"I didn't know you were political, Mopito," she said, laughing, and it was because he never considered himself political, always thought of himself as somehow above politics, that the words felt like an insult.

"Your mother wouldn't have wanted them involved."

"Well, my mother is dead. And you know what?" Nina continued, as though she didn't want to give him the time to apologize. "I'd be worried about their motives if we had our choice of supporters, but we don't. They're it. The Canadian government washed its hands of us and you can imagine the Honduran community. The Democratic Voice found those witnesses, not di Costini. The Democratic Voice saved our store from bankruptcy and paid our way here and they're the only ones who are trying to figure out where Dad will be able to go once this is over."

"Do you mean if he's acquitted?"

"Well, that too, but also if he's convicted. They'll have to find a country that'll accept him. If not, he stays in Holland. That's what Oliveira said."

"Did you meet with him too, yesterday?"

Nina paused. She was no stranger to making blunt appraisals of value, and Patrick felt her weighing the question.

"No."

Fifty yards away, Celia and Paul had become indistinct in the glare off the sand.

"For a long time I felt guilty about not calling."

"What?"

"I didn't call when he was accused of all this. I wrote him a letter after Marta died, but I didn't, you know, give him my support. I feel like I betrayed him."

"There wasn't much you could have said."

"How did he deal with it?"

"Dad? He dealt with it pretty much as you'd expect. He got a lawyer. I was the only one living at home with them and nobody ever said much about it. Isn't that weird? I mean, how sick is that? Everyone is so up in arms about him not talking, but he never talked, never explained himself to any of us. But Mum waited for his explanation. She pleaded with him for months. But he still didn't say anything. And after that, things got worse, Mum got depressed and I was freaking out, but when Celia came back from Toronto it was better, it was almost normal, and it was like we all concentrated on Mum getting better. She just wanted to stay in her room, she wanted nothing except her books. For a while it was like we could avoid even thinking about it. We just kept going. Then, one day, after another article in the newspaper, he sat Celia and me down and told us that the situation in Honduras was complicated but that the story would eventually come out. He asked us to be patient, he told us that we'd all get through this. I remember that word. *Patient*. Even back then I thought, oh boy, this isn't going to turn out well. That was a month before Mum died."

"And Celia stayed."

Nina nodded. "I'm probably to blame for that. My father wasn't saying much, as usual, and Roberto was angry after

Mum died and they started fighting. I needed Celia. It was either I go to Toronto or she stay in Montreal. And if I went, the store would close."

"Is Celia happy?"

Nina looked off in the direction of her sister, shoes off and toeing the liquid edge of the North Sea.

"Dad's in jail. We're in Holland. It's November. Not the recipe for happiness."

"But before all this. Has she been with Paul's father for a long time?"

"She told me not to talk about that with you."

He was pleasantly appalled that Celia had even thought about it.

"Get out."

"No, really. She called you insidious."

"Tell me about Paul's father," Patrick urged, but Nina was a sphinx. "What's everyone so paranoid about? I see you people every ten years. I live in another country. It's natural to want to know what you people are up to."

Nina looked at him. "You didn't ask who I was seeing. Or Roberto."

"I need to take a bath after what you told me about Roberto. And I saw you sending text-messages. But I was being discreet, you know, you're still in your formative years," he teased.

"Pfft. Like you care," she said and smiled. "She was with Steven for three years."

Any pleasure he felt with the past tense soured with mention of the name. *Steven.* An open audition for the part of Steven was called in Patrick's mind. The truth was he had ego enough to allow only permutations of himself, allowing for minor improvements in looks or disposition. Steven, the sensitive boy, pallid and occasionally morose, less a personality than a series of affectations. Well, maybe that was too close. Stevo, then, the polar opposite: purveyor of good moods and possessor of a physique straight from the rugby scrum. Untroubled by doubts or deep thought and no match for her. Then came the brooding visionary Stefan, disdainful of any art form less painful than German expressionist cinema, lowering himself to associate with a commercial artist. Patrick hated them all.

"I'm going for a walk," Patrick said, and Nina just nodded, sunflowering to catch the warmth.

He tried to get up from his seated position in one motion but felt dizzy and so he opted for the staged ascent, leaning to one side and using an arm as a support to get him to a steadier tripod stance and then to his feet. He brushed the sand off and looked around. Behind them, a grand, old-fashioned hotel with a complicated-looking red-tile roof occupied most of the prime real estate on the other side of the Strandweg.

It wasn't far to Der Pier. A small staircase climb from the Strandweg. From the top, it was easier to appreciate the height of the bluffs that backed the beach and the vast expanse of sand to the west. Behind him, he found the hotel he'd seen in the guidebook, the Kurhaus. In the November sunshine it looked like an abandoned temple, an Angkor Wat of beach life. He continued walking on the pier, the North Sea visible below, from this angle a grey slate floor, freshly washed and scattering sudsy foam.

He was surprised by how painful it still was to think about Celia with someone else. He knew this was all nothing more than the conceit of the former boyfriend, that it was only a short dip in emotional maturity to the degenerative sphere of plaintively themed tattoos or drunken, wordless telephone calls in the middle of the night. And while he never expected Celia to resign herself to spinsterhood or wander through the rest of her life mumbling like a shattered Ophelia, the thought of her getting over him, being happy with someone else, seemed to be the most complete form of vengeance. He had no right. She'd say that to him if they were alone. He'd given up any right to even think about her in that way ten years ago.

It would have been easier on him if his relationship with Celia had ended differently. He would have preferred a seismic argument or a parting that followed on the heels of a long-simmering philosophical disagreement. That way, he could have kept believing they were incompatible and the end was coming sooner or later. But they never fought. They were content. Celia spoke in vague terms about going to New York, just as he did about applying for a residency in Boston, and it all seemed so adult, so sophisticated.

Patrick reasoned that for Celia, living in a house with all those voices – Nina now eleven, Roberto still taking pleasure in baiting her – his apartment, with its silence and further freedom not to have to say anything, was a relief. Silence meant no argument, no dissenting voice. No ultimatum. He grew used to Celia being in the apartment, more conscious of her absences, something that he hated about himself, something he promised wouldn't happen. She would stay with him for days and then go back to Harvard Street for a week, without explanation, then he would come home to find her painting in the back room again. He'd asked her to move in permanently, she was already there incrementally, her paints were there, he said. But she said no.

She painted and he studied and there was silence (a *García* silence, he later told himself, although he was responsible for it too). As the time approached for him to make plans about Boston, first the tentative steps of applications and interviews, followed by the irrevocable decisions about visa applications and deposits on new apartments, he grew frustrated with Celia for the silences, for neither of them having any intervening words. And while he could have said something, simply sat down with her and demanded they clarify how they felt and how they were going to negotiate the next five years in their lives, that would have meant him declaring his need for her. It would have meant risking Celia telling him that nothing had really changed since that first day in Le Dépanneur Mondial, that the need wasn't mutual.

Patrick hadn't slept the night before it ended with Celia It hadn't been some long dark night of the soul; instead, like any fourth-year student going through a surgery rotation, he'd been up all night as a third assistant in the OR, getting a good view of the surgical resident's shoulder, and in the morning he'd telephoned Celia to see if she wanted to go for breakfast before he went to sleep. After calling the Garcías', he called home, thinking she'd be there. He listened to his own voice on the machine and then hung up.

He tried to round up a few friends to go for breakfast, but everyone had plans, so he headed out by himself, ending up at a small bacon and eggs place on Park Avenue. It was a busy little restaurant, close enough to the ghetto to be frequented by students and with prices so famously low that it was widely rumoured to be a front used by the mob for laundering money. Or so the story went, but the eggs were good. He was exhausted, yes, he remembered exhaustion being an integral part of the story. He ate alone and watched people. He was seated among clusters of friends and couples, and, as much as he tried, he could not block out the sounds of their conversation and laughter. He would have given anything to have a real grievance with Celia, any hint of betrayal would have been eagerly accepted, but all he had was this, having to eat alone and hear people enjoy themselves. Even his loneliness felt paltry and childish.

He didn't go home. He went back to the hospital and drank coffee in the cafeteria for an hour or two. He phoned the apartment a couple of times, not able to wait until the third ring before hanging up and then spent the rest of the afternoon at a movie, stumbling into small potholes of sleep before being shaken awake by the huge planetary faces on the screen.

It was early evening when Patrick got home. When he tried opening the door, it thudded against its chain. A second later, Jane, one of Celia's friends who was storing some canvases in their spare room, appeared in the gap, looking stark-eyed and frightened. She closed the door to unbolt the chain and then reopened it. Hadn't Celia told him she was going to the de Kooning show in Toronto? He shook his head, he'd been working too much to talk to her about anything.

"Celia said I could do some work here, I hope you don't mind."

He shook his head again.

"I'll be out of your hair by tomorrow, tops."

"Sure. Don't worry about it."

"Are you okay?" Jane asked.

"Yeah. When is she coming back?"

"Tomorrow night, I think."

"Uh-huh."

He made some dinner and ate wordlessly, Jane joining

him, talking and talking. And even though her mood seemed strange, it appealed to him: Jane was energized with the hum and hiss of a person operating on an unnatural level of alertness. It was unnerving at first, and he tried to dispel the suspicion that maybe she was taking something or wasn't well, but he got past that and decided that he liked her fervour, that there was something distinctly attractive about it. She was speaking quickly and effusively about her work, how she had described her work to so and so over the phone and he said he could tell that it had promise, real promise, but that didn't matter because she was developing her own aesthetic sense now and the dealers could go fuck themselves because she'd found what she was looking for, it was inside her, inside her all the time, she said.

Then she brushed the red hair away from where it had fallen over her face and smiled and said, "Do you want to see it?"

He said, "Sure," and he listened to the word as he said it, the comfort of it, how it annihilated silence and erased doubt and made any act that followed seem necessary.

Three days later – a full two days after Celia should have returned but still hadn't, the deep space of that extra forty-eight hours confirming that Jane had admitted what had happened between them to a friend and the news had been duly reported to Celia – Patrick was awakened by full-bodied hammering on the door of the apartment. He opened it to find Roberto standing there and he was transported to Le Dépanneur Mondial back in 1986; Roberto staring him down, jaw muscles contracting and relaxing as if he were gilled as well as angry. A shove to his chest followed, not really that much force, but enough at that time of the night to drive Patrick backwards into the hallway and flat on the floor. Then Roberto stood over him, asking where her paintings were. Patrick remembered being impressed at Roberto's restraint, suspecting even then that he'd eventually pay more completely. Ah yes, in that light the punch on the Churchillplein made perfect sense. Sweeter for the wait, for the self-control shown that night in the apartment. Travelling halfway around the world and across a Den Haag plaza was a detail, just the coordinates of a job to be finished.

Celia phoned him the next week, their last contact until he sighted her in the tribunal gallery twelve years later. She didn't have much to say, except to let him know that Jane wasn't well and she thought he should have guessed as much, and that she expected better from him. Then she hung up.

He squinted to screen out the glare of sunshine. From where he stood on the pier, Nina was clearly visible, still on the blanket, arms straightened out behind her. Further down, near the edge of the beach where the sand flashed a momentary sheen as each wave receded, he thought he could make out Celia and Paul. They were walking. They appeared to stop every dozen or so steps and Patrick imagined the little boy bending down for something on the sand. They were indistinct, the outline of their bodies shimmering, and with each glance it was difficult to tell if they were one or two people. His retinas were capable of discerning shapes from the quarter mile, his occipital and parietal lobes continually parsing the images and creating hypotheses that played against his visual memory. They were real. They were real. They were walking on a beach. Two people. One person. Oh, he realized, they were holding hands. They were coming back.

–

SEVENTEEN

For many people, Holland has always been a tolerant country. *The* tolerant country, modern laboratory for the newest idea: gay rights, sexual freedom, total football. It was no different for Patrick Lazerenko; Holland was famous for its tolerance even among teenagers back in NDG in the eighties, where the concept of the hassle-free bong hit was pretty much the definition of utopian society. *Amsterdam.* It was cool just to say the word, and impossible to keep a smile off your face as you said it. But Holland was more than just hedonism, it was asylum, the embodiment of relief and protection for those who had been harassed. No melting pot. No assimilation. People could live in peace there. Patrick had never spent any significant time in Holland before, never indulged in the café specialties of *de Wallen*, but Holland remained in his mind, more so since moving to America, occupying a necessary place as that reassuring, pluralistic haven.

But, according to the television, Holland was a different place tonight, with the Right Honourable Edgar van der

Hoeven in the ground and his assailant arrested that morning, now being held in an Amsterdam jail. The assailant had been identified variously: as a Muslim extremist, as a North African, as an engineering student, as a Moroccan, or as a man with no history of violence. Parenthetically, he turned out to be a native-born: an *allochtoon* from the Rustenburg-Oostbroek district of Den Haag. The murderer's identity confirmed what everyone had suspected. Every television channel Patrick turned to was a variation on a theme, in strident voices and clipped sentences whose meanings he was able to parse without the benefit of understanding Dutch. Heated debate had become Holland's new national sport, adopted with a vigour proportional to its novelty.

A half-hour of television was all it took to confirm that Van der Hoeven's death had been the necessary cathartic: now people wanted to say out loud, in front of cameras, what they had only ever privately thought. The moderator cut to a city sidewalk somewhere in the Netherlands. The bulb of a microphone breached the frame and a series of faces appeared, uttering one long indicting sentence: the immigrants are trouble and no one tries to speak Dutch, and they don't assimilate and they fill up the jails, and isn't the largest mosque in Europe in Rotterdam? And they have too many children and they'll be a majority in Amsterdam and Rotterdam and Den Haag by 2010, and they don't respect women or homosexuals, and they fill up the welfare rolls, and they have no interest in being Dutch, and they assassinate politicians in the street, and if they weren't Muslims we would just be talking about them as Fascists, wouldn't we?

There was only one story, and Hernan García was not that story. Hernan's story wasn't even *a* story. Even in the week before the arrest, a night hadn't passed without a mosque being burned or defaced, and the Muslim community announced it was going to hold simultaneous demonstrations in the major Dutch cities. When their spokesman was asked what they hoped to accomplish by these demonstrations, the first word out of his mouth was "solidarity." Watching him, Patrick got the feeling that he'd like to take the answer back, that the man already understood the multiple trajectories of the word. But by the time the spokesman had reconsidered, he was off camera and long gone.

Every night he heard the news, the details of the van der Hoeven murder and the escalating invective that trailed in its wake and yet by morning he had forgotten it. For him, Holland could well be the beach at Scheveningen, and Den Haag nothing more than the empty streets he walked through to get to the tribunal building. He saw no sign of discord, no minarets reduced to cinders, no one shaking their fist. But every night it reappeared, a bonfire of reality. It was the amnesia of the strange place, he told himself; it was normal. There was a time when he would have felt guilty about this, this touristic auto-pilot, that ten, maybe only five years ago he would have felt he owed it to himself and others to understand the issue. But he was busy with other things. His head hurt.

The dinner hour news was over and the television shut off with a flash that echoed throughout a newly, exuberantly dark room. He had said goodbye to the Garcías at the beach at around two and had spent the rest of the afternoon wandering alone through Scheveningen and Den Haag. He had spoken to Celia several times in the course of the day. Or tried. Stillborn attempts at chit-chat. By the end of the afternoon, he wished that she had been angry at him, that she'd showed any emotion, but she seemed to be interested only in maintaining a fixed distance between them. He'd come back to the Metropole and left his half-eaten meal on a plate in the restaurant. And now, with the television off, he considered whether doubling the dose of his Valium would allow him to sleep through to the next morning. He didn't move from the bed, but in the place of sleep came sleep's generic equivalent: a less potent mix of exhaustion and excess serotonin along with the fervent wish for genuine amnesia. Sleep would not come. When the phone rang, he answered it unhesitatingly. Welcoming it.

Her voice was different. Almost unrecognizable at first. Over the phone her voice seemed softer, synesthetic in the dark, full of flourishes and adornments. Melodious words. Floral speech. Not the Celia from the beach. He remembered this voice from years before, its tone and diction strumming instrumental memories, a hand that would be happily numbed holding the phone for an hour of listening to such a voice. The voice made no sense to him now.

"What do you want?" he said, the words stumbling down stairs in the dark.

"Are you doing anything tonight?"

Once, he would have been made happy hearing her say that, but his mood was in freefall. "No," he said quietly into the receiver.

"I'd like it if you could meet Oliveira."

"What? No," Patrick mumbled and sat up, repeating "No" like the first bleat of a car alarm. The vehemence didn't surprise him alone; there was a pause on the other end of the line.

"Please, Patrick, listen to me. I've tried to get this done through di Costini, but he's dragging his heels on getting the imaging test you talked about." Celia's voice shed its summer clothes for something heavier. "We have to figure out how we're going to do this."

"With Oliveira? Absolutely not."

"Nina told me you felt guilty – "

"What does that have to do with anything?"

"You'd be doing Dad a favour by meeting with us."

"Us?"

"He wants to meet you. I'll be there. Look, Patrick, I wouldn't ask if it wasn't important."

Patrick tried to focus on the clock, the lines slowly coalescing into digits. "What time?"

"Wait – " She paused and he could sense her hand covering the receiver, that she was speaking to someone. Was she *with* Oliveira? Oliveira was in her room or they were in a hotel lobby somewhere. But he was next to her, listening to her whisper. "What about eight o'clock? Is eight good?"

"Sure. Where?"

"The bar at the Metropole. The one near the lobby."

"What time is it now?"

"A little past seven."

"Okay. Okay, I'll be there," he mumbled, too angry at himself to hear her say "Thank you" before bringing the phone down on its cradle.

The room was familiar enough now that it was negotiable in the darkness. He was able to avoid the compact desk and the wastebasket that always huddled under it, clinging to a back leg like a nursing calf. Right turn, ninety degrees, a bare left thigh that brushed against the television console and then a stumble over a pair of shoes left on the floor. The variables that the temporal lobes hadn't registered. Four steps to the washroom with its orange ambient night light now visible, reflected in tile and mirror to produce a modest sunrise.

He washed at the bathroom sink and searched out his razor. He hadn't shaved that morning and was impressed at how the look of the stubble and the effects of a day at the beach combined with his contusion – now featuring a livid ripe-plum red crescent under the eye – to give him the look of a man sorely down on his luck, a man who might need the shelter of a doorway. So he washed thoroughly, tenderly. The alpine curves of his swollen face took more time to negotiate with the razor, even with the lights on.

It was only a meeting, he reminded himself. For all of his visceral dislike of the Democratic Voice, he could not figure out why it had taken up Hernan's cause. Why would Oliveira want Hernan freed? It was useless to ask the question, he thought, he could just as well ask van der Hoeven's murderer *why*. He would get the same reptile stare of incredulity. They were ideologues and *why* wasn't a question that begged answering. *Why* was a given, a constant in the equation. The only variable that mattered was how. He doubted the Garcías had asked why. The Democratic Voice was a lifeline in a world of dark seas and deadly currents. Regardless of what Oliveira believed, he'd at least been there to help when the Garcías' lives began to unravel.

At that moment he imagined the man who'd been arrested for van der Hoeven's murder, the Moroccan, washing himself in a sink just like this. Even with nowhere to go and nothing to say, there were still the routines of a body, the reassurances of soapsuds and toilet flushes. Something undisputedly human. A heart beat on, lungs bellowing, a gut peristaltically wringing itself like a sodden towel. Because the body was blameless, because the body was a drone flying over a landscape. Holland or home or hell itself; each was just a landscape to the body.

He turned on his computer and checked for the arrival of any of the Globomart data from Neuronaut or, failing that, an explanation from Sanjay, or maybe just an acknowledgement from Marc-André of his reply. No new mail. He should have mail. Any meeting with Globomart would have taken place by now, he thought. If they needed his help, they would have called. And if Sanjay had actually done it – and he had wanted him to succeed in a limited way, still flailing enough to need the guiding hand of his mentor – Patrick couldn't imagine Sanjay not exulting in the triumph. He would have said something. But there was no mail.

With television full of images of a country in crisis and his computer continuing to disappoint him in new and various ways, it was a short step for Patrick to decide to go media-free until he met with Celia and Oliveira. The options were limited. The Metropole's laminated information brochure trumpeted from a stand on the desk across the room, traditionally untouched except for the page that had the room service number. *The Angel of Lepaterique* sat on the bedside table, a clump of García kryptonite whose every annotation was already familiar to him. It was here, in a chapter he'd read repeatedly over the past few weeks, that Marta García was scrutinized most mercilessly. Hernan was still more than two years away from being summoned to Lepaterique, two years of what appeared to be a normal life back home, two years of realizing that his career was never going to amount to more than what it was at that moment. Then the call for him arrived, and while Elyse's documentation of Hernan's choices were well known, she saved particular scorn for Marta, speculating on what she knew as the calendar inched through 1981 and her husband disappeared for days at a time. On page 97, the Garcías were back in Tegucigalpa after their adventure in Detroit.

They are happy and young and they have come home. Hernan is now a successful doctor with a position as professor at the university, settling with two young children and a wife who has put her academic aspirations on hold to run the household on a shady street not a block from the Swedish Embassy.

But they changed during their time in America, and despite having family and friends, Marta and Hernan find themselves missing Detroit and not adjusting to life in Tegucigalpa. Marta García's letters to her sister Ana from those years speak of a "time that was expanding before me and a space that continued shrinking," a sentiment that, according to the letters, she appears to share with her husband. Hernan is occupied with starting his practice, and one can imagine how his expectation turns into disappointment as the months pass.

It is impossible to say what angers him more, the primitive state of equipment or the realization that the prestige of his position does not extend beyond its title to include the power to affect meaningful change. The only clue is in his correspondence with the hospital administration, which details his growing frustrations with what he terms "complete indifference to the plight of the sick of Honduras."

Then the memo from General Álvarez is written, and nine days later Hernan García appears for the first time at the installation at Lepaterique. To all outward appearances, the family carries on through Hernan's absences. Her sister's letters inquire about her health, asking if Marta, who had struggled with post-partum depression after the birth of their daughter Nina in 1980, was having recurring problems with her mood. She writes back to her sister that she is well, getting used to the small community of families of diplomats and university professors that live in her area. She frequently brings her children to the Galería Nacional de Arte, where her daughter Celia takes a particular liking to the paintings of Pablo Zelaya Sierra, and adopts a style, some say, similar to his when she becomes an artist years later. But Marta understands that this life is a facade, a life not only incongruent with the deepening crisis in the streets of Tegucigalpa, but at odds with the anxiety that dogs her. Gunshots are heard most nights. Her husband is called away on business. Tellingly, her correspondence with Ana ends at this point, as though some truth is acknowledged that could not bear repeating.

In Elyse's analysis, Marta García's ability to live through those years meant she was capable of two reactions: denial or complicity. An uncaring bystander or a Lady Macbeth, either way aware of her husband's actions, able to tolerate them, able to consent. Marta García was permitted nothing beyond that, not permitted trust in Hernan. Not permitted innocence.

Marta had followed Hernan to Detroit and back to Honduras, shared a bed and a family and a life with him for more than thirty years; it was logical to infer she must have known. Faced with a husband's sudden absences, Elyse could understandably assume a woman like Marta would have asked questions, and not settled for some ridiculous story about university business – the university had almost no business to conduct and she knew it. She would have even given him the chance to explain himself.

In her book, Elyse wrote that Hernan García left Lepaterique suddenly, after that night in June of 1983, well before Battalion 316 terminated its operations, a decision Elyse viewed not as a repudiation on his part, of course, but rather as an acknowledgement of guilt in the death of José-Maria Fernandez. Within a year the family was in Mexico, having already shed the "de la Cruz" suffix for the shortened, less traceable version of their family name. Another year passed and they arrived in Montreal. When did he admit to her what he'd done? Was it the reason they fled for a corner grocery store in a Montreal suburb? Elyse made her case persuasively. Marta knew the truth long before it came out. Held the truth and managed their escape. A wife would know. A wife would know if she wanted to know. It was a marriage, after all, a two-person secret society. Elyse made the case for complicity: Marta was too smart and she and Hernan were too close for her to be unaware.

But Patrick would disagree.

His understanding of Marta – something not known to Elyse or Lindbergh or McKenzie – came from the summer he spent with her in Le Dépanneur Mondial and from the margins of *Moby-Dick*. Patrick thought of this as he picked up *Moby-Dick* from the side table and let it sit in his hand, a full pound of Americana. When he first opened the book, in the weeks following Marta's death, he was impressed by how the smell announced itself. It was a fairly old book, the Penguin edition from the 1970s, and the pages were predictably yellow and had the sheen and texture that came with heavy, continual use. But the smell hit him like a sweet floral slap. Redolent. A stimulus wired straight to the temporal lobes, sense-memories blossoming. What was the scent that caused it all to bloom? It was vanilla and something else, something from Marta's kitchen, or from Le Dépanneur Mondial maybe, or a scent that she perhaps shared with Celia, his memories of the two becoming confused now. Primordial memory, smells: cut grass and baking bread and Marta, somewhere in the book. Marta. The smell of the book always led to a memory of that summer, in 1987, the summer that he and Marta shared in the store. Marta watching the Iran-Contra trials, Patrick watching Marta. To Patrick, watching her, watching with her, Marta was not a woman weighed down with the knowledge of what Hernan had done. She was a person still deeply curious about the history of her country, still reeling from the ongoing revelations of what was being done to Honduras, amazed and utterly impressed that a society that had done this could then discuss it all in the clear light of day and interrupt the soap operas to broadcast it. Patrick later reasoned a person who had been forced to share a terrible secret with her husband about his role in such lunacy would not, in good conscience, watch with genuine shock and revulsion as the details were made public. They would have kept the television off, bundled up and hidden it in a closet. No, this was the act of a woman perhaps coming to have suspicions, coming to realize the scope of the nightmare they had left behind.

After four years of having Marta's book on his shelf like a totem, Patrick finally read *Moby-Dick* in the last year, initially as a tribute to Marta García, maybe even hoping to evoke a safe García memory, but instead found himself casting the Garcías into the book. Hernan was Ahab, of course, then Ishmael, then the whale. Then Celia and Roberto took turns in a variety of cameos. And of course there was the marginalia, the notes and annotations that Marta had left alongside the text, the parsing of Melville's words for deeper meaning. An extra book, written in the margins, at times chastising or cheering Melville, clarifications, historical or biographical annotations. It was Marta's book, undisputedly; a book that she read and reread and wrote on until it wasn't really a book any more but a document of her life as well.

It was in the margins that Marta made sense of the world, through Melville and her own hard-won understanding. There were other notations whose significance Patrick never understood: on page 26 there was a column of numbers added with the sum – $1,129.31 underlined twice. Celia's name appeared on page 112 with the word "flowers" written beside it, a single word that for the first time he found incredibly sad. He found the phrase "ask Michael Patrick" written in the margins of page 381, next to the underlined passage musing on phrenology and describing how the whale's brain was hidden deep within its head "like the innermost citadel within the amplified fortifications of Quebec."

Eventually, Patrick's gaze drifted down from the title of Chapter 117 – *The Whale Watch* – to the space over the lines of the first paragraph. Below a telephone number with a Montreal area code (now out of service – he tried), Patrick found a line of letters that he'd seen a number of times before, but which now stood out, arranging themselves into initials.

JMF   JG   AO

José-Maria Fernandez, Juan Guererro, Arturo Ortega. Three of the disappeared, according to *The Angel of Lepaterique*, which he had begun to read as a companion to Marta's book, cross-referencing for names and dates, worrying the details like Marta herself. And while it felt like an accusation, like evidence being considered and admitted in the mind of a friend, it could have been anything. He chastised himself for thinking that way, for the overheated Hardy Boys sleuthing.

But there were less disputable entries. On the inside back cover, written in pencil, in Marta's clear script, and taking up most of the empty space, Patrick found a summary of the hearings they'd watched together that summer, a meticulously constructed diagram that tried to make sense of the movement of money and arms and force in central America in the early eighties, along with names of the congressmen who served on the committees and the witnesses who gave testimony. He had joined along then and learned the names of all the principals too, and fifteen years later he found these very names on the back page of her book, a roll call of the Reagan administration. At the bottom of the page, she had written the letters "CIA" and circled the acronym repeatedly, with multiple arrows drawn from the word, indicating her understanding of the extent and direction of the agency's involvement, a hydra of influence. The darkest arrow linked the CIA with the name of Álvarez, a name known to every Honduran, a name that cast the connections further, closer.

On the opposite page were the words "Democratic Voice," written without any clear connection to the other parts of the diagram (although its inclusion on the adjacent page was the first troubling inference Patrick had about the organization). It was also here that he had come across Oliveira's name for the first time, along with the names of the former senators and opinion makers who had founded the think-tank in the early eighties. Marta had diplomatically credited all their names with a large question mark.

Elyse would never know how Marta tried to understand, attempted to come to terms with history. If Elyse had known any of this, Patrick thought she would have at least appreciated the effort and analysis. She would have understood the risk in unearthing difficult truths. Perhaps she would have even allowed a feeling of kinship toward Marta rather than the broader, easier verdict of contempt. What was written on the back page made Patrick want to place the book in Elyse's lap, as much to have the satisfaction of seeing Elyse's smug theories refuted as to have Marta García exonerated.

But there were other things written in the book that made it impossible to give to Elyse. One notation gutted Patrick, physically pained him when he had to think of Marta feeling the need to write the words; it was on the last page of Chapter 73 – *Stubb and Flask Kill a Right Whale; and Then Have a Talk over Him.*

él lo hizo, él lo hizo, él lo hizo

Patrick knew enough Spanish that it registered: *he did it, he did it, he did it.* Not directed at anyone, just a declaration. Words sitting there, demanding Patrick ask who (the penalty for having left the book on his shelf for years) and demanding that he answer. Reading it for the first time a year before had shifted a sentiment inside him, made him come to resent Hernan. He must have let Marta come to the conclusion herself, even then practising the silence he had now perfected. He went about his business in Le Dépanneur Mondial as Elyse arrived and the accusations began. He said nothing as Oliveira slouched into their lives. And this was the response. Words like a fist banging on a door, an angry admission of not just the truth but of betrayal. It was evidence, he thought, circumstantial, but something Lindbergh would want to see. Maybe even something he suspected existed, but couldn't prove. For a moment he thought about the wisdom of having brought the book to Den Haag and considered hiding it, wrapping it in a towel and shoving it behind something somewhere, the way criminals disposed of evidence in movies. But he reconsidered; it had taken him four years to find the words buried there. If anyone thought to look through it, he thought, they deserved to find what she'd written.

He closed the book and was tempted to sniff at it, to remind himself of something else, but knew that any trace of Marta was gone. It had been his book for years by this time. Now it smelled of him.

How do you dislike parts of a man? Patrick asked himself as he went down to the lounge at the Metropole, realizing the distaste he'd already established for the composite parts of Oliveira's persona. A name scrawled in Marta's handwriting, a reputation (itself a mosaic of animus), the look of him as he spoke with Celia in the foyer of the tribunal building. The grandiosity that came with being called Caesar. Even the pronunciation of his last name irked Patrick, with its idiot rim-shot of open-mouthed vowel sounds followed by the animal snarl and spit of the last two. Patrick was in the elevator again – suddenly despairing at the miles he'd covered travelling in elevators, bracketed by time spent in guest rooms and lobbies to form that endlessly recurrent triathlon of hotel life – wondering why he hated Oliveira so. They both wanted the same thing. They had both offered help to the Garcías, the only difference was that Oliveira had actually provided tangible assistance. Assistance for which Celia was obviously grateful.

Despite having seen Oliveira before, Patrick still carried the image of him as outsized, garish in that kingpin sort of way, a veneer of sophistication failing to conceal a man full of coiled, meaty aggression. Patrick attempted to dismiss his preconceptions as he approached them in the bar of the Metropole, tried to imagine a business meeting. Forget the players, concentrate on the proposal. Upon seeing Patrick, Celia and Oliveira both stood up. After he and Oliveira were introduced and shook hands, Celia leaned over and kissed his cheek, a gesture that seemed performative and fraudulent and distracted Patrick with the thought that perhaps love was like hate in that way, as easily constructed from composite pieces.

Up close, Oliveira was pleasantly underwhelming. Slightly shorter than Patrick. A frame that carried a little less weight. Immediately affable, offering the two-pump handshake and the quick release. Professional. Receding hairline and an unlined face sporting a pair of wire-rim glasses, all of which combined to give him the look of an actuary fresh from the floors of one of the larger Den Haag insurance houses. But any reassurance Patrick felt at not being met by a physically imposing presence almost immediately began to have the opposite effect, hinting that Oliveira's reputation and status had to be based on something else, on pure effectiveness, perhaps.

They sat down at a booth, with Patrick marshalled into the spot between the two of them, with Oliveira on his right, up against the eggplant bruise on his face. Oliveira was cool enough not to bring up the bruise, eyes fluttering over it for a second, understanding it was just a feature of another landscape he'd have to negotiate. The bar of the Metropole was accordingly empty for a weekend night – only a couple of single drinkers, both up front, gargoyles flanking the bartender. There was one television in the entire hotel bar, a paucity of screens that Patrick had come to realize provoked a particular, calculable anxiety in his American travelling companions, a screen-deficit that located the bar better than an atlas. But Oliveira had no need to look at the television.

A waitress appeared as if she'd been waiting just offstage. Oliveira ordered a martini – at last, a grudging, partial confirmation of Patrick's preconceptions. The martini had a name Patrick had never heard before, something nonsensical and arbitrarily vulgar, as though it had been christened by the first person who'd become drunk on it. People were meant to chuckle when they ordered one.

"No, two, right Celia?" Oliveira said, and Celia nodded. When his turn came, Patrick wrinkled his nose. He wanted his refusal to have a drink with them to seem like a symbolic gesture of his autonomy, but it seemed like nothing more than a sulk. So he cited stomach issues, non-specific, as the cause for not ordering a third whatever-they-were-drinking. Water would do.

"It's a pleasure to finally meet you," Oliveira said to him from an odd angle, unique to conversations held in U-shaped booths. Patrick felt his lips pull tight against his face, assuring himself this was a smile. Particles of hostility scattered from him like a new form of energy. Fissionable. "I'm very impressed by Neuronaut."

"We've had a good first year."

"I wasn't talking about the business. Success in business doesn't particularly impress me. Your work impresses me, it always has."

Patrick tried not to think about having Oliveira as a fan. "Thank you."

"You're not doing badly, especially with Globomart."

"It's been a great experience working with them." Oliveira listened to Patrick's wooden tone and smiled, not the thousand-kilowatt smile Patrick would have predicted but a slow deployment of a smile.

"As you may know, the Democratic Voice has been involved in Hernan's case since the initial charges were laid."

"They found the witnesses," Patrick said.

"It took some legwork," Oliveira added, in a way that dismissed the fact it wasn't his legs that did the work. "It was just a matter of deposing them and getting them here. And we've played a role, of course, in certain elements of Hernan's defence."

"You got di Costini to contact me," Patrick said, feeling Celia staring at him from another oblique angle in the booth.

"We did," Oliveira answered.

"He said you were asking about brain imaging studies."

"We've, in fact, leased time on the magnet and technical time with Cervotech in Amsterdam. Mr. di Costini tells me that you don't think much of the idea."

The drinks arrived. Oliveira and Celia leaned back as the martinis landed along with a glass of water that the waitress placed in front of him with considerable ceremony.

"As a form of lie detection? At best, it's inadmissible. The technology is too new. It's like trying to use DNA evidence to acquit someone in 1954. I told di Costini that it doesn't have a precedent."

"The case won't be won or lost on one piece of evidence.

This isn't about one test, it's about the accumulation of supportive facts. There's no forensics to speak of. And as for eyewitness accounts after twenty-five years, you know the value of that. Any additional, technical evidence could be vital. Did di Costini mention that?"

"I told him it was ridiculous for me to testify."

"Not to testify. No, no. Just oversee the design of any testing. There aren't twenty people in the world with your credentials. The court would recognize that."

"What happens if the court refuses to admit it?"

"Then Hernan looks like a man willing to take the test, thwarted by the court."

"What happens if he fails?"

"Do you believe he's guilty?"

Celia's face floated like a spring moon over his other shoulder. "I don't know, but you have to be prepared if he fails the test. Hernan has to be prepared."

"Absolutely. But, correct me if I'm wrong: in some ways the technique is imprecise and there is a margin of error. Lie detection alone requires interpretation of the images. Design of the experiment could play a major role," Oliveira said, looking up from his martini glass. "Which is not necessarily a disadvantage."

"Lindbergh is aware of all this," Patrick said, trying to invoke some authority Oliveira might respect. "They know what I do. And if they know what I do, they'll just get their own experts, those without any personal connection to the case."

"I don't think we'd object to that," Oliveira said blandly, and seeing Patrick shaking his head in disbelief, he added, pre-emptively, "Don't you see? That would mean we'd engaged our opponents on our terms. They would be forced to address Hernan's innocence as something that could be proven. Something we could prove."

"Why do you care so much about Hernan? Why is this so important to you?"

Oliveira looked at Celia and then back at Patrick. "Hernan García is a good man. The charges against him are without merit."

"I don't mean you personally. Why would a policy think-tank get involved in a Honduran torture case?"

"The Democratic Voice doesn't limit itself to issues of policy making with regards to Latin America. It's true, we're a think-tank, and as such we wish to promote policy initiatives consistent with certain values – "

"We're talking about Honduras in the eighties. Values like what? Kidnapping? Torture?"

Oliveira turned to Celia, as though remarking on a prediction having come true.

"It's more complicated than that."

"It's not complicated at all."

"Dr. Lazerenko, would you like to get into a debate about ethics? You don't seem to have any problems working for Globomart, but to many people that sort of involvement seems very complicated. Globomart is the subject of how many Justice Department investigations? Bribing, zoning boards, union busting, 'non-competitive practices' – "

"It's not torture."

"People like you frustrate me, Doctor. Democracy doesn't survive because of its inherent righteousness. Athens didn't flourish because of its moral claims, but because it was a military power. It's easy to forget what the world was like in the eighties. But a battle was fought in the Americas, and it was won, country by country. Peru, Grenada, El Salvador – "

Patrick swivelled his head to try to gauge Celia's response, hoping for an arbiter of the world views competing in front of her. She was looking at something in Belgium. "Celia, do you hear this?"

". . . Nicaragua . . ."

"What about Álvarez?"

"Álvarez?"

"Gustavo Álvarez, I've heard the name a few times at the trial. Where do you stand on him?"

"Winner of the Legion of Merit."

"I don't think we have anything more to talk about," Patrick said, and began sliding out of the long padded bench of the booth. He tried to make eye contact with Celia as she shuffled sideways ahead of him, tried to make sense of a person he thought he knew, but it was no use.

Then, as she got to the end of the seat, she turned and faced him, a person summoning reserves for one last stand, "Patrick, wait, just listen to him. For me. For my father."

Patrick was still looking at Celia when he heard Oliveira's voice again. "I expected more from you, Dr. Lazerenko. I would have thought as a scientist you'd have left the ideology and bickering to someone else. Look at the world empirically. Like it or not, the region is more stable. GDP is up. People are living better lives. We're all trading partners now. Forget politics. Our politics are prosperity. We have invested too much of ourselves to let this victory be taken away from us. That's why I'm here." Patrick was sitting at the end of the booth with Celia, and he couldn't help but think that to Oliveira they must look like two rubes playing out a drama.

"Even if you disagree with me, Doctor, it is not me you would be helping. You have to ask yourself how much you want to help the Garcías."

The waitress, circling in a holding pattern halfway between the bar and the booth, returned to her other customers. Raised voices will do that.

"You talk about Hernan like he's a political prisoner."

"All conflicts have a political element to them."

"Does Hernan know you're doing this?"

"We're planning to meet with him."

"What good will that do?"

"We're going to present the proposal to Hernan after the proceedings on Monday. We'll lay out what we plan to do. He doesn't have to say a word. He sits and listens. If he objects, fine, we'll back off. We'll explain that the test is a newer, more sophisticated lie detector. We need you there to speak to him."

"Even if I agree to do this, he'll know I'm lying."

"Don't sell yourself short, Dr. Lazerenko." Oliveira paused. "Think about it. The Garcías need your help. Hernan is a good man. Whatever our disagreements are about the larger issues, I know we agree on that." He emptied his glass and put it down on the table without a sound. "I should be going." He edged out of the other side of the booth, ending up at a place where the logistics of a parting handshake with Patrick were too awkward to even consider. Celia bounced up out of the booth to catch Oliveira and together they walked to the bar's entrance. She said something to him and he nodded. After a handshake, Oliveira was gone and Celia returned. He watched her feet, concentrated on her feet and felt an energy, an anger that he shared.

"What the hell was that? Suddenly, for the first time in your life, you develop political consciousness?"

"Well, we've both changed, then."

Celia leaned over the table. "You asshole, you know this is about getting my father out of jail."

"What do you want me to do, Celia?"

"Maybe not insulting the guy would be a start."

"Jesus, did you hear him? They don't care about Hernan. This is a public relations campaign. It's spin. Your mother –"

"Don't you dare talk about my mother."

"Your mother would have hated that guy. And the Celia I remember would never get involved with idiots like this. What happened to you?"

"My father went to jail is what happened to me. I want Paul to know his grandfather. Oliveira's the only one who's made things happen."

"Sure, between trying to overthrow Castro and bailing out Pinochet."

Celia threw up her hands. "You come here, you say you want to help, and then you act like this."

"'It's not necessarily a disadvantage if the results are tailored to support Hernan's innocence.' Did you even listen to him? He wants me to massage the data, Celia." Patrick waved the waitress over and mouthed the word "beer." She didn't disappoint, understanding the whispered sos, stopping and turning in a moment like it was a dance step.

"He just wants to explore every avenue."

"I have a reputation."

Celia lifted her glass and held it in front of her lips. "You have a reputation for making money."

"What's that supposed to mean?"

She put her hand on his forearm, that demilitarized zone of interpersonal contact, and apologized.

"I know what the Democratic Voice does. Believe me, I know. But there are more things than my feelings. I don't have that luxury. Respect that, Patrick. Please tell me you'll try to help."

The waitress arrived with a prodigious glass of beer, an aquarium of beer, and seeing this, Celia ordered one for herself. This provoked a look from the waitress that could only be described as rueful. He thought for a moment of Birgita and the table at the other end of the bar where they had sat the night before. The waitress returned with aquarium beer number two for Celia, the look on her face unchanged, and he thought she might be the same waitress who had served him the previous night, that this look was really some European form of waitressly disdain for him showing up with a different woman on consecutive nights. Yeah, it was a sisterhood issue, he thought, and he was the bar guy in the equation, the sort of guy he'd always seen and laughed at, a shiner the product of a dust-up with a cheated boyfriend. But the beer was an able antidote to the swell of paranoia. Sweet and yeasty, one sip was all it took to make him want to propose to the brewmeister's daughter. He drained the beer in a series of almost-involuntary python gulps and the froth-veined glass was set free on the table. It was chemical inside him now, a flare of good mood, a window of sociability.

"We'll have to speak to Hernan first, of course," Patrick said, understanding that it was the promise of meeting Hernan face to face that made him agree to the plan, wondering now if it was another manœuvre to get him to sign on. "Then I have to speak to this company that Oliveira's contracted." He paused. "And di Costini's okay with this?" Celia nodded. "I can't promise anything, you have to understand that. The technique is the same, but I've never designed a study to look at lie detection. I study how people respond to advertising, for God's sake, and I'm not even sure the technique works very well."

"But these companies still pay you, right?"

"Oh, yeah."

"If it didn't work, they wouldn't pay."

"Well, I don't know about that. One thing you learn about large retail corporations is that the people who run them are insecure, I mean pathologically insecure. They need to justify every decision to their superiors and their shareholders and industry analysts and so they look for something they can base their decisions on. They need proof. And if the proof is a technique that's new and exotic and exclusive and gives cool pictures, well, all the better. That's the only reason I can think of. I mean, we've never made an unsuccessful store into a successful one."

"Come on, you work with Globomart."

"They were a steamroller long before us. I have no idea if what we're doing actually works for those people. And we haven't tanked anybody yet, either, so it's hard to tell."

"And people buy shares in this company of yours?"

"They step over each other to buy it. Not being able to understand what they're investing in never stopped anybody."

"I never had you figured as a business type."

"Me neither. But if it's any consolation, it hasn't worked out like I planned. I thought I'd have more freedom to do what I wanted."

"Please don't talk to me about freedom."

"You're not the most sympathetic person," he said, bracing himself for her response, but her face was expressionless.

"So what would you like to be doing?"

"Well, you've been kind enough to remind me that I'm not *really* a doctor. It's not like I could just go and start seeing patients. Besides, that would kill me. And I sort of burned my bridges in academics."

"But you run the company. You could decide what projects to do."

"I don't own it," Patrick said, thinking about what Marc-André always said about the tools of production, "not any more. It's a publicly traded company. I can't just do research that interests me, not with other people's money. I imagine it's like doing design work. It pays. You like it well enough and it's *sort of* what you saw yourself doing."

The glasses were both empty and now that they had considerately synchronized their drinking he felt no compunction about having the waitress bring them two more. The beer was delivered and the waitress did seem less angry, enough of a change that he could convince himself that she had been mollified by his gesture. Deep down, amid all the layers of personality, in his beer-drinking self, he was still Canadian after all. It was like a truth serum. No need for a big machine to read people's minds. Maybe they should just get Hernan drunk, he thought.

"I'm a graphic artist. No qualms about the choice. Let's not talk about my work. I just worked on a cover for some children's book by this movie star who wrote it while she was still in rehab. Tell me what you'd do if you could" – Celia curled her index and middle fingers into quotation mark gestures – "break the chains of your Globomart oppressors. C'mon, no limitations."

"I'd probably go back to some of the research I was doing when I left the university."

"The pornography stuff?" Celia said, smirking, until she saw his look. "Sorry."

"Moral reasoning," Patrick said firmly. "Not in the individual sense, not like for Hernan, you know, who makes what decision, but determining what parts of the brain are involved. Stop smiling."

"I'm just surprised that you're interested in that sort of stuff."

"Well, you don't know me."

Celia put her glass of beer down. She had finished three-quarters of it. More than he had. "Could you just drop that?"

"What?"

"The feeling sorry for yourself stuff. It's got to stop."

"Thanks."

"I'm sorry, but you should be happy."

"Do you have any idea how stupid that sounds?"

"Yes. So tell me, how would you do this research?"

"You present the subjects with a scenario, while they're in the machine, and then you see what sort of activity occurs when they deal with the conflict." Celia was still smiling, broadly enough that he knew a buzz was building inside her, helping her to patronize him. It irritated him. "For instance, there's this scenario where we ask the subject to imagine that their town has been occupied by an invading army with orders to kill anybody who has been caught hiding. A whole group of townspeople have hidden in a barn, along with you and your baby – "

"There's a baby?"

"Yes; and it's vitally important that everyone stay quiet. And then the baby starts crying."

"So?"

"Well, it's a question of whether or not you kill your child. The conflict over violating emotional conviction – not to harm your child – or saving the group." The smile disappeared. It worked. It always worked. He edged in, trying not to look too pleased. "So what would you do?"

"I'd breast-feed the baby."

"No, that's not an option. Do you smother your baby or do you let everyone die?"

"That's idiotic. I'd breast-feed the baby."

"You don't understand – we're trying to find what part of the brain becomes active when this sort of reasoning goes on."

"I can't believe people would just answer that. Are these all men you're studying? Did any of them have children?"

"That's not the point. But no, some were women. Most of them are students, so probably no kids."

"Well, there you go. That tells you all you need to know right there."

"It's like talking to a wall."

"Here's an idea: maybe you should do a study to find out what part of the brain is activated to get people to ask stupid questions like that."

"Why don't you just finish your beer."

The waitress clunked down two more beers, which he hadn't remembered ordering. By the third beer he was usually less discriminating, but this third beer was gorgeous, a wave of taste he hadn't appreciated in the first two: a Dutch pastoral, a sweeping vista of flood plains and luridly green countryside, ascetic monks weeping as the hops give themselves up for the glory of God. Then the alcohol hit him like a soft, tidal shove and he was suddenly sleepy. But he didn't want to go.

"I'm pretty certain Lindbergh is going to subpoena me."

"About the testing?"

"No," he replied, freshly stung at the implication that his expertise was the only reason he was subpoena-worthy. "They know that Hernan was treating patients."

"Everyone knows about that, now."

"They think I know more. I'm worried they know about the farm workers he looked after."

Celia shrugged. "Compared to the mess he's in, I don't think any of that is so important."

"The day we went out there with Hernan, to the dormitory with all the workers, one of the workers died. Your dad was looking after him."

"How do you know that?"

"You were outside, but I went back into the dormitory. He didn't know I was there."

"You saw this?" Patrick nodded. "What did you see?" Celia asked.

"I'm not sure."

"No. No, not your opinion, Patrick. I need to know exactly what you saw."

"I saw him carry something back from the car. He told me to stay there, that he'd help the man. But I went in. I was thirty, maybe forty feet away. I saw Hernan doing something, I can't be sure what it was, and then, the man died."

"Have you told anybody about this?"

"I don't know what I saw."

"Have you told anybody?" she repeated.

"No. I didn't see anything for certain."

Celia paused. It was a mistake to have told her. "You would have seen something. You can't mistake that sort of thing," she said in a way he knew was mostly for herself. "If you weren't certain, I think it would be best if you didn't repeat this to anyone."

They were saved by a nightly routine lurching into motion around them. At ten o'clock, the television was turned off and piped-in music started and the bar at the Metropole – now filling: couples at tables, a younger crowd clustering around the bar – revealed its disco aspirations. Celia got up to go to the washroom and crossed the designated boogie-zone as a half-hearted light show started, the equivalent to a grooving airport employee swinging two flashlights around. Patrick couldn't tell the difference between ABBA and ABBA covers and fought the losing battle not to hum to either.

She returned from the washroom and they sat together wordlessly. He didn't have the energy to talk about Hernan any more and he imagined she felt the same. Hernan was all they shared now, and the thought depressed him. He watched her finishing her glass of beer with small sips. There had been a time when Hernan hadn't figured into the way they felt. He could ask her now. They'd had enough beer and talked enough that they knew they were impervious to each other's questions, and if it hurt her, well that sort of thing happened when people spoke frankly. No, it wouldn't seem maudlin if he asked. It would help, too, to know that she had loved him, that she came up to his room that night because she wanted to, that she knew nothing of José-Maria Fernandez or wasn't cajoled or prompted to reach out to him. No, she'd slap him. That's what she'd do, because she was an adult with some dignity left that she wouldn't allow to be shredded by his little dramas and questions. She'd accuse him of calling her a whore and her father a pimp and there would be the definite possibility of another García assault. They had something but it was over. There was nothing between them except the life they'd shared. The words floated in the beer and the music and then they sank. The music was too loud anyway, he thought. She'd never hear me. So they sat in the booth and tipped their glasses back and they appeared like any other couple enjoying an evening of each other's company and silence.

—

EIGHTEEN

He said goodnight to Celia at the entrance to the Metropole. A polite kiss on the cheek and she turned to wave for a taxi and then she was gone, as quickly as if she'd stepped off a riverbank into a fast-flowing current. Oliveira was long gone too, choppered out or whisked away in an armoured Humvee convoy or in whatever way passed for an imperial mode of departure. Patrick stood on the pavement, unsure of what to do next, squinting with the doorman under the marquee lights.

Inside, the Metropole was quiet. Even the bar and its half-hearted disco ambition couldn't shift the mood. He floated through the empty lobby and found several elevators idling in wait, doors yawning.

338
—

Patrick entered the nearest one. As it was about to shut tight on the frame, the elevator door shuddered and recoiled like jaws that had closed on something surprisingly hard. Then four slim fingers appeared, curling around the metal edge as the door opened more fully, and in one deft commando manoeuvre, Elyse Brenman swept into the elevator. Patrick said nothing, the cumulative effects of Celia and beer and listening to Oliveira all inducing a dreamlike state – rendering him entirely suggestible, compliant. Yes, Elyse *would* appear like this. In the elevator. It's Elyse. Of course. Welcome, Elyse.

"I saw who you were talking to."

"Are you stalking me?"

"I saw you with Caesar Oliveira. He's like the *macher* for the Democratic Voice."

Patrick ignored her, spinning in his gauzy beer haze. He felt the elevator start to climb.

"You shouldn't be dealing with people like that. Definitely out of your league."

"I'll decide who's in my league or not, okay?"

Elyse didn't press any buttons, choosing just to watch Patrick, who lifted his eyes skyward, focusing on the array of lights above the elevator door and contemplating the twelve feet per second rate of ascent. Fifteen seconds of ride time. Maybe twenty.

The elevator emoted its gentle keening beep and after a minor geophysical moment, the doors opened. Patrick took off down the corridor and reached into his wallet for the key to the room, all the time hearing Elyse behind him, even though he knew it was impossible with the carpet sucking up all sounds of human movement. But he heard Elyse, he swore he did, footsteps like the beating of wings.

"Where do you think you're going, Elyse?"

"We need to talk."

"Just have them subpoena me. That would be easier for everyone."

"Here's how I figure it. Caesar Oliveira is meeting with you for a reason. Either you know something exculpatory about

Hernan, which I doubt, I mean you would have said something, what, five years ago, or they want something from you, your expertise."

"Maybe it was just people having a drink," he said as he jabbed the hotel card key into the locking mechanism of his door. "Did you think of that?" The little red light on the mechanism flashed. He tried again, with the deliberateness of a man asked to defuse a bomb. Then the green light blinked and the handle gave way and he turned to look at Elyse still standing in the hallway.

"Good night, Elyse."

"Do you know what the funny thing is?"

He sighed. "What?"

"In a way, you already work for him."

"What are you talking about?"

"Sentient Systems." He shook his head in that manner of the truly, hopelessly lost. He needed Birgita, or someone capable of reorienting him on the tour of his life. "They're a multinational – "

"I know who they are."

"But you don't know they've been a major contributor to the Democratic Voice since its inception. That's putting it mildly; 'founding patron' would be more exact." Patrick stood there, a foot against the partially open door, caught in a headlock of semi-drunken, partial recollection. "Sentient bought a sizeable chunk of your company's IPO, and in the last six months they increased their stake to about 26.6 per cent. Roughly. I checked this morning."

"So this company acquires some shares in my company for millions of dollars in order to potentially affect a trial that wouldn't occur for a couple of years. Wow, that's a brilliant strategy. That's just great business."

"I'm not saying they have some grand plan, but their influence is pervasive."

"Do you ever listen to yourself?"

"Bancroft worked for a Sentient subsidiary in the mid-nineties."

"So? *We* hired Bancroft."

"After consulting with your financial backers."

"*We* chose *him*."

"Why are you here? Do you ask yourself that? I know you think you're here of your own free will, personal duty and everything, but who called you? Celia. At Oliveira's urging. You were supposed to be here, Patrick, that's why. The Democratic Voice has their hands all over this."

"Is this how you do all your research? Wild conjecture?"

"Whatever you do, Patrick, whatever you give them, they'll spin it. They don't need to get Hernan off, they just want to create doubt. They want Hernan to go to jail quietly, looking like he's wrongly convicted. Then, they're seen as impassioned defenders, good-guy underdogs. You think they want Hernan walking free and talking to people, naming names? If they wanted him acquitted, they'd have a hundred witnesses testifying that Hernan was a saint and that Lepaterique was a spa and he'd be back at home selling melons. Hernan in jail with his mouth shut is their ideal scenario, and whether or not you want to be a part of *that* is up to you."

Patrick was beginning to envy Elyse. The truth for her was zero-sum; if she had it, then others didn't. She was certain and he was jealous of that certainty. Elyse could speak to him the way she did because she thought he was crazy or bought or scared or any of the conditions that made a person wrong, wrong, wrong.

Elyse stood in the light of the corridor, squinting. It was dark inside the room. The doorway was open enough, closed enough that it was like they were speaking to each other from opposite sides of an animal's mouth. It would be so easy to close the door. Then she spoke and, for a person who before had seemed so certain, it surprised him to hear what sounded like an angry plea: "Do you have any idea how difficult it is to figure out somebody's life?"

"Yes," he said, and closed the door.

NINETEEN

The answer to how long one can look at the *View on Delft* without a break is approximately twelve and a half minutes. Experiments on visual attention indicate that in any non-facial visual image, the edges and silhouettes are scanned for a quick outline of context identifiers and analysis of depth. Then the secondary details are attended to – and in *View on Delft* these details make up almost another entire painting; the play of light on water, the hyperrealist foreground representation and finally, the grey mantle of cloud that frames the entire sky. After surveying that, any attempt at further, intense visual concentration is rewarded with something that feels like anxiety. The painting moves in and out of focus, as if there is some process reflexively trying to avoid the cause of this anxiety. This is no fault of the artist, we are not equipped to stare at stationary objects for very long. Besides, the security guards at the Mauritshuis, ever observant, ever wary of those whose intense study cannot be attributed to pure art appreciation, were trained to intervene at precisely twelve minutes, happy to ask any patron who has lingered that long if they can be of assistance. Patrick said no to the offer, his head snapping up to meet the great tonsured head of a security guard, the hypnotic state broken but the outline of Delft still lingering, echoing through his visual association cortex, playing out like a blueprint against the guard's facial features. He checked his watch, focusing on the novelty of the sweeping second hand at first, then checked the time. Twelve minutes thirty seconds.

It was past noon by the time he'd got up and out of his hotel room. A protracted, beer-stoked sleep was broken by a phone call from an Oliveira assistant. Patrick had been hooked and hauled into a flat boat of midday light, caught speechless, dry-mouthed and aching, but it didn't matter; the assistant did all the talking regarding their new liberate-García project. The call was concerning the follow-up contact – how professional, making it easy for him – telling Patrick what Cervotech's number was so he could call early Monday morning and speak with their scientific liaison, Dr. van der whoever, to make the necessary arrangements. The assistant said, "Okay? You got all that?" at the end of the instructions, the only sign that he'd appreciated it wasn't a machine he was talking to. The call, and its promise of more calls, was enough to chase him from the bed.

The day was overcast and the clouds clung like gauze to a Den Haag morning that ached sympathetically with him. In the distance a church bell sent out its sonic drop kick, sorely testing the effectiveness of the anti-inflammatories he'd downed and making him curse the lack of a more comprehensive atheism in the new Europe. Even with all this, his face felt surprisingly better, the swelling subsiding and the pain a vague sense memory, its appearance giving way to a pageant of discoloured flesh, a craniofacial version of foliage season in Vermont. The staff at the Metropole were now familiar with him and the mysterious evolving disfigurement; the maids felt permitted to smile as he passed by their carts in the hallway. Even Edwin seemed more understanding, more forgiving of this injured man's earlier shortcomings regarding his messages.

It took fifteen minutes to walk to Korte Vijverberg where he found the Mauritshuis with its promise of diversion and solitude that he felt he needed as urgently as another lungful of oxygen. And after three hours, ending with his experiment with *View of Delft*, he felt better. A moment on one of the benches, among the crowd, many of whom clamoured around *The Anatomy Lesson* or *Girl with a Pearl Earring* like obnoxious groupies, and he felt a growing contrarian boosterism for the Delft painting, as ignored as the stucco-faced portrait of Rembrandt. Yes, *Delft* was his painting.

He could have gone to the Gemeentemuseum but instead chose the Mauritshuis. He didn't want to draw conclusions about the decision – the Mauritshuis was a longer walk and he wasn't as certain of the directions – but there was an indisputable satisfaction, a verifiability, in representational art that he found lacking in more modern works. *Delft* looked like Delft. He was as certain of the skill of the painter as he was of any craftsman. Celia would roll her eyes and bemoan his philistinism parading as a more noble sentiment, but she wasn't here. He hadn't looked for her once, hadn't turned at the sight of a stroller or the sound of a child's voice. If he were to come upon her here, swimming upstream through the flow of other tourists mobbing Vermeer's more crowd-pleasing canvases, he hoped he'd just pass by. Not a word. They were strangers, really. Imagining they were something else, something more, was a delusion. Pulling José-Maria Fernandez into it, buying into Elyse's cut-rate psychoanalysis, was doing nothing more than aggrandizing himself, trying to turn an adolescent moment into an epic tale. He wasn't a surrogate for Fernandez. He was barely a surrogate for himself. *Delft* brought him back. There was no interpretation to *Delft*. *Delft* was Delft. It was beautiful and if it weren't worth ten million Euros and as heavily guarded as the main driveway of the White House, he'd wrench it from the wall and run.

He walked through the grand foyer toward the exit, and the estuary of indoor light changed as it mixed with the outside sea of daylight. The sky was clearing and it was warm enough to consider taking off his jacket. The streets had more people. Perhaps Sunday was the walking day, the day out.

The pictures in the Mauritshuis were a distraction, of course, a temporary and insufficient escape from Elyse's grand unified theory, in which, it seemed, every second person in the western hemisphere was in on the acquittal/silencing/ beatification of Hernan García. It was ridiculous, he told himself. He needed the crowds, he needed *Delft* to keep out freshly planted doubts about Bancroft's motives, amazed at how easily his boss's tolerance and amiability mutated into sinister designs. And when his suspicions of Bancroft faded, they were replaced by the depressing thoughts of how Oliveira was going to manipulate the data from the study he felt obligated to arrange. He imagined images mislabelled, key information deleted. It must have happened before, in the early days of fingerprinting or DNA evidence. Now, his technology was new, the science mysterious and compelling enough that it would be difficult to dispute the results. His only hope was that Hernan would refuse the test, that he would understand its inherent fraudulence from the way Patrick explained it (would Oliveira even let him talk? Or would he be kept in the corner, allowed to nod in agreement as a more optimistic sales pitch was used?). But he wasn't even sure what Hernan wanted. Maybe Hernan wanted out.

Throughout the course of the day, whenever feelings of guilt tugged at Patrick for conspiring to free a war criminal, he assuaged them by calling on the standard parole board rationalizations that Hernan García posed no threat to other people. Perhaps justice was less about judgment and more about testifying to what happened, he reasoned, remembering other countries where a tribunal would have gratefully traded truth for amnesty. And had there been any reasonable statute of limitations, Hernan would have never been arraigned in the first place. His children would have their father back. He would see his grandson. Patrick owed Hernan. He owed him this.

Patrick turned left on the Korte Voorhout and crossed the Prinsessegracht where the density of pedestrian traffic steadily increased. For the first time in Den Haag, he had to alter his step to avoid others. Another half-block and there were now people standing on the sidewalks near where the street opened into a large green space. The novelty of a crowd, the planetary density, slowed him as much as the adjustments he had to make in his stride. People ahead stared in the direction of the southeast corner of the park where a stage had been erected and others were speaking. Ahead of him, the overflow from the park blocked the sidewalk completely. At the buckling edge of the crowd there were people balanced on the sidewalk's curb, leaning forward for stability, attention divided between listening to the speakers and eyeing the cars that wheeled past eighteen inches behind them on the busy outer lane of the Prinsessegracht.

Patrick stopped. For the first time in the city he was not surrounded by typical Dutch faces. The women wore hijab and there was nothing he understood in the words around him, Dutch or Arabic; not the words shouted by a man with a megaphone on the stage or the phrases chanted back by the crowd. He couldn't judge the mood of the gathering crowd beyond feeling the tension. That alone would usually have prompted him to an increased pace and a search for a way out, but the crowd had closed in around him, making it impossible to move in any direction. He tried to turn back, pivoting into the face of another man who had been walking closely behind him, and that's when he heard it, the sharp stab of brakes and the *da-daup* sound of syncopated impact against a hollow object. The crowd turned with the sound, a non-vocal sound, then a quasi-vocal sound before it was articulated into a scream, a woman's scream, and there was a torrent of movement that settled into a fixed frenzy of ten to twelve people crouched by the curb and then someone shouted, a male voice this time, a voice calling for an ambulance, it must be for an ambulance, Patrick thought, and three people around him were on their cell phones, one already looking around, shouting. For directions? A cross street? A word was shouted out – a name, he thought – and the man with the cell phone repeated it with harried precision, his free index finger applied to the tragus of his other ear, keeping out the noise of the crowd now that he had his answer.

The crowd convulsed in a sudden lurching movement and Patrick strained to keep his feet. There was shouting and an atonal crescendo of car horns. Patrick watched the crowd around the curb, witnessed the cries and gesticulations as if that was what would bring the ambulance more quickly. And he didn't know why, but he said it then, at first loudly enough only to be heard by the man next to him, who turned and said it back.

"*Dokter?*"

Patrick became aware of the look of confusion he must have worn as the man repeated, "*Dokter?*", this time pointing at Patrick and fixing him with a dead-serious stare. He nodded and the man shouted the word in the direction of the people gathered at the curb who turned en masse, a movement that seemed to catapult Patrick toward them. People moved aside and Patrick found himself standing over a man, unconscious on the pavement, limbs arrayed in a way that confirmed sudden, terrible force applied to a body. Thirty feet away, a car had pulled over, hazard lights pulsing a redundant warning.

He knelt down next to the man and looked into a face that at first appeared remarkably untouched. A man in his twenties, dark-skinned and slender, lying on his side, mouth agape, one eye open. An earlobe newly webbed in blood. He groped for a pulse and the skin of the man's wrist was cool and wet. In the crowd, on the asphalt next to the man, what came next to Patrick wasn't the predictable panic or visceral alarm but only the oddest relief. Patrick looked again at the face and all he could attest to was a remarkable suspension of self-doubt, as though every apprehension he'd had about himself had been sequestered to another part of his body. He could help this person. *I am a doctor; this is what I do*, he thought and the faith wasn't ridiculous, the faith was a fire that he'd never felt before. Looking into that blind eye with its sinkhole of a pupil, he felt such intoxicating certainty, a sense of calm beyond any pharmaceutical, a calm that seemed profane in the tumult of the crowd around him. This was how Hernan must have felt, he thought, imagining a brain bathed in dopamine, a brain revelling, already priming itself, already begging to be tweaked to feel this good again. Any other day, he'd walk away from such a scene just as he'd find a way to duck out of a hospital room during a difficult moment, but his hand was clamped to the injured man's wrist and its impoverished pulse, and he didn't want to go anywhere, wouldn't go anywhere. *I am here. I will help.*

A man in his fifties dropped to his knees beside Patrick, hoarsely shouting some directive at him, indicating in the broadest possible manner that they should turn the injured man over and Patrick shook his head and pointed to his own neck. Across from the man in his fifties was a young woman, squatting on her haunches, wearing a hijab of the most amazing blue, a colour matching her wide eyes, made to seem wider for the fact that they were the only part of her face he could see with her hands brought up to her gasping mouth. Sister or wife. He put his head back down to the pavement to see how the injured man was doing, and he would swear it was another man now, in similar clothes and circumstances, yes, but now a different category of man, a dying man. His euphoria was an airborne memory, leaving him to face the incontrovertible facts of injury and the knowledge that he could do nothing for this man. He was going to die. A crowd of the injured man's friends and family circled in, and Patrick felt the weight of their gaze on his chest like a tightening python. He looked up for any sign of an ambulance, not with hope but for relief from having to kneel there and carry the weight of the crowd's expectation. Patrick lay down again, this time flat on his stomach, ostensibly to be better able to see the man's face. One eye open, its pupil even more dilated, a depth from which no return was possible. The sound of traffic on the other side of Prinsessegracht was a constant dull roar behind him and the voices of the people around him seemed to ride on it, feed off it. The injured man gasped, a shuddering, deep visceral sound, an agonal sound that would have dropped Patrick had he not already been face-flat against the pavement, seeing the man's lips move with each increasingly tenuous breath. He let go of the man's wrist.

The sirens came. Ambulance. Police too, and half the crowd in the park gathered for the demonstration cleared out with their arrival. The injured man was put on a backboard and loaded into the ambulance, which departed with full lights, full siren, perhaps as a concession to the man's family, the woman in the blue hijab and the man in his fifties somewhere among the people wailing behind him. The police waded through the tension in the crowd to take statements from the car's driver and a few witnesses. When they got to Patrick, he explained that he had seen nothing, that he was just passing by. They told him he was free to go. A few steps away, an ambulance attendant stopped him and sat him down, going through the drill of first aid until Patrick explained the bruises on his face were nothing new and the blood on his shirt was not his own.

Patrick opened the taps wide enough that the mirror fogged above the sink. He checked the ridges of his nails and found no visible blood but his fingertips had that smell to them, and so he lathered and scrubbed and drowned them in the blast of water. By the time he was finished washing, his hands were newborn piglets in the sink. He had never told anyone, but an added benefit of research was escape from that never-ending intimacy with death that defined his specialty. The catastrophes were bad enough: mushroom clouds of blood, acres of brain scorched and salted, insurgencies of bacteria and viruses – but he couldn't bear to contemplate a life spent cowering from patients who were aware that death approached. They could see his fear. He knew it. They'd faced it themselves and conquered it or been pulled under, but either way they knew. They'd watch as he came into their room in the morning and inquired about how the night had passed; they'd see traces of it in him as he examined their withering muscles or checked their eyes for evidence of pressure that was building from the little garden of metastases ripening inside their brains. They'd look at him and it would seem that they all knew his secrets and he sensed how it diminished him as their doctor. He had mastered the details of illness, acquired a superior working knowledge of the nervous system, and yet, in the most basic sense, he could not be what these people needed. There was no way to learn this skill. It should have been achievable, like everything else. It should have been fair. It galled him to see classmates almost inadvertently stumble into that sort of confidence, that calm authority that ministering to the ill demanded. It was like watching them be admitted into a secret society from which he'd been excluded. Nothing had been beyond him except this. Not having that ability – and what *was* it, he thought, the delusion of confidence, a benign hubris, the denial of death – had been the biggest disappointment of his life, one that he couldn't admit to someone like Hernan, someone who had been so endowed.

He thought that seeing his father die would have granted him some immunity, something, some understanding or coping mechanism, but the opposite had happened. Every case had that point on the horizon, the approaching end, and every death became a cause for deep, festering panic. There was no disputing it; his patients smelled it, and no amount of washing could get rid of something like that.

He tried to take off his clothes, shivering through the act, having to concentrate on his fingers as they stumbled blindly around the buttons of his shirt. He clattered a hand through the minibar and found a couple of the small bottles of scotch whose contents he shook into a plastic cup. After downing it, a tablet of Valium followed, and then two more and after fifteen minutes the man coiled on the asphalt of the Prinsessegracht wasn't there at all but instead he was safe in a hospital bed, somewhere in Den Haag, the hard work done, the broken bones set and the haemorrhaging staunched, months of hard work ahead of him, yes, but alive. It was with this thought, of a man hovering above his injuries, floating toward a distant but certain recovery, that Patrick fell asleep. He drifted through stages of sleep, surfacing as the last suppressive traces of benzodiazepines disappeared from his system and the loop of images from the Prinsessegracht began its relentless play. He saw the face on the grey plane of asphalt, the open eye and the last breath of the man escaping, drifting up to a white plane that he thought must be the sky or maybe heaven, but which was really only the ceiling.

Patrick finally awoke in a quiet and amniotically dark room. The tremors had stopped and slowly he was able to gather himself enough to get to the window where he separated the curtains to reveal the latticework of Den Haag streets below.

On the Prinsessegracht he had that unassailable certainty that he could do anything, go to any lengths, for a man dying in front of him. Wrong as he had been, he thought of Hernan, and felt he understood him clearly. He understood how a man could have believed in the righteousness of one's actions for so long. Patrick had felt it too. But he had neither Hernan's faith nor skill and so the delusion lasted only for a moment and brought him no place more incriminating than the pavement of a Den Haag street. He understood. If there was no coercion needed to get Hernan to Lepaterique, then he must have wanted to go. And if Hernan was not a man filled with hate, then what, if not a sense of duty, could have brought him there, could have misled him so? In the tribunal, Hernan had come face to face with the people he thought he'd helped, listened as they gave testimony that demolished his notion of innocence. For the first time, Patrick thought he understood the silence at the trial, understood that the judgment Hernan had evaded for years – since the initial charges, since the death of his wife – had finally been rendered. The only problem was a life that continued, a heart that kept beating in its cell ten blocks away.

It then occurred to Patrick Lazerenko that his friend and mentor Hernan García, right there in front of everyone, was trying to kill himself.

–

TWENTY

It was his heart. Hypertrophic cardiomyopathy. A condition characterized by an obstruction to the normal flow of blood out of the left ventricle due to an overgrowth of muscle in the dividing wall, or the septum, of the heart. A congenital condition, affecting less than 0.5 per cent of the population referred for cardiac ultrasounds, it has what is called a bimodal peak of occurrence, meaning that the initial clinical manifestations – as innocuous as fainting spells, as catastrophic as heart failure or sudden death – are most likely to occur in adolescence or in the sixth decade. Symptoms are most reliably brought on by the strenuous beating of the heart; vigorous exercise causes pressures generated in the left ventricle to rise dramatically and arrhythmias ensue: v. tach, v. fib, asystole. Individuals may be completely without symptoms until they are stricken. It is the typical cause when an otherwise ludicrously fit soccer player falls to the pitch in mid-match, dead.

Patrick took a crash course over the next few hours, gathering specific signs and symptoms of the condition from the dozens of medical Web sites, matching each one with what he knew of Hernan: that first time they met, when he seemed on the verge of fainting after chasing him down, the sound of his heart – *he had listened to his heart!* – with the second heart sound splitting and the murmur roaring as Hernan held his breath. But Patrick had missed it all, heard the murmur blowing like a hurricane but failed to understand the cause. A person would know all this if he was a cardiologist, he'd know how to manage his illness and have the credentials to know how to keep the details quiet. A man with Hernan's training and standing would be able to convince others of the surrogate diagnosis – "No need for an EKG, I should know my own heart, Dr. Bolodis, just a touch of angina" – and the need for nitroglycerin, a drug that dilated the coronary blood vessels and eased the pain of angina. It was, however, a drug that had other effects, reducing the filling pressure in the ventricle, and in hypertrophic cardiomyopathy causing a precipitous drop in blood pressure and increasing the probability of the heart stuttering into a final, fatal arrhythmia.

As Patrick ran down Johan de Wittlaan in the direction of the tribunal building, he thought about all the times he had seen Hernan take nitro, all the little leaps. There had been no cabs at the hotel, and he had been too impatient to wait. He surprised himself by keeping up a good pace for someone who had had only a few splintered hours of sleep between checking and rechecking the possibilities of what Hernan was doing and leaving middle-of-the-night messages for Bolodis.

Patrick passed through security and asked a young woman at the tribunal's information desk to have Dr. Bolodis paged, pointing to his face, only too happy to resort to it as an all-access pass. She replied, with serene indifference, that emergencies before ten were typically referred to the hospital and offered him directions. They had a map, she said, and when she looked up to give it to him, he was gone. Down the corridor, the doors of Courtroom One had been swung open, and the crowd, already gathered like bargain hunters of human depravity, entered and were headed directly for their favoured seats. Roberto was the only García in the gallery, taking a seat in one of the middle aisles. He looked up at Patrick, standing beside one of the seats at the back, and tilted his chin up, the Roberto equivalent to a wave. Across the gallery, Elyse Brenman, star student, was already at her desk, fixing her gaze on the proceedings and preparing to create that day's narrative. *God,* he thought – acknowledging that, whatever her motives, she'd been right about so much, seen the Democratic Voice clearly and understood the compromise that he was getting himself into – *I'm such an asshole.*

The teams of lawyers assembled, and a few minutes later Hernan was ushered in and shown to his seat behind the glass. Patrick knew it was probably projection, the effects of the realization the night before or just sleep deprivation, but Hernan was a ghastly, pre-impending-death grey. He could imagine Hernan working the nitropump all weekend, every shot nudging him closer, feeling his heart trill and kick toward a new morning. Did he think about Fernandez or any of the others when he did this? Was this a reparation, his way of repayment for what he'd done or was it nothing more than a desire to escape? Hernan put the nitropump to his mouth, and it could just as well be a pistol for the way it made Patrick wince. He couldn't watch this, he told himself. The justices entered and the trial restarted without much ceremony, indifferent to García's heart or Patrick's billowing alarm. He couldn't watch this, he told himself, but he couldn't look away. Hernan lifted the container of medication to his mouth again and suffered another ebb tide and all Patrick could think about was that behind the glass partition, in full view of the tribunal gallery, was the only time Hernan wasn't medically supervised, the only time he had the opportunity. Bolodis wasn't in the gallery to see this, Bolodis didn't know. Below, di Costini began shredding the partial, halting recollections of witness C-189. Hernan raised his eyes and looked out into the gallery, running his gaze over the first few rows until it met Roberto. A smile from Hernan, more conspicuous than one would expect, but brief nonetheless. Patrick couldn't tell if it was returned.

Patrick told himself that this was Hernan's right, his life. Perhaps Hernan was aware of all the manoeuvrings, all the plans that were being mapped out, and this was his veto, his declaration of sovereignty. And if he wished to end it, to escape the continued hauntings of José-Maria Fernandez and the others who died in his presence at Lepaterique, then Patrick had no right to stand in the way.

Sit still, he reminded himself. *You have no right to interfere.* Hernan could have had him arrested that very first night behind Le Dépanneur Mondial but he didn't. He was a good man, that's all the evidence he had of Hernan, a man who convinced him of nothing less than possibility. Another shot of the nitropump and no one noticed, his plan brilliant for its lack of deceit. But Hernan's head tipped back, like a man trying to keep himself awake reflexively, because the body marched on, unable to accept a rationale for its own death. Hernan turned his head and pumped in another dose and Patrick could feel it in his own chest, the stumbling steps of a heart's journey. This was Hernan's choice, the choice of a rational man. Patrick could understand that. Patrick owed it to him to do nothing. To watch.

It became so clear, watching Hernan's face drain of colour and his head toggle: death was the totalitarian end, in Lepaterique or his mother's kitchen or for van der Hoeven or the man on the Prinsessegracht, it was the cancellation of all possibility, the negation of understanding and acknowledgement. Hernan was dying, and nothing could argue away the fact that death was nothing more, nothing less than annihilation.

Because Patrick was at the very back of the gallery, no one noticed when he stood up. His legs were stilts, the very act of standing provisional, and he watched as if from a great distance as his right hand raised itself in the direction of the defendant's stand. Patrick shouted that this man was trying to kill himself, that he was using a medication to kill himself and every face became a wildly swinging gate, cycling between him and Hernan. He stood and shouted and arms were suddenly around him, a hand tugging at his shirt collar until a button sheared off and was sent pinging against his cheek and another hand now, on his right forearm and he twisted and shrugged them off and shouted out again, full-throated, his lungs great bellows, and he would not be moved and he saw Roberto, a face of incomprehension becoming something else, becoming alarm and he struggled to see Hernan, Hernan disappearing behind a field of limbs, closing his eyes and his head tilting back and that's when someone grabbed Patrick around the neck and pulled him backwards over the seats and out of Courtroom One.

—

TWENTY-ONE

Even though he was expected, Bolodis was the last man Patrick wanted to see when he opened the door of his hotel room later that morning. The doctor didn't have to say anything; from a detention room in the security offices of the tribunal – where Patrick had been taken into custody, his belt and shoelaces and cell phone taken away, all in accordance with a strict policy for dealing with such people – he had heard the sirens like everybody else. A man who introduced himself only as Kuipers – whom Patrick was later told was the chief of tribunal security – had come into the detention room and sat down opposite Patrick. He asked Patrick why he had disrupted the proceedings rather than come to his officers, and he seemed more puzzled than angry at the cause of the commotion in his courtroom. Patrick said he was uncertain, that it was only when he got inside the gallery that he realized what was happening. From there, Patrick said, it was like a reflex. Kuipers paused, and Patrick felt the man's gaze scanning his face, sizing up the bruises and obvious evidence of lack of sleep. Kuipers got up without a word and left the room. Alone, Patrick waited another ten minutes. He listened for the sirens again, a sign that Hernan was being urgently transported. All he could think about was the paramedics arriving, how they would try to revive Hernan, maybe even start their work right there on the courtroom floor, charging the paddles for one last electric stab at a working rhythm. Then there would be CPR, that rib-cracking, vaudevillian effort to bring someone back before they got to the hospital where they wouldn't know his history, and like any cardiac arrest, they'd shock him again before giving him epinephrine, not knowing the peculiarities of his underlying problem, not knowing that, in this case, epinephrine would only make matters worse. They'd be confused, maybe for a moment, before they'd just consider it to be a failed resuscitation and call the whole thing off. By the time Patrick had been released ninety minutes later, on the condition that he would not set foot on tribunal property again (a photocopy of his passport photo had been duly affixed to a wall behind the security checkpoint), the whole main floor had been cleared. Even the young woman at the information desk with her helpful directions to the hospital was nowhere to be seen when Patrick left the building.

Now, in Patrick's hotel room, Bolodis sat down in the one comfortable chair and said nothing for what seemed to be a minute, a silence that would irritate Patrick under other circumstances, but turmoil shouted from the rooftop of every one of Bolodis's gestures, and he sympathized, appreciating their common reaction. Patrick sat down on the bed opposite him.

"I heard what you did in the tribunal, what you were shouting about," Bolodis said. "I didn't get your messages. I didn't know this about his heart."

"I just figured it out myself last night."

"He said it was a little angina. I took his word for it," Bolodis said, smiling but unable to hide the fact that he was seeing his own future collapsing, the letters of official inquest arriving, already smelling the hallways of a clinic in Groningen. "A little angina. Oh, fuck."

"He's dead," Patrick ventured, an inflection between question and declaration. Testing the words for·their road-worthiness.

Bolodis shrugged and stood. "They took him to the hospital. I thought you'd want to come."

On the car ride to the hospital, Patrick had the urge to tell Bolodis to stop and drop him off somewhere. He needed to walk, to take his time before he saw Hernan's shrouded body pulled out of one of those stainless steel man-sized filing cabinets they have in morgues. But Bolodis was on the phone, speaking in Dutch, and they arrived before Patrick could put the thought into words.

They walked through the hospital, Bolodis leading the way. With each floor up, each corner turned, the hallways became increasingly depeopled. Patrick readied himself for the scene in the morgue and for a tableaux of Garcías: Celia weeping and Roberto now stuck in the neutral gear of silence and Nina, wielding her practicality like a shield, thinking about the forms that needed to be signed to ship a body back home, all around the cold metal tablescape of Hernan, and that's when he heard the beep and *shush* of an automatic door being swept back to reveal not a morgue, but an intensive care unit. The incessant digital bips and respirator chuffs, the official soundtrack to his every anxiety back when he was in this world, now sang their hallelujahs as he followed in Bolodis's wake, every face a hero's for having saved Hernan, every hand an engine of technique and wonder. Hernan was here, in a bed, and Patrick wondered if he would be angry with him for thwarting his efforts. Agitation at the thought of this affected his stride, increasing his pace so that he had to restrain himself from overtaking Bolodis. As he walked, he scanned the unit for signs of Hernan's presence, but saw only a repeating, disorienting sameness to it, a coral reef of medical equipment. In one of the rooms off the main unit he saw a flash of colour, an electric blue fish darting away, recognizing it only after turning away as the same colour as the young woman's hijab from the Prinsessegracht. But he was walking too fast and had passed too far to take a second look.

Bolodis stopped at the desk, catching the attention of a nurse, who then turned to the big board behind her where the patients' names were listed. She pointed to another corner of the unit and the room that awaited there. The last corner, they'd run out of corners, and here, as if needing witnesses to the spectacle of being confronted by reality, he found a nurse and a respiratory technologist talking to each other, sharing a joke perhaps, both stopping when he and Bolodis entered, all of them standing over an immobile Hernan García.

The chief of intensive care came into the room a short time later with his white-coated entourage. When Bolodis introduced Patrick as a doctor and a friend of the family, the chief gave a nod of collegial recognition – a complex gesture in itself, an alloy of relief and wariness – and went on to explain that it was most likely an arrhythmic event, the heart tripping into an ineffectual pattern of pumping causing a prolonged period of circulatory compromise. Hernan was intubated, ventilated, canulated, and paced, said the doctor, pleased at his accomplishments, like a man rounding third after hitting an ICU home run. Of course, Hernan was comatose. No, no, coma was too broad a term, too generous; the chief of intensive care looked at his residents and asked, "Does he have brain stem reflexes?" and one of the residents shook her head. No.

Hernan García was dead, after all. Patrick saw Hernan's chest rising and falling with machine regularity. He touched Hernan's arm, fingering the scar that ran down his forearm, looking like an ill-tailored seam. The chief of intensive care, thinking these two doctors in front of him would find a solace in the facts that they could not find in the body, called them out of the room to look at scans of Hernan's injured brain.

Poor Bolodis looked like he was going to crumple as the chief of intensive care showed them the CT scan done on arrival. On the monitor the brain was a washed-out monochrome grey, oxygen-starved from its deep-sea dive of a cardiac arrest, swollen and squeezing down on the vital structures of the brain stem. Measures have failed, they were told. The damage was irrevocable. Hernan wasn't going to wake up.

"The resuscitation was tricky, technically, and not really a victory when you think about it," the chief of intensive care said and closed the window of images with a keystroke. Hernan's name disappeared from the top corner of the screen. After the perfunctory talk about possible outcomes for the patient, where the three of them stood around and traded dismal statistics and nodded, the chief of intensive care excused himself and left.

Patrick walked out of the ICU with Bolodis into a hallway filled with a fine mist of fluorescent light. They'd both been dismissed, that was clear enough, but he was uncertain about where he was supposed to go. Roberto would have brought his sisters to the hospital, Patrick thought, and he stopped at the ICU's family room, wanting to find the Garcías and at the same time relieved to find the room empty. The polar cold light condensed on the walls that they walked past, no destination in mind until they reached a part of the hospital where two pavilions fused, a point marked by a cluster of elevators and a couple of vintage payphones. Bolodis pressed for an elevator.

Patrick stared at the elevator doors opening. He expected something ornate, or at least decorative, an art nouveau flourish or a simple repeating pattern instead of a painted metal door no different than in any hospital in Boston or Montreal. The inside was no less plain, a fact Patrick found irritating.

"He talked to you," Patrick said, and Bolodis turned, preoccupied. Bolodis pressed the button for the lobby.

"Yes."

"Tell me what he said." Bolodis stared back at him, mute. "Tell me," Patrick repeated.

"It's not my business to tell you."

Between the sixth and seventh floors of the Royal 's-Gravenhage Infirmary, the elevator skidded to an abrupt, mid-air stop; but this was the lesser event to Bolodis, who'd been pinned in a corner of the elevator, struggling to get Patrick Lazerenko's forearm off his chest. Bolodis was the smaller man and had been caught off guard and off balance. Patrick leaned into Bolodis, his other hand jammed against the emergency stop button on the elevator panel. Bolodis struggled under the weight of an elbow now forced up against his collarbone. Patrick watched the jugular vein in the man's neck distend with blood. And while the mechanics of assault were as foreign as a cartwheel, and in Patrick's mind already made explicable by grief and disavowed and apologized for, he couldn't help but feel an unmistakable, terrible thrill at the sight of Bolodis's grimacing. This elation was fleeting, and then the act reverted to its embarassing and sinister origins. He was close enough to see the pores on Bolodis's forehead, close enough to detect the smell of tobacco that lived on the back of the man's tongue. "Tell me," he said again and stopped leaning on the man, his own arm starting to tingle as it dropped. "Tell me what he said."

Bolodis was bent over and breathing heavily. He craned his neck and stared at Patrick. The elevator kicked back into dumb descent. Bolodis wiped a drop of saliva that had formed on his lower lip and straightened up. "He talked about his family and the grocery store in Montreal. The rest of the time he told me about the years he spent in Detroit. That was it."

The doors opened up to the empty main lobby of the hospital and it wouldn't have surprised Patrick to see Bolodis bolt or take a swing at him but the man didn't move. Bolodis was breathing more normally now, the only sign of a struggle the small cumulus cloud of reddened skin on his neck visible just under his Adam's apple.

"Do you know if he saw me? Why he thought I was here?"

Bolodis shrugged, then smiled. "I am afraid I cannot help you with that."

He wanted to hit Bolodis again, an urge he realized was based in futility.

"You were trying to protect him," Patrick said instead.

"I didn't agree with him. Understand that. He did things that are inexcusable. And he lied to me, don't forget that. But I wanted to protect him, yes. He was my patient."

"You knew about his heart," Patrick said.

"I thought he had angina, I thought he needed his medication," Bolodis said.

"You allowed him a professional courtesy, you allowed him to cause himself harm."

Bolodis looked thoughtfully at Patrick. "I had no intention of that. Nor did you."

A woman in her fifties entered the elevator and reached between them to select her floor. Bolodis used the opportunity to step outside the door and Patrick followed him to the threshold, where he blocked the elevator door as it started to close. He watched Bolodis walk away, disappearing through the doors of the hospital's main entrance. Patrick stepped back into the elevator, letting the doors finally close and ignoring the glare of a Dutch woman whose journey to comfort the sick had been unnecessarily delayed.

The intensive care family room at the Royal 's-Gravenhage Infirmary was painted a most unusual shade of lavender, a decision no doubt based on one of those psychological studies of grief that demonstrated the superior calming effects of certain colours. But it was ineffective anaesthesia, discounting pain into a more vague discomfort, unnameable and therefore with less promise of relief. It would be difficult to tell if it worked with anyone who truly needed its help; by the time family members made it to a room like this, most were past tears and instead seemed to express their anguish through the more mundane movements like coughing or changing position as they sat and waited. The García sisters were angry; no one had yet explained their father's condition, and it was clear as Patrick listened to them that they blamed Bolodis and the tribunal for neglect in the care of their father. Roberto saw this and came to Patrick, asking him to speak to Celia and Nina. In the lavender room Patrick sat down and tried to explain Hernan's actions to his children, but instead of telling them plainly, he stumbled through a description of the illness and told them their father would have known which medications were dangerous. They understood. The talking stopped. Celia was calm, able to accommodate this discovery along with the events of the day, just as she had accommodated Den Haag and the *realpolitik* of Oliveira's assistance and Patrick himself. Patrick was certain she'd deal with the impending impact of a planet-smashing asteroid in the same way, shifting her son from hip to hip as she figured out what needed to be done. Roberto and Nina were also silent, but unlike Celia, their silence was a bolted door, their grief complicated by anger as they came to understand how respite and severance had arrived at the same time.

Sometime later, the chief of intensive care reappeared, this time on his own. He repeated what Patrick had tried to explain to the Garcías, that recovery was not a possibility, that survival was an absurd term for someone who would never regain consciousness or breathe on his own. It was the hospital's policy to discontinue life support twenty-four hours after the event, and everyone in the room, including the chief of intensive care, looked at their watches, as if they were synchronizing them in a caper movie. Eleven-fifteen tomorrow.

"There is the matter of the organs," the doctor continued, apologizing for having to ask. Dutch law mandated that they have this conversation. "Do you know his wishes?" he asked, and then added, imagining perhaps that it showed a hint of discretion and not a fondness for irony, that they'd leave the heart alone.

—

TWENTY-TWO

The departure lounge was empty. He was early. He thought the train ride to Schiphol would have taken longer, he'd remembered it as quite a bit longer when he arrived, but he miscalculated and now he had an extra little brick of airport time to endure. After a couple of laps around the terminal's commercial court, he decided to wait it out in the executive class lounge, with its big leather chairs and main room more sparsely populated than the western states.

Hernan was still alive when Patrick left the hospital late the night before. He had sat in the room alone with him for fifteen or twenty minutes trying to make sense of a life. Good intentions. The thought that benevolence could be so blindly applied and become so perversely transformed depressed Patrick. It suggested a world where any human impulse could be broken down and subverted to suit another end, that intent meant nothing. Maybe Hernan realized that, too; he must have realized it looking into José-Maria Fernandez's eyes that day in 1983, how his intentions had led him to become part of a larger animal. He must have known it as he listened to the witnesses speak of him as a monster. And, to that end, Hernan lying before him made perfect sense. The ventilator shushed in the corner, as if to chastise him for thinking this way.

And then Patrick said goodbye, a goodbye that he told himself was meaningless, but damn the body if it didn't misbehave, if the sight of the chest moving with each breath didn't stir something inside. He would have stayed, he told himself that, he would have helped with the arrangements or just stood around. He asked Celia if she wanted him to stay. She said no in such a way that he felt neither compelled nor offended.

He wasn't family. He wasn't really a García and he'd never be one. Hernan was a man he'd spent time with for a few years almost twenty years before. He tried to tell himself that Hernan García was a construction, the product of a boy's wishful needs, as much an act of creation as the "Angel" of Elyse's book or the martyr's tale now broadcast courtesy of the Democratic Voice. But he couldn't convince himself. He knew this man, the terrible facts, the kindness, the irreconcilable truths.

He looked at his watch and thought the Garcías must now be gathered around Hernan's bedside, watching, grieving, madly creating a story of their father for themselves that would endure beyond his acts that summer at Lepaterique, perhaps a story that would someday even accommodate those moments, along with his last days in Den Haag.

Until then, the story of Hernan's life was most tangibly the property of Elyse Brenman, who watched the tumult in the courtroom and then spent the evening patrolling the hospital corridors a safe distance from where the Garcías waited, hoping for, or perhaps fearing, an ending to that last chapter. Oliveira staked his claim as well, showing up at the hospital enraged – as enraged as Oliveira could get, a minor-key homage to rage – threatening lawsuits and promising to arrange a press conference from the lobby of the hospital if he didn't get some answers. His tone softened when he got those answers and, knowing martyrdom had come, fully, completely, he left the hospital without further incident. Somewhere in Den Haag, there were witnesses who had been waiting for years to tell their stories of Hernan García, awakening in their hotel rooms only to be told that something unforeseen had occurred and their testimony was now no longer necessary. Thank you. Be well. Goodbye.

After leaving the hospital, Patrick had returned to the Metropole, where he made travel arrangements and packed his bags for the next day's flight. Despite sleeping with unusual soundness, he had still awoken an hour before dawn. At seven, there was a knock on the door and he opened it to find a young man asking his name and brandishing what turned out to be a tribunal subpoena, issued the morning before. He was accompanied by a solemn Edwin, now offering expanded concierge services. Patrick offered no explanation about what had happened to García, and so neither of the men at his door could have understood the obsolescence of the act or the reason for his indifference at receiving the summons. The young man didn't seem to care but poor Edwin looked crest-fallen at the lack of drama.

Patrick wasn't due to leave for the train station for another hour, but after the morning visit he needed to get out of his room, and so he decided to walk over to the Garcías' *pension* on Geestbrugweg with the intention of giving Marta's book to Celia. He had been thinking about it since the night before; it seemed like the right thing to do in so many ways: a gift, a stab at that much-vaunted closure, a chance to see all the Garcías again, making sure they were all right after a night at the hospital. But on the way to the *pension* he reconsidered, worrying that Celia would eventually read the book and find her mother's judgment in the margins, thinking he should instead just put the book on the shelves in the *pension*'s library and have it become lost forever. But as he turned and began walking back to the Metropole, he realized he was acting as much for himself, that the book in his hand was the only thing of the Garcías that he had left and it was something he couldn't relinquish.

The lounge around him now was mahogany-panelled, dark and familiar, with an haute rec-room clubhouse feel that made him wonder where the ping-pong table was. After several tactical seat changes – drawing the attention and curious glances of the waitress – Patrick concluded that there was no place in the executive class lounge to hide from the many giant-screen televisions and so he passed the time trying to avert his eyes from the muted montage of the day's events.

The hour passed slowly, more so because of his obsessive surveillance of the minute hand as it swept away the quarter hours. Patrick opened his computer, deciding that he needed focus, the industrious older cousin of diversion; yes, that's what was missing. He reasoned that the news about the Globomart deal would have been sent by now, and once back in Boston, he'd be patting Sanjay on the back and they'd be well on their way to deprogramming everyone at Neuronaut from the cult of Lazerenko indispensability. The waitress came over, genuinely happy that this new seat was superior in some mysterious way to the other three he'd abandoned. Patrick chose something from the menu and sat in silent contemplation with other monks in the lounge, an order with faces pale before their laptop screens. He checked his messages for the first time that day and found a communiqué sent out late the previous night.

> Neuronaut CEO Jeremy Bancroft takes great pleasure in announcing the signing of a new exclusivity contract with Globomart Inc., Medina, Minnesota, for "continued cognitive analysis of all Globomart marketing" for the next five years, including their soon-to-be-launched campaign – "Amer/I can."
>
> Neuronaut is also proud to announce the appointment of Sanjay Gopal, Ph.D., to the position of Chief Scientific Officer, effective immediately. Dr. Gopal has served in the research and development department of Neuronaut and was instrumental in developing analysis for Globomart's "Amer/I can" campaign.

The next message was from Bancroft himself and had a heading succinct enough – re: personnel change/exit strategy – that he didn't need to open it. The cult of Lazerenko had already ended. He closed his computer.

The waitress arrived with his meal. He thanked her and she left, smiling as she turned away. He wondered if she could tell how he felt. If it showed. Because it hurt, any sense of relief overwhelmed by the sting of dismissal like a punch remembered from a childhood playground. In the end, he hoped that, if asked, the waitress would say that she noticed nothing different about her customer when she came back with his beer, except that his computer was now closed and he looked a little less fidgety than before.

When the boarding call for his flight was finally announced, it surprised him, perhaps because now, he didn't have any reason to go. He could take a flight tomorrow, or board the plane at the neighbouring gate for Barcelona or just wander through the terminal and any of it would make as much sense as going back to Boston. But Boston was as good a place as any and had the benefit of being the quickest way out of Den Haag, so when the second call came he shouldered his carry-on without hesitation and limped into that snaking line with the others, preparing his papers and wanting to see nothing more than the back of an airline seat. When he pulled out his boarding pass, the tribunal subpoena came along with it. Patrick folded the document quickly, and the gate attendant, focused on the boarding pass and matching his face with his passport's photo, didn't notice a thing.

"Ooh, that's a shiner."

"Yeah," he replied, summoning a frat-boy grin that made him want to take a shower.

At thirty thousand feet, the noise of an airplane was a beautiful thing. A seventy-decibel ode to constancy, an anthem to Bernoulli's law, it thrummed its lullaby to him. Close your eyes. Don't look at your watch. Don't look at your watch. The plane tore its way back through time zones, strung on contrails, elongating the day of Hernan García's death. But night would come. Somewhere over Britain the minute hand of his watch would cross the meridian of a particular quarter hour and it would happen, as it must, but Patrick had already climbed inside the noise of the engines, telling himself that it was already over, miles back and years ago.

He closed his eyes and remembered the evening before at the hospital, how they waited, staring at the lavender walls until, one by one, they began to excuse themselves to go on little hatchling expeditions to the washroom or the vending machines down the hallway. They ate in the hospital's empty cafeteria, all of them sitting on the same side of a long table, as if to dissuade attempts at conversation. After dinner, he and Celia took Paul for a walk down the corridor that led away from the intensive care unit, and, finding a sign for the solarium on the twelfth floor, decided to go farther. The elevator doors opened onto a room with walls and a ceiling vaulted in glass. It was a dark and quiet place, the rarest of commodities in a hospital, as rare as a clear night in Den Haag. The sky full of stars spread out over them. Below, the more orderly constellation of Den Haag street lights was hemmed in by the sea. For the longest time they just sat and looked out.

They could have talked about her father; he could have told her that he thought Hernan had made a grave and terrible mistake, a mistake that exceeded any capacity to forgive but an act that they could perhaps one day understand. Yes. He'd try to understand. But at that moment, he hadn't wanted to talk about Hernan. Hernan wasn't really alive any more and Celia was not a person who needed her father defended or eulogized to her.

An older man, a patient in a pale blue bathrobe and pushing an IV pole on its little wheels, came into the solarium and shuffled right up to the glass wall. He looked down at the streets below and then up and around at the city, as if to verify that the scale of things in the outside world had not changed. Then he turned, his hand on the pole, escorting it back to his room. It was only on his way out of the room that the man glanced over and noticed the three of them sitting there. The expression on his face, visibly gaunt even in the low light of the room, did not change as he left.

In the silence of the solarium Patrick felt at ease for the first time in Den Haag. Celia was sitting beside him, and yet he felt no regret that he'd lost her nor anger that he'd spent his life trying to discount that loss. Instead, he wanted to tell her that he'd loved her, from what he understood of the word and of himself, not to change anything between them, but just so that she knew. It was important to him that she knew. But then he watched Celia hold her son in her arms and it all seemed unnecessary. Paul was falling asleep and she wiped the hair out of his eyes and kissed him on the forehead. The boy's eyelids fluttered and closed. Accompanied by the sound of her son softly breathing, they sat in the room looking out past the lights of the city to that point in the distance and the darkness where the sky and the sea must have met.

ACKNOWLEDGEMENTS

–

It was a privilege to work with Jennifer Lambert at McClelland & Stewart. The enthusiasm and intelligence she brought to this book were much appreciated.

I would like to thank my agent, Denise Bukowski, for all her efforts on my behalf.

Thank you to Jim and Maureen Durcan, Bruni and Peter Erdmann, Anne Durcan, Alec Macauley, Maria and Rick Higgins, Andrew Steinmetz, Alain Dagher, and Jim Dixon. Finally, thank you to Florence, Niall, and Julia, for everything.

The following works were particularly important for me during the writing of this book: *The Nazi Doctors: Medical Killing and the Psychology of Genocide* by Robert Jay Lifton; *The Ethical Brain* by Michael Gazaniga; *Neuroethics: Defining the Issues in Theory, Practice and Policy*, Ed. Judy Illes. Details of the activities of Battalion 316 were first published in a series of articles in the *Baltimore Sun* that ran from June 11 to December 15, 1995, and are available through their on-line archives at www.baltimoresun.com.

A NOTE ABOUT THE TYPE

García's Heart has been set in Garamond BE, a modern type family based on types first cut by Claude Garamond (c.1480-1561). Garamond is believed to have followed classic Venetian type models, although he did introduce a number of important differences, and it is to him that we owe the letterforms we now know as "old style." Garamond gave his characters a sense of movement and elegance that ultimately won him an international reputation and the patronage of Frances I of France.

BOOK DESIGN BY CS RICHARDSON